'All around, the Country is tellin
To answer the in

Some time not too far in the future, Australia's ozone layer is dangerously depleted, and the country's water supply is in crisis. For the last one hundred years the depleted supply has been managed and closely guarded by the officers of the Water Board of the Coalition of the Eastern States of Australia, a military-style corporation whose shareholders 'own' the nation's water.

Conway is a whitefulla but his heart and spiritual connections lie with the blackfullas. He is hated by the whitefullas – but they need Conway's abilities as a dreamer and water diviner to survive.

In Docker's radical revisioning of Australia, the country is divided between those who have embraced the Country and learnt blackfulla ways, and those who cling to the imperialist whitefulla imperative of destruction and annihilation. This division has its beginnings in the reimagined moment of the arrival of Europeans in Western Australia when Captain Charles Fremantle chooses to throw off the mantle of Empire and join the Nyoongar people who meet him off the boat at the Darbal Yaragan.

The Waterboys is high-paced and high-spirited, even as it sounds a warning for what can happen if we do not listen to the Country. With humour and with passion, it offers a possible model of manhood and masculinity in a violent and desperate world.

Peter Docker was born in Wiilman Country at Narrogin, Western Australia, of mainly Irish heritage. He grew up on a station in Wudjari Country at Coomalbidgup, near Esperance. He has worked as a dairy hand, hay carter, wheat bogger, window washer, bank teller, lift driver, barman, concierge, seller of adult products, sorter of mail, an infantry officer in the army reserve, singer in a rock band, and has been a professional actor for twenty years.

He lives with his family in Broome (Nyamba Yawuru Buru) in Western Australia.

Peter Docker has had short stories published in Australian literary journals and has written for stage and radio. His first novel, *Someone Else's Country,* was published by Fremantle Press in 2005.

**Book club notes available from
www.fremantlepress.com.au**

THE
WATERBOYS

PETER DOCKER

FREMANTLE PRESS
fine independent publishing

Developed with the assistance of the Australia Council Literature Board.

Developed with the assistance of the Louis St John Trust.

This book is dedicated to my daughter Cleopatra, and her great love for the Swan River (Darbal Yaragan).

Contents

Once, I rested by the Swan River, the Darbal Yaragan. I lay down near the river mouth on the north side. I was not quite awake. Not quite asleep. This dream rose like mist off the water, and settled on me.

I wrestled with the dream until I could write it down in this form.

– Peter Docker

One: Night Delivery

The truck engine howls beneath us, cool desert air rushes past our windows. I'm holding on tight to the console, my white knuckles paler than the stars. Mularabone is driving. He stares ahead into the darkness, a picture of relaxation. Mularabone only knows one way to drive – fucken flat out.

'You still with me, coorda?' he asks, smiling through each word as though delivering the punchline of a joke.

I glance down at my white knuckles: is he taking the piss?

'Wide awake, bro.'

'That's never stopped you from dreaming off.' And this time his smile is like a shoulder hug.

I look out into the dark. I don't know if I can take any more of this wild speed.

'Slow down,' I say through tight teeth and jaw.

'Low down? I'll give ya the low down, brother.'

'Slow down, fuck ya!'

'Nearly there.'

'Nearly where?'

Mularabone laughs.

'There's not even a road,' I say, as Mularabone changes down and guns the big diesel engine even harder.

'Roads are overrated, brother.'

Ahead of us in the darkness stands a lone figure, an old Countryman with a big hat and a white beard. I hear myself swear again. Mularabone jams on the skids. The big rig, with its two huge tanker-trailers, locks up in the loose dust of the desert. The old Countryman in the darkness ahead doesn't move a muscle. He stands patiently as though waiting for a bus. The trucks slides in the dust, with Mularabone fighting the bucking steering wheel. It finally comes to a halt just a metre or so from the old man's cowboy boots.

My head drops and I suck in a big breath. Mularabone is already out of the truck to greet the old Countryman, even as they are enveloped by the dust cloud the truck has stirred up. I gingerly climb down from the cabin and move around to the front, walking unsteadily as though I've been chained in a ship's hold for six months. Mularabone and the old Countryman are still embracing. Then the old Countryman steps away and turns to me.

Uncle Birra-ga.

For the briefest of moments I feel the old Uncle's eyes burn into me through the darkness, and then I drop my gaze and put out my hand. I dunno if Uncle is gonna take something off me with those eyes, or give me something to go on with, like the Country itself.

All I know is it's a little more than respect and a little less than fear that makes me avert my eyes. Uncle Birra-ga takes my hand in a feather-light grip.

'Hello, my nephew.'

Uncle's voice is like a gentle breeze and the dust cloud raised by the truck is gone as quickly as it stirred up.

'Hello, Uncle.'

Without warning, Uncle pulls me in close; that sudden strength always surprises me. He may look frail but I know he isn't. I've heard the stories of Uncle as a young man, when the civil war was raging. His name, Birra-ga, means man-killing stick. Like all of his mob, he is well named. Some men are named after particular ancestors. I'm named for my grandfather. Mularabone too – for his grandmother's brother – in a different kind of way. Some names wait patiently for generation after generation to find the right host. Some names leap out from behind an unfamiliar rock and try to kill you. Like Birra-ga. When his fingers touch my arm as he speaks to me, they are as hard as steel rods.

'We gonna talk later, my boy,' he says to me in his light half-whisper.

I nod, my eyes still down, staying silent in case there is more.

Uncle steps back from me, and turns to face Mularabone. They have a rattling conversation in Language. Then Uncle Birra-ga turns and walks away.

I look to Mularabone. He knows I don't speak. My father couldn't wait to take his sons from the Language program. For three hundred years Djenga bin learning Language in this Country. The protocol was always to start with the Language of where the whitefullas were born. What Country we did our learning in. Whenever people moved around, like we did, it was the Language of the Country of residence – so Djenga and Countryman alike could pay proper respect to Country and elders and ceremony. My father loathed the whole thing. I never knew what made him so bitter. Towards me. Towards the Countrymen. Towards the Country itself.

'Let's get some water flowing, brother,' Mularabone says through his huge smile.

We walk back along the side of the truck. We see the concrete manhole cover set into the ground. It takes both of us to lift it off. Mularabone slides under the truck and unhooks the outflow pipe from the tanker-trailer and connects it to the system beneath the manhole cover. I go up the ladder on the first trailer to loosen off caps on top of the water tanks. Sometimes we have to get our pump going but with Uncle

Birra-ga's system we let gravity do the work. I swing back down and go to the main valves. Mularabone is finishing screwing down our outflow pipe onto the pipe beneath the concrete cover. He is done in a flash and looks up to me. I open the valve and we hear the water rushing into the system below the desert floor.

Mularabone fishes in his pocket and pulls out his ngumari. He rolls a cigarette and holds it to me. Before I can take it, Uncle Birra-ga reaches out and grabs the cigarette. He puts it into his grinning mouth.

Uncle's right hand gestures to me – two subtle, yet distinct movements: fire; question (You got im waru, Nephew?).

I pull out my lighter, flick the flame on and offer it to him. He sucks on the cigarette and it glows red. Mularabone hands me another one. We all stand there smoking, listening to the water flow out of the truck and into the storage system below.

Around us is the desert, awash in the light from the moon and stars. For a moment we are at the bottom of a vast ocean. I look up to the night sky to see a prehistoric marine predator as big as two train carriages turn and flip straight down at us, massive jaws lined with teeth bigger than me, opening to envelop us. I stand like a tree, imitating Uncle Birra-ga in his big hat when we arrived, with over twenty tonnes of water truck bearing down on him in a dusty slide.

I exhale my smoke and there is only the night, the desert night. I glance sideways at Uncle Birra-ga. His eyes twinkle like the stars.

The water stops flowing. Mularabone and I move in unison, it's what happens when you spend too much time together. We stub out our cigarettes, pick up the butts and move in different directions. He goes to the truck cab. I go to the back of the first trailer and undo the pipe. I close the stop on the trailer.

'Yo! Yo-yo!'

Mularabone revs the engine and the truck moves forward. I see his eyes shining in the darkness of the mirrors. Medieval scholars used to believe that our eyes emitted light to illuminate objects, thus allowing us to see. Medical science eventually proved them wrong, but out here in the desert with this mob I always get to wondering. Not that those eyes are like a spotlight, or a candle; more like moonlight shining out through brown billabong water, and the water is warm, like a fire, or embers glowing all friendly without the bald bare light of a flame.

The second trailer is there now, lined up.

'Yo! Yo-yo!'

The air brakes go on with the rush-hiss of a whale breathing. The whale is on the surface, way above our heads, but we hear the rush-hiss as if it is all around us. I move in and attach the hose and screw the valve out. The water rushes through the pipe into the system below. Mularabone comes down to join us at the back of the truck but by the time I straighten up from the pipes, Uncle Birra-ga has disappeared.

Mularabone and I look around as though we are astronauts accidentally left behind by our expedition, standing all alone on the surface of the moon. We stand there unmoving, looking up at the blue planet rising in the clear atmosphere-less sky, until the water stops flowing.

We unhook the pipe, slide it back into position and replace the concrete slab, grunting with the effort. We stride back for the truck, run up the steps, Mularabone guns the engine and the truck starts to move. We are still driving without lights, but in the darkness to our left, we see the old Countryman standing there, like his father, the tree.

'We gotta come back, after we stash the truck,' says Mularabone.

I look over to him.

'We haven't got time,' I say. 'If we're gonna walk out tonight, we haven't got time. We'll never get back to the refugee camp in time.'

Mularabone laughs.

'What's so funny?'

'Dunno, just, I reckon, it's you he wants to see, not me.'

'Won't be funny if the Water Board get us. They ain't gonna be too impressed about the trucks.'

I look ahead into the darkness. Uncle did say he wanted to talk to me. I look over at Mularabone driving. He furrows his brow in mock deep concern-contemplation. His mimic of me is startling in its accuracy. I get the giggles.

'I gotta work on my poker face,' I say, deadpan.

'Poke her face?' Mularabone queries, dry and naughty.

I giggle again. 'You are one bad-ass white shareholder, brother! Poke her face? You're a sicko, bruz.'

'Don't go all virgin on me, brother! You wouldn't say no!'

He looks over to me. I do the tongue in the cheek thing, and I get him. He laughs.

'Yaaaaah!'

'Yaaaaah!'

The truck drives through the trackless night. Mularabone always goes south with his humour when stuck for a response. I spose I do too. It's a hangover from another time. And it works for us. The tension goes. We're both old-school when it comes to women. Lustful thoughts are confusing in our world. You can deny them. You can savour them. As long as you do it quietly where no one sees. We both already know that a woman's trust is a far more valuable thing than her flesh – as valuable as that is to us men. Dying and laughing are connected. Like laughing and living. Lust and fear. Semen and blood. This desert sucks at my mind. I'm still that astronaut on the surface of the moon, gazing up at the blue planet rising, and the vacuum of space is trying to suck my helmet off, so that my body will be obliterated instantly and all that will remain are my thoughts. A thought. A message. A song. Our brains talk to themselves with little song phrases. Like we talk to the spirit world. Like the whales talk to each other. To us.

Ahead, some large rock formations loom out of the desert night. Mularabone glances across to me for confirmation. Behind the rock formations is the dried-up river. I can't see it in the dark – but I can feel the water motion in my veins, I can feel it as if it were still flowing, and not dammed upriver by the Water Board. I give Mularabone a little nod and he spins the wheel left-hand down to back the trailers in. I open the door and jump down while the vehicle is still moving. I hit the ground rolling and then I'm up and running. My hands are gripping an imaginary weapon as I run. I take a few steps then come to a halt, looking down at my hands and the weapon that isn't there. I open my hands and let it drop. Something thuds softly in the dust at my feet. I don't look down. Got to stay out of that dream.

I look to the truck to see Mularabone's eyes watching me in the mirrors. I wave the truck back.

'Yo!'

Mularabone gets the trailer in first time, snugly into the narrow canyon.

'Yo! Yo-yo!'

The big whale breathes again, way over our heads, and the truck stops.

I run in and unhook the trailer.

'Yo!'

Mularabone pulls the first trailer away. We'll put them all in separate spots. I grab the blower off the back of the first trailer as it pulls away and pull-start the engine. It goes with a howl and I aim it at the truck tracks, pulling my facemask up and over my mouth. It only takes a few minutes to do the job. This machine is a ripper. Mularabone modified it from agricultural equipment he stole from the market garden where the refugees slave away on the other side of the dam; he calls it the little wind. By the time I'm finished, there are no truck tracks.

Mularabone jumps down from the cabin. He has the cloaking device in his hands, programming it as he walks. These new ones are so small. He lines it up on the tanker-trailer and initiates it. His fingers are long and delicate and play across the tiny keyboard like a musical instrument. He loves this technology. He scoops up some sand, puts the device into the earth and covers it over again with the sand.

We turn and walk back to the idling truck.

In an hour or so we've parked both tanker-trailers and the rig. We walk backwards for another hour or so with the blower, washing our tracks away with the little wind. We take the blowing in turns. I'm on my second go when I stumble and fall backwards, overcome with exhaustion. I lie there with the blower in my hands, unable to move. The shaft of air points straight up at the stars, the little wind trying to scatter those distant and ancient lights.

Suddenly, Mularabone is there, his face in the airstream, his hair blowing back from the wind. He waggles his head from side to side and breaks into song in this kind of crazy falsetto:

Oh these Waterboys drive round a big old truck
When they feeling that kind they need a good old ...
Fact-finding mission to find that good sweet water
Keep ya sons at home and lock up your daughter
Waterboys always doing what they shouldn't oughtta.

I'm laughing with him. 'What they *shouldn't oughtta*! What's that?'

'Well – it rhymed!'

I'm giggling so uncontrollably that the blower falls down and engulfs us both in a mini sandstorm. Mularabone bends and kills the machine.

A silence comes down on us like a white drug in our brains. There's only me giggling silently, and wheezing for breath, and a million, million stars. I look up to see Mularabone's hand outlined by those shining stars, hovering just in front of me. I take the hand and am hauled up to my feet.

We stand there, our hands still clasped, looking at the stars reflected in each other's eyes.

'Let's walk now,' he finally says.

'How far?'

'Two hours.'

I look at him.

'Tops,' Mularabone affirms with a grin.

We start walking. As we go, Mularabone pulls out a plug of herb and offers me some leaves. I take them. We chew and walk. Walk and chew.

When we were doing our initial training, years ago, before the cadres, The Sarge used to say to us, 'If ya can't do it walkin, it ain't worth doin.'

We used to joke about how The Sarge had sex with his missus. There were all sorts of stories about him marching around his backyard with her straddling him and holding on like a mad Afghan camel driver, especially as his knees always give out when he comes. Even if Mularabone made them up, they were good stories. The Sarge would always demand to know what was so funny, and then laugh his hard little laugh when we told him, may his spirit find peace.

We walk in silence now. Sometimes I think I hear that

ancient whale-song in my head, sometimes I think it is Uncle
Birra-ga. My own breathing is like a sea-mammal, down here
on the desert floor. I am so empty, so nothing, that I almost
forgive myself.

Two: Rainbows in the Tank

It feels like we've only been walking for a few minutes or so when, far away to our left, some tiny fingers of light begin to feel for the edge of the horizon.

We've been walking for hours.

I look up and there is Uncle Birra-ga, standing in the same place where we first saw him. He turns and disappears down into the earth. And this is where we go. Following the old Countryman down under the red skin of this mother of ours. The narrow steps are cut into rock. We go down, following the bobbing, gnarled hat of Uncle Birra-ga before us. There is a heavy scraping sound above us. I look back to see another fulla, smiling down at me from in front of the closed door. I didn't see him at all when I came through that door. I saw no alcove; maybe he was hanging from the roof above like a ghost bat.

We level out and turn a corner, arriving onto a small platform area.

Uncle Birra-ga is being greeted by Aunty Ouraka. She is never in a hurry. Being in her company is like being in a sanctuary. Her name means wait awhile. They're both bathed in this greenish light. I look to where the green glow is coming from and see a glass window into a huge water tank. The tank is illuminated from within. Inside, under the water, two little brown bodies turn over and over in underwater gymnastics. The children are naked, both boys, smiling and looking through the window at Uncle, Aunty, and us. Uncle gives Mularabone and me a big smile. Aunty Ouraka envelops us in a hug. Down in that safe place, with the desert narcotic flowing through my mind, it is like the Country herself enfolding us in her embrace. Aunty releases us without a word. Uncle gestures to the boys in the tank with his lips and eyes and they kick for the surface. Uncle goes over to a sidewall and hits a button. The wall opens and a control panel slides out. Uncle's fingers fly over the keys, then he turns back to face the tank window. The two little boys come down a stairway off to the right side of the tank. They run straight up to Mularabone.

'What you got for us, Uncle?'

'You made something new?'

Mularabone pulls a gadget from his pocket. He aims it at the boys bouncing on the spot before him and clicks on, wait, wait, and then off. They can hardly contain their excitement.

'What is it, Uncle?'

'Can I've a go? Can I?'

'Did ya make it yourself?'

He hits another button and a perfect image of the two boys clamouring for attention, complete with sound, appears next to the two naked boys.

'What is it, Uncle?

'Can I've a go? Can I?'

'Did ya make it yourself?'

The image freezes in the last moment of the record. The nephews laugh. Mularabone holds the gadget out to them. The older one snatches it and they run off down a corridor, leaving wet footprints on the stone floor.

There is some activity in the tank and our eyes go to the window. Uncle Birra-ga throws his arms around Mularabone and me. A whole rainbow of colour flashes through the water tank.

'I love to watch the lights,' he says in English.

Aunty turns and follows the children. Mularabone and I stand in Uncle's embrace for a long time, watching the lights from the purifier flashing through the cool green water.

Uncle's fingers give us both a tight little squeeze, then he drops his arms and walks away, leaving us standing there – the feeling of his touch still a sweet scar on our shoulders. Mularabone and I turn and follow. There is a narrow winding corridor in the rock that slopes gently down. It is dark in here, really dark, but my feet still walk with certainty, like they know where to go. Ahead there is light. The corridor opens out into a huge cavern; a space as big as a footy oval with a high ceiling, with many lanterns and several fires burning. There are many exits and entrances with tunnels leading off and opening into other big underground spaces. There are a few dozen people in the main cavern, going about their morning routine. We follow Uncle over to Aunty Ouraka's fire. She is pulling some seed cakes from a flat stone on the coals. She wraps them in a big leaf, drizzles honey from a label-less tin and hands them to us as we approach. The two naked little fullas are standing near the fire, drying off. They look at me with open curiosity. Not many Djenga come down here, I see by their look.

Mularabone and I sit down on the bare rock and eat. The damper is extraordinary in its richness and texture; dozens of different types of seeds and seed-pods have been ground by Aunty, collected over several days of foraging on the desert floor, way above our heads. After the feeling of being at the bottom of an ancient ocean in the desert last night, to be down here, under the ocean floor, is something else again. I chew the damper. Uncle hands me a piti to drink water from. I drink. I look to Mularabone. He is looking blurry. I don't know if it's him causing that, or me. We haven't slept for three days or so. I look up to see Uncle just over the other side of the fire, talking to two other old Countrymen. They don't look at us, but we know they're talking about us. I finish my damper. Drink again. The traditional flat-cake gives our arrival the air of ceremony. That's why Mularabone and I are trying to feel what the old Countrymen are saying. But we can't. Someone is putting blankets over us. We lie down, and are gone.

Dreaming 44: The Cornfield

After an eternity of icy bump and lurch in the darkness, the ute I'm travelling in finally slows. Ahead of us, behind my head, there is a light source. I don't look around. Couldn't, even if I wanted to. The ute stops. After the manic rush through the desert air, the silence and stillness are almost overpowering.

I get out; the metal thing is still hard against my throat, forcing me to move slowly and with a strange gait. I gradually swing around to the light source, like an insect, reluctant to accept that the pull of the light is as inevitable as drawing breath. I can see dozens of men standing around utes in the semi-darkness. They all have rifles in their hands, or slung over their shoulders. They smoke and drink and talk in quiet, tense voices. They glance in my direction but do not look fully at me. I'm hauled before a huge beer-bellied bloke with thick, square, black-rimmed glasses and a black handlebar moustache, which obscures his top lip. The rifle he holds propped on his hip looks too small for him, like a child who's grown out of his favourite toy. Behind him is a vast field of golden corn, lit up by hundreds of floodlights mounted on tall silver poles. The corn has eared and is standing head-high. The floodlights illuminate us all: me trussed up with metal, and them standing around caressing their rifles like porn stars touching their cocks.

The big bloke looks at me evenly through his thick black glasses.

'Howdy, Boy,' he drawls at me. 'How'r'ya doin? I'm 44.'

The southern drawl goes like an iceblock down my spine. He begins his little preamble. I get the feeling he's done all this many times before. Does that mean I've met him before? He seems very familiar to me. As he talks to me, I'm having trouble understanding him. His blubbery lips move in slow motion and I answer him with 'sir', 'please,' and 'thank you'.

My voice comes out sounding nasal. Almost so I sound like him. Or he sounds like me. I hate myself for this forelock-tugging weakness, but forgive myself too, like a child crying itself to sleep.

I am trying to think. To give myself options.

To run? They have rifles. The only way is through the corn. There don't seem to be any automatic weapons, giving me half a chance. To hide? I could dig a hole. No time. And they'll easily track me on this ground. I could go for 44, put my fingers and teeth into his throat. But he looks strong. And there are so many others. I still can't move properly with this metal cuff at my throat. The only place is in the corn. They want me to go into the corn.

44 is in no hurry. But in the others, there's the beginning of a definite stir sweeping through them. They're restless now. Want their hunt. Their sport. I hear weapons being cocked. I know what will happen if I get caught ...

When I get caught.

There is no bugle blowing or big announcement. Just straight down to business.

Someone removes the throat-cuff and I take off at a dead run. A couple of shots go off and then I'm into the corn.

I hear them take off behind me, baying like a pack of dogs. They tear after me into the corn, swearing, firing, and running – their minds hopeful and their legs strong.

I'm running and running.

I've been hit. I'm falling. I'm making a strange sound. They are hacking into me with machetes. I'm screaming. They're laying into me with rifle barrels. They're propping me up and holding me so they can rape me.

Three: Holy Water

I sit up. The rock floor of the cavern is hard. It was so yielding as I melted into it after Aunty Ouraka's damper. Mularabone is still asleep. The cavern is almost empty. Not far away, I see Uncle Birra-ga and another old fulla, also asleep. I stand up and stretch, going into my salute-the-sun. When I finish I'm really awake. Mularabone starts to stir. I feel eyes on me and look up. Across the other side of the cavern is a small fire. Sitting next to the fire is a woman. Her eyes are on me. I meet her gaze. My muscles still ache from running through the corn. I've got that lightheaded post-adrenalin thing going on.

Even though she is right across the other side it's like she's so close I could touch her. She stands in a quick movement without taking her eyes from me, but not quick enough for me to miss the flash of her chocolate flesh when her robe adjusts to her body's upward flow. The scarring up her torso is tattooed onto my mind now. Between her and me, Uncle Birra-ga sits up. My eyes go down as the other old fulla sits up too. They both look at me. My skin feels peeled off under their gaze. Mularabone makes a noise and I turn to see him sitting up.

'Hey, coorda, where's my coffee?'

'Just going to the café now. You want a croissant, too?'

Mularabone smiles back at me. 'Looks like the café is coming to you, bro.'

I turn to see the old men ambling off to another fire and

coming straight towards us is the woman in the robe carrying a coffee pot. I look back to Mularabone – far too quickly, I realise as soon as I've done it.

He smiles. His voice comes out so low and so quiet, 'Ooooh, bruz. She's got you; she's got you, hasn't she? Eh?'

I say nothing. My mouth doesn't seem to be working right now. When she arrives, Mularabone looks at the coffee pot, and raises an eyebrow in my direction.

What can I say? She gives me a look. I can't pick the emotion but it's a bit like fear and a bit like excitement.

She picks up two empty mugs from by our fire and pours out two coffees. She puts down the coffee pot. On the ground is a tin of sugar. She puts a small fingerful of sugar in each mug and then stirs them with a stick from the fire. She holds the mugs out to us and her eyes fall on me again. I don't mean to, but I smile. In that moment I feel as though this is the most honest I've ever been in my life. She smiles back. Mularabone takes a step back. We turn as one to look at him. He smiles in slow motion. We look back to each other. If I looked down and saw my skin blistering from her heat I wouldn't be even slightly surprised.

'Thanks for the coffee, cuz,' says Mularabone from another universe.

'Thanks,' I hear myself say in a faraway voice.

She smiles again. It is a small smile, a subtle smile, like it's a secret for me. I love her giving me that secret. She turns with a swirl of her robe and sweeps away from us. I concentrate hard not to look after her. Not to run after her. I look up to Mularabone.

'She's got you, all right, bruz,' he laughs and does a little dance on the spot, elegantly holding his coffee mug out and not spilling a drop. I smile. We sip our coffee. We smile again.

'Good coffee, bruz,' says Mularabone.

'Sweet,' I say, 'sweet as ...'

I see through Mularabone's eyes that Uncle is next to me now, on the other side. Uncle Birra-ga nods at Mularabone in that certain way. Mularabone puts out his hand, Uncle takes it, and then they hug. Mularabone steps back.

'I'll see you ...' he says and indicates the direction he's going with his chin and eyes (Over there).

He goes, sipping his coffee as he saunters across the cavern. I turn to Uncle. Behind him on the rock is a massive painting. I don't know how I didn't see it when I walked in. It is a skyscape with spirit figures floating through it. Without taking my eyes from the painting I put my coffee down, fish in my pocket and pull out my ngumari. I roll the fattest cigarette I can and hand it to Uncle. The other old fulla is standing on the other side of Uncle. Uncle takes the fat cigarette and passes it on. I roll another one, just as fat. Uncle takes it. I light both of their cigarettes and then roll myself one. We look at our little fire. I pick up my coffee and take a slug. Them old Countrymen smoke.

'I knew your father,' Uncle says to me.

I nod. I'm looking down. I notice that the little fire is warm. Very warm. It burns far too hot for wood, and too evenly, even though, clearly, some small leafy branches have been burnt. Artificial fire, arty fires, stop people chopping down bush to burn. The leaves are probly just camp smoking, I'm thinking. I sip my coffee. Draw on my cigarette.

'We were not friends. Not brothers.'

I nod. I spose I knew, the moment I knew I was coming out here with Mularabone, that something like this was gonna happen. I wait. But there seems to be nothing more coming.

Uncle nods a couple of times. Too-big-for-normal nods.

'This is Warroo-culla. The Moth.'

I put my hand out. Warroo-culla grips me light as stirred-up wind from a moth's wings.

'Conway. Your name means holy water. You are my nephew. My sister's grandson.'

Warroo-culla leaves a pause. I wait.

'I knew your grandfather. Your grandmother's brother. You are Conway, after him.' He nods to himself.

'Yes ... Great-uncle,' I say.

Uncle Warroo-culla takes a drag on his smoke. I have nothing to say and I sense Great-uncle isn't finished; I know Birra-ga wanted to talk to me. Against the backdrop of the giant painting of the Milky Way, those two old men fit right in with the other floating spirits.

'Some killers-of-men dream of men they've killed,' Warroo-culla says.

I drain my coffee.

'Birra-ga is one of these men.' Uncle Warroo-culla touches Birra-ga on the arm. Birra-ga smiles as though praised for his footy ability as a young man. 'But not you.'

I look up for a moment to see his level gaze coming right through my eyes. He's not using his eyes and he's not looking at my flesh. My heart is beating like a madman.

'You are dreaming now of him in you. The killer. You are afraid of him. You are afraid he will kill you ...' says Warroo-culla looking away.

'Maybe he wants me to kill him,' I say.

'Why?' he asks me.

'To put him out of his misery,' I say.

'Is that why he wants to kill you?' Uncle smiles back.

I stare into my empty coffee cup, as if I'll find the answers there.

'Does he love you?' Uncle asks as innocently as a child; then when he sees these words land: 'Do you love him?'

It was Uncle Birra-ga who told me that the spirit only

dreams of love. That love is the dream. Maybe it was Uncle Warroo-culla speaking through him. Many mouths speak the same words when the message is the truth.

Warroo-culla laughs and with a wave of his hand dismisses this conversation.

'Sit,' says Birra-ga.

We all settle into the dust.

'You don't know who your father was,' says Birra-ga.

'A contractor for the Water Board,' I offer.

'What he was,' says Warroo-culla.

'A grog runner,' says Birra-ga.

'Grog dreaming is all around you,' says Warroo-culla.

I look away to the painting of the spirit figures floating on the cave wall. Are my dreams the sounds of my soul being rusted by the desolate spirits of the grog dreaming? Are the sins of the father visited on the sons?

'There are many kinds of dreams, some of what is coming ... what has been ... some awake ... some in deep sleep ...' says Warroo-culla.

'But you already know this,' says Birra-ga. 'You told The Sarge about your dream premonitions.'

I'm breaking into a sweat.

'You have something,' says Warroo-culla matter-of-factly. 'They want it too. The Water Board.' Uncle Warroo-culla looks away. 'They are already looking for you. And Mularabone,' he says.

'Mularabone?'

'His presence is important. Strength.'

'I haven't got anything.'

When Warroo-culla speaks his voice is calm and quiet. 'Your dreams can be a pathway ... some pathways we can't get any other way.'

Before I can speak, Birra-ga puts an arm on my shoulder

and squeezes me to silence.

'We live in the time of new beginning. To begin again we need to go back.'

'Back?'

'To the beginning ... In the south ... For ceremony ... You and Mularabone have a part to play ...'

Uncle Warroo-culla leans down and extends his finger near my boot. There is a tiny jumping spider there that I hadn't noticed. The spider jumps quickly to the proffered finger. The Countrymen smile.

'Strong totem,' says Uncle. 'Spider. Weaver of past and present.'

'My boy,' begins Birra-ga, 'our people do not share spider totem.'

'But we can share the path she walks, the path she weaves,' adds Warroo-culla.

They both nod. The tiny spider leaps back to my boot.

'To allow for change in this world, we must make changes in the *other place*,' says Warroo-culla.

'The other place?' I hear myself say.

I look to the old Countrymen, but they are both looking away, their eyes absorbed by the colossal paintings of spirit beings in the skyscape mural.

We finish our smokes. We stub them out on the rock and Great-uncle collects the bumpers.

Uncle Birra-ga touches me on the upper arm with his steel-rod fingers.

'Remember this talk, my nephew,' he says quietly. And he somehow makes 'my sister's grandson' float around the word 'nephew' like an invisible halo. I've learned enough about Language to know about what is not being said. I'm still thinking about what I haven't heard, what I don't know, when the old Countrymen get up and walk off.

I look down to the tiny spider. He takes a little step and then jumps again so fast that I lose him in the dry leaves by the fire. I stand up, still marvelling at the speed of that movement, and stride out for where Mularabone is hanging near the steps. As I reach him he starts to go up the ancient steps carved into the living rock without looking back at me. I match his pace and we go up fast. With each step my head throbs like I'm hungover as a bastard.

Four: Can't Remember

We come up through a small opening in the rock and we're on the surface. It takes me by surprise.

'Still dark, bro,' I say.

'Not still, bro.' Mularabone taps his fancy watch. 'We slept all day.'

I nod. Mularabone takes a reading. We start walking. It's as simple as that. The most complex things of all can be broken down like that. Into simple actions. We steal a Water Board truck, get some water – and deliver it to the mob.

Now we have a six hour walk ahead of us, at least. We have to cross the open country, through the low rocky hills, get past the Water Board compound, and into the refugee camp on the other side of the dam. We've gotta be in that refugee camp when the sun comes up and the Water Board troopers do their rounds.

We walk.

'What did Uncle Warroo-culla call you?'

'Nephew. His sister's grandson.'

'Shit.'

I grab Mularabone by the shoulders. 'What does it mean?'

Mularabone takes a big breath. He lets it out slowly.

I shake him. 'What?'

'I dunno,' he says and turns and goes.

We walk.

'They said we have to go back.'

'Back where?'

'To the beginning. In the south.'

'South? What for?'

'Kick-start ceremony.'

We walk.

'What do you know of the grog?' I say.

'The Dreaming?'

I nod.

'Revenge. Sexual jealousy. Hatred. A dark force that unites all dark forces.'

'My father was a grog runner.'

'You ever have a drink?'

'I can't remember.'

'You can't remember any-fucking-thing.'

I take a swing at Mularabone, and miss. Mularabone dances along in front of me like a ballet dancer.

'You can't even remember how to throw a punch!' he says.

'Who is she?'

'My cousin.'

'First cousin?'

'Second, or third, probly.'

'That's all right then.'

'Forget it.'

'What's her name?'

'Don't think about it, bruz.'

'What's her name?'

'Don't think about it.'

'Uncle Warroo-culla knew my name.'

'Proper inkata, him Uncle, maban.'

We walk.

I glance over my shoulder, suddenly not sure if I'm still in the cave; the sky behind us could be the painting, except for the massive floating spirit figures.

'The uncles said nothing about the water gathering?'

'They wanted to talk dreams.'

'That figures.'

'Whatever it is, you're in it with me.'

'They said that?'

'And there's someone looking for us. Water Board.'

'The thick plottens. They tell you who?'

'Maybe they don't know.'

'Course they know. They were probly expecting you to ask.'

'They would've said.'

'Ya gotta learn to ask the right questions.'

'Well, you just left me.'

'Did you tell them about that dream you told The Sarge?'

'I thought you must've.'

'Why did The Sarge believe you? That's what I always wondered.'

'It came true.'

Mularabone shakes his head as though to rid himself of the memory the way a dog gets water from its coat, and walks on.

'You got any herb, coorda?' I ask.

Mularabone looks at me, and smiles his wry smile. He shakes his head. 'Ah, Djenga.'

Of course, any stash he had would have been handed over to the uncles. Sharing Law. Sometimes you can look and see but just not notice what is really going on around you.

We walk.

Off to the north we see a family of wallabies. They stop eating, and look up to watch us pass. Their brown eyes are warm under the light of the Milky Way. Ahead of us is the rocky country we must pass through, to go down to the refugee camp on the other side.

Dreaming 44: Back of the Ute

The ute swerves sharply again and I jostle the body next to me in the back. The driver's head turns for a second. It's Jack! Jack's pissed. Eyes shining, lips as red as sex, cheeks glowing with malice and laughter and alcohol. The man in the passenger side doesn't turn around. But I recognise the back of his head as if it were my own: 44. My arms tighten around the child in my lap. The road snakes away behind us, the black-brown of the hill to the left, the black-black of nothing to the right, and far below us the blue-black of the sea.

'Let's go for two tyres over!' Jack screams, and his laugh comes back to me in chunky wet globules like diseased spit in the wind.

The vehicle beneath us accelerates. My stomach tightens and I feel the tyres go over, for a moment lost, and then yanked back to the road surface by strong hands on the steering wheel. Jack is laughing again. The child is still silent. My fear is as black as the night. The others in the back of the ute loll drunkenly and sway against each other like a kelp forest moving in the ocean current.

As the tyres go out near the cliff edge, stones and gravel fly out into the drop. Even if the rushing night wasn't tearing at my ears, I would never hear those stones hit.

The vehicle begins to accelerate more, the back end swaying to match Jack's casual wrists and dribbly mouth. I twist my head around to get my eyes forward and see the corner approaching. I know we can't take the corner. We're going too fast. I'm trying to breathe, trying to get my mind to work, as the fear rushes through me. My arms are around the child, as tight as tears, and he whimpers for the first time. The tips of Jack's ears begin to glow red. My face cringes in slow motion like a punch-drunk boxer waiting to be finished off – and the ute leaves the road. Leaves the earth. I look back over the waving kelp bed of bodies in the tray of the ute to watch the road and the earth running away from us. Running like a dying man. There is a strange silence, slow-motion silence, somewhere the engine still revs, the tyres still spin in vain, and Jack, Jack with this lopsided confused smile. Which I can see because now I am above the ute looking down, watching it falling. Feeling it falling, and the moment I feel it falling I'm back in it, hunched over the child, falling through the sky, protecting the child with my body against all knowledge of gravity. Falling from terror into nothingness.

There is a big jolt and we're back on the road, the ute swerving this way and that on the winding coast road, which drops hundreds of metres to the ocean on the south side. The back of the ute is full of lolling bodies. I'm comforting the child, and Jack's head is framed in the back window. 44 doesn't look back. Jack still has his lopsided grin. He turns and yells back over his shoulder, 'Let's try for two wheels over!'

Five: Metal Bees

Mularabone touches me on the shoulder. I feel his strength.

'You right, bruz?'

I nod in the dark. Then stumble.

'You sure?'

'I think they're onto us.'

'You see something?'

'Jack trying to kill me in a ute.'

'We gotta keep going.'

We reach the edge of the rocky country. Away to the south there is a vehicle driving. We hear it before we see it. The headlights cut into the darkness, forming a little cone of light, spearing its way through the desert night at speed, and throwing a dust cloud out behind it. It's like the dust is causing the vehicular motion, not the other way around, as though the vehicle is consuming the desert. Mularabone and I stand and watch the vehicle heading doggedly towards the Water Board compound.

'Friends of yours, bruz?' Mularabone asks me.

'Thought they were your mates, bruz.'

We're suddenly weary. We've got that weird underwater feeling; today was our first sleep for days, and like a drug, when you've had a little, and you really need it, it calls to you like a song in your bones. We've been driving and walking through this Country and we haven't seen the sun for two days. This means we're vulnerable. We're once-removed from the realities of vehicles, and what they mean.

Ahead of us, in the rocks, a shadow shifts, a shadow that doesn't belong. Our bodies have already begun to move. We take three steps, maybe four, at full run, and we're throwing our bodies down, instinctively searching for depressions in the earth to land in, as the air is torn apart from the machinegun fire. The earth behind us explodes in dust and rock splinters, the air alive from the angry metal bees. There is another burst of gunfire, the bullets cracking and splitting the air open above our heads. Our bodies are pressed into the earth, and we can't get close enough, deep enough to our mother, in a desperate attempt to keep our bodies intact.

I hear someone swearing. I look to Mularabone before realising that it's my voice. The shooting stops. I stop. We don't move a muscle. They obviously haven't got night-vision gear, or we'd already be dead. They must be sloppy, or we'd never have seen it coming; even just a second or so of warning gives them away as amateurs. We've still got a chance of getting out of this. We glance at each other. A tiny nod. We start crawling backwards, away from the immediate threat. It's not easy to see how close they are, or how many.

The spotlight comes on. It is an intense beam of light to be inside of. Like the light has a texture, a weight, and we feel it heavy upon us. It perfectly encompasses both of us, in our silly little attempt to crawl away backwards. We look at each other, now bathed in brilliant whiteness. Mularabone tenses his body in mock-fear to take the piss out of me. I look down at my offending body, and then sheepishly back at Mularabone. I know I'm still afraid to die. 44 tells me every fucking night. From Mularabone, it is more like love. My brother still prepared to joke and we're both about to die. We smile at each other, naughty schoolboys who know we're gonna get the cane, but it's still gonna be worth it.

'Don't move! Don't move! Don't move a fucking muscle!'

The megaphone blares out as bizarrely in the desert night as the spotlight we're lying in.

Mularabone pushes himself up and gets to his feet in one motion. I follow him half a second later.

'What the fuck are you doing, bruz?' I ask. My voice comes out high and whiny.

'I don't wanna die lyin down, bruz.'

I laugh. Shake my head as if to say 'Crazy-fucken-Countrymen'.

'What are you doin then?' he asks me, looking at my standing-up-ness.

'I don't wanna die alone, bruz.'

He laughs. Shakes his head at me as if to say 'Crazy-fucken-Djenga'.

'I said: don't fucken move!'

A burst of fire smashes into the earth just to our left.

We don't move now. We show them our empty hands. We both wish we had weapons. We'd know we'd probly be dead by now if we did have weapons but we still wish we had them; that's men for ya.

We hear their boots running towards us, maybe half a dozen. The light is in our eyes so we are blind to the night now. Into the circle of light, I see a rifle butt arcing towards me. I step in past it and smash into the trooper on the end of it. He goes down hard. There is another right behind him swinging at me from the other way. I duck deep and strike out for his torso, which appears in the light just in time to meet my fist. Something cracks me from behind and I'm going down hard. I'm hitting the earth and rifle butts and boots are raining down on me.

Dreaming 44: Rotten Inside

I'm sitting in the back of the paddy wagon, chained like a dog. Chained like a rodeo bull – because the ring feels like it goes through my nose. I can't see the driver in the front. But the passenger in the front is 44. I'd recognise that dark crew cut on his big boofhead disappearing up under his black hunting cap anywhere.

There is dappled light falling across my naked torso. I look down. Just above my left nipple is a big ripe pimple. It is almost as big as my nipple, the yellow pus mountain like my nipple, and the red inflamed area like my areola. I get both my hands up to it and start to squeeze. A sharp pain shoots through my left side and erupts through the point of the pimple as the skin breaks. The pus and blood dribble down my chest but the core of the pimple is a dry, hardened yellowish ball. It's left a big hole in me. Inside I see there is another head, just below the surface. I squeeze again and another core comes out. The hole is a little bigger and there are more yellowish balls pushing at the opening. I tear my flesh until the hole is a little bigger and half a dozen or so hard pimple heads come out. I'm getting frantic now. I tear at the hole in me. It is big enough to put a football into, and the hard little off-yellow balls pour out, cascading into my lap, quickly piling up as high as my nipples as my body opens and the hard rotten pimple heads pour out.

Six: Back of the Divvy Van

The motion of the vehicle wakes me. The van rattles, slides and bumps its way along, way too fast for the quality of the road, throwing my body this way and that. We go over a big bump, sending hot pokers into my side. My strides are damp below the waist. I've pissed myself whilst unconscious. Not the first time. The smell of piss fills my nostrils.

I hear a voice in the darkness: 'You back with us, coorda?'

'Mmm.'

'What the fuck were you doing, bruz?'

'Didn't want to die without a fight, bruz.'

Mularabone chuckles in the darkness at my reply.

'What the fuck were you doin, bruz?' I croak out.

'Didn't want to mess up my hair, bruz.'

I try to smile in the darkness but feel myself slipping down again. I keep thinking about The Sarge, and the war. Must be because we're in custody of the Water Board. The Sarge always reckoned that the war was inevitable, may his soul find peace. He reckoned that failure could not abide success – and will always be driven to pull it down. The individual versus the group, said Mularabone. All I could think of was wet versus dry. Nah, said The Sarge, it's just East versus West.

For a moment there are ghosts in the back of the van. I don't know if I can really see them or not. It is true that whitefullas, Djenga, really do look like ghosts. White spirits. If they are there, they bend over me, fiddling with the metal restraining device. If they aren't there, then there's nothin to worry about.

Mularabone and I roll against each other as the van bumps and jumps along the track.

'If they were gonna kill us, we'd be dead by now,' comments Mularabone.

'This is what the uncles were talking about. Someone looking for us.'

'We don't need the Moth to tell us the Water Board is after us – we took their bloody trucks.'

'Nah, but it is connected.'

'I hope so.'

'Why?'

'Otherwise they're just gonna fuck us up.'

'They are very thingy about their trucks.'

'Thingy?'

'Yep.'

We both know we're just talking to keep our shit together.

I breathe the piss smell in deeply through my nostrils to keep myself alert. I'm trying to think about the smoke that Uncle Warroo-culla was blowing out. I'm trying to bring the tiny spider into my heart.

Dreaming 44: The Pub in the Middle of Nowhere

I arrive at the Pub in the Middle of Nowhere and it's hot and dusty and the bar is full of big men. Big arms, big guts, big mouths, big blue singlets, big stubbies, big boots, big lumberjack shirts. Fucken big bastards.

I go up to the bar and they begin to crowd me and I know that very soon I'll have to fight. Fight my way out. By the time I get to the bar, there are men crowding right in on me, touching me on all sides. I really feel like a cold beer but I see now that a drink is out of the question. There is the sound of a can being popped open by someone else. I'm tonguing for a beer. Needing that coldness. Wanting the bubbles. Desperate for the tang on my tastebuds and the blurry buzz in my brain. A thick blue haze of cigarette smoke hangs in the air.

I snap my fist into the man right in front of me. My fist buries itself into him up to my wrist, his skull crushing like a thick-shelled empty egg. I push him off my fist and three men immediately take his place. They leer at me. I punch them down.

Blam! Blam! Blam!

Over the heads of these men I see three black men sitting quietly in the corner. They wear huge white ten-gallon hats. They sit calmly, appearing to take no notice or interest in the action at the bar.

Three more big men turn up. Big white men. They leer. I punch. They leer. I punch. I punch. I punch. The big white men are three deep lining up to attack me and three-deep on the floor with smashed faces and crushed eggshell skulls and I push off the wall of men, and run for the street, grabbing a rifle as I go.

I never get to fire my weapon. I drop my rifle, seemingly unbidden, and it thuds softly into the dust at my feet. They have me. Holding me down. Metal barrels pressed hard against my back and head. Something else is pressed in at my neck, something cold, something metal, something that makes me hold my head at a strange angle and organise my body differently, in a tightened, twisted way. When I attempt any movement it is strange and robotic.

I climb into the back of a grey ute. I'm moving slowly, like I'm in a trance. Like I don't exist. The ute takes off.

Now they have me. I know what is required of me.

I'm just waiting for it. Waiting in the back of the ute.

There are four or five Djenga sitting around me. They all have rifles pointed at my stomach. The night rushes past the ute like a symphony orchestra on ice skates, their instruments muffled, and out of tune.

Seven: The Tank

The vehicle has come to a halt. There's artificial light spewing in through the barred windows at the side. I look down to see Mularabone sleeping. His face is bruised and swollen, and there's blood seeping from a cut under his shirt. I lean in and gently shake him. He doesn't move but his eyes open. He looks at me.

'Are we there yet?'

The back door starts to rattle from the outside.

'Put em in the fucken tank,' a voice says.

Mularabone and I start to get up, the chains at our wrists and ankles rattle on the metal floor. The back door opens.

'C'mon girls, time to get out!'

Mularabone and I climb out. Mularabone falls down. I grab him and haul him to his feet. We're inside the Water Board compound. The place is lit up with permanent ML lights strung on poles. They are powered by the glowing and humming solar storage unit swathed in barbed wire. Just beyond the perimeter is the dam and the expanse of water that the Water Board is protecting. We are so close to the water that I can smell the sweetness.

The Water Board troopers train their weapons on us. But they're standing back a bit. A couple of them have black eyes and face cuts, the legacy of the arrest. I smile at them, gripping a length of the chain that joins our wrists and ankles, willing one of them to get close enough for me to give it to him. I've been in custody for less than three hours and I'm already thinking like a lifer, no care for my own person, desperate to do any damage I can to my captors. The Water Board troopers are mostly Eastern Staters. You can tell em at a glance. Djenga, of course, same look in their eye, same set to their mouth. And the hate. The hate that closes off their auras, leaving only greyish smudges all around them. It's stained them. Stained them as a people, and stained them individually. You didn't see that look on Djenga when I was a child.

They hate me more than Mularabone. Cause I'm white like them. I'm the living proof that they are wrong. So they hate me. And I hate them back. They have no respect for the Law of this Country. They lack the courage to be real men. To face the Law. The Law of this Country can't be beaten with slick lawyers. Can't be bribed off. Can't be tricked by rewriting history. I hate them because of that look in their eyes. I hate that look. I hate them because they are the stupid followers of orders. And I hate myself for hating them. No good can come of hate. I know it in my head but not in my heart. Not in my body. Not in my wild eyes crawling over their features like drunken flies, not in my white knuckles holding the bunched up chain, desperate for an opening. Where is the Law in locking up the water? In locking us up? Shuffling the refugees in and out of their goals and work gangs? Maybe it's that look in their pale eyes that set me to thinking about killing. My memories of fighting them are still so clean, like the stars on a cloudless night. They've got the same look in their eyes as me. They'd love me to try to attack them, just so they could shoot me down. They return my smile with gusto, especially the little dark-eyed fulla with the deep cut on his left eye.

The troopers prod us with their weapons. We pick up our chains, and walk splayfooted, with turkey necks, to the big metal door being opened in front of us. I get to the doorway first. I hesitate. A nightstick cracks into the back of my knees and I fall down. Mularabone doesn't even get a chance to protest before a nightstick smashes into him as well.

Mularabone and I are sprawling in the dust like a couple of barramundi just hauled out of the river. They roll us with their boots until we're inside in the darkness, and then the big metal door slams behind us.

Dreaming 44: Campfire Execution

I'm lounging by my built-up campfire. My back is cold from the frosty morning but my face and chest are hot from the fire. I'm naked. I look up to see her standing there, on a little white sandhill across from the fire. She is still naked. Our fucking is still vibrating in my body. She is looking at me intensely. Her eyes want to hold mine. My eyes want to roam all over her body, drinking in her curves, as though I can claim some ownership with my looking. As she starts to move down towards me, I see the ancient breech-loading pistol in her left hand. She holds it casually, as though it means nothing, like it's a handbag or a purse containing no money. She gets closer and the red fire flickers on her chocolate flesh. I look back to her eyes, but she seems distant, like she wants or needs nothing from me now. She arcs around the fire and out of the circle of red light, coming around behind me. I can't see her. But somehow I see her feet placing themselves one after the other in the white sand. Somehow I see the huge and ancient pistol, already fully cocked, tracking towards me, flowing up and down with the movement of her hips. I'm sitting by the fire and I can see the huge pistol approaching me, I can see it without looking. I look back to where she was when I first saw her on the white sand dune. 44 is standing there. I see him but he is like a shadow too, or a ghost – there and yet not there. I know it's him because the firelight flares on the thick lenses of his glasses. The ancient pistol floats up to the very top of my head, and that finger that was only moments before playing across my body and making me moan, pulls the brass trigger.

Eight: Swimming in the Tank

The tank interior is light now. We sit up with our backs to the metal door. There's a shaft of light that spills in from a corresponding opening in the roof. That glowing corridor almost splits the red dust floor space in half and marches up the far wall. It's still early but the illumination already appears to have a texture, a rich kaleidoscope of heat and danger. The DOz is well over us now. The depleted ozone always makes me think of the vampire legends. Maybe they are legends from our future and not our past? In another hour, one minute exposed to that light would be your last.

There are dozens of blokes in here. All chained at wrist and ankle. All desperate men. On one side of the tank is a mob of Djenga, and on the other, all Countrymen. Separated perfectly by the shaft of light. In this makeshift jail the new divisions brought by the Water Board are being played out in deadly earnest. Why do people fall for it? People are so easy to manipulate, The Sarge would say, may his soul find peace. Maybe they have no choice? The Water Board uses the prisoners as their worker bees, to build their roads, dig their minerals, maintain their dams and catchments, cultivate their crops. And if they can't or won't play the game here on the chain, then they get moved to the underground jail, a whole other level of hell.

I gingerly run my fingers over the top of my head. I half expect there to be a big jagged hole where the ancient flintlock pistol shot went in at point-blank range. Under my dusty hair, my skull is smooth. 44 is using everything close to me to attack me, even my desire for the woman from Uncle's cave. I tried to tell the uncles. I feel like I've been run over by a forty-tonne water tanker. I think if I look down I'll see the bruises on my chest from the thirty-six wheels that went over me. I look down. There is just me. No bruises. Just me, chained like a dog.

Mularabone is stirring too. We're inside a huge disused metal tank. One hundred years ago, this was a water storage facility. The roof has been hacked open, which is how the sunlight is creeping over to us.

The other inmates are starting to notice us now. This big Djenga fulla and five or six of his mates amble over in our direction. They're all tough-looking bastards, covered in scars and tattoos. Across from the Djenga inmates, divided by the light, the mob of Countrymen are also taking a keen interest in us. As the Djenga get closer, Mularabone touches me on the upper arm. We haul ourselves up to our feet without a word. The group of rednecks stops about three metres from us. The big redneck leader, a blood nut in blue overalls, who looks like he was born in this tank, steps out from his gang.

'You're mine, bitch!'

I have this bemused expression on my face, like I don't know he's talking to me, or I don't speak his language. I focus on his mouth as he speaks. His lips are pink and thick, like medium rare rump steaks banging together; it wouldn't surprise me if small droplets of blood flew out with his speech. He takes another step towards me. This time I match him with a step. I'm over it now. His mates behind him might kick the shit out of me, but I'm gonna shove this spare chain in my hands down his throat until he gags on the metal, and spit on him as he's choking to death. I'm locked eyes with him now, no backing down. Out of the corner of my eye I see that the Countrymen have moved closer as well. Blood Nut is trying to figure his next move.

'I said, you're mine, bitch!' he repeats.

'I heard,' I confide with a smile.

One of the Countrymen steps out from his mob. He and Mularabone exchange hand signals. The rednecks barely notice, but all the Countrymen do.

'You talkin to a brother, Mitch.'

Mitch the Blood Nut looks over to the voice.

'No,' he replies, 'I'm talkin to *him*,' and he jabs his finger at me.

I'm poker-faced – but Mitch the Blood Nut is starting to get under my skin.

Don't jab your fucken fingerbone at me.

Out to my left the expressions on the faces of the desert brothers don't change, like their faces are carved from rock.

'You talkin to a brother, Mitch,' that fulla repeats, his voice low and even.

I know that voice. The recognition gives me confidence. Mitch the Blood Nut looks back to me. His eyes burn into me and his hands hanging at his side begin to twitch involuntarily. He takes another very deliberate step towards me. The other rednecks behind follow suit, their big boots stirring tiny clouds of red dust in the golden morning sun. But Mitch the Blood Nut and his cohorts don't even get time to blink. The brothers' expressions don't change. Their feet don't walk. But in a flash they are all toe-to-toe with the Djenga, eyeball to eyeball, blocking the path to Mularabone and I.

Mitch the Blood Nut goes slack-mouthed, the medium rare steaks flapping like wet doonas on a clothesline. The brothers stare hard. The rednecks stare hard. If there's gonna be a go now, it's gonna be big. Big, fast, and furious; there's plenty of old scores to settle. Mitch the Blood Nut shakes them off. Backs down. He goes to turn away.

Phum! The brothers are back where they were standing before. No one's feet have moved. No little red dust clouds in the diffused angry morning sun. No tracks.

Mitch slack-jaws again. He's never seen Countrymen throw images of themselves across a space before. I've never seen it done en masse.

The brothers move in to us now. They light a fire under their smiles. They shake our hands proper way. Young James, the leader of the brothers, comes and hugs us fiercely. He was in the cadre with Mularabone and I and The Sarge. We laughed at death together. We move back over to their spot in the tank. Mularabone is talking in Language to them. The rednecks watch us go.

We sit in the dust and Mularabone reaches into his side pocket and takes out his ngumari. Slack of the troopers. They should've searched us. The brothers slap him on the back and laugh. We each roll a thin one and light up. I look across to Mitch the Blood Nut who is still staring at me, a hungry cat watching the mouse walking away.

I give him a smile: Any time, fucker!

I can read Mitch's thought from here: Who do you think you are? What colour are you? Whose side are you on?

I look around me, the only white face in this tight mob of desert fullas. I've spent my life asking these questions, and reading it in others around me.

Ya can't always get what ya want, I'm thinking as I smoke, and feel a wry, unrealised smile creep into my face.

I catch something out of the corner of my eye and glance down to my right shoulder. There is a huntsman spider perched on my shirt. She has both her front legs up, hanging on with the other six, and is standing up in a challenge stance.

I look at her. I don't move. I can feel her taking me in with her many eyes, feeling my mood and texture through her feet, trying to read my intentions. I stare back. She suddenly jumps off me without warning, freefalling for a moment, and then floating down as if she has an invisible parachute. She hits the ground running and takes off, heading under some rotting wooden crates lying on the tank floor. Only then do I feel the silky-secret touch of her web brush my face. She spun a web as she dropped, that's how she controlled her speed. What a piece of beauty, wrapped up in that single action. She wasn't afraid of me. I was afraid of her. And that dismount; huntsmen don't build webs but hunt in the open – but she could spin one to abseil off me like Water Board Special Forces going down a building with their ropes and carabiners.

I look up to see that Mularabone and a few of the other desert lads are looking at me. I wonder what they saw? Wha'd they reckon?

From the other end of the tank there is suddenly a big commotion as the steel doors are opened and Water Board troopers in full riot gear start pouring in.

'Here he comes,' I say.

'Who?' asks Mularabone.

'Jack. Fresh from my ute dream.'

'Is he the one looking for us?'

'I doubt it. Jack would be battling to find himself.'

When a dozen of them have formed an open-ended perimeter, Jack steps in. He isn't in riot gear, but wearing the dress uniform for Water Board officers. Apart from his enclosed helmet, he resembles a bona fide member of the original Rum Corps of New South Wales.

I turn to Mularabone. 'Nice entrance.'

'Didn't know ya could still get away with jodhpurs, bruz.'

The group around us laugh.

Jack turns to the sound and marches towards us.

'Uh-oh! Look out!' says one of the brothers.

More laughter.

Jack strides towards us with renewed purpose. He is just about to get to the end of where his troopers are, when a low voice sings out, 'Watch out, brother.'

The sound of the voice chases Jack across the sand and latches onto his flesh like a word spoken-hummed through a didj.

Jack stops.

'You wouldn't wanna get too far away from your boys, Jack ... No telling what might happen ...'

Jack looks to the speaker. Young James is like a king brown snake that's been sleeping all winter, storing up venom, and is woken by the sun and an unpleasant vibration against his belly.

Jack stands his ground and turns his eyes on me.

I can see him clearly through the greenish ultraviolet protection glass of his helmet. He hasn't changed a bit. He should be handsome still, but the ugly shit inside him is really starting to show on his face. I catch myself wondering the same about myself. Why do I never look in the mirror? Am I frightened that I'm worse than Jack? It'd serve me right for thinking I'm a better man than him. He surely thinks he's a better man than me.

He's trying to read me. 'Conway.'

I'm trying to read him through the UVP. 'Jack.'

'Now why aren't I surprised?'

He doesn't really want an answer. He's always needed an audience, though. He hasn't thought of anything smart to say. I change my mind and decide to answer him.

'I'm not surprised to see you either, Jack.'

'Come and have a chat, Con*man*.'

'Are we going for a morning trot? Or a gallop?'

There is a moment before the brothers get my meaning. It's like a wave curling, that moment that suspends time, when the wave peaks, hangs and then crashes. There are giggles all around me. The brothers are laughing openly at the jodhpurs now.

Jack spins on his heel.

'A nice canter, perhaps?' I offer up meekly.

Jack strides back to the guarded doorway, speaking to his troopers out of the corner of his mouth as he goes. 'Get em both out. Separate em.'

And then he disappears through the metal door in the tank wall.

The Water Board trooper on the end turns and stares at me. He raises the visor on his riot helmet. I see his black eye from last night. He doesn't look happy. Small but dangerous.

'Come on!' he says through gritted teeth.

'Come on Aussie, come on, come on,' one of the brothers sings under his breath. The trooper doesn't take his angry grey eyes off me but strides out to our right, to where this other young brother is standing on his own. He's only fifteen or sixteen and a bit unsure of himself. He is frozen like a roo in a spotlight. We all are. It's the weapons. We know that these troopers will kill us all. It's happened before. And the truck bearing down on him is the angry little trooper, with the black eye from last night. Before we can move or even make a sound, Black-Eye-From-Last-Night clubs the youth a terrific downward blow with his weapon on the head and neck. The others troopers have read his intentions exactly, and as the young Countryman crumples into the red earth floor, their rifles are already coming up to aim at us. We see their fingers push off their safety catches. Our eyes zone through the drama of the big picture to read the details that we need.

'Come now!'

A nasty thrill thrums down my spine. I should've stepped out before. That young lad took the hit for me. I try to keep this feeling at bay so I don't lose my focus. It's done.

Mularabone and I step away from the group and walk out towards the troopers. I'm a couple of steps closer and I'm going to get to the trooper first. I can hear Mularabone thinking, 'He's gonna go for a hit, bruz.' He probly hears me thinking, 'Yeah, bruz.'

I know it's coming because everything has already begun to go in slow motion. If I fight there could be a bloodbath. I know what these type of fullas are like, the Water Board troopers, I mean.

But I can't go down. He's holding the rifle across his body. His left foot is forward. He's gonna butt-slam me in the face. I hold his gaze. There is an almost imperceptible movement from the toe of his front left foot. Here it comes. I'm going forward. Straight at the threat and under it to my right side. The butt of his weapon slips past my face, and I'm in close now and low, with both my hands I'm grabbing his arm and yanking hard in the same direction as his own momentum. He's overreached and is easily pulled off balance. He goes past me and lands in a heap, dust flying, at the feet of one of his trooper mates. Mularabone and I do not stay our pace and are both past him and heading for the door by the time he can get to his feet. The inmates erupt with cheers and howls of delight, Countrymen and rednecks alike. We've done this move before. It's exactly the drill to overrun a fortified or dug-in position. But now we have no grenades or automatic weapons to do the damage inside the wired-up perimeter.

I'm almost at the door when the troopers' nightsticks slam into my head, neck, and back.

Nine: Boxed In

I'm in a much smaller cell. A box more than a cell. I've been in these metal boxes before. These cells are defence issue. I'm cuffed to the metal bench The Sarge used to call 'the couch' with more than a hint of irony. Like the walls, floor, and roof, it is plain metal, buffed but dull. Like my captors. My head is aching. Pulsing like a molten lead jellyfish; like coming up those stone steps only hours ago, my mind trying to compute what the uncles said. I know there is a part of me that recognised the conversation. But there is a dark cloud obscuring memories of my father. For the coming ceremony down south – it makes sense of the Countrymen wanting to smash the power of the Water Board. To smash it, not with guns, with something more lasting. The ceremony will make the venture not about diminishing the invaders, but about increase for us. The ceremony in the south will surely be held at a place of increase. What about what was not said? Who is looking for us? How do we escape the Water Board, and operators like Jack? I've never taken part in a Countryman ceremony in my life. My mind is jumping about the place like a half empty drum of fuel in the back of the ute. I'm tired and hungry.

My right hand is cuffed down tight but my legs are free. I slip my buttocks down the bench, carefully slide my right arm down onto the couch, and place the outside of my elbow down flat on the metal. The metal is already beginning to lose its overnight coolness. I allow the movement of my arm to pull my shoulders and then my head down, taking the weight across the back of my shoulders; and I lift my pelvis and push my legs and feet up over my head so that I go into a full headstand on the couch, braced against the back wall. I close my eyes and listen to the deep song of my head-throb. As the blood rushes into my head and my energy centres are inverted, the throbbing rises in pitch. It rises until I think I can feel my brain beating like my heart, rattling around in the bone cell of my skull. I wonder if my heart is resting for a moment, letting my brain keep the blood flowing, or maybe they've swapped and my heart is having a good think. And then it is like the tide is going out. I stand on the shoreline of breath, and watch the pain gently receding from me. I see it as the tide going out. Only it isn't the clear blue waters of the Indian Ocean – but some dark oily liquid of unknown derivation. When the pain recedes there is nothing on my beach. Just the pain oil-stain. A few small rocks. A metal box slowly warming in the morning sun. How strange it feels to be in this metal box on the beach of pain. These cells were designed to be picked up and dropped by helicopters. That was years ago, before the helicopters stopped flying. A moveable jail. The Sarge always said, may his soul find rest, that the trouble with the Water Board, the trouble with the Eastern States was that they began as a penal colony and just can't grow out of that jailer mentality. Here they are, putting us in jail, and not giving us access to our own Country, our own water. Time isn't a straight line. Isn't even a circle: kind of orbs that intertwine across universes and dimensions. This is what the uncles were talking about.

The metal door slides back, and Jack steps in. He's changed into desert fatigues. The UVP cloth composite hangs down to obscure his face. His hands are gloved. He looks like a zombie trooper. Even though I'm inverted, I know it's him from the way he holds his shoulders: reminds me of someone.

I squeeze my eyelids to blink away the sweat. When did I start sweating? The box is getting hot. Or is it my pain? Or my fear?

Jack quite deliberately takes off his hat, and with it the UVP, revealing his face. In the confined space I can smell the grog on his breath. The diffused smell of that liquor circles my heart like a pack of dogs, hungry and wild. I have to really concentrate to keep myself here in this moment with Jack, and to keep out those memories and half-forgotten dreams crowding in on me, salivating like those starving dogs. Jack's eyes stay hidden behind his shades. He appears surprised to see me. Maybe just taken aback to see me upside down. He stays in the doorway. Maybe he's worried about me launching myself off the wall in a kicking attack.

'You stink, Conman.'

'You going soft, Jack?'

He smiles at my jibe. His shades are thick and chunky but I can still feel the hate burning behind them. Everyone's hatred takes a different shape. Jack's is an insolent child sitting inside the rim of his eyes. The Insolent Child of Hate is doing something with his hands: fishing, or, no, maybe it's a yo-yo. I can still make out the movement through the dark glasses.

Jack loves his luxury but perversely envies my wretchedness. He's never had anything to believe in: just the warm and soothing false bed of comfort.

I slowly disengage from my headstand and allow my body to retrace its steps until I'm sitting back down on the couch, looking at Jack.

'What are we going to do with you, Conman?'

'Who? You and your Eastern States mates?'

Now Jack's smile is gone. His face is blown clean like a desert dune, just the fishbone ripples to show that some force of air has passed that way.

'Don't think I won't do what I have to do,' he says.

'Are you threatening me?'

'This is serious.'

'You don't have to do anything.'

'You know I do, Conman.'

'I know you will. You choose to.'

Jack takes a breath. He gives his head an almost imperceptible shake. I wonder if he is trying to shake something off, or allow something to settle on him more completely.

'History is history,' Jack says.

'Whose history?'

'There is nothing between us, Conway.'

I keep looking at him evenly. I know he's right. There's nothing between us. Look at him there in his Water Board fighting rig – our ancestors worked so hard to keep this Eastern States thinking from corrupting our community. I can't keep the scorn out of my eyes.

Jack is holding a small remote control. He taps it with the finger of his right hand. Suddenly my jaw clamps down, my muscles thrash, and my joints rattle like train tracks. The electric shock throws me to the floor. I look at Jack's boots. Notice the rubber soles.

'What do you reckon?' he is asking me.

At least he's enthusiastic about something.

'It's new,' I say, struggling for control of my tongue.

'My idea.' Jack positively beams. 'Got the idea up on the islands. They converted it for me.'

Prack! Snapple! Cop! The charge pulses through me again.

Fuck, it's a weird pain. I'd rather be hit.

'I'd rather be hit,' comments Jack.

I wrestle my tongue back to the floor of my mouth and breathe in through my nose.

'Jack. Are you angry with me because I saved your life?'

Jack rips out an extending baton with his free hand and smashes it into my right shoulder.

'Or because now you owe me?'

The baton thuds into my other shoulder. Jack folds up the baton and sheathes it.

'You stole my trucks.'

'I didn't know they were your trucks, Jack.'

'Ya fucken know now.'

'Do you think I did this to hurt you, Jack?'

'Do you know how much shit I've had to take for those trucks?'

'Ya gotta expect to lose a few trucks.'

Smash! Frapple! Strop! Another charge hacks through me. I can't get my eyes open now. It feels really bright in here. So bright. I hear his voice in my light-bathed pain cloud. I try to get my eyes open but can only manage a tiny crack against the streaming light. He is a huge blurry silhouette. Like the god of the setting sun.

'It's not about the trucks, Jack. And you know it.'

'What?'

'Who sent you to get us?'

Now I've really got his attention. The Insolent Child that lives in his eye is having a fit, raging around inside that eyeball like he'll destroy the place.

'Who is looking for us, Jack?'

'Just me.'

'You're a bad liar. Which is funny, you've had a shitload of practice.'

He takes a couple of steps and slams his right boot into my guts. I should've let him die when I had the fucken chance. He grabs my hair and lifts up my head. He leans in close to me.

'He can't get you if I don't tell him I've got you!'

'Who?'

'They don't know what it's like out here, dealing with your kind.'

'What do they want with us?'

'Doesn't matter, does it?'

'That's why you can't kill us.'

'He can have you when I'm finished. If there's anything left.'

He hits the remote again. His whole countenance shakes as the charge goes through me, as though he is generating it out of his own body. He's trying to restart my heart. Stop my brain from pumping the blood. Stop my liver from thinking. The Insolent Child is swinging his outside leg back and forth from all the excitement. He's a fidgety little bastard.

'I'm going to hurt everyone you have decided to side with against your own people. Starting with Mularabone. Hurt him good.'

'Don't you mean hurt him *bad*?'

'And you're gonna take me to them. I'm gonna kill them all.'

I try to manage a smile. 'Fuck, Jack – I thought you were gonna kiss me.'

He punches me in the face. A short, sharp blow. Kind of wakes me up a bit.

'Jack, you sound like an Eastern Stater.'

'And you look like a white man.'

I'm sure Jack is trying to smile as he says this but his face muscles rebel against his heart and can't quite make the right shape. This is like those white men who took the other path to my ancestors; those on the other side of our continent who couldn't respect Law and Country. It is said they laughed as they watched the Countrymen dying in front of their eyes from the poison they put in the blankets and flour. As the strychnine threw the afflicted bodies into the terrible rictus of the dance macabre, and the screams would come, the white men would watch and laugh. But I see now from Jack's face that it wasn't real laughter, but the noise of a soul rusting away at high speed, being corroded at the source by greed and hate. This is the origin of the fidgety little bastard spirit that lives in his eye. Some type of memory, of passed-on pain.

'Seriously, Jack: I really thought you were gonna kiss me.'

Jack's hat settles back onto his head, the UVP covering his face. His boots turn and disappear from my sight. The door slides shut behind him.

I pull myself back onto the couch. Jack's gone off to organise the drugs; I'm fucked now. The Sarge warned us this is how they roll, bless him. Ya gotta summon up something to resist. Something beyond the physical. If them uncles were right, I've gotta find the pathway. Stop waiting for it to happen to me. Gotta go after it.

What The Sarge was talking about – about holding out – wasn't about not giving any intel you have; everyone will do that eventually. That's why the cadres were set up in small cells that don't know the big picture details – so you can't give it up. The cell you are in is all you can give up. The Sarge, may his soul find peace, was talking about not being destroyed by the interrogation.

I close my eyes. Focus on my breathing. Focus on feeling myself in this cell. My body sitting here on this metal couch. The light kiss of blood on my face, the dull sting of bruises down my back and legs. I breathe in. I breathe out. I do nothing. Allow my breath to come in through my nose. Out through my mouth. I'm spinning coatings around myself. Spinning from my deep web. The core. The spirit animal that cannot be destroyed. Will not allow itself to be destroyed. I know my totem is a spider. That I am descended from people who lived a totemic existence long before my ancestor arrived at the Darbal Yaragan river mouth, south in Nyoongar Boodjar. This is what Birra-ga was talking about. In the spaces around his words. And now that spider is spinning to protect me. I invoke her by speaking her secret name. Quietly at first and then I am singing the secret name over and over until the box is humming with her presence. With her power. Her power to weave across the worlds. Her power to weave across time, to weave the past, present and future into the same web, whichever comes first. The secret-name-song spirals up and out of my throat like a willy-willy. I sing a secret incantation that I didn't know I knew. It is like I have remembered it from another time, from another life. To weave in the spirit and dream world with this one we can see with our eyes, touch with our flesh.

I breathe in. I breathe out. In. Out.

Rise. Fall. Wet. Dry. Black. White. Up. Down.

In. Out.

Waking Dream Memory: The Eyes of Spiders

I'm lying flat. The weapon in my hands still feels new. The feeling hasn't become second nature yet. The Sarge says that will come. I'm trying not to grip the weapon too tightly. My hands are sweaty from the plastic and metal, and the new anxiety of guard duty. The responsibility has come down on me like a weight. The Sarge says that eventually it will be a fuel, the protectiveness for my fellow warriors. I'm ten metres higher up than the others camped in the little valley. I can just make out their sleeping forms in the darkness. The Sarge is at the back of the others in the small patrol. It's quiet. So quiet. I could be the last person left on earth.

A shooting star catches my eye and I look across the hilly edge of our little valley. Then I see them. Five or six redback spiders as big as helicopters are picking their way slowly over the top of the ridge. My eyes flick to the top of the rising ground where I am, to see more giant redbacks. They move slowly and surely. They can't miss us. It's as if they know we're here. Maybe they've smelled out my spider-ness, even in the darkness. They make no show that they've seen us but their line is so direct. I glance back at my sleeping comrades. They're depending on me. But where there were bedrolls, the ground is empty. I quickly pick up movement just beyond. I see my comrades as spiders, too. The five daddy-long-legs with their oblong bodies and impossibly long spindly legs are backing away down the valley. The redbacks are still slowly converging on me from both sides. I can see the starlight glinting on their fangs and the tiny bristles on their long slender legs. The bright red marks on their backs don't seem quite right. They are too uniform, like some kind of crimson insignia. I put my weapon into my shoulder and hit the 'ready' on the electric firer. The tiny red light winks at me. I am good to go. I take aim at the nearest redback. Our eyes lock. It's not like looking into anything recognisable, but like staring into an unknowable chasm. There can be no exchange, no understanding here – just the emptiness of confrontation.

'Brother.'

The whispered voice is right in my ear. I don't know how I don't pull the trigger. It's the recognition of the voice in the same moment of the panic-fear gripping me that stops me. Mularabone.

'Brother. What are you doing?'

He kneels down next to me. 'Did you see me get up?' he says.

'No, I ...'

'Were you sleeping? The Sarge will kill you.'

'I wasn't sleeping.'

I look around. The helicopter-sized redbacks are nowhere to be seen. Mularabone is looking at me hard.

'You fucken better not be.'

'I had a dream.'

'You were asleep!'

'Not a sleeping dream. A waking dream.'

'What's going on?'

We look up. The Sarge is there. Neither of us heard him coming.

'What now?'

'I had a ... vision.'

'A what?'

'I have dreams when I'm awake.'

The Sarge kneels down. He and Mularabone share a look in the darkness.

'What did you see?'

'Redback spiders as big as helicopters surrounding our camp. You mob were daddy-long-legs – and you all backed out down the valley and left me here.'

The Sarge turns to Mularabone and they whisper in Language. Then he turns back to me.

'Daddies kill redbacks, yeah?'

'Yeah,' I say.

'Get the others up. Leave our rolls. Make it look like we're still here. Ghost camp.'

Mularabone and I nod.

'Where are your defensive perimeter mines?'

I point with two fingers at the locations. I show The Sarge the clacker attached to the stock of my weapon with two lacky bands. He nods. We move down and wake the others. We quickly pad up our bedrolls with branches cut from the scrub. The Sarge hangs his jacket over a low branch near his bedroll. Then we start to move away down the valley the same way I saw the daddies go. The Sarge comes up to me.

'In your dream you watched us go.'

I nod.

'You're staying. Dig in.'

'What?'

'You haven't got long. Dig in.'

The fear of being left behind in the dream comes crowding back in on me. 'Sarge?'

'I'll stay too,' says Mularabone.

The Sarge waves him off. 'Not your dream.'

Mularabone opens his mouth to protest but The Sarge jumps in.

'We don't have time. You convince them we're still here. Icing on the cake. When they start – fire everything. We'll be coming down behind them for a sweep. Don't leave your hole.'

Then he is gone, shepherding the rest of the patrol down the valley in the direction I gave him. They'll go a couple of hundred metres and then hook back around. I grab my short shovel and start to dig. I'm sweating hard in the darkness. I never saw the resolution. Just me abandoned. Is The Sarge punishing me? Does he think I was asleep? The ground is hard. My shovel noises are loud as a bulldozer in my ear. I dig. I've seen those new rocket-propelled grenades go off on the range; I don't wanna be above ground. I thought The Sarge said that this was a training patrol, that there were no Water Board within cooee. I sweat. I dig. Further up the valley I hear an owl hoot. I stop and listen. They're coming. If they're not already here. I reckon I've got a few minutes. I check my watch. Dawn in an hour. They'll be taking up fire positions. Aiming at the empty bedrolls, and me. I've made enough of a hole to just get my body below ground level. I attach the shovel to my pack and look out. From somewhere up the ridgeline I hear the tiniest of metal clicks. They heard me digging. Soon they'll send a probe. If they have infra-red they'll only find one heat signature. Mine. They'll still want to kill me. I settle into my shallow hole, put my finger on the red switch of the clacker, and wait. My heart seems too fast, my breathing too loud. With my next in-breath I consciously slow down the release.

Out to my right I see some movement. The form is indistinct in the darkness but much closer than I thought. Shit. Inside my mine placements. Gotta go. I raise myself to my knees and take aim.

Crack! Crack!

I fire the double-tap and then drop flat into my shell-scrape.

The bush in front of me erupts with firing. I hit the clacker and the anti-pers mines go off with an earth-shattering ker-rump! There is half a second of silence and then three or four weapons open up on me again. I'm hugging the earth in the bottom of my hole, holding my weapon above my head and firing like crazy. Up on the ridge to my left the rest of my patrol opens up and within moments the fire coming my way ceases. I hear The Sarge moving them down the hill. The Sarge was right: training, training, training.

I raise my head and look out. The first light is coming now.

'You right, Conway?' The Sarge calls from up on the ridge.

'Yo! Yo-yo!'

Then out to my right flank I hear a distinct whimper. I swing my weapon, and before I know it, I'm running at the sound. The Sarge would tear shreds off me: I should've been firing. Right in front of me a Water Board trooper stands up. I stop, and we both prop, looking at each other over our barrels and sights. Jack. I haven't seen him since my mother ...

His body tenses. I take up second pressure on my trigger. We can both hear The Sarge and the rest of my patrol getting closer. Looking into Jack's eyes is like staring into the chasm of the giant redback spider. Except for that dark wriggling thing in there turning over and over itself like a bucketful of maggots.

Crack! Crack!

There are two shots fired from behind me. The Sarge won't take prisoners. I lower my weapon. In another thirty seconds it'll be out of my hands. Jack glares at me, and this time there is a flicker of something more distinctive in his eye – like all the maggots have formed into one being, and I see the flash of the tail of something that was on the surface, flicking as the unknown thing dives down to the depths. He turns, and disappears into the scrub. I squat down. My breathing is ragged. In a moment, The Sarge is standing over me.

'C'mon Conway. Gotta go.'

The others are fanned out and facing outwards into the scrub, on high alert for a counterattack, each with three or four confiscated weapons slung over their shoulders. I get up and dust myself off.

'You hit?'

'Nah.'

We move off. My hands are still shaking.

Ten: Watchin the Footy with Me Mates

We're watching telly. Me and the other Water Board troopers. I look around to see us all lounging around in uniform. My mates and me. We're drinkin beer. I'm drinkin beer. On the piss with me mates. Maybe my brain has forgotten that soon my body will get sick. Or maybe my body has forgotten that soon my brain will get sick. That the disease will grow like a living shadow within me. The other troopers around me, me mates, they seem to know. They know the grog road and walk down it as steady as pelting rain. Their heads are up, but slightly too high from the arrogance, and never held straight on, always at an angle, from the crazy mix of guilt, lies, greed and righteousness. These troopers walking. Walking in the rain of alcohol in my brain. I know the grog dreaming. We all do.

On the telly is the footy. Maybe we're walking to the footy. We would be if we weren't slumped on a couch. I'm more slumped than the others. The drugs they've injected me with keep me down here like a long-necked turtle curled up in my shell. I look from the beer at the end of my arm to the 3D images in front of the wall. Footy. Brown-skinned players with flashy skills flowing across the faraway green of the MCG.

'That's real grass,' comments one of me mates.

'Bullfuckenshit!' retorts another.

'It is!'

'Whadda they water it with, Banzoil?'

Laughter.

'Euuagh!' I add (to which they've got no answer).

The camera suddenly goes tight on the only white player. Me mates all get excited. He's the first Djenga for twenty years to play for Collingwood! The fullas all marvel at him. Toast him. Yell their hopes and dreams into the 3D picture in front of us. I hear myself laughing and I don't know why. Even here, in my drug-dulled state, wearing the Water Board uniform, there is something else. I know this is a lie. That the heart of the grog dreaming is about lies. About self-delusion. I'm not a trooper. I never played footy. I don't drink grog. Before the Water Board there was no grog here for a hundred years. That old grog will smash me to bits. Will destroy me and all the possibilities of me, and my children, and my children's children.

One of me mates slaps my back. I look down at the brown bottle of beer in my hand. That hand is so far away. So totally foreign to me. Like it's in a different culture. I concentrate and the bottle slowly begins to travel up towards my face. I fix my eyes on the bottle as though breaking the stare would destroy the levitation trick. As it comes close I see it is too high, I've lined it up to my eyes not my mouth. I adjust the thought and down it comes and clatters into my teeth. My front teeth.

At least I've still got them, this thought says from a tiny lost corner of my mind. The cold beer tips down my throat and the bottle is travelling back again, until my arm is extended and it is fucken miles away. I don't remember giving the order to move the bottle away again. There is some kind of spring-loaded thing going on. I stare at the brown bottle in my hand, as though I'll wear it down, and it will confess its allegiance through my withering glare.

From somewhere outside of me I think I hear Mularabone. I can't tell if he's laughing or weeping. Then I know for sure it is Mularabone; something in my reaching drunkenness finds something good and strong to hold onto. I can't tell if

I'm laughing or weeping. I know for sure it is Mularabone. He is straining a scream through a grunt as the pain flashes through his body. Fuck! He must be close. Real close. The cell next door.

My sloppy grin is lopsided and fake. I notice that I'm dribbling beer and spit on my trooper's uniform. I concentrate on the mouth of the beer bottle. As I gaze at it, it becomes Mularabone's eye. Pupils wildly dilated but still fiery bright. The eye winks at me. That wink fills me with strength. Like I've been injected with it. And I know what I'm talking about; I've been injected with a lot of shit lately. My muscles tingle as they come alive and stand by. I shift my gaze to my fist. I balance the bottle on the arm of the couch and change my grip to an underhand one. It's like watching grass grow, watching my hand change grip. I turn to the trooper next to me. He laughs and takes a swig from his beer. But the grog gives me a power too. I know that. A power pushing me to the strength of chaos and havoc. I've got to open myself to the grog power.

I remember my intact front teeth, and bite down hard on my bottom lip without warning, without giving myself a chance to think about it and back out. I bite down hard until my skin splits and the blood mixes with my beer dribble, and the pain gives me enough cut-through-clarity to see myself as a warrior again. I flash on my grog warrior and smash the bottle into the trooper's face. The other bottle smashes too and he reels backwards, his face a mask of blood and glass. Something hits me from behind. I swing around and slash at the other trooper with the shattered beer bottle in my hand. It hacks into the flesh of his cheek and he screams. Adrenalin is coursing through me now, waking me up. An alarm is sounding all around us. Something else hits me. Glass, beer and blood run down my neck. I turn to confront a third trooper. He smiles at me. I lunge at him, going straight for his throat. We both make contact with our bottles and he goes down. The side of my head feels ripped open. I'm really waking up now. They haven't given me pain for a few days; it's new and fresh. I'm shouting something. I don't know what. Then it filters through.

'I'm not your mate.

'I'm not your mate.

'I'm not your fucken mate!'

The white footballer is tackled heavily and drops the ball. I take a half step away from the screaming crowd and the blurry shape of a trooper blocks my way. He is saying something to me but I can't make out what it is. He is reaching out to me with his electric shock baton. Right as the end touches me, I place my hand on his shoulder as if we were old mates helping each other to stand up during a big session on the grog. He hits the shock button and the charge travels through me to him, sending him flying backwards out the door. I bend down and grab the baton from his grip.

'Ya can give it out – but ya can't fucken take it!'

I stand swaying in the doorway looking out into the brilliant sunshine. The trooper lies on his back. His skin is blistering and he is screaming and trying to roll over. I turn back into the cell. There are helmets and gloves hanging by the door. I jam a helmet down on my head, shouting away the pain from the helmet going over the wound. I grab some gloves. A trooper staggers towards me with a beer in one hand. I whack him with a shock from the ES baton and he goes flying. I grab his near-full beer, and lift the UVP visor to drain the bottle. I pull on the gloves. Outside there are weapons firing. I step over the screaming, writhing trooper. I can feel that grog surging through my veins. A trooper steps out of the cell next door. He throws a weapon to his shoulder and fires. I look to where he is firing to see a figure in Water Board fatigues running towards the gate that opens to the dam. I know that run. Mularabone. I crack the trooper with the ES baton, and he goes down. I grab his weapon and pull off his helmet.

'Burn, ya dog!'

My mouth seems to have a life of its own. No wonder Jack is so full of hate if he drinks grog every day.

Mularabone is at the gate. He is fast. I take aim and fire a long burst at the guard tower. I must've hit something because there is no more fire from there. Mularabone is through the gate designed to stop vehicles from the outside, and he is running for the dam. I'm laughing and dribbling. Blood is running down my neck from the wound under my helmet. I grab a spare mag from the downed trooper and rake the vehicle parked near the gate with fire. The troopers seem confused. I'm laughing and firing. I'm running towards the gate and firing at any trooper I see. Mularabone does not slow his pace until he is out on the concrete of the dam. There are two troopers out there on the dam. They are momentarily unsure. Mularabone and I are in Water Board uniforms. Jack's great plan to play with our minds. I aim and fire, and one of the troopers falls. I'm shouting at the troopers:

'Youse are weak as fucken piss!'

Mularabone launches himself off the top of the dam, and does a perfect swan dive into the deep water below. I'm laughing.

'Good dive, brother!'

A massive electric shock smashes through my body. I fall to my knees; the weapon thuds softly into the red soil in front of me.

Eleven: Keepings Off

I'm being flattened against a hard metal wall – but there's something different about it as well, something indefinable, a duality giving it a web-like quality. The water is relentlessly pushing me into the wall. I try to remember the secret chant of the weaver. I'm inside something. Something unknowable.

The grog power seems to have left me. Like the tide has gone out too fast, leaving me stranded in a shallow rock pool and easy prey. Whatever the true nature of the grog dreaming is – I know I was born to it. That's what the uncles meant by telling me about my father. Did I already know this? Before the Water Board there was no grog here.

I've got no intel for Jack. Intel is just an excuse. He'd torture me anyway. He's a prisoner of his own hate. All I've gotta do is hang on. He can't kill me. Someone above his head is looking for me. The uncles were so certain. Maybe his madness will blow itself out. Maybe he'll get bored. Just gotta hang on.

There is a torrent of water smashing into my face. I try to shake it off but it is coming from outside of me and I can't. The stream of water travels down my body, buffeting my arms and torso. It seems like only moments ago I was in the dry heat of the desert and now here I am with all this water. My hand automatically goes to protect my genitals but not fast enough and the pain stabs up into my belly as hard and unforgiving as a bayonet. I get my hand across and the torrent is in my face again. A big flap of skin and flesh has peeled away from my head. I'm like a spindly eucalypt shedding bark. My hand pushes it back into place against the wall of water. The screaming stream hits my exposed balls again. My hands go back to my groin and the stream hits my head. This game goes on forever. Like big kids keeping the ball off the littlies, the troopers never get sick of it. I try one hand over each spot. It's a little better. But not much. They laugh.

Ghost of History: Welcome to Country

I'm swimming in water. Smashed around by its power. In its power. I'm becoming water. Maybe returning to my proper state. In the blackness I'm reaching out to my extremities, my flesh, to soften and open to the spirit of the water. This water is from a place. A specific place. A place anchored in time and space.

Feel for the spirit. Link to the liquidity. To melt into the water. Dissolve in it. Consciously choose it. To flow down the drain, rush through the pipes and amble into the luxury of the tank. Spread out even more. Drawn to the uppermost boundary where the sun glints on the surface.

They haven't enclosed the tank. It'll evaporate like a reverse flash flood this time of year, I think. Not really think, but watch the thought drift by. I ease up into the surface and flatten out. Spreading myself thinly. Then I feel that old sun begin to heat the tiny particles at my extremities. It builds like a frenzy. Tiny bits of me race round and round until finally bursting free from my surface tension. It goes on and on until I am gathering in a little cloud above myself. Waiting for the rest of me to break free as a gas. There is no accounting system here logging the arrival of each tiny particle of spirit-flesh – I just feel I am whole. I cannot look. It is not the world of earthly faculties. It is the world of clouds. I feel myself start to drift away. To gain altitude. Up where there is already a mass of moisture building. The particles of my being spread out until I lose all notion of a solid form and become a mist.

A cloud. The cloud me. My consciousness is spread wide too, like a blanket where the weaves no longer exist. The material is still all there, but loose and wide and not joined. Each tiny moist droplet in the cloud me is a complete me but cohesion can occur when we react as a group. It is the nature of things.

The cloud me is already being sucked up by the vast open sky as the sun heads for the horizon. I am dragged straight up, then given a shove by the hot air over the land at my back, sending me racing toward the sea, leaving the red earth far behind.

I'm being drawn out over a mighty ocean. And travelling at terrific speed. Days or years or millennia pass – or a fleeting instant, a millisecond. If there is any time here, it is in me. It is me. I am turned over and over upon myself and find myself gathering with a momentous mass of swirling moist air. We are all moving at great speed and suddenly start losing altitude. Ahead is a landmass, rising out of the blue plain of rippling ocean. Below me the sea is bubbling and boiling onto the endless sandy Nyoongar beaches. The clouds around me drop down, pulling me with them and I feel myself begin to gather together. It happens so fast I feel I might perish if I fall whole from the sky. But the instant my particles are gathered together enough to be droplets, gravity tugs me down, one drop at a time. I rain down, coming out of the afternoon sky at an angle, exhilarated by my own falling.

Below me there is a wooden boat. A cutter and gig. There are fourteen men in the cutter. Djenga all. All wearing side arms. The bayonets on the muskets are like a small forest of steel cacti. Yet they move across the ocean with the movement of the boat. Burnham wood. Burnham steel. Burn em clean. The oars dip and pull. The marines look afraid. There are two men at the stern. One is from the ship's company. The other blurry shape is a lieutenant in the Royal Marines. Onto this shape I fall. Into this shape I fall. Slapping into the flesh, into myself, as I become human.

Captain Fremantle sits in the bow. I know it is him. I have the knowledge of this Royal Marine lieutenant body that I've fallen into. I have his history. Does he have mine?

I blink against the rain. I look forward at Fremantle's back. The man next to me speaks.

'Bloody storm came from nowhere, sir!'

I look up. Not only has the storm come from nowhere but it seems to be local to us. We have our own little dark cloud.

Them old Countrymen are already beginning their Welcome to Country for us. Beginning their mystery.

On the shore we can see a big mob of Countrymen, each having about six spears, which they carry in one hand, holding them vertical, with the woomera in the throwing hand. The mob are all painted in distinctive line designs, with white, red, and yellow ochre. As we watch, they drop all but one spear, and shake out into a formation. Other Countrymen are tapping sticks. They all start to sing now, and do this swaying dance. Then they are fitting their spears and stamping down the beach. They raise their spears and fit them to their woomeras like they will throw them straight at us in the culmination of the dance. They lean back into it in the dance like it's going to be a big throw, and then at the very last moment they drop their spears down, hooting and laughing, and then a final stamp-out dance.

Captain Fremantle gives me another look. Did you see that?

Yeah, I say, just with my eyes.

Fremantle is dressed in his finest. Dressed for a ceremony. He's gonna get that all right. We're already well into it.

'Trim that sail! Into the river, helmsman!' Captain Fremantle slings back over his shoulder. 'We'll land down the river!' His eyes do not leave the large mob on the beach. There are many senior Countrymen there.

The nose of the boat swings away from the beach and into the mouth of the Darbal Yaragan. The group of Countrymen follow our progress by walking along the beach. They move at a leisurely pace. No one is in a hurry.

The wind from our own little storm fills out the sail and pushes us along hard. The boat is beginning to go in beyond the land when we slam into the limestone reef guarding the entrance. The marines at the front of the cutter are hurled into the drink, and the oarsmen and the rest of us are thrown onto the deck. There is a moment of panic from the hands in the water before they realise that they can stand. On the seaward side of the reef it is chest-deep. I go to get to my feet when a big wave crashes over us. The boat is upended and this time we all end up in the water. Under I go, feeling the texture of the salt water all around me, sliding over my just-solid flesh. I come out of the water to the extraordinary sight of dozens of Countrymen all around us in the water, grabbing blokes and getting them to their feet and securing the boat. And that's how we come ashore for the first time: in disarray, and helped by Countrymen.

Captain Fremantle is telling the men to grab their now useless weapons, and that he wants his trading chest recovered. He looks over to me, as though expecting me to be involved in this. I'm not confident yet, here and yet not here. I wade to the shore with the other marines.

We come out of the water slowly. There are now over a hundred armed Countrymen on the beach. They wander down to us.

Captain Fremantle must've swallowed some water. He's still spluttering as he makes his way out of the water. The marines and sailors are shaken by the ordeal. No one is quite themselves. The light around us seems different. The marines and sailors are soaked and so are their weapons and spare gunpowder.

Fremantle recovers his lungs and turns to me. 'Form the men up, Mister Conway.'

The use of my name baptises me and hurtles me fully into the dream. Wakes me up – spewed up by history at this exact moment. I know I'm really here. History can be whatever it wants to be; can travel any path, old or new.

'Company, fall in!' comes my Royal Marine's voice from nowhere.

The marines fall in and stand to attention, with the sailors behind. A couple of marines are missing boots, and most are missing their hats. Captain Fremantle casts an eye over his troops, and then looks to me.

'I can only hope they won't be too terrified of our power,' he remarks drily.

I look back at him. I feel like laughing.

The Royal Marine part of me wants to question the wisdom of proceeding. It is too late in the day and we are far too few in number to be able to account for ourselves if there is trouble. We are within cannon range but I doubt it will be any consolation to us if we are attacked. The Royal Marine thoughts in my mind are like having a running commentary going on underneath in another language. I am him and yet still me. It's good to hear them, though; it means I'm going deeper here.

We both turn back to face the Countrymen. This young fulla with bright eyes comes to the fore. He speaks to us in rapid-fire language.

This young man, his paint-up – with his nose-bone, the layered scarring on his muscular torso and arms – transfixes Captain Fremantle.

'Do you suppose he is a king or a chief, Mister Conway?'

I shake my head, indicate with my lips the older men standing up the back. Fremantle follows my gesture and sees the old Countrymen standing there. Then his head snaps back to me. Now he's wondering who I am, where I got that gesture language from. He must be open to this. The past is the future. Is now. All woven together.

Fremantle turns back and repeats my gesture to the bright-eyed young fulla who spoke. The younger Countrymen part slowly to reveal the old fullas. Fremantle gives me another little look: the gesture worked.

The senior Countrymen get their first good look at us Djenga. They only look for a moment before they all burst out laughing.

We are struck catatonic by this wave of mirth.

Captain Fremantle is the first one to join in. Then I go up.

The whole group of painted Countrymen with spears are laughing too.

This wave of laughter washes away any remaining formality in us.

Look at this funny little army of invaders with hats that won't stay on and weapons that don't work. Captain Fremantle starts taking off his soaking wet dress uniform. I follow. We get our jackets and shirts off.

Now a collective 'Oooh' comes from the Countrymen.

Our paleness is a shock to them. I can say for myself that their blackness and scarring are a shock to me, the Royal Marine me. They all look fit and strong and would surely make formidable adversaries. The scars are in various patterns, groupings on the chest and arms, each scar at least half an inch thick, in lots of sixes slanting diagonally across chest muscles, and others on the upper arms running down the limbs. Each man has a bone threaded through his nose. It is an impressive sight.

Fremantle turns to me. There is a crazy look in his eye. He smiles his unexpected smile at me.

These old Countrymen indicate for us to go with them.

Fremantle grips his still-sheathed sword and follows them. I do the same.

'Come on you lot, stick together,' I throw over my shoulder.

The marines grab up their useless wet weapons and follow us, not marching or anything, just ambling behind us as though the attitude of the young Countrymen on the beach is already getting to them: that unlikely mixture of discipline and freedom. We are pressed-ganged into the former with little hope for the latter. They seem to have easy and open access to both.

The marines walk in a group. They are nervous. Most of them look certain that soon we will all be dead. Especially with Captain Fremantle and me acting so strangely.

The Countrymen stare at us intently. As we move through them, quite a few of them reach out and touch us.

We come up to these three old Countrymen. Their beards are huge; their bodies are rivers of shining scar tissue. The Countryman in the centre is older. He is slightly shorter than the other two and his beard covers most of his chest. He has a prominent bump on his forehead. He looks at Fremantle. At him. Around him. Through him. Like he's measuring the way his atmosphere accepts the Djenga aura.

When he speaks, his language is so foreign to us that it is a few moments before we realise his mouth is making speech.

'Ngullak nyinniny kooralong koora ngullak noitj nidja Nyoongar Boodjar.'

Then I almost stagger backwards as something pierces

the veil of my mind, and his voice is right inside my head. And inside my head, I understand him perfectly well.

(*From the beginning of time to the end, this is Nyoongar Country.*)

I look to Fremantle. I see from his wild eyes that he is hearing this too.

'Ngalla djoorapiny maambart boodjar ngallak bala maambart quop ngalla koort djoorapiny nidja ngalla mia mia nyinniny Nyoongar Boodjar.'

(*We respect the earth our mother, and understand that we belong to her – she does not belong to us. In all her beauty, we find comfort, wellbeing and life that creates a home for everyone that has become a keeper of Nyoongar Country.*)

Fremantle and I are held in the spell of this man. It is the same feeling of having strong firm hands on our shoulders.

'Djinaginy katatjin djoorapiny nidja weern Nyoongar Boodjar ngalla mia mia boorda.'

(*Look, listen, understand and embrace all the elements of Nyoongar Country that is forever our home.*)

Fremantle is momentarily struck dumb. Lost for words.

I want to help him. Our great hero. A visionary. A prophet for our people. But I do not know how to respond to this welcome from the old man with the prominent bump on his head, with his obvious mantle of power. Fremantle should be responding with official words, as the representative of His Majesty's great authority. He doesn't speak. Already he is making different decisions.

The old Countryman turns his attention solely on me. As his aura touches mine he flinches. He looks up at me and smiles. He steps in closer to me and I look down. He reaches out with his left forefinger, not pointed at me, but curled curiously back towards himself, and touches my chest with the rounded knuckle joint. His curled knuckle goes into my flesh as if it were water. When he withdraws it, it is wet. He sniffs the water and nods his head. He gives me his tiny smile like a throwaway gift and turns to talk to the other Countrymen.

They look at me and nod. Then they turn and walk. The Countrymen behind indicate for us all to follow them. We were going to anyway.

We travel through low sandhills and scrub by the river until we come to an open flat area only ten metres or so from the river's edge. It has been flattened by thousands of bare feet over thousands of years. The old Countrymen get to lighting a fire and the younger ones settle in to the earth all around us.

'What's happening, Mister Conway?'

I turn to Fremantle. He already looks different. Many said he shouldn't have taken on this assignment. That he was a changed man since the Portugal campaign. But he had to. He left London in disgrace. And now here he is, sitting with the Darbal Yaragan mob on the other side of the world to the Empire he once believed in. And I recognise that look in his eye. Even here where part of me has a history that is not mine I can still see it. Reminds me of someone.

Already all around us there is a stirring in the spirit world. These old Countrymen are building up a big mystery now.

Fremantle is sitting by the fire. The old Countrymen are singing. The next outer circle of Countrymen are on their feet and dancing. Singing and moving. And they are pressed close to us and to the old Countrymen. They travel around us, stamping out that sacred circle.

The old Countrymen sing a different song back to them. An older song. A secret song. They tap sticks to keep their rhythm. Beyond the circle of stamping Countrymen, there are other circles dancing and moving around them. Moving, stamping, singing.

The old Countrymen suddenly look up and straight at me. The old Countryman with the big wide beard and prominent forehead bump reaches out to me. They keep singing. Around us dance the Countrymen and the Spirits of the Country. His hand grows as it reaches around my face, then my whole body is scooped up and held in the palm of his hand. As soon as I feel the cool smooth dryness of his flesh, I stiffen, and all moisture is instantaneously drawn from my body. I start to crumble. Those fingers close in and crush me. Crush me until I crumple in on myself and crumble into a pile of dust. A pile of deep golden-red dust. But not dust. Tiny crystal shards, like soft glass. Balga sap.

Fremantle doesn't even notice. I'm a pile of grass tree sap dried and crushed and being held in an old Countryman's hand, and he doesn't notice.

The hand suddenly flicks itself and I'm flung through the air – spreading and arranging myself, biggest granules back to the tiniest of fragments, dusty fingerlings reaching out for the flames. I hang in the evening air, suspended in time, defying the pull of the earth, spread-eagled and glittering red-gold – then I slam into the heat of the fire. I explode outwards into a shower of sparks and up and out as sweet, thick, grey-blue smoke.

As smoke, I play over the bodies and spirits of the old Countrymen and Fremantle – and then I'm gone, floating in a white haze above their heads, looking down on the mystery. The old Countrymen grin up at the smoke-me as the song swirls and dances all around them.

Twelve: Dispersing the Natives

I'm swimming in morning sunshine. It comes through the protective dome above me with an orange tinge. It's like those glorious mornings just after the DOz has moved away, and we have the promise of three months of freedom light ahead of us.

I'm sitting in the back of a vehicle. I cast around to see three other desert cruisers. I'm handcuffed to the vehicle. There is a large wad bound to the side of my head with bandages. I can't move my hands to touch it. It feels like I've got a football gaffer-taped onto the side of my head. The wound beneath the wadding desperately wants to be scratched. Must be starting to heal. How long have I been under?

I'm looking at Jack's back.

'Jack! Jack? That you?'

Jack spins to look at me. 'G'day mate.'

'I'm not ya fucken mate!' I say – but he predicts it and joins in to say it with me – and then laughs.

'Yes you are,' he confirms after his laugh.

'Is this a planned conversation?'

'I said, "You are my fucken mate." '

'It is planned.'

'Fuck off.'

'Do you rehearse out loud?'

'Where are we, Conman?'

'Desert.'

Jack turns back around to face away from me. I see that we

are looking at a small hill ridged with a line of twisted trees. I know those trees. Just through the trees we can see a wisp of smoke from a fire in the valley we can't see. Jack hears my intake of breath. He will've been listening for it. My sharp intake which is me saying, 'Noooo!'

'Yeeees, mate. You told us how to get here.'

He turns back to face the front and says something into his headset.

The cruiser lurches forward and picks up speed quickly. We race toward the small opening in the twisted trees at the southern lip of the hill.

I hear myself screaming. Jack swivels quickly and, using his turning momentum smacks me across the mouth. The blow snaps my head sideways but I keep screaming. Jack is facing me now and screaming himself, screaming into my face, screaming through his cat-got-the-cream smile. My head feels light and cold, there is blood seeping through the dressing and running down my neck.

The cruiser races through the trees and over the lip we go. The gunner at the front swings his big weapon to bear.

Ahead of us in the shallow valley there is a mob of people near their morning fire. That moment is like a photograph. Uncle Birra-ga is looking up and straight at the camera. Straight at me. Aunty Ouraka is over the fire. There are a couple of Countrymen sitting a bit apart and a big group of Countrywomen and kids on the far side. There are two little girls skipping up the hill towards us.

Then they are all gone.

The valley is empty. There is no one there. Not even a fire. The little bit of smoke in the sky maybe drifted in from somewhere else.

Jack is speaking frantically on his headset.

The cruiser comes to an abrupt halt.

I lean forward, straining against my bonds. 'Watch out Jack! It might be a trap!' I yell, and then I'm laughing like a madman.

Behind us the other two cruisers fan out. Now they're nervous. Not so sure.

Jack is talking.

Our vehicle starts to edge forward.

'Watch out! Watch out! We're going to be killed by savages!'

Jack turns and glares at me.

'Dangerous women and children! Killers!'

Jack is pointing a handgun at me now. I see in his eyes that he is going to kill me. That insolent child that lives in his eye is positively quivering with anticipation.

I go silent. I slump. Slump silently. Jack wants to see my fear. I try to look as terrified as I can. I'm not sure if he believes me but he doesn't fire. When he turns away from me again I have to really concentrate hard to stop myself giggling like a schoolboy who's been told off in front of the class. I know enough about men to know that Jack will kill me under such circumstances, despite someone high up looking for me. Out here, I mean. Not back in the Water Board compound. The rules have always been different out here. In the scrub. In the desert.

I'm slumped like a sullen teenager. I'm bored and disinterested in everything around me. I'm looking over Jack's shoulder without much interest. I'll be bored with whatever we find. I'm thinking about telling Jack that this massacre is boring, they haven't even killed anyone yet. I look down at the trooper's uniform they've put me in. *We* haven't even killed anyone yet. Yeah, that's what I'll say.

Then the front of the cruiser disappears as though driven into some invisible curtain. The driver panics and slams on

the skids and the big vehicle slides to a halt. Ahead of us, we can see the Countrymen again. Now ya see em. Now ya don't. Now ya do.

The last of the mob are disappearing into a hole in the earth. Someone has put the fire out with an extinguisher. They've gathered up everything and gone. Gone down into the earth our mother.

'Fire!' screams Jack.

The gunner leans on his trigger and the big weapon explodes in his hands, killing him instantly. Jack is thrown backwards out of the commander's seat and lands heavily on me, swearing and cursing. He is still holding his handgun. He pulls his UVP balaclava down, pushes off me, and jumps down from the cruiser. Jack takes off towards the mob, hopeful for a shot. From the earth in front of us rises up a young man. He is shirtless and holds a nulla-nulla in his left hand. It is Young James. He's disabled the machinegun with some kind of plug he slipped into the barrel as it came through the projected image. That's a cool head.

Jack is lifting his weapon to fire when Young James knocks it from his hand in an underhand blow. Jack goes into a martial-arts stance. Young James smashes his front knee and down he goes. Jack is looking back up the hill now. He can see the other two cruisers waiting, full of armed men. But they can't see him. The mob are using a hologram projection system to mask themselves. Jack half gets up and opens his mouth to yell orders. Young James can read his thought as surely as I can. The next blow collects Jack on the side of the head and he goes down hard. Young James looks up at me.

Maybe I'm still drugged cause all I can think about is seeing Young James yesterday in the tank. But even as I'm blinking in slow motion, I'm thinking that can't be yesterday, as all these other vague yesterdays are yapping at my heels like camp

dogs, hungry and hairless. Maybe those yesterdays are fiction, planted in my mind by Jack. I remember watching the footy with me mates, and drinking beer, and there was a huge fight right on the siren. Fuck, we laughed. Then I'm down south, arriving at the Darbal Yaragan river mouth in Nyoongar Country with Captain Fremantle. But that was three hundred years ago. The possibilities of yesterdays are endless. It's the tomorrows that are the most hammered down.

Down in the valley, Mularabone stands up, too. I knew he couldn't be far away from such a brilliant high-tech defence for the bush camp. He looks bad. His whole head looks puffy and swollen. He is holding some bush medicine against his side. He smiles at me. I try to stand and am yanked back down by my cuffs. Jack is messing with my head. He wants me to feel guilty. Whoever tells the history positions the emotions of the receiver. I tell myself it's the drugs they've given me to excite my paranoia. I breathe.

The mob turn and move down to where the fire was, and quickly disappear into the earth. I want to be with them. I'm on the wrong side. This Water Board trooper's uniform puts me on the other side of history. Maybe that's what my history dreams are about. Putting history right in my head. Showing me which side I'm on. If there is such a thing as different sides, different worlds, different views of history. Of now. I brought these killers here today. This is what Jack's history-telling will say. The photos will always show me in this Water Board uniform. Lies are easy to sell, said The Sarge. It is the truth that is hard to swallow. I breathe.

The driver revs the engine and reverses. The projection is gone and all we've got is the empty valley with no morning fire and a lot of Djenga with unfired weapons.

The troopers run down and grab Jack and get him onto a stretcher. He hasn't moved a sniffle. Young James really

cracked him one. They get Jack into the back of the cruiser. They leave me handcuffed up on top and turn around and head back. As the three armoured cruisers turn to head back, I see Mularabone standing in the shadow of a twisted tree. There must be another hatch there. He's trying to send me his strength. I reach out to him with my spirit. He watches me. I am free. He is chained. No. I am chained and he is free. Then the woman from Uncle's mural cavern appears at his side. Our eyes meet across the space. She makes a hand signal to me, two fingers almost pointed at me, then gathered in a basket back to her breast: I'm coming for you. That hand signal travels across the space and lodges in my breastbone. I put my hand over the place where it lodges.

I twist my head and look back to them until they are indecipherable shadows in the tree line.

Dreaming 44: The Disappearing Track

I'm walking. Barefoot now. Red dust. Desert. My muscles are dog-tired. It's only my bones moving me around. Something way ahead of me is pulling me toward it. Like there is a cord attached to me, drawing me steadily toward the never-getting-closer horizon. In my mind the cord is a single strand of unbroken spider's web that would shine with dew if it were early morning and stretch out before me like a tiny silver airborne highway with no end in sight.

I see no web. No dew. Just my feet moving rhythmically under me.

Is the cord attached to my eyes? They feel free. I tell myself I could flick them from side to side and look around if I wanted to. I just don't want to. So I gaze ahead unwaveringly with my soft and free eyes.

Is the cord attached to my heart? My heart feels uplifted; alive at least, pounding merrily away in the front of my chest, thumping out a beat for my feet to follow, the rhythm that ties me to all other living creatures, to this land, this greatest of all the instruments. This is not a heart with encumbrances.

Is it my gut being pulled? My soft eyes drop to observe. Posture appears fine. Bones stacked on top of each other. Belly seems fine.

But there is something. Past my belly, where I am looking now, at my feet – all is not well. I watch these feet lift and place down, push off, lift, and place down for a few cycles as I search for a clue to the wrongness. I look up again. Everything appears to be normal.

I notice the heat, beating down on me in waves and pulsing up at me in great shimmers from below. The horizon. Never getting closer. Fine. No birds or animals. Pretty quiet. Fine. My track. Fine.

How can there be a track in front of me? I haven't walked there yet. But there it is. A perfect set of my own tracks stretching away to the never-getting-closer horizon. I look down to see my feet carefully and nonchalantly placing themselves in their own print, push off, lift, and into the next one.

I hear this sound. The insistent whine of a truck in low gear. My head swivels to see what is behind me. There is nothing on the sand. No mark or sign of me having passed by. As each of my feet lift out of my prints, the prints dissolve into the desert and are gone in a moment. Maybe two hundred metres behind me there is a truck. It's one of those ten-tonne water trucks, sprinkling water out the back to keep the dust down. Behind the wheel is that big ugly redneck bastard with his black-rimmed Coke-bottle glasses and his handlebar moustache, humming some obscure tune, with his rifle laying within reach on the empty seat beside him.

Thirteen: Talking With Rednecks

The lift doors open. Rough hands grab me and drag me out. The doors close again behind me and the lift makes its way back to the surface with a jerk and a whine.

I hear them talking over my head, but I can't tune in, too bone-tired and spirit-weary. Here I am, swallowed again by the earth our mother. But now her womb is not bursting with the warm blood of life but is cool and dry and hard, and stinks of fear and death. Maybe she can no longer nurture us. The privations of the Water Board crawling over her red earthen flesh and sucking her dry have left her without the means or the desire. Or maybe she *is* still warm and moist and bursting with life, *always* warm and moist and bursting with life – but I've come in on a hypodermic – and she thinks I am foreign matter. Soon she will make antibodies. And they'll come for me.

I open my eyelids to let in a tiny sliver of light. We're in an underground cavern. Maybe old diggings. I'm against the rock wall. Down past my feet is the platform where I was dragged from the lift cage. There are drag tracks in the dirt that lead into my prone body like freeway ramps. There are a few lights up high on the walls but it is generally pretty dim. The cavity in the rock is big and there are small groups of people everywhere.

There are two men squatting near some blankets loosely stacked against the hard rock wall.

'He's dressed as a trooper, he could get baccy sent down.'

'He's a fucken trooper. Let's just hurt him.'

'You used to be a trooper.'

'And you can see how well they've treated me?' the second man spits.

Shit. I know that voice: Blood Nut from the Tank. How many prisoners does the Water Board have being shuttled around their chaotic system? It's not only the mob in the refugee camp that needs to be freed.

I glance up through my slitted eyelids to notice the dim light touching his flame-head. He glances in my direction and I squeeze my eyes closed: a child playing hide and seek, trying to wish away the forty-tonne tanker bearing down on him.

I hear Blood Nut moving back over to me. His meaty fingers grip my shoulder and he shakes me like a rag-doll.

'Eh! Shareholder! Wake up! Wake up!'

I open my eyes slowly and peer out from my hazy pain daze.

'What?'

'We dragged you in.'

'So?'

'Are you a trooper?'

'Are *you*?'

'Got any baccy?'

'Side pocket,' I say, with no real memory of how it got there, or how I know.

Blood Nut rummages in the pocket at my thigh and pulls out the small pouch. He peeks in like a five-year-old looking inside his Christmas present.

'Enough for a couple,' he announces with glee.

He pulls out my papers and rolls three thin ones. He passes one back to his mate and hands one to me. I put it in my mouth, prop myself up and accept his proffered flame. We all inhale.

'I'm Mitch. This is Torby.'

I nod at both of them. There is a strange silence while we smoke and look out into the chamber at the other prisoners.

Then their eyes snap back to me in unison.

'What's ya name, Trooper?' asks Blood Nut.

'I'm not a trooper.'

'Let's call him Trooper,' offers Torby.

'That all right by you, Trooper?'

I try to manage a smile. They both look away, satisfied.

I look out as well. I've never seen so many white people in jail. People are wrapped in blankets or sitting close together for warmth. There are a few arty fires in drums, surrounded by frail-looking men warming their hands. I feel the bandage which still holds the flesh to the side of my head. It's why he doesn't recognise me.

'They catch ya stealin water?' says Torby.

'The water is ours,' I say.

For the second time both their heads snap around to face me with the precision of dancers. Or maybe soldiers.

'Who told you that?' asks Mitch the Blood Nut, moving in on me.

I push myself up a little higher, and pull hard on my thinnie. I want to look him in the eye.

'Them that look after it.'

Mitch the Blood Nut grabs me by the throat and pulls me up to him. We both drop our thinnies.

'Do I know you?'

Torby goes to grab our two discarded thinnies. Mitch sees him move and instantly drops his hold on me and gives Torby a 'don't argue' shove in the chest. Torby and I hit the deck at the same moment and Mitch scoops up the two thinnies.

'I thought youse were finished wiv em,' says Torby.

Mitch scowls at him and restores the thinnies to his mouth,

and then to mine. We both drag in the smoke, looking at each other.

'What sort of man would try n take ya thinnie before ya finished?' says Mitch.

We smoke.

'What if the Countrymen are right, Mitch?'

I pitch my question like the ultimate slow ball and it hangs in the air for an eternity. Mitch is considering what I've said. This is all I can hope for. How can he still be loyal to the system that put him here? How can we not be on the same side? I should just shut up. I can't help myself.

'The water belongs to the Water Board,' Mitch says. 'The Company owns the Water Board. It is the Company. If you're not a shareholder you don't deserve shit.'

'Are you a shareholder, Mitch?'

Mitch looks at me like I'm a maggot crawling out of his mother's corpse. He spits a dark globule onto the rock dust floor. 'We got duped. In the East, the white man took everything, lived like gods, and gave the black man nothing. For hundreds of years.'

'Listen to yourself, Mitch. The "black man"? What the fuck's that? That's not our language. Fremantle said no to that. They brought that. The Water Board. And what they did over East was fuck the Country up. The Country and the Countrymen. They stopped all ceremony, brought in European farming large-scale, and poisoned the rivers.'

'That's bullshit. Propaganda shit,' says Torby.

'Did Jack tell you that?'

'You know Jack?' asks Torby.

'Jack's a legend,' says Mitch.

'He's my brother.'

'Whadaya doin down here, then?'

'What are you doin down here?'

'Rotting.'

'Yeah, well, me too.'

I suck on my cigarette. I'm talking social political history with Mitch the Blood Nut who wanted to rape me a week ago, or however the fuck long ago that was.

I'm suddenly thinking of old Captain Fremantle. Once his heart has been opened to the spirit of the Country, and he's felt the power and serenity of the oneness of all things – how does he sell it to a couple of hundred armed Englishmen, whose stated aim is to annex this land for Empire, and all get fucking rich in the process?

My head is all over the shop. Maybe Jack has dumped me down here to hide me from whoever's looking for me?

Mitch and Torby finish their thinnies. They stub them out and watch me take my last drag. Always been a slow smoker. I stub out my thinnie. Blood Nut stands. Torby follows. They look at me. Maybe they expect me to stand. I just keep looking out.

'Goin for a walk,' announces Blood Nut. As if I give a shit.

'Righto,' I say, hoping to get the right subordinate tone. It satisfies them. I lie still. My right hand retrieves the hand signal from the woman from Uncle's mural cave from its breastbone hidey hole and caresses the movement – two fingers almost pointed at the subject, then gathered back to the chest in a basket of fingers: I'm coming for you.

Ghost of History: Planting Tears

I wake before Fremantle. We're curled up like dogs on a little
sandy beach. In front of us a freshwater stream tumbles down
from the sandstone rock to form a pool. We are shirtless. Our
swords are gone. Captain Fremantle's pack is open beside
him; the top of his leather-bound journal protrudes from the
canvas bag. As I watch him, he too sits up. I can see that like
me, though stiff from being unused to sleeping on the ground,
he is refreshed and alert. Up behind us there is a three-foot
lizard moving down the rocks. His head moves from side to
side, his tongue flicking out to taste the air. He is completely
unhurried and untroubled. He heads straight for the journal
sticking out of the canvas bag, and tastes it with his tongue of
deepest blue. He walks on top of the journal with his clawed
feet and pauses. His eyes are small and dark, his belly skin has
a deep fold running the length of his body; he's still got plenty
of growing to do in this skin. He flicks out his tongue again
and heads off.

Fremantle looks up the little beach to the darker sand
above. We're on the shore of this large bay. From the look of
it, we are probably in the vicinity of Garungup, the place of
anger. I don't feel particularly angry. What is this place named
for? Maybe hasn't happened yet.

There is another course of water flowing over the river soil,
staining the sand, and eventually draining into the Darbal
Yaragan. This slow water has attracted dragonflies. It is in this
direction that the lizard travels. He moves in his unhurried

way, and moments later, grabs a big dragonfly in his mouth. The dragonfly struggles, trying to flap his wings. The lizard chews methodically, his jaws moving faster than the eye can see, and each time he crunches back down on the insect, he is arranging it in his mouth until finally he can swallow it in one big gulp. Only the wings are a problem. He has to get the dragonfly really aligned down his throat to fold those wings in as well. In the last flash of the wings, before they disappear, they seem to be red-tinted on the underside. The lizard licks his lips perfunctorily and keeps walking. His attitude is not changed. He ambles off into some dying low-lying scrub at the base of the rock.

Fremantle takes out his journal and quickly sketches the lizard eating the dragonfly with his charcoal pencil. His sketches aren't bad. He easily catches the essence of that lizard out hunting. Then he jots down a couple of notes under the heading *EDEN:*

No hoofed animals.
No shame about our flesh.
Abundance.
The Angel is in the detail.
Freshness of observation.
Wealth but no money.
Discipline and work but no transaction for private gain.
God is ever-present.
Present in the Peace of this place.
Present in us.

Fremantle stops writing. He can feel me watching him. He looks up quickly. He looks around. He doesn't see me. I stand up. He looks for a bit longer, and then goes back to his journal. He can't see me. I'm not here.

Fremantle has ochre painted on his chest and face. There are cuts on his upper arms. I watch him feel the wounds with his fingers. The cuts have ash packed into them, and although swollen, are dry and cauterised.

Suddenly I am gripped from behind by some unknown power. This force has me in its unfocused but specific grip. A force that effortlessly overwhelms me. Both my hands are pinned and also held fast at the neck and shoulder. I am rushed forward straight at Fremantle. I open my mouth to yell a warning but no sound comes. I smash into him with unbelievable speed. We go face down onto the sand. Into the sand we fall. And when we stand – it is just I: Captain Charles Fremantle.

My head is bleary. I don't know how I got here. It was a long night. There was a fire. There were Countrymen dancing. Old Countrymen singing. The best sleep I ever had. And now here I am. On a river beach somewhere in Walyalup Country. I remember that much. I don't remember these cuts on my upper arm. Like sad mouths cut into my flesh. I have been wounded before, and I marvel at the simplicity of the ash poultice, how perfect a solution. It's still sore though. Even a light touch of the wound sends hot needles stabbing through my flesh. I don't remember how I got the wounds. I cup each dry wound with the opposing hand and press as hard as I can.

The pain drops me to my knees. I'm light-headed. I fall face forward into the exact print in the sand. The print I just vacated. But my face doesn't rest there, confronted by the grainy crunch of the sand. Down I go. Into the sand. Through the sand. I'm accelerating through the Country. It's agonising, crashing through rocks and dirt. Making a pathway where there can be no pathway. Crashing and thrashing my way through – and then up and out!

I come up into this clearing in the forest.

Some English colonists have set up a ration station – to introduce the natives to our food. Sitting on a horse behind the cart is Captain Molloy. He rests his rifle on the pommel of his saddle as he looks on. His uniform has been patched together with some kangaroo skin, and his beard is wild and woolly. Only his boots shine. The rest of him is dull, like dried blood. There is something familiar about him.

Up to the cart comes this old Countryman. His proud bearing gives away his boss-man status. His two sons and nephews hang back. These are not the Nyoongar people I know. If Molloy is here then I am much further to the south. The language and appearance of the natives is similar but different. The boss man goes up to inspect the colonist's wagon, horse and loaves of bread. Over behind these Djenga, the old Countryman can see their sheep watched over by two or three shepherds in a makeshift yard. The old Countryman calls over his two sons and two other nephews to discuss the sheep. They point and talk animatedly. The old Countryman comes up to the wagon where the bread is. He pulls out a loaf and breaks it open. The young Djenga by the cart is happy. The Countryman sniffs the opened loaf. He has a taste. He likes it and so grabs a few loaves.

The young Djenga is trying to tell him, 'One loaf each!' He repeats this loudly. 'One loaf each!'

The young Djenga looks back to Molloy for approval. Molloy gives him the nod to proceed. The young Djenga gestures at the old Countryman. When this doesn't work, the young Djenga tugs on the Countryman's beard, and shoves him hard in the chest. The old Countryman falls backward, his beard floating up to expose the silky scar ridges completely covering his torso. One of the younger Countrymen, the eldest son, fits his spear into his throwing stick, and slams it into the chest of the young Djenga at close range. Captain Molloy fires his rifle and the spear-thrower is thrown backwards, a huge wound appearing in his chest. Molloy drops his rifle, and a large pistol appears in his fist. I know that pistol. He fires, and a warrior falls. The other Djenga are raising rifles and firing and people are going down as the lead slaps into their bodies. The Countrymen throw spears and run in to grab their Patriarch. One of the shepherds raises his rifle and shoots the old Countryman in the chest. Molloy's horse appears to be fetlock-deep in blood that flows around him like a creek after rain.

Down into the earth I fall and race along again. Not sure if I'm being pushed or dragged. Tearing through the earth's crust, shredding through the rock with each out-breath, and reforming again, and shredding again at unbelievable speed.

I come up and I'm galloping on a horse across a shallow river. Ahead of me the Countrywomen and children run for their lives. Out to my right I see Captain Stirling, the Governor, also at full gallop. Even at full gallop and swinging a sabre, Stirling doesn't have a hair out of place. He looks at me for a moment, his teeth bared in something between a smile and a snarl.

And then we are into them. Pistols. Clubs. Whips. Sabres. Down they go. There is a young Countrywoman running straight ahead of me. Her feet flash across the riverbed sand, her hands pumping the air as she runs, and I gain on her. I am at full gallop and am only just gaining. She is fast. I get to know those muscles in her fine back in such detail, as they tighten and loosen, side by side, as she sprints along. And then my sword is arcing back across my body; my horse draws level, and down the cut goes. The blade goes in just above her ear and splits the top of her head open like a melon. The body of the Countrywoman is flung sideways and lands in the growing puddle of gore at her head. My eyes are looking forward to other targets and the bloodied blade dances at the end of my arm like some carnivorous metal plant, arcing around in the endless sightless quest for flesh.

'Where are the men?' I'm screaming. 'Where are the men?'

The blood stains us like sticky black river mud of Pinjarra.

I'm dragged down into the earth again. I tear through the Country until I come upon another scene. As I come racing up through the dirt and rocks I can see and hear the action unfolding on the earth's surface.

There is a contingent of the 63rd Regiment, the bloodsuckers, drawn up in formation.

'Ready!'

The rifles of the soldiers go to slant position, across their bodies.

'Aim!'

I burst free of the earth's crust right next to them to see their rifles level at the old man with the prominent bump on his forehead, who is tied to a tree. His eyes appeal to me for help. This is the man that put his Welcome To Country right inside our heads, that first day after we all went into the water. The leader who welcomed us with song and dance and ceremony. I look around. Where is his bright-eyed and burly son? Where is the Governor?

'Fire!'

The rifle balls slamming into the old Countryman's naked torso dull the booming report from the twelve muskets, and I am flung back underground.

I'm standing back on the little beach by the river. I press in on the scars.

I know my people. I know what is coming. How can the bond between human beings be so flimsy? We're in never-traversed-before territory, Djenga and Countrymen alike. Countrymen know their Country. But never before with us on it. Us, the inevitable tide that cannot be turned. The tide of history. How can this tide flow out from our estuary of existence and wipe out Countrymen rights? Whilst upholding our rights? Djenga. European. Tides come in. Tides go out.

The look of the Countrywomen's faces as we rode down on them. The fine ropey muscles in the back of that Country-woman as she sprinted for her life.

This is all about sheep and cattle. I'm a sailor. An officer. What do I care for livestock? For new colonies? For anything? For this bloody Empire? I am not my father, the Admiral of the Fleet. I am not my brother, Lord Cottesloe. He will say that I owe him because he pulled strings to make my trial go away, to save my honour. It was his honour he was protecting. This price is too high.

When my tears start to come, each one of them is a child. A child born of agonising birth. Pushing their way out of my birth-canal tear ducts and scalding my skin as they crawl down my face and fall to the sand below. Child after child, tear after tear, forcing their way out. They need to be born, my salty children. They roll down my face, drip onto my chest, and fall onto the sandy beach of Garungup.

These tears of mine, tears for that slaughtered family, fall like seeds into the earth. Not dead but alive. Alive and contained. Waiting to grow. Tear after tear. Child after child. Seed after seed I cry. I weep. I plant my tears deep into this Country. A feeling swells back up to me from the Country as each tear hits like an orchestra building to a crescendo. The sound that comes out of my mouth I don't recognise. It might be a sad song suggested into my heart from the rhythm and melody of the waterfall. I howl. I weep. I sing. I plant. Plant my tears. Plant them deep into the Country.

Fourteen: Swim the Sick Mother

I'm under water. Inside a huge rectangular fish bowl. I'm on the bottom of the tank, my head jammed strangely in the corner. I have expelled all the air in my lungs. The only thing keeping the water out of my mouth, throat, lungs, and stomach, are my lips, pressed firmly shut. I inherited this thin top lip from my father. My mother had beautiful full lips – I missed out on them. The water pushes in on me insistently, daring me to try to breathe liquid like my fish ancestors. I run my fingers down the outside of my breastbone to feel for the warmth of the hand signal. It's still there: I'm coming for you. Above the surface I see Mitch the Blood Nut and Torby standing over me. Over the fish bowl. I try to shake off the water but my head is jammed solid in the glass corner. I'm stuck in this watery-grave-fishbowl dream.

Mitch reaches down, grabs me by the scruff of the neck, and hauls me up. My head breaks free of the fish bowl water and I gulp in beautiful, dry, rotten-body-fear-stinking air. Even through my loathing, I could kiss Mitch. But he doesn't even know he's saved me. His hands are dry. There is no water for him. No fish bowl.

Mitch holds me easily with his big angry red hands. His face is twisted into a leering grin. 'I do know ya, don't I?'

The dressing from my head has fallen off. It's lying in a heap on the rock-dust floor. The wound on the side of my head is exposed, revealing my face as well.

Dry the wound out a bit. Do it good.

Mitch punches me in the face. I fall back in a heap.

'This little girl don't know which side of her toast to butter,' snarls Mitch.

Torby gives a little giggle through clenched teeth.

'Get his pants off!' says Mitch.

Torby goes for my fly buttons. I try to knock his hands away and Mitch kicks me in the belly.

'Ain't got your brother-boys with you now, Bitch!'

Torby is pulling down my strides. The air in the underground chamber is cool on my buttocks.

'Get his shirt off, too.'

'You gonna suck his nipples, Mitch?'

Mitch backhands Torby across the mouth. The power-lust is upon him now, crouching over him like a giant, twisted scorpion.

'Shut up! If ya want seconds.'

Mitch kicks me again and I feel Torby ripping off my shirt. Now I'm naked and scrabbling around on the dirt floor. Mitch is laughing, Torby is chuckling his clenched-teeth-giggle.

I wait for Mitch to lower his strides. He gets his cock out and is stroking himself to get hard. I steady myself with my hands and sweep my right leg straight through his legs. It's a good foot-sweep given my weak condition, and down he goes. I flip myself onto my feet and jam my heel into Mitch's groin. Mitch screams. Torby goes to step in and I joint-kick his front knee. His knee snaps with a loud crack and down he goes. I jam my heel down onto Mitch again – this time his throat. Training. Training is what will get you through, The Sarge always said, may his soul find peace. They're both writhing on the floor as I take off, still naked, across the crowded chamber. I don't alter my pace for a few minutes, threading my way through the bewildered Djenga inmates. The faces look pale and sick and confused. They're shivering, even though I am the naked one. Their limbs are swathed in makeshift bandages as though the whole place is a subterranean leper colony.

At the far end of the massive chamber there are several smaller passageways leading away into the earth. I choose the opening at the far left and run straight in. Once inside I slow to a walk. The ground is cold and hard on my bare feet. My feet are soft from the years of boot wearing.

Outside in the main chamber I hear a big commotion starting. Mitch will come again. With mates. I keep walking and the rocky corridor opens out a little and there is a big pool of dark water. There are some artificial lights in here. There are five or six inmates getting water from the dark pool in old Water Board ration tins. They stare at my nakedness, my anxious face. Outside, in the chamber, the big commotion is getting closer. The water gatherers look at me as if to ask what is going on.

'Get out of here and you won't get hurt!' I say.

They hoof it out of there. I get down to the water's edge.

I look around for weapons. There's a rock as big as a grenade near the water's edge. I grab it. I can see there is no way out. Around the corner come Mitch and Torby with four or five blokes in tow. I start to back away. The only way is into the water. They arrive at the water's edge as I am about waist-deep. Mitch clocks the rock in my hand. He pauses. He knows that I have training.

I feel the hand signal lodged in my breastbone begin to heat up until I am warm all over. Then I notice the tiny bubbles popping up out in the middle. There's something in here!

The water abruptly breaks open and the Countrywoman

from Uncle Birra-ga's cave bursts through. She swims straight to me and stands up.

'Grab em!' yells Mitch, and the chasers thrash their way towards us.

She is holding me firmly and pulling me back into the deep.

'Get em! Get em!'

'Come on,' she says. 'The first swim is the longest. We get to breathe after about three minutes. After that it's two two-minute sections. At the first hole only one can breathe at a time. You go first. Then we swap. Then we go.'

'Grab them!'

She turns, still holding me, and pulls me under. We dive in and swim down. Straight down. She keeps holding my arm as we go down. We've gone four or five metres down when she takes a torch off her belt and turns it on. There is a white cord in that dark water which shines in the torchlight and disappears through a hole in the rock. The white cord is like the watery version of that single thread spun by the huntsman spider who abseiled off my shoulder in the tank. She goes through first and I follow. The hole is only marginally bigger than the width of my body. We grope our way along the rock, following the white cord that winds its way into the future. We pull ourselves along the rock above our heads. The torch is a tiny light in the vast inky blackness. The rock is pale grey in the torchlight.

I follow the light, struggling to keep up with the wet-suited Countrywoman, fighting the feeling that at any moment a huge subterranean monster will chomp into my nether regions. Jack's drugs are still fucking with me. Mitch the Blood Nut is real. The water is real. The monster is in my head.

Then she is there, shining the torch up into a tiny hole in the rock just big enough to get my head up into.

Up I go. With my bare shoulders jammed against the rock, my face comes into the air. I suck in oxygen.

In. Out. In. Out. In.

Down I go and wait for her to breathe. She's faster than me. She comes back down, and we take up the cord with our fingers to follow to the next breathing hole. It is the feeling of clinging to my mother that envelops me now. The warmth from the hand signal is wearing off. I'm cold and I can feel how weak I am. I close my eyes and follow the white cord blindly, playing it through my fingers like a fishing line. Her hands touch me and I open my eyes and kick up into the next hole. We come up together, breathing like whales. I think I hear them singing out in the dark water way below us. She shines the torch at me.

'You right?'

I check myself. I feel weak and tingly all over. Like I might faint.

I nod. I'm good.

Back under the skin of the water she goes.

I take a breath and follow her. She plays the white cord through her fingers as she follows the rocky passageway. The walls start to close in on us now, as it gets tighter and tighter. I bump my head on the rock for the umpteenth time. I swear, even under the water, and a mass of bubbles escapes my unruly mouth. My eyes are blurring out a bit from having them open too much in this cold water. She doesn't look back but seems to speed up. I drag myself along behind her.

There is a big light ahead of us. I kick out my feet behind me. There are fingers of sunlight dancing along the bottom of a shallow pool just ahead. I kick for it and burst into the filtered sunlight.

I come up just behind her. It is so bright that I squeeze my eyes shut. I can hear her breathing evenly in front of me, even as I am blindly sucking and gasping. We're in a pool, still underground, with this beautiful shaft of sunlight coursing down from above. I pull myself out and lie wheezing on the rock. Above me, bathed in the golden light, are Mularabone and Young James.

'Love ya traditional dress, bruz,' says Mularabone.

I remember my nakedness and her presence. The blood rushes to my face. Young James has a blanket that he drapes over me. I'm shivering now, my whole body shaking.

I can smell the paste that they've daubed themselves with for UVP. It's a secret herbal handed-down recipe, which gives the wearer one hundred per cent UVP and a strong odour. Uncle Birra-ga says totemic ancestors who could see the coming danger from the sun, as the global industrialisation changed the atmosphere, gave the recipe in dreams to the mob a hundred or so years ago. I remember the first time I ever saw Mularabone, how shocked I was to see his bare skin during the day. He looked free, whilst I was confined and constricted and afraid to burn.

'I – I just strip down to fighting rig, brother. Ya wanna go a couple of rounds?'

I try to stand but can't. I crumple back down from my parody of a fighting stance. They laugh at my weak attempt at humour. They bend and help me up. They steer me tenderly up the slope to a set of well-worn steps.

At the top there are two small tents. I'm ushered into one. It has silver plastic lining. There is a Countryman in there in a sealed-up suit. He turns a strong hose on me.

Oh, fuck. Not the hose.

I try to scream. To struggle. Strong hands wrapped in plastic hold me firm. A heavy brush scrubs my flesh with some kind of pink foam. I fall to my knees. I'm sobbing now. The water cannon is relentless. The scrubbing is horrendous against my flesh, which has been denied sunlight and clean air and sustenance for so long. If they rub me any harder, my flesh will come away like a pot-cooked roast, leaving only my gleaming bones. Through my sobs I think I hear something. It's at the periphery of my comprehension like the tiny misty droplets that spray from the nozzle of the hose and aren't caught up in the main jet. Even if they still floated onto my flesh, I would never feel them next to the colossal rage of the main jet of water. It is a sweet sound above the throb of the water pump. I focus in on it, cutting out that scrubbing and the terrific thrust of the water pounding me.

It is her. It must be her. She has only ever spoken a handful of words to me but I know that it is her voice lifted in song. She is singing a lullaby. I can hear in her voice that she is also being hosed and scrubbed. The power of her lullaby obliterates the sensation of the jet of water for me, and caresses my face like a soft rain. I allow the drops/notes to fall on my open face. Some drops/notes run down my skin. Some drops/notes hit me like I am a puddle, going into me, and sending out concentric waves across my surface. I lick my lips to taste the sweet free water.

Ghost of History: The Empire Has Not Forgotten Us

The water pouring off the canvas is loud and insistent, as if it is flowing right through my soul. I'm standing in the entrance to my tent, my head bowed, looking out. The rain beats down. It has poured all night, since Fremantle and I left the Birdiya's fire to come back here to sleep. The old man with the prominent bump on his forehead and his son with the bright eyes like to sing and dance every night. Fremantle calls it the old man's court, and compares it to King George's. The old man is the Birdiya, or Law boss, for all the lands south of the Darbal Yaragan down to the island of Meandip, known as Beeliar. Fremantle says the old man has more land than his brother, Lord Cottesloe. Fremantle calls the old man 'Beeliar', as in the Duke of Beeliar, which seems to please the Birdiya. The fireside court can be a raucous affair, Beeliar and Bright Eyes, his son, being men of relentless energy.

Straight across from me is Fremantle's tent and the flaps are pulled back. Inside there is a group of Countrymen. They've got a fire going inside and, oblivious to the smoke, they crowd around the flames singing a morning song. Fremantle is nowhere to be seen. The sun is just up, although completely obscured by the heavy clouds crowding in on the land. I sit on the edge of my makeshift cot and pull on my boots. It's cold. The wind tears at the heavy canvas. I shrug on my woollen coat, jam my hat down onto my head and step out. My face is itchy from the remnants of the ochre applied last night and I rub my features with both hands. In another tent I see a couple of marines sitting with some Countrymen. They've also lit a fire and I can smell the fish cooking through the rain. This looks nothing like a Royal Marine encampment. Smells nothing like it.

I step out and on a whim head up to the high ground of Manjaree. The limestone cliffs jut out into wardan, the ocean, with the river mouth just to the north. Even before I get there I see Fremantle standing alone. The wind buffets him and the rain lashes his person but he stands as steady as a mighty jarrah tree. He has his glass up to his eye. I pick my way carefully up the sandstone ridge until I'm standing next to him, following his gaze out across the wild ocean. After a long time he lowers the glass.

'The Empire has not forgotten us,' he says, without taking his eyes from the raging sea, and passes the glass to me.

I raise the glass to my eye and make out the *Parmelia* standing off the coast of the island of Wadjemup several leagues directly west of our position. I lower the glass.

'Captain Dance's *Sulphur* can't be far behind,' I say.

'And on board, Captain Irwin, and the 63rd Regiment.'

'The bloodsuckers,' I hear myself say.

'You know the 63rd ?'

'Apparently.'

Fremantle grunts. The swells crash into the beach down below the headland. The spray arcs up into the air to join with the rain flinging itself against us on the shoreline. The long arm of the Empire is reaching out to us.

'We have two days,' I say, sensing his dark mood.

'He'll make a run in today.'

'It's too dangerous with such a sea.'

'Have you ever met Captain Stirling?'

'Captain Luscombe is the commander.'

Fremantle grunts again. We both knew this moment was coming. Time has stood still for us since we arrived here. We don't yet have the language to describe what has happened to us. To accept what has happened to us. What is happening. We've had six weeks of hunting, fishing, dancing, singing and dreaming here with the Countrymen. With the Country.

'Where did this weather come from?' I ask.

'The senior men have gone to the other place for ceremony,' says Fremantle, and his phrasing causes me to look at him. I look at him, trying to read his thoughts in the cold rain. I hand the glass back to him. He raises it to his eye.

'Ready the cutter and gig, Mister Conway.'

'Sir.'

'He is coming.'

And as we watch, the *Parmelia* weighs anchor and begins turning towards the run down to the safe waters of the sound. Even from this distance, we can see the ship struggling with the howling southerly and the monstrous swell.

'Perhaps it is his fate never to make landfall, sir.'

Fremantle turns to look at me as if I have spoken a profanity.

'Clearly, you have not met Captain Stirling.'

I can't meet his gaze. I have not met Captain Stirling. But I know him. I know him as Fremantle knows him – with horses, sabres, pistols and clubs.

The wind and swell appear to pick up. We struggle to stay upright as the rain pelts us. Fremantle watches through his glass. We only have a few minutes to wait before the *Parmelia* is clearly in trouble with the big sea. The front sail is torn away by a sudden gust and for a moment the vessel flounders. Then she is turning away to the north, and heading back to her anchorage off Wadjemup. We see the rest of the sail coming off.

'Will you be taking the cutter and gig, sir?'

'No, Mister Conway. You shall have that privilege.'

I look out to where I can just make out the *Parmelia* each time a major swell dips. I haven't been out in a sea like this since we rounded the Horn.

'You shall inform Captain Stirling that if he does not have the patience to wait for conditions to become amenable, then he will surely be lost with all hands.'

'Shall I use that tone, sir?'

Fremantle claps me on the shoulder, and dazzles me with his smile.

'You may take whatever tone you wish, Mister Conway. As long as Captain Luscombe and Captain Stirling accept the folly of attempting to enter the sound in such seas and winds.'

'I'm sure they've learned a valuable lesson today, sir.'

'Indeed.'

'Are you going to find the Birdiya?'

'I am returning to my ship. I am still an officer in the King's navy.'

Fifteen: What You Bring

We're sitting between two fires, my brother and me. I'm chewing a johnnycake made by Aunty Ouraka. Mularabone eats too, stuffing the seed cake into his smile. Uncle Birra-ga sits just beyond Young James. The young woman from the cave is here too, sitting with Aunty. Her hands rest in her lap. Every time I look up, her eyes are down.

I'm hungry.

I am trying to decipher the images in my head. I remember swimming. Swimming through an underground river. I blink my eyes repeatedly, and suddenly I'm not so sure.

I really need this food but my throat is tight with emotion, so I have to chew the seed cake finely. It's a good chew. The little muscles at the corner of my jaw and those at my temple are burning. Doggedly I chew on. As soon as I get to wondering what Mularabone is smiling at, I realise it is my chewing that is causing him mirth. He starts mimicking me, much to the delight of the rest of the mob. They all start doing it. So I exaggerate even more, my cow's cud rising and falling in a substantially embellished circular motion. Little bits of cake fly out of my mouth and into the fire. The tiny cake particles burn up like meteors entering the earth's atmosphere. This sets everyone off into a fresh round of laughing. The laughter is like another bigger, warmer fire engulfing all of us. The coldness of that underground chamber and that swim is finally beginning to seep out of my bones, sweating out like a bad inverted fever, and I start to feel warm and alive again. I can feel my mind, coming home to roost like a wayward homing pigeon. I take a final bite of Aunty's seed cake and get into the last chew-down.

They laugh. I chew. I laugh. I swallow with a flourish. Everyone cheers. I laugh.

Then the laugh is stuck on something, a fishing line caught on seaweed, and won't come up.

'I thought ...' I start to say to Mularabone.

His hand on my forearm checks my thought.

I look up at him with my eyes even though my head will not do as it is told.

'You're right, brother,' he says.

I look into the reflection of myself in the fire. I am starting to melt.'I thought ...' I begin again and can't finish again. My head is down.

'Brother. You didn't give us away. We knew you'd come. With troopers. We shoulda bin stay underground. But Uncle wanted to come up.'

We look over the fire at Uncle, who smiles back in response. 'I wanted to see you, Nephew.'

I break into open weeping and my tears fall straight onto Country, here between the fires. I can't stop weeping. Weeping for what has been lost. For what has been saved. For my own weakness. For what I know is coming in my dream country. For it is already past. And I will feel the responsibility as surely as that old Royal Navy captain. I must. I weep for the families. My tears soak the Country. They go in, and go down deep.

Uncle rocks back and forth and claps boomerangs together as he sings. The others drift away from the fires until it is just the Old Man and I.

'Planting tears,' says Birra-ga. 'Again.'

I look up to see him watching me closely. I smile.

'This is good. Connects you.'

Uncle Birra-ga reaches out and touches the jagged scar on the side of my head. He nods as though he can see the broken bottle going into my flesh. 'Them old spirits recognise what you bring to the table,' he says.

'Water Board was trying to turn me.'

'Into what?'

'One of them.'

'You are one of them.'

I smile, and almost laugh. 'Tried to get intel from me.'

'You don't know anything.'

This time I do laugh. 'Uncle, I don't know how ...?'

'The dreams? Sometimes it is sleep. Sometimes it is a change of pressure in the brain between sleeping and waking. Sometimes it is the story chasing you down from the other place.'

'Uncle, I want to help you but ...'

His laughter is sudden and loud. His hand touches me on the upper arm. 'Your dreams are not for me. For you. Your people. We need to meet in the middle. We walk out from our camp. You from yours.' He laughs again. 'Help me?'

Sixteen: Nayia-Nayia

We walk below the level of the ridgeline. An old habit for us. The sounds and smells of the desert morning are drifting to us from every direction. The earth is cool beneath our bare feet. We breathe out, the scrub breathes in.

The sun is fully over the horizon now, even though the ghost-ball of the new moon can still be made out in the sky of the opposite horizon. They balance us out, these two unearthly orbs that hang over us like promises of things to come. A promise of nights. Of days. Although for us and them right now there is only today. Today is every day that has ever been and every day that ever will be. Today is the day. That old fulla Sun accelerates as he comes up out of the earth, and then punches up a gear and backs off the juice to cruise up to midday sky. He does it same way every day.

Mularabone and I stop and sit. Neither of us has spoken yet. Mularabone rolls two thinnies and holds one out to me. I hesitate.

'Swore I'd give em up.'

'In jail?'

'When I was swimming through that tunnel and couldn't breathe.'

'That was just cause you were following Nayia.'

'What?'

'Nothin.'

'What is her name?'

'Nayia. Nayia-Nayia.'

'Nayia-Nayia,' I test her name on my lips. I give him a question look.

'Angel. Angel from Above. Nayia.'

I smile. Mularabone looks away.

'Angel?' I say.

'We got angels, too, bruz.'

'What's all the secret for?'

'Nothin. You want ngumari, or not?' he says, indicating the thin cigarette in his fingers.

I hesitate, the smile perched on my face like a half-told joke – waiting for the punch line.

'You might as well,' Mularabone adds, holding out the ngumari again.

I give him a careful look. He is suddenly hard to read. Maybe I was enjoying his discomfort too much. I don't know why he's been holding back. Is Nayia married, or promised, not straight, or first-cousin taboo for Mularabone, and therefore me? I don't want to admit to thinking about her so much after the first meeting in Uncle Birra-ga's cavern-camp.

I take the proffered thinnie from Mularabone and we both light up.

There are two bush doves dancing around in the shade of the bush in the gully at our feet. At first I think they're fighting as they throw their little bodies into the grapple, turn over and over, and then spring back to their feet, throwing up little kicks of morning dust. Then I see the little fulla fan out his tail and go into his strut. He is good. His timing is excellent. Maybe she's been put slightly off-guard from the play wrestle and ready to be dazzled by his splendour. He struts up and down; four paces west, six back east in a figure-eight movement. And she likes him, we can see that. Her little eyes twinkle as she drinks in that fanned-out soft chocolate and white tail. Maybe the colours excite her too. Then off they fly without warning, at exactly the same moment – them both feeling the crescendo of the dance and the energy between them.

'Country looks different,' I say.

'You bin away two months.'

I smoke. Two months?

'Time flies when you're havin fun,' I say through a stream of smoke.

I feel the side of my head. Aunty Ouraka has packed bush medicine into the wound and it feels better already. Lost its nasty sting. It's gonna leave a big scar, though. Mularabone sees me touching the old wound.

'You no longer beautiful, bro,' he says.

'I was never beautiful, bro.'

We smile. We smoke.

'Nayia is beautiful,' I hear my voice say.

'Yes. Nayia is beautiful,' Mularabone agrees with a sigh.

'What you sighin for?'

He doesn't answer me.

'She bin in my dreams,' I say.

Mularabone expels smoke carefully. He nods.

'You know something that I don't, bro. About Nayia.'

'It's nothing, coorda. Just protocol.'

'What, to keep us apart?'

'I don't make the rules, bro.'

'Is it cause I'm white?'

'You're not white, coorda. I told ya, don't think about it.'

I drag on my thinnie.

'You bin livin in dreamland, coorda. It's written all over you.'

'What do you mean?'

'You got that faraway look in your eye. Only yours looks far, far away.'

I take him in. 'You bin dreaming up big too, bruz.'

'In a different place. You're going back. I'm going forward.'

'Two camps,' I say absentmindedly.

We finish our smokes. Stub them out. Put the ends into our pockets. We watch the sun just cruising now he is in the open sky a little. I touch my bare face to feel the paste Aunty rubbed into me earlier. Mularabone sees me.

'DOz moved on too, coorda. While you were underground. Aunty was just being careful.'

I nod. It's funny how our bodies or minds can sometimes be aware of time passing, and sometimes not. Once all outside references are gone, it is almost impossible.

My head is full of blurry memories of being a Water Board trooper.

And there is something else haunting me like a half-forgotten tune. I can't quite get hold of the tune and I can't get it out of my mind. The feeling I had with that grog twisting its way through my veins, as I watched the troopers burning up in the full sun, and falling to my bullets, as Mularabone sprinted for the dam – I felt strong. I cared nothing for the carnage. That grog transported me to another place in my heart. A desolate place. It feels now like the killing and death amused me in some way. I remember laughing.

'We have to get more water,' Mularabone says.

He suddenly seems all light and loose again. He drags me effortlessly along with him. This is what we do best.

We walk.

Shared Waking Dream Memory:
Secret Water

I'm coming back from a long walk. I'm about fifteen or sixteen. As I come over the rise I see the van parked there by the little spring. My throat tightens when I see that my father's dusty vehicle is there. I didn't know he was coming back. Mum didn't say anything. Maybe she didn't know either. I edge down towards the van. As I get closer I can hear him shouting. Her voice is in the mix too. I come up to the vehicle, keeping it between me and the van, and creep along the side. I gently open the front door. There are empty grog bottles and shit everywhere in the cabin. It looks like he lives in this vehicle. There's a swag in the back. I open the glove compartment. There's pair of leather gloves sitting there. I tentatively lift the well-worn gloves to see a large pistol crouching underneath like a big black scorpion. I reach in and place my hand on the cold metal. I rest my hand. When nothing happens I lift the weapon out. It is huge and black in my hands.

I hear him shouting. She is moaning. I push off the safety catch and creep to the van window. There is a tiny slit I can see through at the edge of the window blinds. Inside the van it is much darker, the only light spilling from those red military lamps. He is naked and standing over her, thrusting into her on the edge of the bed. I look down and shrink back from the van. I slip the safety catch back on the weapon. I turn and walk, retracing my path back over the rise, the pistol hanging from the end of my arm like a bad afterthought of my creator. I'm trying to keep the image out of my mind. I couldn't see her face, just a section of her bare torso, and one breast wobbling back and forth, the nipple dancing this way and that, in time to the rhythm of his thrusts.

I was suckled on those breasts, I catch myself thinking. This memory lives on my lips.

I have this strange grin twisting my face, which is red and hot from the quick-skin blood of shame. It reminds me of Stirling's snarl-grin as we rode down on those unarmed women and children on the riverbank at Pinjarra, after I was dragged through the Country in the Garungup dream. Time is weaving in and out of itself, and I can feel the web humming with life beneath me.

I thought they were arguing, him bashing her, but they were fucking.

I career away from the van and walk, almost running, for a long time, before I remember the heavy weight in my hand. I take aim at various rocks and trees and pretend to fire the weapon,

'Pee-ow! Pee-ow!'

It takes a two-handed grip for me to be able to hold the weapon steadily. I imagine the rounds hitting my targets in explosions of rock shards and splinters, and the sound of the shots repeating dully in the hot air all around me.

The sandiness of the earth starts to disappear and all around me the Country is getting rocky and hard. I walk on. The gullies are deep and boulder-strewn. It doesn't seem possible that a force of water rolled these boulders as big as cars and trucks here, but I know it's true. I can feel it. That flood was tens of thousands of years ago. Water has a song that echoes through my veins, but this song of that water is so old, it is just the ancient ghost of a flowing hymn. I go downhill and then turn and walk up one of these ancient watercourses. There is a little fine sand at the bottom but it is still pretty rocky.

Ahead of me I hear what sounds like a fight: the smack of something hard into flesh, grunts and strangled cries. I proceed more carefully, stashing the pistol into my belt at the small of my back, like I've seen my father do.

I turn a corner and there is this young Countryman about my age. He smacks his fist into the huge flat rock one more time, then grunts and cries out in pain. He dances around, rubbing his aching knuckles. He is deep in this self-flagellatory dance and doesn't notice me approach. I'm only a few metres away when he spots me and jumps back like he's seen a ghost. And I'm a hidden ghost, all my flesh being swathed in the UVP cloth composite. He is bare-chested, bare-armed, barefaced, barefooted. We're from different universes.

'What you sneaking round for, fulla?'

'I wasn't sneaking.'

'Yes you was, if I hadn't bin dancing, I woulda seen you before you seen me.'

'Is that the famous rock-punch dance?'

'I'll punch you if you're not careful.'

'I wouldn't if I were you.'

'Why not?'

'I'm armed and dangerous.'

'Bullshit.'

'I am.'

'I oughtta flog you now for lying.'

'I wouldn't try it.'

'Who are you, anyway? This is my Country.'

He takes a step towards me.

With a flourish I take out the big pistol.

'Holy fuck!'

'Yeees. Holy fuck. Still think I ain't armed?'

'You ain't dangerous.'

I grab the pistol with two hands, lift it to eye level, aiming off to the side of him, flick off the safety catch, and let off a round.

Boom!

His eyes go wide. He smiles. 'I was wrong, brother. You is armed and dangerous!'

'My father says we ain't brothers, we're shareholders.'

'That's cause your father is an ignorant immigrant, brother. He don't know any better. What's ya name?'

'Conway.'

'Mularabone.'

We shake hands.

'Can I've a shot?' Mularabone asks quickly, as if the whole sentence is one word. In his Language it would be.

I offer him the pistol without hesitation.

Mularabone's face lights up, and he grabs the side arm.

I say, 'My father's not an immigrant, we been here since Captain Fremantle.'

'Immigrant is in his mind, not where he's come from.'

Mularabone grabs the weapon, spins, drops onto one knee and lets off two rounds.

Crack! Crack!

He comes up smiling. He likes it. He shifts it from one hand to the other like it's a football, feeling its weight. He looks back to me, and hands the weapon back.

'Whatcha doin out here?' I ask.

Mularabone looks away. He kicks the red dirt with his bare feet. He walks away a bit.

'You all right, brother?' I hear myself ask.

I've never called another person 'brother' before in my life. But then I've never met a Countryman before.

My father says they own nothing. That their respecting of the Country and therefore the Country producing food and wealth is all bullshit. That our side of the continent simply fared better than the East under the massive climate changes. That there is no Law in the Country. In the plants. Animals. Rocks. The Countrymen.

'I'm sposed to find water,' he says into the ground.

'Out here?'

'My grandfather is a water man. Can make rain. Find water hidden in the earth. He says I'm the next one.'

I watch his mouth closely because I'm not used to the Countryman accent. We all love that accent too, us Djenga. If ever I use it, my father flogs me. He's one of the special contractors recruited by the Water Board of the Coalition of the Eastern States of Australia. He's always going away. Mum kids herself that he's doing some type of construction work. We all do. We have to. He has construction helmet and tool belt in his vehicle. As well as the huge pistol. And the crates of grog. He has a shotgun in the van as well. He doesn't feel comfortable unless he has guns around.

A silence hangs over us.

I know exactly what Mularabone is going through. My father always makes me find the water. My grandfather told him that I could do it. My mother's father. The man whom Warroo-culla knew. My father can speak Language as well. I know it even though I've never heard him.

'How does he do it?' I ask.

'What?'

'How does your grandfather find secret water?'

The young Countryman gives me a sharp look, his head still half turned away from me. Then he smiles.

'I'm not telling you.'

'You don't know.'

'Yes I fucken do.'

'No ya don't. That's why you were punching the rock.'

'It's my rock, on my Country, and if I feel like punching it, I will.'

I say nothing.

'It doesn't work when I try it!' he says.

Now I start smiling. He catches my smile like it's a thrown ball and smiles back. I turn and start to walk away.

'Hey, where you goin?' he calls after me.

'Well, if it's anywhere – it's back there,' I sling over my shoulder.

'What?'

'The water.'

Mularabone grabs up his digging stick and runs to catch up with me.

'What you talking about, Djenga boy?'

'I thought we was all brothers.'

Mularabone bends and picks up a tennis ball–size rock, tosses it up, and whacks it with his stick. I whip out the pistol and line up the flying rock, following its trajectory with the barrel.

'Pee-ow! Pee-ow!' I sing out.

'You woulda missed.'

'Bullshit.'

We walk.

'How can you expose your skin and not die?' I ask finally.

'Secret.'

I look to him, trying not to seem eager, hoping for an elaboration. There is none. We walk.

'My grandfather is a secret water man,' Mularabone reiterates.

'Mine too.'

'What are you talking about?'

'Yep, it's the next valley for sure.'

'How do you know?'

'I can feel it.'

'Feel it where?'

'It's like I can hear it flowing in my own blood.'

Mularabone goes quiet. He's heard someone talk like this before. If I've heard someone talk like this before, I can't remember it. I don't know where my voice is coming from, or who is directing my speech.

'Sometimes it is like a song in my head. Sometimes it makes me feel warm, sort of under the ears ...'

Mularabone is giving me a strange look. I'm already starting to learn that these looks are part of our conversation. I start to walk quickly as the sound/feeling/heat gets louder, more intense, hotter. I run up the little ridge in front of us, and cascade down the other side in a shower of small rocks and dust. There are two fresh saplings in the creek bed. I fall to my knees between them and start to dig with my hands. Mularabone falls down in front of me. With his digging stick he goes down twice as deep twice as fast as me. Half a metre down, clear water floods the hole.

We stop and look up at each other. Mularabone shouts for joy and pulls me into a hug over our water hole. Our first one. The suddenness of his movement surprises me and pulls me off balance. We both end up in a laughing heap in the wet hole, caving the sides in as we go. We drink, cupping the water in our hands and lifting it to our mouths.

Mularabone breaks into a dance and song in Language. I join in his dance and he laughs at my clumsy parody of his movement. The song swirls and then finishes. We stop. We look at each other.

'You knew it was here,' he says tentatively and watches my eyes for his words to land.

My mouth tightens but I don't speak. We look into each other's eyes.

I did find the little spring near where our van is camped – last year when my father wanted us to move out here – which means there could be more water – but I hadn't come looking. I didn't know where it was. Not until I knew, anyway.

Mularabone eventually smiles (You knew I had to ask, brother, didn't ya?).

I feel like we're standing chest deep in a torrent of water. We are trees or rocks in that terrible current, standing strong, so that the spirit water has to swirl around us to continue on its headlong rush.

I blink, and it's just a Djenga boy and a young Countryman standing in the bush, having met for the first time.

Seventeen: Reward or Punishment

Mularabone and I make our way back to camp, each carrying two bush turkeys from his overnight traps, and each wearing secret smiles from our shared waking dream memory of our first meeting. The power from our hearts linked for the dream has left a tingling feeling all down my spine. When we get back the billy is boiling. We pluck the fat birds, throw them on the fire, and heap coals on top of them. Uncle Birra-ga is talking to Uncle Warroo-culla who arrived in the night with Cuz Mortimer. Nayia and Aunty Ouraka are putting on a damper. Nayia barely notices me. I don't know what I was expecting. Young James and Cuz Mortimer have automatic weapons. The presence of the weapons changes something for me. Mularabone too, I can feel it. Maybe it's because Mularabone, Mort, Young James and I were in the same cadre. Mort's name means still water, and he was the one who coined the phrase the Water Gang: Muddy Water, Still Water, and Holy Water. Even Young James, whose name means supplanter, reckoned he belonged. Can't be a coincidence we're all together. Nothing is.

By the time the uncles are ready to talk to us, our bellies are full of rich turkey flesh, and we're feeling like another thinnie. We both roll an extra smoke and hand it up. Sharing Law. We all light up. What a strange little council, sitting out in the peaceful desert morning, dreaming up the future, or the past, whichever comes first.

When I look up from my smoke business Nayia and Aunty

Ouraka have gone. When I've seen them out walking, they seem to just amble, but that pace is so deceptive. They have completely disappeared as though swallowed up by the Country herself.

Uncle Warroo-culla makes an expressive speech in Language. After months in Water Board custody I struggle to follow Uncle's drift. I try to pick out words I know – or even words that sound like words I know – and thread my own meaning. Uncle is talking about Country, I think, and strong men, and joining things up. I concentrate intensely on the glowing end of my thinnie, as if the red light will open up my heart to the Language. Then I think he's talking about big holes in the ground, how certain nuts are hard to chew with old teeth, and why we need more good pairs of boots and more egg-laying birds who can fly.

Everyone is nodding at Uncle's speech. Me too. They must think I'm silly.

Uncle looks into the fire while he finishes his thinnie. Uncle Birra-ga comes over and sits near me.

'We will go to the big meeting,' says Uncle Birra-ga as if we are both expecting this information/instruction. Mularabone nods so I nod too.

'You will take care of all water business,' says Uncle Birra-ga.

I look to Mularabone. He is looking into the morning fire and makes no attempt to meet my gaze.

'The Djenga from the south Country was here looking for you. Your brother Jack kept you hidden,' says Warroo-culla.

'He's not my brother.'

The two Countrymen elders look straight at me as if I have blasphemed. I feel their power drill into me. I feel the shame of denying my brother.

'When I was young, there were two brothers who fought

with us,' says Birra-ga in a measured voice.

'One of these brothers fell to the grog ... and crossed over,' says Warroo-culla. 'He was the most vicious, ruthless enemy we faced. He sometimes worked with your father. We think your father turned him onto the grog path.'

'When his brother, our comrade, was killed ... he came back to us. Now he is our man inside the Water Board. He is the one coming for you. His name is Greer, the Guardian. His brother you knew. He was The Sarge. Now, you will complete the circle with Greer,' says Birra-ga.

'All around, the Country is telling us it is time to speak. To answer the invasion,' says Uncle Birra-ga.

Uncle lets his words settle like a flock of sulphur-crested cockatoos, and even though they've landed on me and settled on my branches, they continue to squawk and call out questions and jeers into my heart.

'We need you, Nephew. We need both of you. We need the connection to the ceremony in the south. The spirit path must be walked to free up this world. Free us to grow again.'

These words are cockatoos squawking in my boughs, breaking off small branches, picking the seeds out of the nuts, and then casually discarding the broken off nut-bearing branches.

My throat is constricted. I have broken into a heavy sweat. I don't look up now. A terrible fear grips my guts. I feel certain the uncles must look right through me and see my treachery, see what I am keeping locked away in my underground bunker. I remember too well the grog that passed my lips the night The Sarge died. That was what I remembered when the troopers got me drunk. That ache. That emptiness.

From across the other side of the fire, Uncle Warroo-culla speaks up.

'You are afraid of the troopers, Nephew.'

The electricity and the drugs and the smell of grog fill my mind like wild dogs, jaws and teeth dripping with eager saliva.

'You have your dreams now.' Uncle Warroo-culla is looking right in on me so that I feel small, like my body is hollow and my vantage point is way down in this hollow body, so that I have to strain my eyes and arch my spine backwards to look up through the opaque eye sockets of my own skull, to meet his gaze. 'You are dreaming your own story now. Searching for it in the heart of your spirit,' he says.

Mularabone is very still. Young James and Mort look outwards, their weapons bracketing their bodies like punctuation.

'Where you are going there is great danger,' says Warroo-culla.

'The dam?'

'Below the dam. Not far from where the truck is hidden,' says Warroo-culla.

'After you deal with the dam,' adds Birra-ga.

'Ambush?' I say.

I am really struggling to stay in this exchange. My mind wants to sink into the blurry safety of self-pity. This is a hangover from the grog. I bite down on the inside of my lip to keep myself bright with the pain.

'Not the ambush you are thinking of. This is a strong place. A danger place for you. Because of the grog.'

'Grog dreaming?'

'Yuwai,' Uncle nods. 'You will need Mularabone.'

'Why don't we get the water from somewhere else?'

Uncle Warroo-culla looks at me as if I've understood nothing.

'We need the water from *that* place. You need it.'

I get the feeling there is more coming, so I wait.

'Water from that place to heal you.'

I look to my thinnie, which has gone out.

'You know the grog dreaming is a story of two brothers ...' says Uncle.

I wait. But Uncle is looking away. He has said his piece.

Every moment in time encapsulates every other moment. My dreams are teaching me this. Each past. Each future. Each future for that moment. This is the nature of being. I knew about my connection with water from my maternal grandfather and uncle, but I'd put it away, or allowed it to be pushed aside to make room for other stuff barging its way in.

'What about Nayia?'

'Nayia-Nayia. The Chosen One,' says Uncle Warroo-culla.

I try to find Mularabone's eyes but he's concentrating on the fire.

'The Chosen One? What happened to "Angel From Above?"' I say.

'Interpretation,' says Mularabone with a shrug.

I look to Uncle Birra-ga. His eyes are fiery but somehow faraway for a moment – but then he focuses on me with a suddenness that makes me want to pull away. But I don't. I open up my heart and pour it back at Uncle through my eyes – meeting him head-on with all my spirit.

'Nayia chose to swim through the Sick Mother for you.'

'The Sick Mother?' My voice is calm and strong.

'They stored nuclear waste in those rock holes a hundred and fifty years ago,' says Mularabone.

'Who did?'

'It was the Eastern States mob. It was stored underground just over on their side of the border. We didn't know what they were up to.'

'Under the water?'

Mularabone nods. 'Yuwai.'

'Are they compromised?'

'We think they might be. Uncle's father wouldn't drink water from there. The story was that it made everyone sick, made them die.'

'But the inmates are drinking it,' I stammer out.

Radiation sickness. Blackness. Slackness. Sleepless. Senseless. Shortage. Shortfall. Rainfall. Walk tall.

'It was the only way out,' Mularabone says with a shrug, patting me on the shoulder.

What starts to creep into me now is a smile. Nothing like old Stirling's killer snarl. From down where I was trying to look out my eye sockets before, comes a wave of unexpected joy.

Nayia and I are bound together forever. She volunteered to save me. To swim to her certain death to save me. And by saving me, condemning me to certain death. But I'd been in the mine jail for days. I was already fucked. And the death will be slow and painful and sickly, not the brave, heroic, flashy kind. I remember the strange sickly appearance of all those Djenga prisoners in that old mine, shivering by inadequate fake fires.

'Is Nayia my reward, or my punishment?' I ask.

The Countrymen all laugh.

'Aaaaah,' says Uncle Warroo-culla with a dismissive wave of his hand, causing them all to laugh again.

I laugh too. The romantic aspirations of young men are always funny. Even my own. Love reduces us all to fools. I like the sound of my own laughter. We are all born to die. And I'm definitely dying. We all are. That's a laugh.

Eighteen: The Smoky Man

We all laugh for a long time. Then the laughter dies down. Like the fire. No one feeding it wood now. That old laughter dries up like an ancient riverbed strewn with huge boulders.

The old uncles nod and get to their feet. Young James and Mortimer are away and moving, the weapons held at casual readiness.

I look at Mularabone. He gives me a little giggle. I return it. Then we get up and skip away in the opposite direction.

We've only walked a few paces when Mularabone sings out, 'If ya get blisters and wanna stop – just let me know!'

I laugh but my fingers tell him to fuck off. My body is still weak from my subterranean captivity but I know I can walk. Djenga can walk too: if ya can't do it walking, it ain't worth doing!

'What did Uncle say?' I ask.

'He was saying that once the dam is gone, the lower river region can recover,' Mularabone says.

'He spoke for a long time.'

'The place where he was born is now under water. He is worried for that Country.'

We walk for a long time. We're heading back to the dam. We'll have to get the truck to cart some water for the meeting of the Law bosses. The water covering Uncle Warroo-culla's country is another matter. There's Jack and the whole Water Board compound protecting that dam. But we'll know what to do. It will come to us when it comes. I wish I could keep my thoughts all on one line.

Then Mularabone's head goes up, and he is completely still for a moment, before he takes off like a madman. This bungarra goes running this way and that with Mularabone in pursuit. Finally the lizard goes racing up a stunted desert oak with Mularabone hard on his heels. I run up to the other side of the tree to flank him. Then Mularabone dances in, as though all the moves are rehearsed, nulla-nulla out in one graceful movement, and thud! Thud! Thud! He whacks that old goanna. Mularabone smiles. He sings a thank-you prayer to that bungarra spirit.

We don't stop walking. We're following a snaky tree line. It's hot. Really hot. I glance over at Mularabone. The heat and pace don't bother him. I'm thinking about the dam. About the water. I remember the strong song in my blood from the dried riverbed beyond where we stashed the truck. Something tugs at my memory from that strong old water song, a feeling that I can't quite get hold of. That feeling of recognition, like seeing Molloy the killer handing out bread to the Nyoongars in the dream of Fremantle at Garungup.

Mularabone takes off again with the bungarra hanging from his belt. My eyes go up and out. Way out to the shimmering east there is a movement of grey on the red-dust horizon. Running out towards the barely perceptible movement – Mularabone's right hand flashes an instruction to me, a pumped flat pushdown movement away from his body. I fall back to the shade under the thin trees and lie down on the warm earth. In this landscape we suddenly do not exist. The desert is so big and we are so small.

Mularabone throws himself down and pulls off his backpack. He takes out a gadget, unfolds the dish-shaped aerial and places the little unit on the ground. He hits a button and a control panel lights up. Mularabone keys in a sequence and then flattens himself on the earth like some reptile soaking up the heat from the ground to give him more energy. He's masking our infra-red signature. Another of his own devices. He's a bloody genius in the boffin room.

I lie in the little hollow between two grass trees. I can hear a little rhythmic tapping. At first I think it is some sound generated by Mularabone's little black box. I look over and see a chunky brown beetle in the shade of a fallen branch. The beetle is clicking against the wood, maybe burrowing into it.

I lie on that earth and listen. The vehicle out on the horizon causes vibrations. Mularabone must have felt them before he saw it. It's way too far off, even for his keen eyesight. The Country is alive with vibrations. With music. Anything that interrupts the song is out of place. Discernibly different. It changes something and that is what is felt. The whole Country is a living, breathing instrument, like an orchestra with infinite musical devices in play, which all connect and react to each other. This is what Mularabone calls the *oneness*. Mularabone can't find water but he is the most creative military matériel technician I've ever come across. And in combat he is the best. He excels. Has saved my arse so many times I can't count. I always wondered why he wanted to. I always wondered whether I was really worth saving. I'm drifting off. The heat. I look up and Mularabone is coming back over to me.

'We'll go for another hour, then rest up,' he says.

I can't even open my mouth to say, 'Why don't we rest here?' before he is off again. Mularabone is the real soldier out of the two of us. In another hour the tree line has petered out and we move into real open country. There is only a click or so to cover before we come to the sunken rocky canyon area where we'll rest up. This rock formation doesn't rise up but sinks away into a valley you can't really see until you are right on top of it. Down we go and it is cool. The floor is river sand

and the walls are high and tight. Down in the bottom of the canyon there is a flat shady area. We sit. Mularabone comes over to me. His hand signals 'water' and his eyes ask me the question. With my lips I point to the far end of our little area. Mularabone wanders down there. As he gets close he sees the tiniest spot of dampness in the river sand just behind the two big boulders. He crouches behind them and digs. He fills up two cups and brings them back and sits next to me, offering me a cup and holding one for himself.

'We'll sleep when we get there,' he says.

'When's that?'

'Tonight, maybe.'

I nod. Those 'maybes' used to worry me. But not anymore. Not trying to get anywhere. Not anymore. I am somewhere. On a road that I can't see. Going to a place to steal water we already own and take it to a place that I can't talk about. To meet Countrymen I don't know. Speaking in languages I've never heard before. This is the way of things. Even getting the water is not the main thing any more.

I take out my makings and roll two thinnies. I hand one to Mularabone.

'You will get strong, bruz,' he says.

I light Mularabone's thinnie and mine. We smoke.

As I blow out my smoke it appears to cling to me, as if the mass of tiny particles rising from the tip of my thinnie can read my thoughts. I'm sitting in a little cloud of Conway-shaped smoke, swirling and flowing with my movements, and totally keeping my shape. I take in more air and try to exhale my smoke forcefully away from me but it makes no difference, it just clings more and more. Soon I can't see Mularabone. Can't see him through the smoke. I can still hear the clicking. Mularabone has joined the beetle, and is tapping a small rock on a twig, and gently intoning an ancient rhyme.

The smoke begins solidifying into some kind of grit on my eyelids and I have to close them or be swamped by the growing mountain of grey powder. I close my eyes. Squeeze them against the accumulating smoky powder, squeeze them hard, and then relax them into the mellow darkness coming. I close them and slip away. I want to go. From what Uncle has said to me, I am happy to go into this dream, to face what I have to face, to learn what I need to learn from old Captain Fremantle.

Waking Dream Memory: Wrong Place

The smoke starts to clear. I look down to see that I'm still holding a cigarette. It's a defence force–issue thinnie. The sun has gone down. I see the other glowing tip in the darkness and follow it up to young Jack's face. We're leaning up against the vehicle. We can hear our father in the van behind us. He is drunk and shouting at invisible people. Shouting abuse and threats. Jack catches me looking and turns to glare at me.

He's nothing like me, his features dark and his body thick. I start to wonder who his mother is. How my father came to be Jack's father. How I knew nothing of his existence until a few hours ago. I look away.

The van and vehicle are parked exactly where they were when I first met Mularabone. My throat and chest feel sore. I don't even smoke. This is my first one. I always thought Mularabone started me smoking. But he doesn't smoke yet. And he's not here. Jack sneaked the smokes from our father. We couldn't stay in the van any longer. And we might not be safe out here if he remembers we are here.

'What was your mum like?' Jack asks in the darkness.

My head snaps around to look at him again. He is younger but only by a year. I can see he really fancies himself. I take a drag on my def-thin and try to act as tough as I can. I hardly know which way is up. My mother is dead. My father was unfaithful to her and me. I have a brother I didn't know about. My father has little or no love for me. My head is spinning from the nicotine and all my extremities appear to have advanced pins and needles. Jack is still looking at me intently. I finish my def-thin and stub it out with all the manliness I can muster. I walk down to the front of the vehicle and open the door. I lean in and carefully open the glove compartment. I lift the gloves and feel for the weapon.

Nothing.

My body stops, suddenly unsure.

'Looking for this?'

I turn to see Jack holding the big pistol.

'Give it here.'

'It's mine.'

'Bullshit.'

'He taught me how to use it.'

'Bullshit.'

Jack drops the magazine out the bottom, cocks the weapon to get the round out of the spout, reverses it, and in three quick moves, quickly disassembles the weapon, placing pieces on the vehicle. He then reinserts the spare round into the magazine, and quickly reassembles the weapon. His sure, quick movements betray many hours of practice. Finally, he slams the magazine back in with a flourish, cocks the weapon, and points it at my head.

'Bang! Bang! You're dead.'

I hold Jack's killer gaze. I can see something moving in his eye, something wriggling like a mosquito larva being born from an egg in the dark pool of his iris. He holds it for just a moment too long, and then lowers the weapon, slips on the safety, and smiles.

'She musta been still young,' he says with a snarl.

That snarl slashes at me like a homemade shiv. I launch myself at Jack but he slams the pistol into my guts and I drop. He was waiting for me to do that. Goading me to do it. He's definitely his father's son. I look up to see him walking away, laughing. He has the pistol in one hand and a bottle of clear grog in the other. I don't wanna be here. I don't remember any of this. I'm not asking for this.

With Jack, my father got what he always wanted – an apprentice, an accomplice, an open vessel to pour the dark treacle of his soul into.

I lie where I fell. No point getting up. I hear Jack moving around above me but I don't move. This is the message from the possum, Jack himself. I hear the plish-plish of the burning liquor in the bottle as it travels up and back to his lips. I lay there feeling the vague new warmth of the burgeoning bruise on my abdomen.

After a long time, there is finally silence. No breathing, no scratching, no smoking, no drinking noises from above. There is just this formless music playing, somewhere off in the distance. I move my head off the gravel. Some of the small round gravel stones stick in the indents in my face that they have made, and I have to brush them off like hard little burrow-less kangaroo ticks that have sucked my poison blood and been turned to stone.

I look down and I am lying on the grave, the mound of bright new dirt rising from the earth. The dust is hard and dry in my nostrils and throat. Six feet down is the body of my mother. The earth is pressing in on her, and now my weight too.

She loved me. She just made the mistake of loving him as well.

My tears sting my eyes as they wash the smoke grit onto her grave. Into her grave. Into her. My stomach is cramping from all the body-wracking sobs. My head is dull with the ache of those heavy tears. My eyes are grenade holes in a bombed out winter moonscape. I feel a noise and look up. Uncle Warroo-culla is there. Passively watching me. There and yet not there.

I pull myself up onto my haunches. I wipe tears and snot away with my sleeve. My stomach is churning like big surf on rocks. I'm a whale swimming in the open sea, feeling those first black pangs of desire to beach myself – hurl myself onto the land where I know I cannot survive. I stand up and stagger back towards the lights from the van. Uncle is gone. He fades away, or maybe I walk right through him. The generator is a dull thud against the low hills. It feels like that thudding is right inside my head. Between my ears. It's like that water pressure that wouldn't stop. No respite. No rest for the wicked.

I come up to Jack slumped on the front tyre of the def-for vehicle. The grog in his bottle is nearly gone. There are half a dozen butts on the ground next to him. He must've lifted a whole packet. He has the big pistol in his lap.

'He made me,' Jack slur-blurts out.

'What?' I stop and look down at him.

I'm looking hard at him. I'm trying to sort through his syllables to decipher his meaning. It's like I'm struggling to understand my own language.

'But I would've done it anyway!' spits Jack.

I bend down and snatch the pistol from Jack's ashed-on lap. He tries to grab it back off me and I smash the weapon into his face. Jack falls back against the front tyre, bleeding from a gash in his forehead.

I stride to the van and sling open the door. I can't see my father so I step up into the van – the weapon held out in front of me, ready to fire. I turn into the van and there he is at the computer terminal with his back to me.

There is a hologram image of my mother, naked and dancing, in front of him. She is singing:

Come on baby
Come on baby
Come on baby

He swivels his head and tries to smile at me. Maybe he can't see the pistol. His grief is a horrifying thing to behold. He no longer resembles himself but some tortured monster attempting to morph into human form and failing, destroying itself in the process. He reminds me of that sinister figure birthing itself in Jack's eye. He sees the pistol now and it causes his whole body to swivel on the chair without his head and eyes moving from their focus on me.

In his hand he is holding a hunting knife. He has cut himself along his inner forearm. Both sides. He is bleeding freely into his lap.

He opens his grotesque mouth to speak to me. The colours in his mouth so bright: the yellow of his teeth, the red-purple lips, the red-pink gums, the white and grey snow of tongue-fluff, the angry crimson of the back of his throat. It is into this cacophony of colour that I fire the weapon. His eyes pop out towards me as the back of his head explodes through the image of the naked body of my mother. He slumps back onto the terminal, and my mother disappears. I drop the weapon and slowly back out of the van.

Nineteen: Right Questions

The smoke clears. The little breeze that has sprung up simply blows it away into the fresh darkness of the coming night. Mularabone is still tapping out his beetle rhythm. He smiles at me.

'Don't you ever sleep?' I ask.

'You Djenga love the cot.'

'I wasn't asleep.'

'What did you see?'

'I killed my father.'

He lets his little beetle rhythm go.

'Someone had to,' he says.

'Shouldn't we get going?' I ask, and my voice comes out sharper and harder than I intended.

'Not until we eat this fat fulla,' he says and dumps the bungarra on the sand between us. He gets up and collects some wood, and in no time there is a fire going. He pulls out his infra-red masking gadget, pulls out the aerial, and quickly activates it.

'We got far to go?'

Mularabone looks up from his gadget.

'How can you be so close with water, and not have a fucken clue where we are most of the time?'

'I got you to tell me where I am, bro.'

Mularabone shakes his head. He must know that I'm not quite myself but he isn't going to play it. 'We're coming up on the dam from the top end. You'll be able to feel that water soon.'

'We'll be seeing Jack before the night's through.'

He pokes the little fire. 'Was Jack there?'

'He was trying to tell me something about my mother.'

'Was she there?'

'No. Finish,' and I do the finish-up hand signal.

'You got a plan?' he asks after a while.

'Maybe.'

He looks over at me, and smiles, just with his eyes. 'We need to get the truck?'

'Maybe.'

He nods again. This is our favourite game. Solve the puzzle. Search for the possibilities. He prods the fire again. When he is happy with the shape he puts the bungarra on.

'It's gonna be too hot,' I say, knowing he hates me to pass comment on his cooking.

'We gotta eat, brother – so we can get going!'

He says it with such conviction that I am shaking my head, as the smell of the burning bungarra flesh fills our nostrils, and causes our mouths to water.

'Where is the uncles' meeting place?'

Mularabone makes a vague directional point with his lips. I consider this answer. I didn't ask the right question. That place is not a place that I can ask such a direct question about.

'A meeting place?'

'A healing place.'

My lips go tight and loose again. I wait.

'Two hour drive. Maybe.'

'From where the truck is now?'

'Maybe.'

I have a sip of water and hold it in my mouth for a long time.

'How far back to that little gorge? The one where those Other Fullas live? Those Strong Fullas?' And I make the signal with my eyes and lips so that Mularabone knows who I mean: spirit beings. He nods. This is that strong old water song place that is floating around the edges of my heart.

'One hour. Maybe.'

Now it is his turn to turn it over in his mind.

'But that place is dry.'

'Is now,' I say, and keep my tone light, almost non-committal.

He looks across at me and gives a smile.

'Knew you had a plan. You Djenga can't help yourselves.'

'Ha!'

Soon we are tucking into that lizard flesh and feeling the strength flow into us. We eat. We smoke. By the time we are climbing up and out of that sunken place the stars are starting to come out and I am tingling with the now-ness of being alive. The light breeze that blew away the smoke is still blowing and I can just smell the water on it. It is faint, barely there – and I know it would be stronger if the Water Board didn't have their anti-evaporation skin stretched across the surface of the dam. But it is there all the same.

'Country gonna start speaking up,' Uncle Birra-ga said.

Now we are thinking about what the Country will say. How she will say it. We are made of this Country. Soon we'll know.

Twenty: Riding the Skin

Mularabone was right. We were closer to the top end of the dam than I realised. I should've felt that water. I always feel the water when it is close. As we come down the slope the vegetation starts to thicken up immediately and the whole place is buzzing with nocturnal life. The heat of the desert is replaced by the thick blanket of the humid air. But this isn't old water, I try to comfort myself. This water should be flowing down through the river system, not trapped up here. This dam is the brainchild of the Water Board; as soon as the Company got control of the Country it was one of the first things they did. As if to prove that they'd learned nothing. They flooded the whole valley by damming the river down near where the compound is, condemning kilometres and kilometres of sacred Country to the watery depths.

Our boots start to squelch in the new mud of the shoreline. We break through the line of trees and find ourselves on the shore. The massive expanse of trapped water stretches out before us, the filmy skin clinging to the surface, almost allowing us to think that we could walk right across. Mularabone walks out into the water up to his knees to the edge of the skin.

'What is it?'

'Some kind of synthetic polymer. Cuts evaporation to nothing.'

He bends down to feel the light plasticky texture of the skin. 'It wasn't there when I dived into it.'

'They had it retracted; routine maintenance.'

'I forget that your father was Water Board.'

'That was a nice dive, brother. Classy.'

'You saw my dive?'

'Who do you think was giving covering fire?'

'I thought you were drunk?'

'I was.'

We laugh.

Mularabone looks back to me and does the question hand signal (What now?).

'What time is it?' I say.

'Nineteen-fifty hours.'

'We've got ten minutes.'

'Ten minutes?'

'Maybe.'

'Til what?'

'Every night they retract the skin. Gotta let the water breathe. Otherwise it overheats.'

Mularabone shakes his head at my explanation. The dam is madness enough – but this? He grabs the edge of the skin and pulls at it with his other hand to test the strength of the film.

'We roll ourselves in it. The Sarge reckoned he saw a croc do it once. We can get pulled right across to the dam.'

He looks back at me.

'That's your plan?'

'You wanna walk around?'

'I thought you'd have a proper plan.'

'This is a proper plan.'

'I'm not a crocodile.'

We get down to the edge of the skin. I go to grab the edge of it. It is smooth and slippery, and hard to get hold of.

'Just grab hold of it, Mr Croc,' says Mularabone.

'He said they rolled in it.'

I scrunch up a tight handful, and then I feel it start to go tense. Looking out, the whole surface tension is starting to ramp up. Out there in the dark on the wall of the dam, they are taking up the slack. I lower myself onto the water and roll myself into the skin, wrapping it around me like some unholy prophylactic blanket. Mularabone is following suit. The skin is so thin and slippery that it just unrolls me again. We are both splashing and thrashing as we try to get some purchase and wrap ourselves in the film. Behind us and to the left there is a dull splash. Something else coming into the water. Something big enough to make that deep dull splash. Mularabone hears it too. He pushes himself out onto the skin, flattening his body, slithering as far as he can out onto the surface, and at the same time gathering the skin before him so that he's got some bunched up skin to hang onto. I try this method, hurling myself out across the skin with the sound of that dull splash behind spurring me on. Then the whole skin starts to move. It is so sudden, and building up speed so fast, that for a moment, both of us lose our tenuous grip and feel ourselves sliding back. I'm scrabbling across the skin, and bunching it in front of my chest so that my arms wrap the bunched skin, and my fingers dig into it. Then we are moving, being dragged through the water much faster than I imagined. That old croc must've been a thrillseeker. We are on a manic ride to the dam wall, and the Water Board compound. We cling to the anti-evap skin like parasites and plough through the water. The water rushes past us and now the challenge is to stay up and out of the water, as we leave little phosphorescent wakes behind us in the darkness.

'All right for the crocs,' Mularabone calls out, 'they don't have to breathe as often as us!'

And the last word of his sentence is almost drowned out by his head being dragged under the water. I use my fingers to continually scrunch the skin up under me as the water rushes past. Now across the skin on the water I can hear the faint whirr of the machine that is hauling us to the dam wall. Already if we let go we would be in big trouble. Too far out to swim back. And we aren't alone.

The waterfall sound of the water starts to take me over. It buffets me and usurps every other sensation. The water passing beneath me is like a solid wind. And that sound is constantly building, thudding into my ears with relentless velocity. I close my eyes and give all my energy to my fingers to hold on, as we fly across the surface of the great dam like two fat pelicans who can never take off. I try to keep my breathing even. The water flows on and on until it's rushing right through me.

Ghost of History: Waters off Wadjemup

Even though my hands are making fists in the pockets of my coat, the rain in my face feels like a friend. Each rivulet on my skin is like a kind word. I stand looking out to the island of Wadjemup, called Rottenest by the Dutch. The *Parmelia* is still having a rough time of it as she attempts to come into a safe anchorage. She is hidden from the swell and the brutal southerly by the island. To the south, the *Challenger* is still riding peacefully at anchor in the calm waters of the sound, protected well by the island of Meandip.

I turn and head back down from the high ground of Manjaree. I am still an officer, and I have my orders. As I come down into the camp I meet midshipman Sutton coming towards me with the Birdiya's eldest son, Bright Eyes, carrying fishing spears with their distinctive three-pronged barbed heads. With the rain in his face, Sutton greets me as though we are passing each other at Ascot on a spring day.

'Morning sir.'

'Morning.'

The Birdiya's son imitates Sutton's tone exactly.

'Morning sir.'

'Morning.'

Bright Eyes takes my hand and pumps it enthusiastically.

'Morning sir.'

'Morning.'

'Morning sir.'

'You don't have to call me sir.'

'Morning sir,' he cries triumphantly and finally lets go of my hand.

'Lovely day for ducks, sir.'

'Indeed.'

The Birdiya's son pounces on this new word.

'Indeed,' he says. He shakes my hand again. 'Morning sir. Indeed.' And he laughs at his own attempts to get my language.

'You all right, sir?' says Sutton.

'Stand the men to. Ready the cutter and gig. Fishing will have to wait.'

'Are the French coming, sir?'

'Captain Stirling is standing just off Wadjemup in the *Parmelia*. We are going to pay our respects.'

'Sir,' he acknowledges, clearly disappointed, and turns on his heel to march back into our camp.

Bright Eyes remains and looks directly at me, holding my gaze. Eventually he turns and follows Sutton down to the camp.

I get back into my own tent, reach under the makeshift mattress and retrieve my Marmeluke from where I had hidden it. I open my trunk but there is no spare uniform or hat in there. I look down to see how filthy my trousers are. At least I can give my boots a shine. I pull out a rag and drag it back and forth a few times before I realise my heart just isn't in it. I buckle on my sword and stand straight. I examine the blade of the Marmeluke. Bright and sharp – the only thing a true marine needs. Outside I can hear the hustle-bustle of Sutton rousing the men to action.

By the time I emerge into the rain again, the place is alive with activity as the men ready the cutter and the marines sort themselves out. Even though the small vessel is still beached, Bright Eyes and two other Countrymen have climbed aboard.

They sit up forward, pull their kangaroo skin cloaks around themselves, and hold their distinctive stone axes in their laps.

'Let's go, Midshipman Sutton.' My Royal Marine voice booms out from nowhere.

I clamber aboard, and the sailors manhandle the cutter into deeper water and climb on. The draft is shallow so it doesn't need much. We will be feeling that shallow draft when we hit the big sea beyond the river mouth. We grab the wind and skirt the reef to head into the open sea. Bright Eyes and his companions stand up as we come into the big swell. He points out the reef to his companions where we came to grief on that first day. The cutter rings with their raucous laughter above the tearing wind. That seems like several lifetimes ago now. We come belting into the big swell, and now all of us are holding on for dear life as the midshipman shouts orders and fights the bucking helm, throwing it this way and that, his steady eye on the mountainous seas charging in on us. Bright Eyes looks back to me as he realises the insanity of putting to sea in such conditions. I give him a grin, and his eyes get brighter in response. The midshipman takes a course that will bring us just to the north of Wadjemup and then tack back in to meet the *Parmelia* at her anchorage on the leeward side. The boat slugs into the big swells, crawling up the face, and crashing down the back.

I start to feel faint. My head is reeling from the motion of the boat. My fingers in my pockets ache with cold and they keep cramping up, making claw-like shapes. I throw up at my feet, leaving a little puddle of white muck. I wipe my mouth with the back of my claw-hand. I hold the hand out to consider its claw shape and tightened pain. The rain that is sleeting in goes right through my flesh as if I am a shadow. I look up to see Bright Eyes watching me. I grab onto the gunnel to steady myself.

'Take in sail!' the midshipman is calling, and the swell levels out as we swing in and come under the protection of Wadjemup.

The four hundred and forty-three tonne barque *Parmelia* looms up out of the rain as we come alongside. Ropes are thrown and tied off as sailors call back and forth. I go to stand, and Bright Eyes is next to me offering his hand. I take it, and we both go up the rope ladder on the hull of the *Parmelia*. On the deck there is only a marine sergeant to greet us.

'Welcome aboard, sir.' He salutes me. 'This way, sir.'

He shows us the way to the captain's quarters towards the stern. I hesitate for a moment, glance at the Countrymen, and step inside. Bright Eyes follows me in. Inside the cabin it is warm and dry. Stirling and Luscombe stand at a table, poring over a chart. I come to attention and salute.

'Sir. Lieutenant Conway from Captain Fremantle.'

They both look up.

'Conway, eh?' asks Captain Luscombe.

'And where is the good captain?' asks Stirling.

Outside it may be the waters off Wadjemup – but in here it is the Empire of King George IV.

'On board the *Challenger,* sir.'

Stirling is older than I expected but he carries himself with such erectness that he gives the impression he still commands physical power as well as position. He takes in Bright Eyes, standing just behind me to my right.

'Why is your prisoner not secured, Lieutenant Conway?'

'This man is not my prisoner, sir.'

'Your guide?'

'In a manner of speaking, sir.'

My tone causes them both to look at me hard. Stirling moves unhurriedly to sit behind the table. He pours himself a drink. He looks me up and down and my shabby appearance is reflected in his snarl. I'm thinking of my still-sharp blade.

'Are you here to guide me in, Lieutenant Conway?'

'No, sir.'

Stirling takes a drink, savouring the wine. Luscombe stands to his right, ramrod straight.

'Then why are you here?' asks Stirling.

'To welcome the new governor?' asks Luscombe.

'Captain Fremantle is still the governor.'

Their eyes flap around like the Union Jack on the flagpole in this heavy wind.

'And why have you brought this savage before us?'

His eyes flick to Bright Eyes who steps forward right on cue. Under his kangaroo skin cloak, his hand rests on the handle of his stone axe.

'Permit me to present Bright Eyes, the eldest son of the duke of the lands south of the river mouth, known as Beeliar.'

Stirling and Luscombe take him in more completely. When Stirling was here mapping the potential settlement location, the closest he got to the natives was a deserted campfire. Bright Eyes is physically the most impressive individual I have ever met, with his thick muscles packed into his burly frame. Their eyes linger on the distinctive scar tattoo on his right shoulder, the mark of his high rank. Stirling turns his eyes back to me. He dismisses my introduction with a curl of his lip. Maybe his snarl is him trying to smile.

'Am I to presume that Captain Fremantle is otherwise engaged with native girls, so he sends you in his place?'

Stirling and Luscombe share a smile. I address Luscombe.

'Captain Fremantle wished me to convey the absolute folly of attempting the passage to the sound until the seas and the winds are more favourable. There are many hidden sandbanks, and with your draft, Captain Luscombe ...'

'I shall be piloting the ship in, Mister Conway,' Stirling

says. 'Perhaps Captain Fremantle forgets that I have been here before; that I charted this whole region; that I was the one who lobbied the ministry for this settlement.'

'Sir, Captain Fremantle wished me to impress upon you in no uncertain terms –'

'That will be all, Lieutenant Conway.'

'Sir?'

'That will be all. Please thank the good captain for his undue concern.'

I salute them with my cold claw hand.

'Captain Stirling. Captain Luscombe.'

They do not return my salute. I about face, and Bright Eyes opens the door for me. We share a conspiratorial smile. We step out into the cold sheeting rain, and are enveloped by the roughhouse sounds of the big seas crashing into Wadjemup just beyond.

Twenty-one: Smash and Grab

'Brother!'

I hang on. Through the waterfall flowing over me and through me, I hear the voice again.

'Brother!'

My eyes snap open. I'm hanging onto the skin and being pulled across the surface of the water. Swirling around my neck is the white vomit mixed with dam water.

'Brother! Let go!'

I look up to see the concrete wall of the dam looming up out of the darkness, and on the surface of the film-covered water are two spotlights dancing towards us.

'Let go, bruz!' Mularabone calls again, urgency in his voice without volume.

The edge of the spotlight is almost on me. I open my claws and let the skin go. It is pulled out from under me like the old tablecloth whip-trick, and I am the quivering china left behind. I drop my head into the water; my forward momentum takes me straight down into the depths, pulling my feet in quickly as I go. I kick out immediately for the wall. The lights zigzag back and forth on the surface above us. I kick out for the wall. I look sideways but I can't see Mularabone. I swim and swim. Finally, my reaching fingers touch the rough concrete of the wall. I brace myself against the dam wall by spreading my fingers wide and applying pressure. I can still hear the hum of the retractor machine from down here. I ease up the wall. I look up. The spotlights are further out, where I just came from, scanning the now open water. I ease my face out of the water and take a long slow breath. Mularabone is already on the surface. He gives me his smile. He has one for every occasion. The retractor machine hums for a moment longer, and then is switched off. The silence comes down. Then we hear the Water Board troopers up on the dam as clear as if we were standing next to them.

'There's nothin.'

'Must've been a snag.'

'Or a croc?'

'Crocs don't worry me.'

'Bullshit.'

Laughter. The spotlights get turned off. There are still a few work lights illuminating the top of the dam. Mularabone signals to me to follow and he moves along the wall to our right. There is a ladder out in the centre of the dam. He gets there and waits for me. I get to the rusted ladder and grab on.

'You right, coorda?' he whispers.

'Yeah.'

'Ya chucked up.'

'Seasick.'

'Bullshit.'

We breathe. We listen.

'What now?' Mularabone asks.

'Smash and grab.'

'Wait here.'

He goes up the ladder the three or four metres to the top. He slips his nulla-nulla out of his belt. I go up the ladder slowly until I am just below the lip of the dam. I hold on to the ladder. My head rolls forward to rest on the concrete wall. Above me I hear a scuffle, a muffled shout, and the dull thuds of heavy wood on flesh. There is movement in the water below and I look to see a big gnarly form sliding away into the darkness of the water. Then Mularabone is above me at the ladder.

'Okay, coord.'

I go up the ladder. There are three Water Board troopers laid out on the concrete. Mularabone quickly grabs their weapons, handing one to me. Over on the edge of the dam is their vehicle, and beyond that the short road to the lit-up Water Board compound. We stride out for the vehicle, dripping and squelching as we go. We are still thirty metres from the vehicle when a trooper steps out from the driver's side. He has earphones in. He gives us a funny look, and pulls out his earphones.

'Are you blokes gonna take all night?'

Then he really clocks us. 'Who the fuck are youse?'

He glances into the cabin. The Sarge would tie our weapons to us if he ever caught us without them in our hands, may his soul find peace. We are close enough now to see the dilemma on the trooper's face. Our weapons are in our hands, and coming up, and that front seat is a long reach away.

'Don't do it, trooper,' Mularabone warns. But Mularabone's voice galvanises him and he dives for the weapon on the front seat. We both fire and the trooper is blasted backwards as our rounds smash into him. We take off for the vehicle.

'Didn't you trust me to get him?' asks Mularabone.

'I want to do my bit.'

'You drive. I'll shoot. We need something to hurt this concrete.'

I jump in, hit ignition, and gun the engine. The onboard system lights up and I hit MANUAL ALL. Mularabone has two spare weapons at his feet. I drive with mine in my lap. I head straight for the compound. The radio comes to life.

'H20 6, this is H20 1, sitrep, over?

I hit the transmitter.

'H20 1, this is 6.'

'6, this is 1, we heard shots. Sitrep, over?'

'1, this is 6, we have taken fire. No CAS. We are coming in hot. One terrorist shooter on north side of dam.'

'Roger 6. Gate, this is 1. Open up.'

'1, this is gate. Open up.'

Ahead of us we see the crash barriers being removed behind the gate. Mularabone gives me a grin. 'Open sesame.'

I gun the vehicle for the opening. We are a hundred metres out and moving fast when the radio fizzes into life.

'Gate, this is H20 Charlie Oscar. Shut the gate. I say again, Charlie Oscar, shut the gate.'

Mularabone and I know that voice. But Jack's too late; they'll never get the barriers back in time to stop us. There is a spotlight swinging onto us. Mularabone gives a burst of fire and it explodes. He rakes the tower on his side with fire, and then leans out across the bonnet to hit the other one. The gate tower men are fumbling for their weapons as they go down. Sloppy. We smash through the gates.

'Is that you, Conway?' comes Jack's voice on the radio. Inside the compound there are figures running everywhere. Mularabone is finding targets and putting them down.

I hit the transmitter. 'Surprise!'

Mularabone and I both clock the Armoured Fighting Vehicle just inside the gate. Must be their quick-response fire team. The AFV has machineguns and a heavy gun mounted forward. Fire starts coming our way. I start to swerve this way and that, as random as hell.

'What now?' I scream to Mularabone.

'Power. Then tank. Then out again in that rig with the gun.'

'Hurtful.'

'Life is pain.'

Now Jack will be sorry he ever brought us in here. His HQ

is over the far end of the compound but the solar storage isn't far from the tank and the metal boxes where we were kept. I switch off our lights as I see the storage cell system dead ahead.

'Hang on, bruz!'

'Where'd you learn to drive?'

'I didn't.'

We both brace and the vehicle slams into the storage structure. There is a massive electrical hiss-pop. And the whole camp is swathed in darkness. All around us the troopers are running and firing. This is why Mularabone is the best. He grabs me.

'You good?'

'Yeah.'

We pile out of the wreckage and run for the doors of the tank. When you've crashed a few of those junior cruisers, you just know how it's gonna go. At the tank entrance there is a big chain threaded through the steel outer doorhandles. Mularabone steps back and I go back with him. Mularabone empties his mag into the chain. At point-blank range the ricochet is terrifying and I can't believe we aren't hit. The chain falls away. Mag change. A couple of rounds come our way from over near the gate. I throw up my weapon and fire at the flash until it stops. Mularabone is kicking down the doors. They burst open. I step in. Mularabone stands at the door and fires a burst back the other way towards HQ and our burning vehicle up against the solar storage facility. Illuminated in his muzzle flash is Mitch the Blood Nut.

Mitch yells at me in the darkness: 'What the fuck's happening?'

'You got parole, shareholder.'

He steps up close to me and I smell his off breath.

'I know you!'

Mularabone turns and thrusts the spare weapons at him.

'We're not the enemy, brother.'

Mitch grabs the weapons. He hands one back to Torby.

'Thanks, Trooper,' he spits back at me.

'See ya later, shareholder.'

Mularabone turns and sprints back for the AFV by the gate. Behind us, Mitch is firing and moving. By the time we reach the AFV there is a serious firefight going on behind us. We throw ourselves onto the ground at the rear of the AFV and look back to the exchange of fire ripping through the night.

'He's good, your mate,' grins Mularabone.

'Not my mate.'

Inside the AFV we hear the voices of the nervous troopers. The engine is switched on, and the spottie on top lights up. Mularabone clambers straight up onto the shell of the vehicle and pumps two rounds into the light. Inside the AFV we can hear them swearing. The top hatch is suddenly thrown open, and out pops the head of a trooper. Mularabone smashes him in the face with his nulla-nulla, and the man slumps back. He slips the club into his belt and swings his weapon forward and fires a burst down into the vehicle. I sit up. The back hatch opens and three troopers pile out. I am so close to them that I can smell their stale vinegary sweat. I shoot each of them once in the head. Mularabone is clambering down the hatch. I go straight in the back. He jumps into the cockpit, slams it into gear, and we lurch forward. The trooper that Mularabone nulla-nullaed groans. I shoot him in the back. Mularabone guns the engine. I drag the body into the rear, and slide into his seat. I hit the screen and bring the weapons systems online. Mularabone doesn't turn on the lights, and we smash through the last barrier with a rolling crunch, and burst through the front gates. I'm in imaging now, and bringing up the picture of the dark road in front of the AFV, and feeding it to Mularabone's screen. He is going fucken flat out. A few rounds slam into our hull but no serious fire. In moments, the dam appears on my screen.

'Surprise!' yells Mularabone and laughs with the exhilaration of the moment. 'Ha! They weren't expecting that!'

'I wasn't expecting it, coorda!'

The dam is on my screen. I target the centre of the concrete mass, as low as I can go. 'Steady, brother. Steady. Stop!'

Mularabone slams on the anchors and the AFV slides to a halt in the pindan.

'Firing now!' I warn, and hit multiple-fire-max, and the gun opens up.

Whump! Whump! Whump!

Whump! Whump! Whump!

In the imager the HE rounds slam into the concrete wall one after the other. Almost instantly I see the concrete darken with moisture.

'That's it! We're out!'

Mularabone puts the AFV in gear with a bit of throttle, aiming it to the road going across the top of the dam. I turn and pile out the back door with Mularabone right behind, and we roll hard into the dust. We are up and running, sprinting for the scrub just on the water side of the dam. There is a depression in there. We throw ourselves down and crawl into the scrub until we are on the edge of the slope down to the water. Coming out of the compound is another AFV.

We duck down. Mularabone is into his backpack. His heat signature-masking device is still wrapped in its waterproof coating. The AFV is firing at the empty AFV rolling out onto the dam.

Mularabone rips off the plastic, pulls up the aerial, and keys in the GO. We press into the earth. They pour their fire into our AFV. It has reached the edge of the dam.

Whump! Whump! Whump!

They hit it, and up she goes. Mularabone puts his device down on the edge of the decline. The AFV is burning fiercely. There is an almighty crumpling sound, and the ground beneath us shakes. The dam gives way. The smoking AFV is gone in a moment, and so is most of the dam, as a couple of billion gigalitres of water surges down into the parched valley below.

Ghost of History:
Finest Navy the World Has Ever Seen

Even in the relative safety of the sound, the swell is big. The howling wind has swung overnight from the south and is now blowing directly east. The winds come direct from below the coastline of Africa, picking up the chill and power from the colliding Antarctic systems to batter the shores of this island continent without mercy. Fremantle stands on the bridge and sips from a steaming mug.

'He is coming, Mister Conway,' he says, and I try to find the sail of the *Parmelia* above the heavy swell.

I stand next to Fremantle, whether to give comfort or draw it, I cannot say. The rain does not let up.

'The Governor cometh,' I comment.

'The Governor is dead, long live the Governor,' says Fremantle.

Bright Eyes watches us. Fremantle notices him. He wants to say something, but then thinks better of it. He drains his mug and puts it down. He retrieves his glass from his coat pocket, and twists it over and over with his hands.

'Hardly a robust endorsement for the virtues of the Empire, Mister Conway.'

'Captain Stirling is an experienced pilot, sir. He has traversed these waters before.'

Fremantle has the glass to his eye. Bright Eyes comes over and wants to look through the glass. Fremantle directs him how to hold the piece to his eye. He looks through, exclaims loudly, and then checks the image again with his naked eye. He repeats this process several times. Then he turns the glass on Fremantle, and shouts with joy when he sees the magnified image. He pulls a nulla-nulla from his belt, and hands it to Fremantle. Fremantle stands there holding the club and looking at me blankly. Bright Eyes aims the glass at the mainland, shrouded in rain.

'Good trade, sir.'

'Indeed.'

Bright Eyes hears our exchange and comes over.

'Morning sir. Indeed!' he exclaims. And when we laugh, he adds, 'Good trade, sir.'

Fremantle holds up the club, and swings it a few times to test the weight. He gives a satisfied nod to Bright Eyes who smiles and holds up his glass.

Our eyes go back to the *Parmelia*. She is coming in from the north, trying to angle slightly east to keep the swell at her back. But she is too fast, and too close to the small island of Ngooloormayup. There are several big sandbanks right there. They may not even have been there the last time Stirling was here. That was two years ago – and even in the six weeks we've been here we have learned that you cannot depend on conditions to remain unchanged.

'Ready the longboats!' calls Fremantle, and the order is repeated down on the decks.

There is a slippery scramble of sailors working in the rain to comply. Our eyes are on the *Parmelia* as she appears and reappears in between massive swells. Then we see her slam into the sandbank. She hits and slews sideways so that the huge swells are hitting almost side-on. She looks fast on the bank; her sails are torn away and the foreyard gone. Waves crash over the decks of *HMS Parmelia*.

Fremantle cannot stifle a wry smile as he sees Bright Eyes

watching the ship hit the sandbank, and then reach for his glass and put it to his eye to have a closer look.

'I am quite looking forward to meeting Captain Stirling again,' says Fremantle.

'Bright Eyes must be completely awed by our sailing prowess, sir. I wonder what he'll report to his father?'

'The finest navy the world has ever seen.'

Twenty-two: Going Over

The water boils over the rubble of the demolished dam. We can still hear sporadic firing from the far end of the compound.

'Your mate is still going.'

'Not my fucken mate.'

'Where's your loyalty, bruz?'

I look down to the dam. The level has dropped at least twenty-five metres over the last few hours of darkness. As the light comes up, we can look up the valley to see huge tracts of land that were under water last night, emerging.

'Uncle will be happy,' I say to Mularabone.

He grabs his masking device and swathes it in its waterproof covering. He stashes it in his pack. We go backwards down the slope to the retreating water's edge. Jack will be here soon to survey the damage and, depending on how long he takes to quell Mitch and Torby, to look for us. Either way, we have to be gone. We get down to the water's edge, and now the roaring of the rapids fills our ears. There are huge clouds of spray crisscrossed with new rainbows filling the air where the dam wall used to be.

'We go feet first, for snags, sitting upright.' Mularabone reiterates the drill to me. 'You hold the pack – it'll keep you up. I'll hold you.'

We get up and start to wade out into the water. It's cold. I'm thinking of the dull splash behind us last night as we were both getting onto the skin. The water in front of us explodes as rounds slam into the surface.

'Go, bruz! Go!'

I run for the deep water. Mularabone crouches in the water and fires back up the slope to the two troopers standing there firing at us. He puts the first one down immediately but the other trooper drops to the ground and continues to fire. The current has hold of me and I push off the muddy bottom and start to pick up speed. Rounds are hitting the water. Mularabone is still firing and backing into the water. He ditches his weapon, turns, and dives down. I submerge myself, holding onto the bottom of the floating pack. I kick out for the deeper water and feel the current pushing me along. The backpack is nearly torn from my grasp as two rounds hit it. I just hang on by getting another hand onto the dangling strap. Under the water I feel Mularabone next to me. I feel along his arm until we are holding hands tightly, and now we are in the current proper. We pick up speed very quickly. In a few moments Mularabone gives me the double-squeeze signal and we both breach the surface. Above and behind us there is some shouting from up near the remains of the dam. There is some more firing. I grab the pack and hold it to my chest, and swing my feet around so they're in front of me. Mularabone keeps holding my hand, and uses the leverage to swing his feet forward in the current. There are more shots fired but we don't hear them hit. Now we can see the drop. Beyond the initial drop of forty metres there is a series of deep pools forming, and boiling rapids that disappear around a right bend after another two hundred metres.

'Can't we walk around, bro?'

'This was your idea, coord.'

'My idea?'

'You're the one reckons we're the Waterboys!'

We hold hands and race towards the opening in the dam wall. We wrap ourselves in our water blanket, go through, and slide into the drop.

Ghost of History: Cavorting with Savages

The day is overcast but warming gently. The clouds are high and have no intention of dropping rain on us. We could be in England, were it not for the strange foliage all around. As we make our way unhurriedly down the slope we can see the large group of Englishmen already assembled at the designated place. Fremantle walks ahead with the three boss men. The Birdiya of Mooro – the Country north of the Darbal Yaragan – and the Birdiya of Beeloo – the lands east of the Darbal Yaragan bordered by the Dyarigarro River and the hills – walked into the Beeliar camp before dawn. Beeliar seemed to be expecting them. They each brought twenty warriors at least. Then we marched up the river to this place. Fremantle is in full dress uniform, and the birdiya are all painted up, wearing their prominent nose-bones, and carrying their stone axes. How these birdiya knew to come in today, Fremantle would not say. Behind us is a large group of young warriors carrying spears and woomeras.

As we approach the Djenga, a clear ripple of consternation spreads through the red-coated soldiers of the 63rd under Captain Irwin's command. We see one of his subalterns confer with him, and a clear nod from the Irwin. Captain Stirling steps away from the group to greet us. More like to impede our progress towards his gathering. He is a naval officer after all.

'Captain Fremantle.'
'Captain Stirling.'

It is six weeks since we had to rescue Stirling and his passengers from his ill-advised attempt to run into the sound in arduous conditions.

'I was beginning to believe you overslept, Captain Fremantle.'

'Not one of my vices, Captain Stirling. I was conferring with the representatives from this Country, which took longer than expected.'

Stirling takes in the three birdiya, as if seeing them for the first time. They are unflinching under his vice-regal gaze.

'May I present the owner of the Mooro Lands, on which we stand, the owner of the Beeliar Lands near the river mouth, and the owner of the Beeloo Lands east of the river upstream.'

As each of the boss men is introduced, he steps forward as if this moment was rehearsed. Stirling turns his gaze on Fremantle.

'I hope that you have impressed upon these … gentlemen … that the new power in these lands is His Majesty – whom we both represent.'

Fremantle stares back at the new Governor as if he has not heard or understood. The birdiya are unreadable. The spearmen behind look on impassively. The redcoats beyond look distinctly nervous. Stirling steps in close to Fremantle, their noses almost touching.

'Don't be a fool. Do not shame your father and your brother. You have been given a second chance. Do not bite the hand that feeds you with this nonsense.'

Fremantle stares him down. 'You know nothing of shame … How dare you presume to speak to me of my family,' and his voice is like ice.

Captain Irwin approaches to break the stalemate: 'Shall we begin, gentlemen?'

Stirling steps back.

Fremantle says, 'The Birdiya of the Mooro Lands wishes to officially welcome you to his Country, Captain Stirling.'

'Then you had best explain to him that he is now a subject of His Royal Highness King George IV.'

'Why don't you explain it to him?'

The birdiya watch this exchange with interest.

'The natives may watch ... if they behave.'

Stirling turns and walks back down to the assembled soldiers and settlers. One of the junior officers hands him the parchment with the official proclamation. The three boss men and Fremantle follow.

There is a colonist all dressed in white just off to the side making a sketch of the scene that Morison will develop later into a painting. His sketch will never include the Countrymen present. This is our history. You can tell yourself it's not really a lie. But you can't tell yourself that it is the truth. These men of Empire need no instructions to reconstruct history towards a narrative that better suits civilised invasion; it comes naturally – an unspoken contract that they have entered into freely.

One of the settlers begins to ready some bottles of wine from a basket. An animated murmur races through the assembled Countrymen when two metal axes are produced by one of Stirling's men.

The Union Jack flutters in the breeze at the end of a long pole held by one of Major Irwin's men. Captain Stirling is clearing his throat to speak. Captain Dance of the *Sulphur* nods to his wife, Helena. Mrs Dance, dressed all in white, steps up to the tree, and an axe is handed to her. This was meant to be Mrs Stirling, but the Governor's wife refused at the last minute to venture so far up the river into the untamed wilderness. The Mooro Birdiya steps forward, holding his stone axe, and starts to shout at Mrs Dance.

Stirling remains unperturbed and begins to read: 'In the

name of His Royal Highness, King George IV of England ...'

Mrs Dance looks uncertain. She changes her grip on the axe. The Birdiya continues to shout, moving forward like he might grab at the axe. Irwin is nodding at his men, and the redcoats rush forward with their weapons to come between the Djenga and the Countrymen. I can hear the soft clacking of wood on wood as the warriors behind me are fitting their spears into their throwing sticks and the distinctive metal on metal clicks as the soldiers cock their muskets.

Stirling leaves off reading, and strides over to Fremantle.

'I warned you, sir.'

Fremantle says nothing but his own hand lies on the hilt of his sword.

'You may proceed, Mrs Dance,' Stirling calls back over his shoulder without taking his eyes from Fremantle.

Captain Dance's wife swings the axe into the meat of the wood. The sound rings out in the bush by the river, and the Countrymen all go very still. Fremantle turns to the Birdiya. They exchange a long look, and then they turn and start to walk away.

'Do not give me your back, Captain Fremantle!'

Fremantle stops and turns. 'A man who cannot navigate should not call himself a sailor, Captain Stirling.'

'A man with no honour should not call himself an officer, Captain Fremantle.'

'You cannot change. None of you!'

'One would only make a change if something needed to be rectified,' says Stirling. 'If something was wrong.'

'Something *is* wrong. Can't you feel it?'

'The sooner you put to sea the better, Captain Fremantle. Your display of cavorting with the savages in front of your own men is preposterous beyond sanity.'

Fremantle draws his blade in a moment. 'Cavorting?'

'You, sir, are a disgrace to the Navy and to the Academy! Oh, I stand corrected, you never attended the Academy!'

'Cavorting?'

Fremantle moves towards him with his blade held out. The soldiers of the 63rd are taking aim. Stirling draws his sword.

'Gentlemen! This has gone far enough!' booms out Captain Irwin.

Behind us we hear a song start up with slow-slow clapsticks. The two captains face each other with their bare blades almost touching. I have fenced with Fremantle and know his power and speed only too well. The slow song creeps up on us all and wraps around us all like a mist. After a long time Fremantle is backing away, and sheathing his weapon. Irwin and Stirling turn their eyes on me. I look down to see my own blade in my hand.

'You would do well to remember your place, Lieutenant,' snarls Captain Irwin.

I look away towards the song origin, and the retreating Fremantle. Captain Stirling sheathes his sword.

'Wherever you go, Fremantle – the native stink will follow you!'

Behind us we hear the metal blade of Mrs Dance's axe smacking into the tree. The song sucks us all away like minnows on an outgoing tide.

Twenty-three: Red Balloons in the Guts

It's fully light. My face is hard up against the river sand. My body is flattened beneath me. The water tugs at my feet like an insistent child.

'Where are we?'

'Ssshhh.'

I pull my feet out of the water. Mularabone is above me. He speaks in a hushed tone.

'Don't move. Don't look up.'

Behind my ears, and the base of my skull, is burning. Mularabone bends over me and rubs sand all over me as if he's salting a pork roast. He rubs sand on my feet. I try to pull them away but he holds me firm by the ankle as he does each foot.

'Don't move.'

'It tickles.'

He finishes and lowers himself onto the sand next to me.

'You good, coorda?' he asks.

'Never better.'

'You liar-boy.'

I try to smile. 'Where are we?'

'We're in *that* place.'

That's why he's covering me with sand: protection. This gorge is humming with a secret power. There are dark forces here. Dark forces that can take over even an unwilling host. My father was willing enough. The Sarge's brother, too. Something happened here. Something that stained the Country. Behind us the water is still hurrying away to invigorate the lower riverland. Above our heads the morning birds are singing out the joy song for the return of the water. My heart is still beating fast from the rapids and my knees are burning with fresh bruises.

'We gotta move,' he says.

'How?'

'You tell me.'

My stomach feels like it is full of big red balloons rubbing against each other and making that rubbery slippery sound. I squeeze my eyes shut and listen.

'There's a tunnel,' I hear myself say after a while.

Mularabone gets up.

'Don't move,' he tells me, and moves off.

I lie there trying to slow my heart, listening to the fast flowing beauty of the reborn river at my feet. It'll take days to empty the dam. Maybe longer. They won't be able to attempt repairs until the water is very low. By then it'll be too late for the Water Board.

Mularabone comes back. 'I found it – but it's too small,' he says.

'We have to crawl to start with. Then it'll open out to a chamber,' I say.

Mularabone grabs the backpack, and I slowly get up, careful not to look anywhere but at my own feet. I know better than not to obey Mularabone when it comes to such instructions. If there are things here that I can't see – then I can't see them. It's as simple as that.

At the end of the little spray of river sand the walls of the gorge are sheer. The tunnel entrance is about a metre over our heads. Mularabone makes a stirrup with his hands and boosts me up, and I scramble into the hole in the rock. I start to crawl. It is tight. I hear him clamber up the rock face and come in behind me. The back of my head is burning. This is the right one. Formed by the passage of old water. I crawl with my head down. The only time I try to lift it I hit the rock above me. This is more claustrophobic than the Sick Mother, but drier. I have to fight to stop the closeness of the rock making me feel trapped. Just keep crawling.

After a while I think I hear voices. Women's voices talking Language. My elbows are red raw from the rock crawling and the red balloons are rubbing away in my guts, almost drowning out the water song burning through my head. When I finally stop, unsure of whether or not I can continue with this crawling, there are the voices again. Then Mularabone is standing over me, and we are in the larger chamber. He turns me over, pulls me up to a sitting position, and then slings me across his back.

I think I see a fire. I think I hear Nayia. Aunty Ouraka's voice is there too. I see the fire. I see weapons standing nearby. My eyes are open but my vision is blurry. The red balloons in my guts start to deflate with a soft hiss.

I feel Mularabone's feet walking beneath me as if they are mine.

Shared Searching Dream: Grog Bunker

Around me are strong arms, holding me up, cradling me, warming my bones, defying gravity, and moving me along. The movement comforts and confuses me. In this bewildered perambulation we go along and then down, down steep steps.

I'm dumped onto the cement floor like a bag of root vegetables. The air is close and putrid. That smell reminds me of the underground prison, before I swam the Sick Mother. There is some light down here. Some kind of open flame that I can't see from my vantage point on the floor. An unknown smell invades my nostrils, flaring them involuntarily.

The first thing I see is the blade. It catches the light and twinkles silver and white. I recognise the hunting knife. My father had it in his hands the night I shot him through the mouth. He'd cut himself with the blade, letting blood whilst watching a recording of my mother dancing. Now he carefully rubs the blade on a small flat stone, spitting on the stone to achieve the desired wetness. As he concentrates on the blade, I see Jack in him clearly, and the nature of passed-on pain in families. The noise of the blade scraping across the wet stone dominates the cramped space. It's some kind of concrete bunker.

Strapped onto a steel morgue bed is a small girl. She is tied down with defence force plastic ties. Against the far wall is a young boy, tied up, and just above me is a woman. All Countrymen. All naked. All have tape across their mouths.

Stacked against all available wall space are crates of rum bottles.

I'm not tied up: just a pile of bones with skin on them, lying in an untidy heap on the floor. He doesn't think I'm a threat. He doesn't acknowledge me in any way. I have that feeling of having intruded on something secret and personal, like peering through that slit in the van, seeing my mother's nipple moving back and forth. I can't move my skull, just swivel my eyes in their sockets, to look around. Feels like 44's metal neck restrainer.

How did he get that steel trolley hospital bed down here?

He opens a crate, pulls out a flagon of rum and takes a big swig. He goes to the naked woman chained to the wall and forces her to drink. She swallows and coughs. Her lip is bleeding.

He starts to speak. War suits him. Especially this war. I try to focus on his voice. In the end I only get it when I zoom in on his lips with my vision and really concentrate. They remind me of the lips of Mitch the Blood Nut, the lips of 44. Nothing like Jack's lips or mine. I can hear his tone and the melody of each sentence – but I still can't get any meaning. His words are greasy, smoke-like worms with no eyes or features.

I change my focus to the girl prisoner. She strains against her bonds in a silent and useless struggle that knots her little muscles and tightens her face. Her eyes are wide with fear. There are tears pouring from her eyes and mucus oozing from her nostrils, making her breathing loud and laboured.

It is Nayia. Nayia as a child. The boy is Mularabone.

I know it all now. I can see it with my own eyes.

Who is the Countrywoman? I can't see her face clearly in the half light. The mother of Nayia? Of Mularabone?

Why is my father taking so long to sharpen his knife? The

plastic ties holding the prisoners can't be that hard to cut through. I blink my eyes and his words in English come through to me.

'We're gonna play a game. All you have to do is watch me. If you take your eyes off me, I stab her deep. Starting now. Watch me!'

I look to the Countrywoman. She is watching him. He takes the hunting knife and cuts the girl on the arm. Her little body arches on the table and a strangled scream comes out through her nose, her mouth working against the tape.

'You still looking? Good.'

He cuts the child again. The Countrywoman is trying to yell but is stifled by the tape. From her taped-over screams, I can tell that it is Ouraka. He cuts her again. The child is howling behind the tape now while my stomach is churning and my head is engulfed in icy flames. He reverses the knife and runs the hilts along the thigh of the child Nayia, his smile growing as the Countrywoman recognises his rape intention. He runs the knife hilt up her thigh. The Countrywoman's head rolls around.

'Oh-oh. You looked away! Yes you did! You did, I saw you! Come on! We've gotta be honest with each other. You definitely looked away. I'll just do a little stab because it's your first look away. Maybe you didn't mean to. I'll give you the benefit of the doubt.'

He turns and stabs little Nayia through the left shoulder, carefully missing organs. Nayia tenses and then passes out from the pain.

'Oh, dear. Don't worry. She's only passed out. We'll get another shot at her when she comes round. Are you mob big bleeders?'

My father wipes the blade of his hunting knife. He looks over at young Mularabone. His eyes are burning orbs of hate.

'What do you reckon, little matey? Do you reckon she'll wake up so I can fuck her? Yeah, she'll wake up.'

He comes over to the Countrywoman.

'Now, what about you?'

She is trussed with her hands behind her back. He reaches out to touch her naked flesh. She tries to pull away but can't. He cups one of her breasts. 'What about you, eh? All this is probly making you horny.'

He forces her to drink more rum. The smell of grog goes into my nostrils like smoke from burning plastic.

I look over at young Mularabone. He is the closest to my eye-level. He's noticed me. He is beseeching with me with his eyes. I look back with just as much of a plead. He looks wild and lost.

I killed him, I say in my mind as I concentrate on Mularabone across the space. I killed him.

As soon as I think this thought, Uncle Warroo-culla is there, standing near the table, and the unconscious bleeding child Nayia. There and yet not there. Uncle purses his lips and blows. A cool breeze licks at our bodies, our extremities sharpening from the cold.

There is a noise above us and the steel blast-door is slung open. Above us is a howling dust storm. Dust swirls into the concrete bunker, stinging us with its gritty touch. On the morgue bed Nayia Child is stirring.

There is gunfire. Someone yells down to my father in English. He goes running up the concrete steps and out into that storm of dust and bullets.

The door closes; the flame is blown out, and we are plunged into darkness. I try to soften my bones into the concrete floor. The Countrywoman is humming through her taped-up mouth. She is soothing her wounded child on the morgue bed. Doing all she can. That tune hummed through her taped-up mouth is all we have now. It envelops us with kindness in this dark place. I've heard it before. I search my spirit for the memory. There is pain, water crashing into me, and Nayia's voice singing that song.

Twenty-four: Scars, Weapons and Free Water

Nayia hardly seems to move her lips as she sings. She sits very still and looks at me across the fire. Her voice fills the little river cave.

I have a big drink of water from a bottle placed by my side, unfold myself, and sit up. I grab a big stick and place it on the fire. The coals are still red and the wood quickly catches. I put on two bigger bits of wood. My hands are shaking. The dream clings to me like old scabs. Uncle Warroo-culla warned me. I let the notes from Nayia's song stroke my scars. I want to ease Nayia's scars from her flesh with my lips. I want to kill my father again. Drown him in a vat of grog. Nayia sings.

Nayia and I look at each other. Look into each other. Mularabone and Ouraka stare into the fire. We have the feeling of slowness, and togetherness, as if we've all shared a song, and gone through the change from tight to loose and uninhibited, all in close proximity to each other. Mularabone takes up a tight roll of dry leaves he has gathered for the purpose and lights the bundle. He lets it burn for a moment and then blows out the flame, leaving thousands of tiny red embers smoking languidly. Mularabone throws smoke out to the four directions, and then up and down, calling out the Language names and asking for cleansing from the smoke. He moves around the fire, running the smoke over each of us. When the smoke dies down a little he blows on the end gently, and the smouldering leaf-ends respond to the extra oxygen by flaring up and throwing out the desired smoke. When finished, he returns to his place and dances a few steps on the sand, grunting and chanting. He lets it go as easily as a man takes off a shirt, and sits back down, tossing the smoking bundle of leaves casually in the fire.

Aunty gets a billy and puts it over the flames.

The river cave air is cool on our faces, reminding us all of Uncle's breath-wind in the concrete bunker. We know each other well now, like soldiers who've faced death together and lived to laugh about it. Even if it's not funny we can still laugh about it. Especially if it's not funny.

Mularabone rolls up his blanket.

'If we head off soon, we'll be at the meeting place tonight,' Mularabone says.

'With the water,' I add.

'Yeah, bruz. With the water from the place. Living water. For the healing.'

I roll up my blanket. I feel better. Mularabone opens some defence force ration tins from his backpack and puts them on the edge of the fire. He has two automatic weapons with him.

Aunty makes some tea. We all sip. There's something else in the air as well. A kind of naughtiness. Mularabone and Aunty are enjoying the energy between Nayia and me. They love it and mock it at the same time. And under their scrutiny, Nayia and I have become twelve-year-olds.

After a while we eat the tinned meat that Mularabone has warmed up. I make four thinnies and we smoke by the fire. The flames leap and dance. We're all light-headed from our night. Mularabone and Ouraka get up and go off towards the cave opening.

Nayia's gaze is direct. 'We are connected, you and I. Conway Holy Water.'

'I belong to you, Nayia-Nayia,' I whisper.

'We are two souls spewed up by history to find ourselves together in this place,' she says.

I want to laugh. Then she drops her robe off her shoulders to reveal her naked arms and torso. My breath goes in sharply as if I've just been slapped. Carved into the curves of her rich dark beauty are the knife scars. High on her left shoulder is the stabbing scar, a thick, rough, brutish thing compared to the more delicate lines of the cut scars on her arms and chest and belly. And amongst this chaos, those butterfly scars down the centre of her body that I first got a glimpse of in Uncle Birra-ga's cave. Then she is covered and looking at me.

'I belong to you, Conway Holy Water.'

My head races. I know from Mularabone's behaviour that there are protocols in place, even if I don't know what they are. I want to learn. I'm hungry for it. I undo my buttons, and then drop my shirt off my shoulders, hoping that I'm doing the right thing. The fire shines on the ridges of scar tissue on the side of my head where the trooper got me with his broken bottle, the marks from the chains on my wrists, the cuts inflicted by my father on my arms and shoulders, and the old bullet wound just above my left hip. I watch Nayia's eyes, and see that she is surprised at my many scars. We have lived in a war zone for all of our lives. Standing here shirtless, and under such scrutiny, I think I understand the protocol. Then I cover up.

We're still separated by the fire, and now our spirits reach out for each other over the flames. I move forward. She moves forward. She opens her arms and hugs me to her. It is such a joining that for a moment I think we are standing in the fire, or floating just above it. Nayia pulls her face out of my neck and shoulder and kisses me. The fire is inside us and burning/melting us into one new body.

We are oblivious to Mularabone and Ouraka returning, so involved are we in our kiss. Finally, it is Aunty singing joyously by the fire that brings us back. Aunty shuffles a few dance steps and sings. Mularabone is laughing.

'What are you laughing at?' I ask, still half in the fire.

'We thought you two would take forever!' says Aunty, and she and Mularabone howl with laughter. Mularabone runs over and hugs me, then hugs Nayia, shouting for joy. Aunty shuffles in the dust, singing about love. Aunty hugs me too, nearly swinging me off my feet.

'All right – you boys better get going now,' Aunty announces (Now that *that* is out of the way).

'Come on,' says Mularabone and lifts the automatic weapons. He holds a weapon out to me. I hesitate.

'You don't have to,' says Mularabone.

Nayia steps over and takes the weapon from his hand.

'I'll hold it for you,' she says. Then kisses me again.

I look into her brown eyes. Is this a test?

I put my hand on the weapon. 'I'll take it.'

Nayia hands the weapon to me and our hands brush each other lightly. My hands fit around the automatic weapon unnervingly. I can still remember The Sarge's words, may his soul find peace, in our very first weapons instruction class.

'Just let the weapon hang natural,' he said, showing us his easy grip.

I pondered that for years – the 'naturalness' of the metal and plastic automatic weapon in the flesh hands of a man.

'Aren't you coming?' I ask Aunty.

'Where you are going, to get the water for the meeting ... We cannot go. We go to another place. Women's place. We will sing for your safe passage.'

I nod. Acceptance is more important than understanding.

I turn and go with Mularabone. I'm careful not to look

back. I have to fight it as we come to the opening of the cave and are about to disappear from her sight – and I can feel her eyes still on me.

I walk after Mularabone out to where the truck is hidden.

Twenty-five: Blood and Dust in the Water

We approach the rig from the opposite direction. The canyon walls are close, and it is cool down here where sunlight rarely penetrates. We split up and circle the cab, looking carefully at every part of the vehicle. It wouldn't be the first time that the Water Board had left something intact and booby-trapped it. Another tactic they learnt from us. It looks clean. I dive underneath to look up at the chassis. There are a lot of spider webs but no taped-on packages that don't belong. Mularabone does a half-circle out to the front to look for any sign of interlopers, old or new. He comes back, gives me the nod, and we climb up and into the cab. The effort we went to in blowing away the tracks has worked.

It is late afternoon. Mularabone has timed it so that we do the run to the old fullas' meeting in darkness. He quickly goes through the pre-ignition sequence on the keyboard and then hits START. The big tanker engine roars into life. Mularabone hits MANUAL ALL, slams it into gear, and we take off.

'Just need one trailer, I reckon,' he says, and I nod in return.

We pull out into the open country and go south for ten minutes to where we stashed that first trailer. Mularabone drives with the throttle wide open, with the big rig jumping and sliding across the desert floor, throwing up dust behind us. He slows the machine, I jump down and run back into the tight little canyon and he reverses in using his mirrors. I quickly run around the trailer but can see no sign of interference.

'Yo! Yo-yo!'

The brakes hiss and Mularabone jumps down and we hitch her up. Then we are back in the cab and heading back north following the line of the river that we can't see but know is there. We've done this so many times it is a drill our bodies know without reference to our minds. Our eyes scan the open red country for any sign of dust or movement. The weapons lie on the seat between us. We end up at a spot just north of the river cave. We jump out. Mularabone walks to the lip of the gorge to check the ground. The water in the gorge must still be rising. I stand at the front, holding my weapon and looking out.

'Back in to here,' he says to me, making a mark with the butt of his weapon on the dry earth. 'We'll drop the pipe straight down.'

I move to the mark without looking at the river. I haven't forgotten. The sand he rubbed on me is still itching my neck, and coming out of my hair. I stand on the mark as he jumps into the rig and takes her forward so he can back in. He does this flat out.

'Yo! Yo-yo!'

The brakes hiss. Mularabone jumps down and goes for the pipe, unravelling it, and feeding it over the edge. I prime the water pump and turn it over. I climb up onto the trailer, walk along the top until I'm standing on the roof looking out. I hear Mularabone engage the pump and the water start to flow. I stand there on the roof scanning the horizon, with Mularabone down by the pump. There's no wind but I can't stop my body from swaying back and forth. I try to go with it, as if I am standing on the deck of some sea-going vessel and the swells are gently rocking me. I scan. I sway. Behind me, the pump engine throbs away, filling the big water tank. I hear a little noise and turn to see Mularabone climbing up next to me. He hands me a thinnie.

'Why don't you sit down, bruz?'

'Sitting down on the job; what would The Sarge say?'

'Never stand when you can sit ...'

'Never sit when you can lie ...'

'Never lie when you can sleep ...'

He lights my smoke, and we sit on the roof, dangling our feet in front of the windscreen. I look away to the plain of red soil stretching away from the river so that Mularabone has no chance to read the emotions that churn through me at the mention of The Sarge, may his soul find rest.

'Would've been less exposed to get the water from further down,' I say.

'Has to be from here. That's what Uncle said.'

We smoke.

'Anyway, be dark soon.'

Yeah.'

We smoke. The silvery liquid mirage from the heat of the day still lingers on the flat desert country to our front. We watch the glistening mirage and finish our smokes. Then we hear a little higher pitched whine above the throb of our water pump. Mularabone snatches up his weapon and leaps from the cabin roof to the top of the trailer. He runs crouched over to the back of the tanker and I'm right behind him. Down in the river we see a metal dinghy with four Water Board troopers in it. From their angle, they can't see the tanker but they have spotted our hose, and can hear our pump. Their electric motor strains against the current to push their dinghy towards our pipe. Two of them are readying grappling hooks. We throw our weapons to our shoulders and fire a burst at them. Our rounds smash into them, throwing two of them into the drink, and dropping the other two onto the floor of their aluminium dinghy. One of these troopers manages to pull a pistol, and a couple of rounds go whistling past us. Mularabone fires a single round that hits him in the middle of the face, and he slumps. With the tiller man floating dead in the water, the electric engine still whines but is completely directionless. The boat is borne away downstream by the rushing river water.

'We gotta go,' I hear Mularabone say from faraway.

I can't move. There is a willy-willy in my guts. Mularabone turns to me to see that I am transfixed.

Straight across the boiling river are the rock paintings that Mularabone had been protecting me from down on the beach. The two brother spirit figures stare back at me from the living rock with their all-seeing eyes. These spirits hold me in their gaze as if I were trapped in a massive spider web. As my mind struggles against them, I am held faster. Their images quickly become obscured by a dust storm that springs up from nowhere.

Mularabone slaps me hard across the face. My head snaps sideways from the force and I drop to my knees. He is yelling in Language, his voice not aimed at me, but lifted up and out. We crouch on the top of the tanker with the water of the rushing river below us, and the water pump of our rig throbbing away. Even with my head down I can feel those rock-painting eyes on me. Mularabone drops his weapon and takes out a small knife with a sharpened bone blade. He rips up my sleeve and plunges the bone blade into my forearm. The pain hits me and I double over as he plunges the blade into his own arm, and our bloods mix. He jumps down from the tanker, and I follow, landing hard and going forward onto my face. He is still yelling as he disconnects the pipe and shuts off the pump. I get myself up and drip red blood all the way to the cabin. Behind me, Mularabone picks up a handful of bloodied dust where we both bled, and hurls it out into the river below, yelling out in Language all the while. His calling out is urgent, and I only understand a little. He asks for protection for his white brother. He calls out that we are on the sacred story path, and that we respect this place.

Where our blood has dripped onto the red earth, dark crimson willy-willies spring up. The blood dust spins and grows, pursuing us with its unknowable darkness.

In a moment Mularabone is there in the cabin with me, and starting up the big rig. I tear off my whole sleeve and wrap the cut tightly. Then I tear off my other sleeve. Mularabone holds his arm out to me, and I bind up his wound. The crimson dust storm envelops us completely, blocking any vision through the windscreen. The wind power is incredible, and it feels like the whole rig could be lifted and flung back into the river at any moment. The storm is all around us, in us. The willy-willy in my guts is threatening to lift me off the seat so I belt myself in. Mularabone guns the engine and drives flat out.

Blood Dust Dream: River of Blood

The night races down on us. It envelops the landscape like smoke. We're at that moment when our shadows blur and melt, losing their connections to our bodies, and are lost in the all-shadow of the all-alone.

In this moment I hear the horses walking behind, and see the burning torches just ahead.

'Captain Molloy?'

'Sir,' I hear myself answer.

'Is it him?' he asks quietly.

I glance at Stirling. He is leaning forward, peering ahead at the meagre light-spill from the burning torches. That sneering half-smile is almost permanent upon his countenance now, his teeth as sharp and flashy as the oiled blade of his sword. He feels my eyes touch him and glances back at me, then his eyes snap back to the front.

He doesn't like what he sees in my eyes. No one does. I get those whores in town just so I can look into their eyes as I'm fucking them, more than for the fucking itself. When I am fucking them, my cock is really my sword – and when I am hacking into the blacks at full gallop, my sword is really my cock. Looking into someone's eyes just before they die is another thing altogether, even though orgasm and death are relations so close that they couldn't marry. Especially if I am the one bringing the death. The early death. The late death. The clean death. The messy death. Any fucking death. They're all the fucking same, in the end. Or the beginning. I need a drink.

'Is it him?' Stirling repeats.

I've drifted off. I wrench myself away from hypnotising swords and cocks, and push my eyes to search the gloom ahead.

'It's him. He's erected a pavilion.'

Stirling looks again and sees the paleness of the canvas behind the flickering red-orange light. That square shape doesn't belong. That paleness doesn't belong either. That tent could be made from the skin of a hundred Djenga. There is a slight movement to my left. A shadow shifts against the steady random rhythm of the dancing fire-shadows. I pull the big pistol from my belt and level it at the sound, thumbing back the hammer, stepping forward so that I am exactly between that sound and Lieutenant Governor Stirling.

Must be one of Bunbury's men. That's who we've come to meet. Bussell won't be faraway. I have Molloy's knowledge. Taking it with me to the congress of killers.

The shadow steps out of the darkness. He is a cruel, thin man holding a rifle low across his body. He sneers at me, and my pistol. My cold eyes drill into his. I see that his sneer is a lie, a cover, a mask. He glances back to the tent. By the time he glances back to me my pistol is away. He shifts on his feet.

'They're here, sir!' he yells back to the tent.

I pull my pistol again and level it at his head. His yelling is a crime I'll shoot him for. It wouldn't be the first time. At this range the weapon will rip his face in half.

'Leave it,' says Stirling under his breath as Lieutenant Bunbury comes out of his pavilion. It shocks him that I would level my weapon at a white man. Especially in front of Bunbury. I can still remember those Frenchmen falling to our blades, and cannon, and shot. They were as white as fucking white. Cancer is cancer.

'Another time, then,' I snarl at the thin man who seems to have completely misplaced his sneer. With his blank face I see the lost child within, almost begging me to help him; to help him get out, to play again, to be loved.

I follow Stirling, but with my pistol still cocked and pointed at the loud-mouthed, cruel, thin fool.

Stirling and Bunbury shake hands.

For a brief moment I think the part of me that knows what I am witnessing will speak up, will know what to say, will galvanise this hard little body beneath me into some dynamic and terrible action, but then the dark mud of anger and despair multiplies itself and clogs up my entire being. I need a drink.

'Would you care for a drink, Your Excellency?'

'Good job, good job,' says Stirling and they go inside.

I lower my pistol and stand near the tent.

Thin-cruel-loud-mouth-fool-boy has a mate, and they stand off a little way and consider my countenance.

I give them a smile.

They think they are hard men. I can see they're all ex-soldiers. I'm still a soldier. Always a soldier. Just new wars. New rules. No rules. Bloody fools.

'Are you the one?' asks Loud-mouth-fool-boy.

'Which one?'

'The one who is always with him?'

There are other men standing there now; eight or so blokes who were sitting away from Bunbury's tent a little bit. I feel their scrutiny.

I look down at what's left of my Royal Marines uniform. I've patched it in several places with kangaroo skin, and the remaining scarlet has faded to dark brown. I can't replace this jacket. I'm superstitious. I have two pistols in my belt, a knife in my boot, and a double-barrelled rifle slung from my shoulder. My hair is long. My beard is matted. With mud? Blood?

I stare back at them. No inner child in me can they see. Unless their eyes could go around corners and down into deep, deep holes, and even then it would only be the vision of a torn and bloodied corpse. There is nothing so shocking as to view the torn-up body of a child. I look back at them and my gaze is withering like rifle-fire.

I catch snippets of Stirling speaking from within:

'... Retaliation for the pertinacious endeavours of these savages to commit depredations of property ...' There is the clinking of crystal glasses. '... Not one savage would be allowed to remain alive on this side of the mountains ...'

Behind me the tent begins to glow red from within. A thick rivulet of blood starts to flow from the tent and right over my boots. I took these boots off a dead French officer. That man could have been my brother. His boots fit me perfectly as though I had been measured up for them in the backstreets of Paris. He walked on the inside of his feet whilst I walk on the outside and always wear away the very rear of the heel. It is a marriage made in heaven, because the more I wear them, the better they level out.

The blood flowing from the tent is thick like crimson syrup. Bunbury and Stirling are wellsprings for that blood – bringing that filthy gore up from deep in the earth. Fremantle has sailed away. The time of blood is upon us. The killing time.

The sum of the parts is greater than the whole.

The scum of their hearts is rusting up my soul.

I stand there, facing those men down, in that river of blood.

They turn and try to get away from the horror.

The river of blood quickens. The tent behind me dislodges, and begins to move away in the blood torrent. I wade to the side to let the tent pass me. It spins drunkenly to the side as it passes me and then collapses completely into the blood, and is quickly submerged.

Stirling and Bunbury are gone. Melted by the scarlet torrent. Everyone is gone. Just me with my swirling blood. Me as the killer. 44 has more shadowy depth than I could've imagined. We all have a history. We all have a shadow.

I draw the pistols. If I see someone, anyone, I will fire – in case I don't get another chance to kill, if I'm going to drown in this blood, that is.

What will I do if I see a woman?

Will I still want to kill?

A child? A woman? A white man?

The blood is rising swiftly. A flash flood. Blood flash flood. Flash blood. It swirls around my chest.

I take a breath and duck under the surface of the blood and suddenly all is quiet. But there is something else now. There are even darker shapes gliding through the blood. Shapes large and ominous.

I wonder if my weapons will fire. I aim at a passing murky form and pull the trigger. Nothing. I drop both of them and slip the rifle from my shoulder. I try to move but can't, weighed down by my clothes. I pull off my boots, rip off my clothes, and let them be snatched from my hands by the strong current of rushing blood. My lungs are yearning for breath now and my head is dizzy with panic. I fight my way to the surface.

I'm swimming like mad now, not passive but fighting the blood. I'm in a vast sea of blood – and ahead, there is a beach. I kick for it and a little blood wave dumps me on the shore, slamming my face into the gravel beach.

I land naked and exhausted. I pull myself out of the stinking, snarling blood river and lie there, trying to get my breath back.

I'm disturbed by the sound of voices and look up to see a large cohort of blacks. They aim their spears at me and yell at me in their gibberish. I don't understand. Can't understand. I try to get to my feet.

They menace me with their spears. They shout at me.

'Warra! Warra!'

They push me back into the blood.

I don't want to go. They jab at me and hurl insults at me. I turn and dive back into the blood river and sink to the bottom, allowing my heartbeat to slow, and a great stillness to come upon me.

Twenty-six: Here and There

The truck has stopped. I look out but can't see anything. I've gotta get out. I open the door and fall into the red dust. My weapon thuds softly next to me. In a moment Mularabone is standing above me.

'Where are we?'

'We're here.'

'The meeting?'

'Listen,' he says. I listen, and can hear many songs being sung. Somewhere close by. This is the big Law meeting going on. I rub my eyes. They're full of bloody dust.

'I'm going to get help,' he says.

'Don't leave me.'

'We've gotta hurry. That dust storm will be seen. We haven't got long.'

'That blood dust was real?'

'I'll get help. Don't go to sleep.'

'The blood ...'

'Trying to protect you, bruz. Don't go to sleep.'

And he is gone. I look down, half expecting to see my clothes bathed in blood and gore, but they are dry. Nondescript is the word I'm searching for. That's how I feel. Nondescript. Like I'm non-describing myself out of existence. How much blood have I lost?

I sit hunched over. A huge yawn takes me over. As my jaw locks open I hear the rush of blood in my ears. It feels like every cell in my body opens up its skin and yawns in the fresh, cool desert air. The yawn finishes. My muscles relax. My head slumps down onto my chest. I lie back on the earth. I look up at the stars. The weapon is by my side. My hand stays on the pistol grip. My eyelids are heavy. Can't go to sleep. I sit up and cradle the weapon on my knees. Gotta do something. My hands start to disassemble the weapon. It feels like it was many lifetimes ago that I last did this. But I know it's only been a few short years. Taken apart and set out on a rock like this, the pieces of steel and plastic could almost be something else: a toy, or some vital medical equipment, or a machine that does something useful. The Sarge used to call it 'the peacemaker'.

'Makes peace by killing your enemies.'

I feel his presence all around me. I try to shut him out.

Mularabone and I and all the other soldiers know: killing your enemies can be the least of your worries.

Before I know it, I'm snapping the weapon back together.

The bottom half of my body is warming up. I'm drifting off. I'm in a bath of blood, all warm and sticky. My chest cavity wheezes in and out, up and down like bellows. I'm stuck inside my own punctured lung, filling with blood, drowning in my own liquid. The air pocket above the lung bloodbath gets smaller and smaller. I keep my face up above the blood to suck in precious breath.

My eyes open a sliver, and I see the flickering light. A fire crackles nearby. I hear Mularabone's voice talking Language. I feel something tugging at me. It's like that feeling of getting operated on under a local anaesthetic – there is no pain, but a strange feeling of understanding that there should be pain. My eyelids flutter like butterflies, and then fall open to tiny slits. I have my own darkness, all aflutter from the blood coursing through my eyelids, and don't need that smoky dark from the real night. The fire is built up.

Through my slits I see an old Countryman above me. I don't

know this ancient Countryman but his features give him away as Young James' father, uncle, or grandfather.

Old James, I'm thinking.

He has hold of the weapon in my grasp and is gently pulling it out of my grip. My hands don't want to let go. The old fulla is as insistent as he is gentle, and gradually the tension in my fingers gives way to looseness, and the weapon is eased from my grasp. Like that lead bullet being pulled from the deep and secret recesses of my flesh, I feel relieved when it is gone.

I adjust my body on the earth. The pool of blood I'm lying in starts to recede, like I am a giant sponge that has been squeezed and wrung out before being placed here, and now I'm sucking the rich ruby river back into my body. Old James hands the weapon to Uncle Birra-ga, standing just behind. Mularabone takes the weapon from him.

Old James' face is close to mine. 'When you go,' he says, 'you can be both here and there.'

Twenty-seven: Secret Healing Water Song

I'm lying here, shivering. Feels like I'm lying over there. Near the fire. The built-up fire. Someone built that fire up. But it's here. The shivers are here, inside myself. They start somewhere in my belly and radiate outwards through my body. I vomit again. The vomit looks like I've been eating vanilla ice-cream. Mularabone bends down, and, using a yandi as a shovel, he scoops up the vomit and some red dirt. He walks away a bit and buries it. He comes back and squats.

'It's the radiation, bruz. From the Sick Mother.'

'I know,' I croak out.

I know the radiation can't be bad. Must be under five hundred rems. Probably under two hundred. I'd be dead by now, or have a third arm, or something. No, that's my kids. I don't have any kids yet.

'Where's Nayia?'

'Keep drinking, brother,' he says, and holds a piti to my mouth.

My eyes roll around in my head unbidden. I see Old James above me again. He has water in a shallow piti. This is water from the truck. Water from the strong place. The danger place. The grog dreaming place. Mularabone has passed it to him. He sings gently over the bowl of water as though it were his own precious child. His eyes play across the water in the same way that he would massage his grandchildren by the fire at night, to pour his spirit into them, and strengthen them with his loving touch and incantation.

He holds it to my lips and I drink from it. The water is cool and sweet. Living water. The sensation I get when I feel the underground water comes upon me. My ears become warm, my whole psyche is agitated and revved up by that water coming into me, like it is all around me, and I'm swimming in it. Old James drinks the last of the water. As the water enters him, he too is transformed, and I see what the Birdiya saw in me on the ceremony ground near the Darbal Yaragan south in Beeliar Country. His flesh takes on the texture of the surface of a billabong. If I dropped a pebble in him it would surely make a plopping sound and send out little concentric waves. He sits back for a moment and I see his eyes roll back into his head, as though there are some vital instructions written on the inside of his skull that he needs to read. A song begins to fall out of his mouth like the first trickle of a waterfall after rain. His eyes come back and focus on me, and he spits the water from his mouth back into the piti. Other Countrymen behind him peer into the piti and nod and murmur their prayers. Old James sings. His voice starts up high and spirals down through his register to finish in his deep, croaky, chest voice. Each breath is a whole song. His clapsticks keep time with his heart.

'Keep drinking, brother,' Mularabone says and holds the piti to my mouth again.

I gulp it down. My mouth feels foreign and chalky.

He is saying something else.

Old James' song rocks me back and forth as steadily as ocean swells, as though I am swinging in a hammock in a ship on the high seas.

Ghost of History: Arriving Again

It's the noise up on deck that disturbs me. I'm tired, having completed a long night-time watch.

'No one ever died of tiredness.' I hear Fremantle's voice ringing in my ears. He would've got on well with The Sarge.

From the shouting, I'm guessing we've made landfall. Captain Fremantle and I have not been able to bring ourselves to speak of it, but now I realise that, from the moment we sailed away from the Darbal Yaragan and our new friend the Birdiya of Beeliar, we were destined to return. It is the way of things. Coming back is our chance for peace within ourselves. We know now how far outside the thinking of Empire we are. I sit up in my bunk and pull my boots on, grab my jacket and head for the deck. I bound up the stairs and the fresh salt air hits me. And there's something else: the smell of that bush, still miles away, is sweet and dry.

'Smells like a pint of ale,' remarks Captain Fremantle on my approach to the poop deck. He turns and trains his new glass on the smouldering coastline. The Countrymen are always burning one patch or another. If you could fly over the whole country like a bird, from coast to coast it would appear like my aunt's patchwork quilt.

Fremantle's face is ruddy and beaming as if he's just stepped out of a steam bath. He offers the glass to me without taking his eyes from the land. I take it and put it to my left eye, squint my right, and the land jumps into sharp relief. There are two ships standing off the river mouth, and it is in this direction that we plough on.

'Did you dream, Mister Conway?'

'Yes, sir.'

'I would have stayed awake if I could have,' Fremantle remarks, almost under his breath.

I lower the glass and turn to him. We're standing very close. Two men on a precipice. In and around his eyes, ugly dark spirits circle. They are worms that burrow under his flesh and feed on him as they travel. His ears are red from the howling of the dog spirits.

'Do you think me strange, Mister Conway?'

'No, sir.'

'They call me. Call on me to honour my word.'

'Yes, sir.'

'Are you a man of your word, Mister Conway?'

'I hope so, sir.'

Captain Fremantle's eyes are drawn back to the Country. The deck rolls under us; that feeling of the riding swell flowing up through my feet and thighs and the answering downward pressure is why I wanted to be a sailor. The power in that water, that is not the water itself, but a wave moving through, and simply using the water particles to continue itself, that power always thrills me. It is indefinable, untouchable, and yet tangible, and inevitable – all in the same moment.

'What if I have made a contract I cannot honour?'

'Then you have to make it right,' I say.

I say what he already knows. He looks terrified by the knowledge.

'There is no running from this,' I say.

The captain's eyes go sharp. He searches me thoroughly, as if sifting through my possibilities. Captain Fremantle seems to have grown a halo of rich golds and greens.

'You give good counsel, Mister Conway.'

'History has spewed you back on shore at this precise moment.'

'Do I know you?' he asks suddenly.

I look at him. I know him. I cannot say if he knows me. I offer him my face, wide open, so that he can search for his answer.

He searches me, sorts through me like going through his sea-trunk. Eventually, he breaks our intense mutual gaze and looks back to the land rising before us like the sun coming up on a brand new day.

'Get the cutter ready, Mister Conway. I want the gun loaded with grapeshot, and a dozen of your best marines. Men you can trust.'

He smiles at me suddenly as he feels that sense of destiny come flooding in from his boots up. 'We are sailing off the edge of the map, here. You could excuse yourself.'

'That isn't possible, sir.'

'I need loyalty from them, Mister Conway. The Lieutenant Governor is not going to be overly amenable to our presence here.'

I'm nodding like a schoolboy. We're coming to the turning point, and I'm going to play Captain Fremantle's offsider.

And I'm scurrying off to my 2IC. I tell him to prepare the men. I give him a list of names. I open my mouth and the names come out. They seem to make sense to my 2IC. I tell him there'll be action. I need men who will not hesitate, who will not question.

Captain Fremantle is dreaming. Captain Stirling is killing.

There will be clouds and blood and sparks between them.

Minutes later, we're in the cutter, and belting for the river mouth again. I look out over the stern and up to see the little storm following us. Just like the first time we arrived. That's how it is for us Djenga, constantly arriving, leaving, and arriving again.

On the shoreline we see Countrymen. They've got up from their fires to consider our approach. Maybe they recognise us from the trim of the sail, the determination of our precise course.

We come skidding in toward the reef, then at the last moment we take in sail and tack south, to come around the reef through the shallow entrance. Two brown hawks circle overhead. I look up to see them coast on over to check us out. Their motion on the wind is determined by their wing and tail angles, which operate independently of their chocolate and white bodies, constantly adjusting the flow of air across the feathers. It is birds who have given us the gift of sailing.

On the south bank there are several springs flowing out of the limestone and tumbling down into the Darbal Yaragan. We pass through Walyalup and at Dwerdaweelardinup we tack back to the northern bank and beach the cutter. Captain Fremantle is staring back at the southern shore. I cross to him.

'The dogs,' he says and I follow his gaze back to the shore.

There is nothing there now. But we have both felt the power of these spirit guardians of the river mouth. On the full moon, they will be ranging up and down the river at Dwerdaweelardinup, howling, and drinking from the fresh-water springs in the rock. Fremantle knows full well that those howls can reach out to you across vast oceans; like the songs of the blue whales, they echo around the world in deep watery recesses, unheard by any except those who know how to listen.

The men are jumping into the shallows and pulling the boat up. The captain and I turn and jump off the boat. As we alight onto the beach with the wetlands beyond, we see a work party of Stirling's men towards the top of the first hill.

'Mister Conway?'

'Sir!'

'Go and find out where Stirling is. Take two marines. You four, with me. The rest stay with the boat.'

Fremantle turns and charges up the beach, back toward where we saw the Countrymen, with the four nominated marines shaking out behind him and struggling to keep up.

I step out in the direction of the work party, with two marines falling in behind me. There is a track of sorts, where the settlers have walked along a kangaroo road. The sand gives way beneath my boots, making my walk laboured. We go across the hundred yards or so to the base of the hill. There are marks on the ground where something has been dragged.

By the time we get to the top of the rise, the four Djenga have stopped working. There are two soldiers there too, holding muskets. They must be Captain Irwin's men from the 63rd. When they see me they come to attention and salute, 'Sir!'

The Djenga work party look at their soldiers for a moment like they are watching strange insects killing each other in a jar.

'As you were, men,' I hear myself say, as I try to follow the non-verbal communication amongst the Djenga.

The head of the work party is a short and chunky red-haired Scot.

'Ye be in the wrong place, young sir.'

'How is that?' I ask.

'Cap'n Stirling is at the barracks.'

'Barracks?'

'They're not finished yet.'

'Of course.'

One of the other men steps forward, a young man from Kent with a scrappy beard.

'Are you the one?'

'The one?'

'The one who's always with him?'

I look to him, and a wild cry wants to tear out of my throat but I clamp my jaw shut tight, and swallow the fire down. It burns my throat as it descends to the pit of my belly to smoulder. The dream of the river of blood with Captain Molloy, the shadow-ghost of 44 and his bloody thoughts, circles me slowly.

'Captain Stirling?' I hear my strangled voice ask.

They all look at each other with nasty little grins on their nasty little faces.

'Captain Fremantle,' he corrects, a strange look crossing his countenance.

'How do you know this?'

'There was a rumour, that Captain Fremantle would come back ... That you would come back ...'

The Scot looks sharply at the Kentish. I watch this play between them.

Down in front of us is a massive rivergum. In the topmost branch sits a crow. Wardung. He looks at us, then looks away upriver, and calls out his fading pattern, 'Aaarrr! Aaarrr! Aaarrr!'

I follow his gaze and look upriver.

'Captain Fremantle has gone to speak to the Countrymen.'

'The who?' asks the red-haired Scot.

I look straight at him. Then take in the four of them. The two soldiers, as well. Something isn't right. The way they're all looking too hard at us. Something too formal and yet too casual in their body language.

'The owners of the Country,' I hear myself say plainly.

Several of the Djenga shift on their feet.

'We're the owners now.'

I look from the red-haired Scot to the two soldiers who are

now levelling their muskets at us. My own two marines look to me.

'Did you buy this land?'

The Djenga glance at each other. They look like they're about to giggle.

I gaze at my boots and see a tiny caterpillar making its way from my ankle to my toe. This little fulla's green body is see-through, so that his tan-coloured insides are visible to me. He has feet at the front and back of his body but nothing in between, so he moves by creating this high, tight arch with his back, then reaching out into the unknown with his front grabbers, then bringing the back end in, and then repeating the whole process.

I don't look up at the rifle barrels pointed at me.

'You men better lower your weapons now.'

They respond by lifting their weapons to their shoulders.

'They have their orders from Cap'n Stirling,' says the Scot.

There is a big commotion down at the cutter and I swivel my body from the waist to observe the action. Captain Fremantle is down there with a big mob of Countrymen. They're pushing the cutter off the beach, and fullas are jumping into the craft. They quickly get the cutter out and up goes the sail. Already the good captain is only wearing his white shirt, and the Beeliar Birdiya wears his Royal Navy jacket. As the boat takes off, the strange ship-fellows of the marines and the Countrymen mingle on the wooden deck. The Countrymen are all over the boat, investigating wood and rope and canvas. They look out, and yell. The forest of spears and muskets with bayonets are stacked around the centre mast. One marine takes up his post at the gun in the bow.

Captain Fremantle suddenly looks up at me, as though he's just remembered my presence, or he felt my eyes upon him. I stand here with the two muskets pointing clearly at my belly.

He makes no gesture but holds my gaze for a minute, maybe more. It's as if we are standing only a few feet apart.

Down below me, west of the beach, is the ceremony ground where we first met the old Countrymen. Where I went from water to flesh to smoke.

'It don't appear that Captain Fremantle has got your back, Lieutenant Conway,' says the Scot. 'Cap'n Stirling says he's gone native. He's dangerous. You better have your men lay off those muskets.'

I nod to my men and they hand their muskets to the Djenga.

'And your sword, Lieutenant Conway?'

I hesitate, concentrating on keeping my breathing even.

'That's if that is your real name,' adds the Scot with a snarl.

I look to him. Now he has my attention. I feel like I know him. He reminds me of Mitch the Blood Nut. When I do speak, my voice is surprisingly calm. Thank God and St George for my English officer-class upbringing.

'If you attempt to remove my sword, I shall be forced to defend myself.'

'It would be a shame to kill an Englishman,' says the big Scot, 'a real shame.'

This time the others do snigger. Behind them, I notice the big ceramic grog flagon on the ground.

Down on the river, the cutter disappears around the corner, towards Garungup.

'I am going to draw my sword.'

I lock eyes with the Scot. My hand goes to the hilt of the navy cutlass.

'Shoot him!' he says, way too loud. I notice the tiny white bubbles at the corner of his mouth.

In the next moment, the two soldiers and the two armed

Djenga suddenly sprout branches, bloody and dead straight, from their upper torsos. They look as surprised as me as they topple slowly into the sandy earth. The Scot and the Kentish turn to face the threat, just in time to receive terrific blows to the head from nulla-nullas, delivered by Countrymen at full sprint. In three blinks I'm standing on the sandhill with my two marines, surrounded by two dozen Countrymen – armed and quivering with adrenaline. Bright Eyes is there, beaming at me. The warriors quickly dispatch the Djenga with their nulla-nullas and retrieve their spears. I realise that I am quivering too.

Twenty-eight: Whale Song Blessing

I lie still and try to orient myself to the space. My body feels light. Almost empty. I'm propped up against a large boulder. I remember a big scramble at the meeting. I remember being carried. I remember some firing. Small arms only. In front of me is Mularabone's back. He is as still and settled as the rock at my back. He is the rock at my back.

'Where are we, coorda?'

'They're here,' Mularabone flings back at me over his shoulder.

My hand grabs for a weapon that isn't there and I don't really want. Instead, I grip the rocky ground to prevent myself from floating away.

'Who?'

'Troopers searching for us.'

We're up high, the plain stretching out before us to where the sun goes on his daily journey. In the half-light it's like looking over the ocean. Way out to the north a small wave crashes over a stand of desert oak, sending lazy foam arcing into the sky. Maybe a hundred metres or so in front of us is a rock formation rising out of the surface of the sea. My eyes are drawn to the rock formation. I know this is where Mularabone is looking, even though I can't see his eyes. There is something about that big rock. It is huge, as big as ten of my father's vehicles stacked on top of each other. I focus. The rock is the perfect granite shape of a southern right whale, frozen in the act of coming up to breathe.

My eyes investigate the form, searching for anything not adhering to the whole shape. This is how we were trained in the cadres – fault picking, The Sarge called it, may his soul find peace. I find nothing. It is like I am swimming in a shallow bay with her, this massive aquatic mammal with a brain almost as big as my whole body. My eyes play over the beautiful and colossal contours of her body.

And then she breathes! The very moment I have that thought, she breathes. A puff of dust shoots up into the air, accompanied by the distant, releasing hiss of air-brakes as the rock whale ripples into life. In almost slow motion, her enormous, barnacled head lifts from beneath the surface of the blood-red soil and looks directly at us. It is her eyes that give away her gender, beautiful, long and curved, fine rock eyelashes that hover, and then blink. She speaks, and her words reach across the space to us with a mother's gentleness. I see her words go into Mularabone. His body receives them like me sipping water from Old James.

Her words tumble into me and lodge themselves down deep.

A shot is fired from a big weapon. A terrific explosion tears the night open only a few hundred metres to the west of the Rock Whale Spirit Woman, and the vicious white-light shockwave arc cuts across the desert floor, the gentle ocean waves, and she is gone, that Rock Whale Spirit Woman. All that is left is the granite, still as rock in the perfect frozen moment just before she breathes, and descends. The water truck below us burns fiercely, washing the now empty valley with oranges and reds. Now we see the Water Board troopers, who fired from the cruiser with their spotlight.

We flatten our bodies into the earth. Moments later the inquisitive pool of light plays across the boulders above our heads. We breathe while the light source moves on. They're heading down into the little valley where the dry creek bed is. We watch them stop at various dead campfires where the old Countrymen had been. Gone now. Even from here, we can hear Jack swearing.

Them Djenga still impatient after all these years.

Then Mularabone is grabbing me and pulling me gently backwards, until the fading light of the early evening is replaced by the real darkness of the tunnel. This is the vast network of tunnels north of Uncle Birra-ga's mural cavern. There is a scraping behind us as Mularabone completes the closing of the tunnel opening. He comes back down to me.

'You right, coorda?'

I stand straight up. The movement surprises both Mularabone and myself.

'Yeah. Let's get into it.'

Mularabone goes past me, ripping the top off an ML, casting garish green shadows on the rock walls around us.

'What was the meeting for?'

'To prepare for the big ceremony down south.'

'Jack get anyone?'

'He's definitely off his game, your brother.'

We walk. The greenish light from the ML makes me feel like I'm under water, walking along the bottom of a river. The tunnel we're in goes down, down for another hundred metres or so, before it levels out. It's cool and dry underground.

'He's like a dog with a bone, your fucken brother, coorda.'

'I'm not my brother's keeper, coord.'

'I spose we gotta expect him.'

'Cause of the two brothers?'

'Maybe.'

We walk. In this part of the tunnel we can walk side by side.

'What about that Whale, hey?' I ask.

'She had a calf we didn't see,' says Mularabone.

I nod, the feeling of protecting that child in the back of Jack's ute flooding through me.

'I feel different.'

'Old James did a healing on you, bro, don't you remember?'

My memory is a strange series of burbling creeks, converging on a river whose name I can't pronounce. A dream I just can't get back. The water is murky, or there's not enough light to see by. I remember song phrases going round and round, and cool, hard hands touching my body, right inside my body, inside my veins, my creeks, inside my webs, right inside me. Old James drained out my blood like it was contaminated grain, threshed it, and winnowed it, before funnelling it all back into me. I remember drinking water from a piti. Very particular water from a special wellspring. Living water. I remember Old James spitting out his water, his cool, dry hands on me, or in me, I can't decipher which.

'She gave us a blessing, coorda.'

'The blessing was from the calf we didn't see.'

'The child.'

The tunnel closes in on us. I glance sideways a few times, like I half expect the Rock Whale Spirit Woman to be down here with us, and to burst out of the depths of the rock/water all around us. The moment I think this thought, the very rock we are walking on vibrates and the whale song breaks over us like foamy waves.

Ghost of History: The Soul of Our People is Burning

We hear the singing long before we get there, broken in parts by the gusting wind. The Countrymen in our group, and even the marines, are glad to hear that singing. We feel like we're coming home. It's early evening when we finally traipse into the camp at Goologoolup, the place of the red clay where the Waakul came down. The wind has blown us all the way here. On the other side of the world it is called late August. Here it is the time of Jilba, the time of warming after the cold, wet, westerly gales of Mokur. The half-finished barracks stand out, the red clay of the bricks such a strange colour to see up in the air, stacked on top of each other, rather than underfoot. There are fires everywhere, the smoke curling away down the hill towards the island in the river.

All along the way we had to stop while Bright Eyes took great pains to tell me the name of a place and its chief assets. We couldn't move on until he accepted my pronunciation. At the last few stops, the marines joined in and were also trying out the new language and the new names, to help me get through. I've always thought of myself as pretty fit, but I've struggled with the twelve mile march through Country, whilst the young Countrymen seem to cover the distance with so little effort that it doesn't seem right.

Fremantle is at a fire with a group of Countrymen. He sees me approach, jumps up and runs to me like a child.

'Mister Conway!'

'Sir.'

'I'm glad you made it.'

He looks like he's going to hug me but then suddenly he doesn't. He stops and stares at me. Behind him, everything goes quiet, and all eyes turn to us.

'I want you to meet the Birdiya,' Fremantle says.

Beeliar gets up from the fire and comes over with another senior man. He is a bit older than Beeliar. His body is also covered with ritual scarring, and he wears a permanent smile. He was here the day Mrs Dance chopped at the tree whilst Stirling read his proclamation.

'May I present the Birdiya of Mooro, lands north of the river. He can speak for this country.'

'Another duke?'

'Precisely, Mister Conway.'

The Birdiya of Mooro shakes my hand lightly. 'I am made from this Mooro Boodjar, from this Country,' he says.

'He is a fast learner of English,' says Fremantle.

'What have you done?' I ask, my voice measured.

'We have stepped off the world,' he says.

I nod, still waiting. I'm wondering if he's speaking for my benefit or his own. Not that he looks like he needs convincing that he is no longer walking with his feet in our old world of uniforms and empires.

'Where is Lieutenant Governor Stirling?' I ask quietly, and now my voice sounds like it is coming from a long way off, as if I already know the answer to this question, as though I can read it in the faces and bodies of the Countrymen around the fires and that of the captain.

'We have stepped off.'

'Stepped off?'

'The Empire.'

'Can I see him?' I ask, the rain starting to fall into my face.

It's not Stirling I want to see; but the other one, the one who is always with him: the killer. The killer from the river of blood. His power is what I fear. That he is the power behind 44. I'm not looking directly at my captain when I ask, in case he reads my deception.

But Fremantle has turned away from me. He is churned up in the guts, like he is wrestling with some demon emanating from his own innards. When he does turn to face me, his face is flushed and shining like a madman, or a prophet.

The Countrymen around the fires read me from where they are sitting. I see them exchange tiny knowing glances.

'Don't you see? This is the chance. It's got to stop. Let's stop it here. You and I. Let's make a stand. The soul of our people is burning. I see you reading your Bible, Mister Conway. You are not like the bosun: you really read it, search for it. I see you searching. That's why it is you and I who stand here, spewed up by history into this precise moment. We rape and pillage and steal and kill without mercy and build an empire and become wealthy and become heroes and all the time it is our spirit we have sold to the lowest bidder.'

The rain hits my face. Behind the captain, someone throws a handful of grass tree sap powder and there is a whoosh of sparks and a big puff of smoke rushes out. For a moment the wind is reversed and the thick sweet smoke blows straight through the captain and I, as though the consistency of our flesh is no more solid than the smoke itself. Then the wind rights itself and the smoke flows around us and down through the Countrymen.

I struggle silently with myself, like I'm back in my bed as a young man and the angry faces come in at night to press their heaviness down on me; I try to move and can't, eventually concentrating all my power on raising one paralysed eyelid, and finally succeeding, and then my power of speech comes back.

'What are they waiting for?'

'For you.'

'Show me.'

Captain Fremantle calls over a marine and says something to him. The warm rain falls on us all. Near the fires are shelters made from trees and shrubs. They look warm and dry. Suddenly I want to sleep. My feet are cold lumps of lead in my boots. The marine turns and I follow him down the hill. All the Countrymen at the camp get up and follow. I feel like I'm in some theatre show; I take a few steps and stop, and the Countrymen all stop. I repeat the process a couple of times. Some of the Countrymen crack a smile. I take a step and stop and spin round to see if I can see anyone moving. They all freeze. I turn back to the front then snap my head back. Nothing. They are grinning brown statues in the rising dark. I turn to the front and the marine is rapidly moving away from me. I quickly go after him down the winding path and hurry to catch up, my leaden appendages clomping heavily in the sand.

After a little while we come to a flat area. There are a number of solid tent structures and a few beginnings of what might be brick cottages. Captain Fremantle is beside me.

'Where are the Djenga?'

'Fled into the bush.'

'Cold night for them.'

'Indeed,' Fremantle agrees.

'Indeed! Morning sir!' beams Bright Eyes.

He goes on ahead and disappears into a tent. There is a lantern in there. I follow the captain in. The big mob of Countrymen all crowd in behind us. The air is close in that canvas enclave.

Lying on the earthen floor are the bodies of six Djenga and two Nyoongar warriors. One of the warriors has a grotesquely swollen neck replete with rope burns, and the other has a bullet hole in his stomach still oozing purple.

Captain Stirling is furthest from me. He has a huge bloody hole in his throat, and a surprised look on his face.

'You shot him? I thought it would be a duel at dawn with navy cutlass?'

'Turns out Captain Stirling was right. I'm not much of an officer and a gentleman.'

My eyes travel down the faces of the other dead men. My eyes go back and forth over them, searching and not finding relief. I turn back to Fremantle.

'Who are these others?'

'They made a choice. Wrong choice.'

'Indeed.'

'Indeed! Morning sir!'

Fremantle's tone reminds me that he is a Royal Navy officer, a warrior, and a man who has fought many bloody campaigns for the Empire. He is no stranger to the choices men make in battle, or politics.

I can't take my eyes off the dead men. He's not there, the one I saw, the one I *was*, in the river of blood. I wanted to find him here. Find him dead. I wanted 44 to be here, to be dead.

I nod to Fremantle, unable to hide my disappointment.

'What about the Countrymen?'

'As we arrived Stirling was hanging one man for stealing flour. The other was shot in the ensuing exchange.'

'Did he steal the flour?'

'The flour was on his Country, his Boodjar. He believed he had a right to that flour, that it was to be shared.'

The Birdiya of Beeliar steps forward and makes a sharp

hand gesture.

'Finish!' he says.

Beeliar comes to me and shakes my hand. He hugs me. Fremantle puts his arm around my other shoulder. My head is spinning.

'Let's go and talk, Mister Conway. You hungry?'

I nod. I feel embarrassed at the touch of the other men. I'm not used to it. Mooro says something in Language and all the Countrymen cheer.

We head back to camp and when we get there the place is full of women and kids. We go out of the rain and have a feed of wallaby.

That meat is so sweet. I can still taste it now.

Twenty-nine: Same Water Me

Walking through this ancient tunnel, I get the feeling that we're deep inside the Rock Whale Spirit Woman, and moving along her arteries, or winding our way through her lower intestine, with her gently extracting the goodness from our spirit-flesh all the while, to nourish herself and her child. It's the opposite of the feeling that I had in that other cave full of incarcerated people, with the escape through the belly of the Sick Mother. All things evolve and change into other things. Us. Feelings inside us. The air we breathe. The rocks we walk over and through. The water that flows through the earth and sweetens our people-clay. No beginnings. No ends. Just constant changing.

We take it in turns being the front man, the point. We step off and stop in complete unison, stepping into each other's tracks. The darkness allows us to whisper, at best – but mainly we are wrapped in her warm, thick blanket of silence. The freedom in that silence allows us to be together and alone. The man behind rests a hand lightly on the point man's shoulder, to read the transfers of weight with each step, the pace, the breathing. We match each other like hypnotists until our bodies are blended into one flesh vehicle for moving us along in the dark safely. It is so dark that we close our eyes on point, and reach out with other antennae to feel our way along. We aren't ourselves. We are no longer our thoughts. We are not even our flesh. Our senses cannot detect what we are. In that tunnel we become our walk. The walk. There is nothing else.

We come into Uncle Birra-ga's cavern camp from a different direction this time. We've grown so accustomed to the weight and closeness of the rock walls of the tunnel that the open space of the cavern is a surprise.

There is a figure near that fire we first sat by and a big mob over by the far fire. Everyone is still, like they're waiting for something. For someone. Our ML has long since gone out. We followed the tunnel in absolute darkness for the last three hours at least.

Now here at the edge of the cavern, the space and light are terrible to behold. We both hesitate. Is the child ready to be born? Are the parents ready to be parents? Is anybody ready? There's only one way to find out.

Mularabone has been point. My right hand still rests on his shoulder. His left hand comes up and then down on mine, and rests there. A long rest. And then a gentle squeeze. Our hands drop to our sides in unison.

'Wait, my brother,' Mularabone says quietly.

'What's goin on? Who this mob?'

'Your new in-laws.'

'But I thought ...'

'There's gonna be some business. You just listen. Don't speak. Don't react. No matter what. Repeat it back.'

'Just listen. Don't speak. Don't react,' I repeat.

'No matter what,' Mularabone prompts.

'No matter what,' I repeat, adding, 'don't react.'

Mularabone gives me his cheeky smile. I watch him amble away from me until he is in the centre of the cavern space.

There is some muttering amongst the people at the far fire. Two Countrymen stand and face Mularabone. They have spears in their hands.

In Language, Mularabone asks for the blessing of the old people, and the spirits of Uncle's cavern. He then addresses the far-fire mob in a loud clear voice. He speaks for a minute or so, and then looks back to me. He motions me forward. I stand still. He motions for me and calls out to me in Language to come to him.

I don't move. I'm made of stone. I breathe out in a rush of dust, hissing like a whale. Mularabone turns back to the far-fire mob. That mob are all on their feet now. Mularabone gestures back to me with his lips and a head-raise.

'This is Conway Holy Water! He is my brother! He is a man! His soul is from the same water! Same water me!'

I know this is for my benefit because it is in English. I want to rush to him now, my brother, and hug him. From the far fire, two Countrymen break away from the group and go up to Mularabone. There is a heated exchange between them. Mularabone isn't calm. He talks wildly and gesticulates like a mad man to match his adversaries. Just when the yelling of all three of them hits fever pitch, they fall silent. The cavern envelops us with a silent ohm, pressing us with the firm love of a mother to her screaming infant.

The two Countrymen peel off Mularabone and wheel over to me. They are both shirtless, their chest scars shining in the half-light. One of the Countrymen fits his spear to his woomera and steps closer to me. I watch him. The spear point comes up and wavers in the air four metres out from my chest, while his eyes burrow into me. I am ready for this scrutiny. I came through Jack's drug and electricity realignment. I don't exist. I am a walk. A walk standing still. He reads this in me, the spearman. He retreats a step or two. He looks at me from around the corner that isn't there. He shouts at me in Language. The Countryman behind him fits his spear to his woomera and shouts his agreement. I walk without moving. Only my breathing gives it away.

The two Countrymen consider me. The spirit of my walk.

Standing still. They lower their spears and simply walk away in silence. The others from the far fire join them, and they leave the cavern.

Mularabone looks back to me.

Is he wondering if he did the right thing? If I'm worth it?

He turns away from me and goes. Goes out by a different exit to the far-fire mob. It's a real labyrinth down here. I gaze after his departing figure, before I feel the strength of the other being still in the cavern touch the edge of my vision, and my focus shifts to the figure by the fire.

Now, I'm not sure if I can move? If I can walk?

The fire in front of her crackles. She throws on some powder with a flash of bare brown arm, and the flames rear up bright yellow and orange, before sinking away to leave a heady puff of sweet smoke. Even from this distance, the sweetness strokes my nostrils lightly like a feather. My feet begin to complete me with their steps.

And I am in front of the fire. In front of her. I've had to come around clockwise in a wide circle, so she could see me all the time.

I'm swimming in the dream by the sandhills but now there is no ancient pistol, and 44 can't touch me. I am walking to her. I am on the web of the spider. She sees me stuck here. I am joyous to see her, stuck here as I am. I feel her vibrations on the web as she comes towards me. She is huge. When she smiles her fangs show and even the venom forms tiny droplets on their points. We come together in a joyous crunch. I am her. She is me.

Thirty: Water on Scars

Her eyes are direct. Under her gaze my flesh and blood become transparent. Her eyes are like the water in those precious rock holes, appearing to be dark and mysterious, but pure and clear when scooped out with cupped and clean, dry hand. At the bottom edge of my sight is the fire glow. Her smile appears slowly, and is easy and fathomless. I want to test the depth in those pools, but the sticks in my heart, feeling for the bottom, touch nothing but the emptiness of more liquid. For a moment I'm back in the escape tunnel from the underground jail, with that unknowable depth sucking at the fear in my belly as I go up to breathe.

'I thought you'd never get here,' Nayia says in English.

'Why are your relations so angry with me?' I say, indicating with my lips the departed group of shouting spearmen from the other fire.

'Angry with you? They love you! You are Conway Holy Water.'

'Must be hard kind of love?'

'They just want to make sure you respect them ... and me.'

'I will,' I say with a grin.

The fire picks out the dry highlights in us, like we are two fresh new hills in the desert experiencing sunrise. Nayia slips her robe off her shoulders. I feel as if I'm looking at a piece of country, something sacred, something secret. I undress without hurrying. We watch each other over the fire. And then we are lying down together on rugs made of skins.

We are two dry stretches of country. We carry the marks of millions of years, from the volcanoes, the ice ages, droughts, fires, floods, cultivation, and mining. There are dry creek beds winding through us, patiently awaiting the arrival of water. Without water, the creek beds could be taken for scars, old wounds cut into the crust of the country with knives; the rock holes up and down my arms could be taken for ciggie burns if they weren't brimming with pure water.

I start to feel the warmth behind my ears, which gradually builds to a low hum. In each of the countries now, spring water begins to bubble up from deep within, and the creek beds begin to run wet and cool with the ancient sweet water. Her hands touch the scars on the side of my head and my fingers dance over the healed-up holes where my father's knife went in.

The creeks flow side by side and winding for a thousand kilometres, for a thousand years, before they turn suddenly, and cutting a new pathway through the red earth, join forces to become a mighty river. And this is us, this boiling pool of swirling water, this joining.

Dreaming 44: Love on the Web

I'm crouching in the bush. I'm not alone. There are three or four of us here. We are all naked apart from hair belts. We are all painted with ochre. Just ahead, through the scrub, we can see the surface of the water, flat and dark in the rock hole. None of us moves a muscle. Breathing is a quiet, private affair. We are waiting.

I watch a dragonfly hovering over the water. He reminds me of the gunships all those years ago. In my hand is a carved nulla-nulla. It is heavy. Must be jarrah. A Nyoongar weapon – no jarrah this far north. My mind is processing the environment, the other men beside me, and the tranquillity of the water.

Ahead of us there is the tiniest of sounds, a deep sigh – and all of our eyes go forward. Focus. Us, the hunters.

The first emu is like a ghost drifting down to the water. He pauses, his half-raised foot stops dead, his head goes up, and listens. Nothing. The deep internal bell/drum goes off in his breast, and there are two of his wives moving close in behind him. They bend to drink the sweet water from the rock hole. I look to the others beside me.

It is Young James and Mularabone, and the third one I can hardly make out. The third one smiles suddenly without mirth and I see it is Jack. Young James makes a sign with his left hand and we erupt out of our hiding spot like crazy white cockatoos, making a huge ruckus. The large birds turn and belt through the scrub with us in hot pursuit, yelling like mad bastards.

The emus are faster than us and quickly put a few metres distance between us, until they crash into our net strung up between several eucalypts. They thrash about and struggle against the vegetable rope. Then we are on them with our nulla-nullas. Crack! Crack! Crack!

We are ecstatic. Dancing around like children. So much tucker now. We got all three. Enough for the mob.

I go up to Jack. 'What are you doing here?'

Jack smiles. In our ochre we are the same colour as Young James and Mularabone.

'What are you doing here, Jack?'

Jack steps in close to me, like he is going to whisper his response, but then shoves me hard in the chest with both hands. The shove takes me unawares, and I stumble back into the bloodied net. Only now it is not the sinew trap that we painstakingly wove but a huge spider's web. I stick fast to that secret protein weave. Jack's handprints on my chest glow a whitish green colour in the fading light.

Jack steps back.

The web begins to vibrate.

I turn back into the web to face the spider. I can't see her yet but can hear her percussive eight-footed song on the web getting louder. The web is as thick as my wrist so I know she is going to be big. I wriggle a little and, instead of being further entrapped like the hapless emus we were hunting, I am suddenly freed from the web. Only my hands and feet are touching and I am in control of my own traction.

Then I see her. It is Nayia. A spider. She is huge. Huge and black and beautiful and terrifying. As soon as I see her I am aroused. She is spider. She is woman. She looks dangerous but now I am the hungry one. My eyes drink in her breasts, her throat, her belly, her thighs. I see her fangs glinting. She is coming at me too fast. She thinks I'm prey caught on her web. I stand up on the web and start to dance. She slows her approach.

She is so close I can hear her breathing, smell her skin. She sees my erection, and she is ready to couple too. I can see her engorged sex. I want to dive into her. She moves closer, and I start to shoot web over her many feet and hands. I dance, and shoot out web, and dance. I offer myself in the dance, over and over, until I am sure she is ready.

Then we are fucking. It is the most glorious fucking. Glorious spider fucking. This is the fuck I've waited my whole life for. This beautiful fuck. I don't notice her hands get free, so subtle she is with her movements, so joyous am I within her flesh and surrounded by thigh and breast. My little spider bottom pumps and pumps as she gently ties my hands with her web. I don't notice until I can't move.

'Coorda! Chuck an emu on the web! She's hungry!' I call out.

All I hear back is laughter. 44 laughing. He is pacing back and forth, sucking his teeth, and laughing.

I open my mouth to speak again and she shoots a plug of silk into the hole.

'Ssssssh,' she seems to whisper, 'ssssssh.'

She rears back and sinks her fangs into me, the left tooth going into my heart. I feel the warmth of her poison flood my chest.

Thirty-one: Memory of Spiders

I sit up. I'm alone on the rug. The little fire still burns. I feel weightless and heavy all at once like a big river moving slowly. I'm looking at the river and I am the river. There was big rain upriver two days ago. I focus on two floating eucalypt leaves on this huge mass of moving green. On one of the leaves is a little red-brown jumping spider. He rides the leaf boat with patience and acceptance as though he'd booked a ticket on this ferry. He knows he can't survive in the water, he doesn't have his cousin's ability to run across the top, or his other cousin who can trap an air bubble and walk along the bottom. He doesn't have to because he has his leaf. His memory goes back two hundred and forty million years, so he can take solace in his survival. He was here before us, and he'll still be here when we are gone, weaving the past, the present, and the future with his silken thread.

I look up. There is Mularabone, sipping at his coffee and smiling his huge white smile.

'Jeez, you Djenga mob like the cot.'

The light in the cavern has a gentle bluish hue, and a dense texture like we are actually inside the giant mural on the rock wall behind and above us.

'She's left with Aunty already,' Mularabone says in answer to the desperate question in my eye.

'She coulda woken me.'

Mularabone looks at me like I am a child who knows nothing.

'Wake a sleeping man? Wake a dreamer? Not our way.'

He hands me a mug of coffee. I nod. The love in my heart and on my skin has overwhelmed me. 44 is still trying to take away my joy. To hurt me in my dreams. Him and Jack thought that they'd be getting me in my core with the spider-fucking-death. Jack is as weak as piss. And that mammoth spider lover, and that eight-legged boy with his silly little penis – that's all me.

Mularabone seems to understand. His nature is gentle and consoling, even if there is a huge grin waiting to be set free. Understanding can be overrated. Acceptance is more useful. Mularabone has taught me this. I've learned it because it awakens in me those deeply forgotten ways from another time. Forgotten things can be remembered. Them old people have taught me that. It doesn't matter how long since they were last remembered since time doesn't work in a linear way, no matter how much we try to fool ourselves that it does. What matters is that real truths, the real way of things, can never be truly lost; only forgotten to be remembered again. This is the nature of these bodies that our spirits must live in, to be constantly in this cycle of remembering and forgetting.

Mularabone hands me some cooked meat. I take it from him and bite into the emu flesh. My mouth explodes with saliva and my stomach floods with juice as I chew the meat.

'We got a long walk,' says Mularabone. 'Got to eat.'

'Can't we get a vehicle?'

Mularabone's grin bursts out from behind the clouds and floods me with light. 'You're just not a morning person, are ya, bro?'

'Is it morning?'

'Who knows?'

There are two packs close by; Mularabone is serious about this walk.

'We'll have to get another water truck,' I say.

'Uncle Birra-ga needs us to go back to the refugee camp.'

'To organise more fighters?'

'To wait.'

'Wait?'

'For the pathway south to open up.'

'Jack will kill us.'

'Jack is as weak as piss.'

I finish my meat. I pull my clothes on and lace up my boots. I look up and Mularabone is watching me.

'Watchu lookin at?' I fire at him.

'Hain't worked it out yet,' he fires back.

'If you need a hand with that thinking thing, just let me know, bruz.'

'Why, do you know someone?'

We laugh.

'How ya feelin?'

'Snapped back and cuttin slack, brother. I'm a bit tired but we ... She ...'

My voice trails off. Mularabone has this funny look on his face.

The blood floods my pale Celtic skin and I blush to my toes.

He got me. Got me good.

'You weren't asking about Nayia, were you?'

'You're right, coorda,' Mularabone says more gently, he's had his fun, and now doesn't want to cross a line.

We both slowly nod at the fire as if it is telling us something.

'Old James did a healing on you. But you still swam through the Sick Mother.'

'Which means she birthed me. I am the Son of the Sick Mother.'

'That's what them old fullas were talking about. If you and Nayia both came through her, and both survived …'

I chew down some emu meat, swig black coffee from my tin mug.

'Am I healed, coorda?'

'You're changed.'

Mularabone pulls out two pre-rolled thinnies. He hands one to me. It's the fattest thinnie I've seen for ages. He must have a truckload of that ropey old defence-force tobacco buried in the hills somewhere. We light them off the small fire at our feet.

'We'll finish these and get a wriggle on.'

'Country gonna start speaking up,' I add with a voice from faraway.

We suck on our thinnies. I stare into the fire.

There's a small red-brown jumping spider near my left boot. His head bobs quickly and he jumps onto my trouser leg. He moves so quickly that to my eye he is only visible again when he lands, like he has disappeared into another world and reappeared again. When he lands he holds his front two legs and back two legs together on each side so that he only appears to have four fat, long legs. He does this to fool his prey that he is one of them. I look back to the fire for a tiny moment. Suck on some smoke. When I look back to my trouser leg the little jumping spider has gone. Disappeared into that other place. I blow smoke.

I want to thank Mularabone for standing up for me last night. There are many Countrymen who believe that nothing good can come out of any associations with us Djenga, the white spirits. Mularabone and his old fullas are still pioneering a new way, even after all these years. Uncle Birraga says it is the Country. If us Djenga had been here for as long as his mob, we too would become deeply affected by the Country. Affected to the point that Country and people become indivisible: that the people are the Country's way of moving itself around, to look after it, to make music to resonate with.

We finish our thinnies and throw the stubs into the flames. We grab our packs and head for the surface.

Thirty-two: Neanderthal

Young James is at the inner door at the end of the tunnel near the surface, standing with a stillness that is only ever a heartbeat away from explosive, devastating action. He gets us through the door, and then silently drops back down behind the inner door, leaving Mularabone and I alone in the pure dark below the heavy steel outer door. We get up onto the ledge and put our shoulders into the steel door to slide it across. As our bodies bump together I feel the weapon Mularabone has in his belt, one of those nasty little death-spitters imported from South-East Asia. He never offered a weapon to me. Nor mentioned that he was going to be armed.

Does that mean it's official – that I'm no longer a soldier? I'll fight if I have to, I tell myself. Anyone will fight if they have to. Trouble is, I'm not sure if I'm telling the truth. And if I'm not a soldier, then what? A water finder? A dreamer? I don't wanna get killed. I wanna be a man. This is a new beginning for me. I have to see Nayia again. Our destinies lie on the same dreaming path. And if I don't wanna get killed, it's good to be with Mularabone. Mularabone and his nasty little death-spitter.

The door slides across and the cool desert evening air rushes into the space. After the close heat of being underground, it's like a sea breeze. A hundred thousand years ago it might've been a sea breeze. Mularabone would be here to smell that salty air but not me. I'd be scratching across Europe all the way from Africa, my skin and features evolved into something paler and sharper to suit my new home and diet.

We go up through the hole and slide the cover across behind us. We get to our feet on the surface and just breathe for a moment. The sun has already gone down but there is still a little bit of light about to stroke our skin.

This time, and the time just before sunrise, are my favourites. The sun and the moon seek each other in an endless courtship around the earth, and it is these times when they must come together briefly, before going back to that endless circling and tremendous longing. They can never truly consummate their love, just these rare moments at the beginning of the night and the end of the day, and the beginning of the day and the end of night, where they can enjoy the soothing touch and the gentle poetry of the other. I feel cleansed by it as though love itself is the water of life, the elixir of everlasting existence, and the constant reinforcement that nothing is born or dies, but all things are in a continuous state of change from one thing to another.

'Ssshhh,' says Mularabone quickly.

'I didn't say anything,' I whisper back, too loud like a petulant child.

'Don't fucken *think* anything!'

In the bottom corner of my eye I see his hand drifting to the small of his back to where the death-spitter is, and then I hear *that* voice.

'Evening boys.'

Suddenly there are a dozen Water Board troopers all around us, rising out of the sand like wind spirits, weapons pointing at our hearts. Mularabone's hand hovers for a moment, caught in the middle of his movement. The drugs and grog and electricity flash through our bodies in a spasm of memory.

'I'll take that,' says Jack, and the moment of decision is

gone, as Jack grabs the death-spitter from Mularabone with the barrel of his weapon touching him right between the shoulder blades.

'Face down, gents. You know the drill.'

Jack knows that his Eastern States colonial act gives us the shits like nothing else on earth. We are both smashed from behind and find ourselves sprawling in the dust. Mularabone is spewing.

'They learnt that off us,' he spits through sandy teeth.

'Get the hatch off,' we hear Jack say.

There is a scraping and two troopers drop into the hole.

'There's another door, boss,' one trooper calls out.

'Blow the fucken thing!' Jack yells.

There is a terrific thud as the booby trap goes off and the two troopers are skewered on ten or so short spears that Young James has rigged up. They don't even have time to scream, they're already dead.

'Get back! Get back!' screams Jack.

'Maybe youse were expecting a cuppa tea?' says Mularabone into the dirt.

Jack rounds on him and puts his boot onto the back of Mularabone's woolly head, pushing his face hard into the desert floor.

'Maybe they'll be havin a cup of tea in a couple of days when half a dozen deep penetration missiles rain down on this spot, ya fucken Neanderthal! I've got your coordinates now!'

Mularabone and I both enjoy a secret smile; he couldn't keep up his Rum Corps accent very long. Typical Jack, as soon as something goes wrong, he goes to shit.

Jack strides back to the hole, and shines a torch onto the speared troopers. He takes out his PersNav and double checks the coordinates.

'Let's move, or they'll be up our arse with ready-react force.'

Jack knows he can't take the uncles' perimeter defence for granted. He's just found out the hard way. One of the troopers speaks into his radio and we see a vehicle start up about a kilometre away from our position and head straight for us at full pelt. Jack comes over to me.

'We won't leave you alone, Conman. Not until you accept whose side you are really on.'

'I've already accepted that, Jack.'

He kicks me hard in the guts.

'You're a child, Conway.' He kicks me again.

Even with the sudden pain in my ribs, I feel like laughing.

In Jack's voice I hear the inner tremble. He is my younger brother. He thinks he hates me. He just lacks the courage to believe in anything. Our father saw to that. Each time I meet him he seems further away from himself. The gulf between us is wide – but not as wide as that terrible lonely distance contained within him. Now he's gonna get expansive, he won't be able to stop himself. It's like a child's comfort blankie that he carries around.

'There is a new world here, boys,' Jack says. 'You just haven't been in it.'

'No, it's still comin, it just ain't what you think, Djenga!' Mularabone fires back.

My eyes go to him. It's not like Mularabone to feel the need to speak. But he doesn't look at me; he is concentrating hard on Jack's boots. Jack strides the three steps and one boot goes back for the kick. The boot goes in but at the very last moment Mularabone spins his body on the earth like a dance move. His knee coming up knocks away the barrel of the trooper's weapon at his back, he catches Jack's kick, and twists. Down comes Jack; the fool has forgotten how fast Mularabone can be, and the PersNav falls from his hands. Still on his back, Mularabone jams his boot hard into Jack's groin and grabs the death-spitter from Jack's belt and brings it down hard on the handheld navigation computer. The blow smashes the gadget open, spilling wires out the side, and in the same movement Mularabone tosses away the weapon.

Three troopers fall on Mularabone and blows rain down on him while he lies still. I'm blinking and almost smiling. Fuck, he's good. His mind never stops. Of course he is willing to die to delete those coordinates.

Jack gets to his feet.

'Fuck! Fucken Countryman bastard!'

He kicks Mularabone hard.

'How's ya missile coords now, Jack?' Mularabone laughs at him through the blood and the dust mixing in his mouth.

'Shut up. We found this place once! We'll find it again!'

The vehicle comes roaring up and we're bathed in the headlights before the machine slews to a dusty halt right next to us. A figure jumps out of the dual-cab and strides towards us through the dust.

'Jack! Jack! What the fuck are you doing?' he booms.

'He attacked me, sir!'

'Leave it!'

'We lost two troopers down the hole from his fucking booby trap!'

'Your orders were to arrest these two and nothing else! If you sent two men down there, it is on your head.'

'We couldn't let the opportunity ...'

'Shut up! Your entire fucking command is hanging from a thread!'

'He smashed my PersNav, sir.'

The big man strides right up to Jack like he might strike him.

'If you mess up one more thing, you'll be cleaning toilets in the officers' mess at Port Fremantle for the rest of your pathetic fucking life! Understand?'

Jack doesn't respond.

'Understand?'

'Yes.'

'Yes, what?'

'Yes, sir.'

Mularabone and I share a look. We can't see the big man's face clearly in the glare of the headlights – but we know that voice. We know it even though we've never heard it before. Whether it is genetic or environmental, siblings always have a sameness of making language. Even if they haven't spent much time together. Some malicious emotion is clawing at my guts but Mularabone is as light as a feather, in spite of the beating he's just taken.

'I think he's been *damming* up his feelings for too long,' says Mularabone, indicating Jack with his lips.

'Damming things up can be bad,' I agree.

'Damming stops the flow.'

'No flow, that's dam hard.'

The fidgety little bastard in Jack's eye is throwing televisions out the window.

Greer the Guardian turns to us. 'On your feet, gentlemen.'

The troopers covering us step back.

'Jump into the vehicle. I have a proposition for you.'

I get up and help Mularabone up. He took a good beating but he's pretty pleased with himself. He flashes a bloody smile to Jack. 'Out of my way, Neanderthal boy, there's a new world coming.'

Ghost of History: Djenga Gods

We sit near the fire not saying much, listening to our stomachs growl. Fremantle is in his own world. He looks like he's been sitting here for millennia. The trees have grown up around him and the wind blows right through him.

We've been waiting back in Beeliar's camp down near the river mouth. The Countrymen have gone off somewhere to perform death rituals and sorry business for the young fullas killed by Stirling's men. They've been gone for days, maybe weeks. Occasionally we hear singing and clapsticks from somewhere up the river, but mostly it is quiet. The wind is still blowing off the ocean but the rain has dissipated. We buried Stirling and the others up the river. The bosun read from the Bible. Fremantle didn't stay for the burial but wandered off somewhere.

When the Countrymen come back to camp one morning, they come noiselessly with no warning. One moment we are all alone by the Darbal Yaragan, the next we are surrounded by painted-up warriors with short, stout spears. The Beeliar Birdiya nudges Fremantle with his spear, and the good captain surfaces from his thoughts.

'My nephew – your brother – finish!' says Beeliar.

Fremantle looks to me. I wonder who he sees.

'Your brother – Stirling.'

'No. Not my brother,' says Fremantle.

'My nephew – your brother – finish!'

'He sees you both in navy uniform,' I tell Fremantle. 'You

have the same ceremony – so brothers. He is saying the deaths cancel each other out, honour way.'

Fremantle is giving me that same look from the first day on the beach when I gave him the pointing-with-my-lips gesture.

Fremantle nods. 'Finish,' he agrees.

The spears are put away, and the men sit around us. Fremantle launches into a dissertation about the coming of the white men. This is what he has been thinking about.

'Many, many Djenga will come. They will be like the reeds by the river.'

I say nothing to assist, as Fremantle acts out the soldiers, the convicts, the lumberjacks, and the farmers. In mime and broken English, he presents the methodology of colonisation and how the English have been doing it for hundreds of years. Fremantle's oration is a cold appraisal of likely events, clinical appreciation by a commissioned officer of the Royal Navy.

It soon becomes disjointed, not so much because of the translation issues, but because the Countrymen cannot accept the probable behaviour of the Europeans. And anyway, the Law is the same for all men, and our spears are sharp and straight and strong, they seem to be saying. The conversation keeps coming back across the fire to Fremantle:

Why?

Why would they do that?

They don't need to bring sheep and cattle; we have kangaroos.

If they cut down the trees, the forest will die.

How can they kill more whales than they need to eat?

This discussion rages back and forth for an hour or so.

Then Fremantle looks across at me as though seeing me for the first time.

'He doesn't believe me, Mister Conway.'

'It does sound a little far-fetched, sir.'

Fremantle looks quickly back to me. He can't hold his serious face for a moment longer and breaks open into laughter.

'You're right, Mister Conway. It does sound a little far-fetched.'

We both sit there, laughing like madmen, with the Countrymen looking on with bemused expressions.

This time Fremantle really lets go. He is close to the edge. He's been around death, and even killed before, but I venture to say he's never before put a pistol to the throat of a lieutenant governor of one of His Majesty's colonies and pulled the trigger before. I can see it tugging at the corners of his eyes. The Birdiya sees it too; some dark shape crouching there and, with long claws grabbing at the edges of those wet orbs, hanging on like a hungry crocodile trying to drag its prey under.

'History has spewed us up, Mister Conway, at this precise moment.'

Silence.

We listen to the bush.

Fremantle suddenly sits up, his face calm, and leans in to the Birdiya.

I lean forward to hear what is said. But right at the crucial moment of Fremantle speaking, there is an eruption of noise from some young Countrymen just over at the next fire; they hoot and jeer as two fullas have a play wrestle. Fremantle is sitting back and the Birdiya is smiling and nodding.

Fremantle stands and, motioning for me to follow, moves away down towards the river. I get up, excusing myself from the company of the senior Countrymen with a nod, which they don't acknowledge. I always get the feeling that my body language amuses them in some way.

Fremantle stops. We're on a beach in Walyalup, looking out across the vast expanse of the Darbal Yaragan. It is quiet and still. And yet so full of life that it is bursting. We sit on the sand and look out across the water to where the river flows out to the open sea.

'If you were God, or at least, a god, what would you do?' Fremantle says.

'Do?'

'Exactly. What would you do?'

'I could do whatever I wanted?'

'Precisely.'

'Nothing. I'd probably *do* nothing.'

'What would you want?'

'A quiet life. A family. Some land. Abundance. Freedom.'

'But you could have the whole world?'

'I've seen a lot of the world, sir. The old world is all the same, and the new world is being harnessed by those same powers. If I am a god, I don't need it, and I want no part of it.'

'I thought you would say that, Conway.'

'What if I'd responded that I want a tonne of roast beef? A million gallons of German beer? And a hundred of the finest Parisian strumpets in the business?'

Fremantle laughs. His laugh is so contagious, I'm soon laughing too.

'Do you have any brothers?'

'Yes,' I say, and then wished I hadn't been so hasty.

There is a scurry of activity in the water just in front of us, and the surface explodes with small silver fish in a last ditch attempt to evade the predator beneath the surface.

'Why do you think Cain really killed Abel?'

'Jealous for their father's love,' I say.

'How could a loving father allow for one son to feel neglected?'

'Perhaps Abel was caught in his own trap?'

'I believe that it was between the brothers.'

'Do you think Cain was a drinker, sir?'

'Absolutely.'

'What about Abel?'

'Probably.'

We laugh. The half-moon peeps over the high country across the river.

'We need to bring something to the table, Mister Conway. The Countrymen need to benefit from our presence; otherwise Stirling's death is in vain.'

'If you hadn't killed him, the Countrymen would have killed you.'

'That's not why I did it.'

'They will send ships for us, sir. His Majesty will seek justice.'

'Then we must be ready. Ready for his justice.'

And that's when it was born: two Djenga men standing on a river beach in a Country where they did not yet belong. We would have to earn our place.

'And why "Parisian", Conway?'

'Have you ever been to Paris, sir?'

'I wish you'd stop calling me sir.'

Thirty-three: Taken In

Mularabone and I sit in the back seat of the dual-cab, with Greer in the front seat next to the driver, and Jack in the back tray with the other troopers. I want to yell out to Jack, but that's just impulses from the boy in me, the wounded child wanting to hit back, to taunt, all those things that I despise in him. We stare ahead, past the trooper driving, and into the shaft of light cast by the headlights. Jack will have to sit in the back with the other troopers and deal with the rushing desert air without any acknowledgement from me.

Greer swivels in his seat and faces us. In the reflected muted glow from the nav screen and the weapons screen on the dash, we can see Greer clearly. He is bigger than The Sarge, a little heavier in the face, but unmistakeably his brother.

I struggle to meet his eye.

'My name is Greer. Greer Sargeant. I know you were both in my brother's cadre. It is an honour to finally meet you both.'

'We respected your brother,' says Mularabone.

I look past Greer into the desert illuminated by our headlights.

'You ever go up against us?' asks Mularabone.

'Once,' says Greer. 'No, twice.'

We listen to the sound of the engine of the vehicle.

'Come on. What?' says Mularabone.

'Not much to say. The first time, only Jack and I escaped with our lives. The second time ... I found my brother dead.'

'Greer ...' I begin.

His eyes flick to me, pouncing on my tone. His right hand makes a loose fist and does one small downward movement: stop/pull up/silence. His eyes flick to the driver, who hasn't noticed anything.

'We will have time to talk, Conway.'

Greer turns back to the front. Mularabone and I exchange a look. It's two hours in the vehicle back to the Water Board compound across the open plain. We settle back into our seats to sit it out.

The motion of the vehicle takes me straight back to another time and place, not far from here. That time my father took me pig hunting: I get caught behind, and as I'm running with him to the wounded feral beast, I fall, and cut my knee deeply. My father doesn't wait for me and yells abuse back at me as he sprints through the scrub, rifle in hand. I can hear the two dogs, Clacker and Bindi, barking like crazy at the cornered pig. I hobble on with the blood oozing down my leg. There is a gunshot. My father has caught the pig. Then another shot. I try to run, sensing that something isn't right. By the time I get there he has already cut the pig deep to bleed it. I go almost right up to him before I see the other furry body lying in the long grass. Clacker is licking the blood from the kill, so it's not him. Bindi. I go to her. She is shot through the head.

I turn and he is staring at me. He knows I love Bindi. And Mum loves that little dog too. He's done it on purpose. I bend over Bindi and insert my finger into the wound. The little shards of skull are crunchy and the blood is thick and sticky. My finger goes in like my fist into the skulls of the rednecks in the front bar of the pub in the middle of nowhere. I extract my finger and wipe the blood in a single line down the front of my face. My father watches me with a strange look on his face.

I shake these dream memories out and force myself to be here, riding in the Water Board dual-cab with my brother, staring into the darkness beyond the vehicle. I feel a twinge of fear in my guts because 44 is crouching at the edge of this darkness. I'm heading to the Water Board compound. He can remember my fear of this place. I have to rid myself of him. It's coming. I can feel it.

No one speaks again until we are inside the compound. The dual-cab eases its way through the main gate, past the guard towers, and goes down to the far end of the compound. We drive past the now repaired solar power unit, and park next to a donga. These are the quarters for the troopers and their officers. As soon as the vehicle stops, Jack and the other troopers jump down from the back. They stand a little way off, cradling their weapons and watching us get out. Greer shows us to the door of the donga.

'Sleep here. In the morning we fly south for our business,' he says quietly.

Mularabone and I go in and the door is locked behind us. There is a light on and we have control of the switch. We sit on the cots facing each other.

'You alright, my coorda?'

'Yeah,' I hear myself lying.

'He's like The Sarge, isn't he?'

'Yeah.'

There is a long silence. We can hear the hum of the powerlines, and a vehicle driving off in the distance.

'There is a power, a strength, a connection between the brothers … Could you feel it?'

Mularabone looks at me. 'It's between us, coorda.'

I go over to the light switch. Mularabone swings his feet onto his cot. Out of the corner of my eye I think I see Nayia standing by my bed with a smile on her face. For the first time since leaving the cavern I allow myself to think of her. I snap my head around to face her but there is just Mularabone and me in this small box-cell with artificial light.

I hit the light switch and cross back to my cot in darkness and lie down.

The box is so completely dark, it's like the air has a different texture – two sides of a coin, which impossibly both show at once, lightness as though I am in the void between the worlds, and a heaviness that presses down upon me. Even in this absolute darkness I can feel the tightness of the space. I could be anywhere.

I hear the evenness of Mularabone's breathing. I feel how big his spirit is – all around me, filling up this black box like a gas that can take on the shape of any space that contains him. I am reaching out to his spirit. I know we can share dreams and memories. Now I have to draw him to me consciously. I dare not speak of this secret to my brother. I have to let him see and judge for himself. And if there is judgement for me to face – so be it. I close my eyes and reach out to my Countryman brother with the watery limbs of my spirit.

Shared Dream Memory: The Sarge
(May His Soul Find Peace)

It is hot. Even without the sun, and with the vast starry night sucking up the warm air, it is hot. In that moonless night I creep down with The Sarge, and we set charges on absolutely everything. Exactly as The Sarge said, there are only four troopers in the compound. The Sarge and I are humping heavy charges and, by the time we get inside their wire, the troopers are already dead. We hadn't heard a thing. Young James had taken care of all of them with his nulla-nulla.

The base is standard – concrete dongas dug into the earth surrounded by wire-walls and huge mounds of dirt to block our RPG attacks. We set the charges; then the lads get into the Water Board uniforms, including The Sarge and me. We had no choice, as the only Djenga in the ambush party. We're giving Young James shit, because our uniforms are covered in blood and gore. I'm just finishing the activation code for the charges on the earthmoving equipment they had in this sandbagged hangar – when I hear the distinct scream of a child. Mort has discovered her walking around, apparently lost, a little Djenga girl, aged about ten. She is dragged into the hangar, and everyone assembles.

Then we hear them coming. They're flying across the open ground in their AFVs, lights blazing. Heading for home. Heading straight for us. We look at the little girl. Everything's turning to shit.

'We gotta get rid of her,' says The Sarge.

'Hide her?' asks Thanpathanpa.

Then everyone is talking at once. The adrenaline is coming onto us early, because the plan is out the window.

'There's gonna be a firefight now.'

'The plan can still work – but they have to dismount.'

'Keep her with us.'

'Tie her up.'

'She's only a child.'

'Come off it.'

In the silence that falls on us, we can hear the AFV engines revving in the distance.

'We'll draw straws,' says The Sarge.

He gets six sticks, and makes one short.

The little girl is crying now, her tears sparkling in my torchlight and then hitting the red dirt at our feet.

We draw straws – and The Sarge gets the short one.

The AFVs are still a long way off when they fire their first round, and we hear it drop short.

'They know we're here!' says The Sarge.

'They don't know we're here. How ...?'

The Sarge turns on me; he's holding the little white girl by the shoulder, his weapon in the other hand.

'Why are they fucken shooting? Course they know we're here!'

He slings his weapon. 'Now, move!'

We switch off our torches, and quickly move out of the hangar to our pre-arranged positions. The Sarge heads off in the other direction, back towards the dug-in donga, which is our fire-everything position. I'm sprinting for my shell-scrape on top of the earth mound above the main hangar when their twenty-five millimetre cannon-fire starts raking the ground of the base. The AFVs are closer than we thought, and coming on at speed. In the dark I see Thanpathanpa get ripped apart by the big shells. I hit my controls, and the big charges out the front go off; the leading AFV is destroyed. That should slow them down. But it doesn't. Three more AFVs are still coming hard.

Behind me, in the direction of our FE posi, I hear the distinct 'whump' of a grenade. HE rounds start falling in the compound. We gotta move. Get back. Fire everything. Get out. We can leave the girl here. Their attack helicopters will be here in fifteen minutes. I roll, and crawl back down the mound, and into the hangar. I'm running back past the big dozers when I see The Sarge coming back the other way. As I get close, I see his weapon is still slung, and his big blade is in his hand. The same type of knife my father carried. As I get to him he doesn't seem present. Faraway. To start with, I think he might be hit. He is dazed. My eyes roam over him looking for the wound – but there is nothing there. Then I see the blood on his blade.

'Where is the girl?'

He doesn't answer. Outside, shells and cannon-fire are raining down.

'We can leave her for them, they'll be here soon. Come on, Sarge! We gotta blow and go!'

'They had their wives here,' he says. 'Wives and kids. One of them was on the radio, calling them back.'

'Let's leave them all and go!' I'm screaming – but I can't take my eyes off that blood on his blade. 'Where is she?'

'Let's turn and burn,' he says.

A big round hits the front of the hangar, and we are both thrown down. We hear Mort fire the big charges on the perimeter. They must be right here.

I'm grabbing The Sarge by the shoulders. 'Where is the girl?'

He goes to sheath his blade but I grab at it.

'What have you done?'

'Wha'd you think I was gonna do? Why did we draw straws?'

'We'll leave her.'

'She's gone. They're all gone. Let's fucken go!'

I punch The Sarge right between the eyes. He goes backwards, and falls, and I jump on him. He punches me, knocking me off him, and his blade comes for me. I smash him with my weapon, right as he slashes at me, opening up a big cut in my leg. My weapon goes flying, and I pull out my knife, and jump on him. With his massive strength, he gets to standing, with me hanging on. Up close, I see that his eyes aren't just weeping – but tearing themselves apart from the inside.

'Conway ...' he starts, and before he can stab me, I stab him, my blade going right into his guts. Goes in deep. We're standing, hugging like brothers at a funeral, and his blade with her blood and mine, drops to the dirt floor.

'Finish me, brother,' he whispers.

My blade flashes across his throat. His body slides down mine. The cannon fire is smashing into the outside of the building. I turn and run. Outside it is chaos. I have to get to the FE posi. I take a chance and sprint across the open ground. I am almost there when I start to draw fire. I go down into the entrance at full sprint, and trip over something in the dark. The door to the dug-in donga is open, and I go sprawling and sliding into the room.

'Report?' I yell.

'Mort.'

'James.'

'Down!' I scream.

I yank the control from my webbing and hit FE. Outside, everything we set goes off, and the explosions chuck us around inside that donga like a handful of gravel. I'm bleeding from the mouth and I've lost my weapon. I switch on my torch to find it, and then me, Young James, and Mort – we see them all. All the women and kids The Sarge grenaded.

I go back up the sloping entrance to where I fell. I am still on my hands and knees. Then I see what I tripped over. The Sarge had cut her throat.

'Come, brother!' yells Mort, and he gets us all moving.

We go up and run for the pathway we cut through their wire earlier on. There is still one AFV on the far side of the battered compound, trying to negotiate a path through the debris to our position. Not to our position, but to that donga. Mort urges us on, running, running, as though I could outrun these demons that are now swirling all around me. In the distance, we hear the attack choppers.

Thirty-four: Keeping Enemies Close

It feels like early morning. Hard to tell exactly what time it is in our windowless metal box. Time is a trick, anyway. Like history, and genetics, and skin pigment. Mularabone and I sit on my cot with our boots on, holding hands. After the shared dream, we haven't slept. We have sat, holding hands like we are conducting a sorry business vigil. With the darkness and the silence, and the touch of our hands, skin on skin, we have cocooned ourselves in our hope for understanding and acceptance.

'Why didn't you tell me, coorda?'

'Shame, brother.'

Eventually our hands disengage, and Mularabone goes back over to his own cot.

'Hurry up and wait' – The Sarge taught us that lesson well. Not that we have any routine to do in our cell. No water to wash with. No food to eat. No shaving gear. No weapons to clean. Just our boots. And our UV paste. Mularabone hands me a small woven bag, ingeniously lined with plastic and filled with the secret paste made by Aunty Ouraka. The Countrymen aren't caught up on who caused the ozone depletion, just the reality of dealing with it. Mularabone and I have heard it is much worse down south.

I give my exposed skin a good coating, my nostrils flaring at the sharp smell of the herbs. Like a surgeon washing hands before an operation, my digits move over all my exposed skin in a strict pattern, replicating that ancient journey of the ancient creator spirits of the land, painstakingly taught to me by Mularabone when we were still young. Without the commitment to the spiritual protection, the science will never work. Us Djenga have had to relearn that in this Country. When Aunty Ouraka applies the UV paste, she sings the soul protection charm. For her the charm is more powerful than the science. I see them as equal, maybe even the same thing. Any mistake can mean a black blister that won't go away for years, or even a slow painful death as all your flesh is sucked and burnt inward through the tiny black blister.

My head is already scarred up from that trooper's broken bottle, from watching the footy with me mates, so it isn't vanity for me, just basic survival. We sit on our thin unforgiving beds with our paste on.

Neither of us took our boots off to sleep. Neither of us would've been remotely surprised if we'd been dragged out in the middle of the night for interrogation, or brainwashing, or gender reassignment, or just plain old-fashioned torture. Human beings behave very strangely when given absolute power over other humans. My father taught me this. Maybe strange, maybe predictable.

I sit in half-lotus, and stretch myself out along the length of my bed. I love the feel of those back muscles stretching away from my hips. I wriggle my toes in my boots. My feet always feel like they shrink a little overnight when I sleep with my boots on, and I awake to this turtle-in-a-shell feeling, until I can get the blood flowing through them again. My forearm still aches from where Mularabone cut me with his bone knife.

Where we are going I have only visited in dreams of future past. Whilst I can guess what the Djenga want from me, I have no way of knowing what the Country may demand. I have dreamed of the birth of the thriving new culture, with the best of the Europeans and Countrymen swimming together in the pot. I feel lighter after the shared dream memory, as though the weight of my shame has been shared with my brother.

Without warning the door slides back and there is an armed trooper in the doorway. He wears full UVP, a helmet, and holds a weapon slanted across his chest.

'Come on! Rise and shine!'

We both stand smoothly. Mularabone steps out quickly and nearly knocks the trooper over. We haven't turned on our light so the trooper's eyes haven't adjusted to the darkened space and he doesn't see Mularabone coming. I follow as the trooper staggers back a couple of steps trying to regain his balance.

Outside the sun isn't up yet and the compound is bathed in light from LLG bulbs set up high on bare metal poles. The trooper comes back at Mularabone, raising his weapon to strike him a blow.

'Stand down!' a voice booms and the trooper lowers his weapon, slumps his shoulders and steps back like the schoolyard bully caught in the act.

'You'll keep,' the trooper mutters.

The booming voice belongs to Greer, standing by a vehicle with Jack. Mularabone steps towards them with a big smile.

'You sure got a discipline problem, Jack,' he beams.

Jack shifts on his feet and stares at the offending trooper. If looks could kill that man would be face down in the red dirt with a wooden stake protruding from his torso, low, where his liver is.

'Sleep well, gentlemen?' asks Greer.

'Like a baby,' says Mularabone. 'Woke up every two hours looking for a nipple, and then pissed and shat myself.'

'This vehicle will take us to the runway,' Greer says, indicating a cruiser nearby. 'We'll board a plane going south. We'll eat on the plane.'

'Thought there were no more flights?' I say.

'You been in the boondocks too long, Conman. Lost touch with reality,' says Jack.

'Mount up. Let's get this show on the road,' says Greer.

'Have a nice trip,' says Jack.

There is something about the way he says it, like that snarl he shivved me with about my mother. The fidgety little bastard in his eye is visible even through his dark sunglasses, pacing and swinging some nasty little weapon back and forth.

We look around. Down near the gate where the dam used to be are three heavy cruisers. Troopers are moving all around them, refuelling and loading on ammo. We know we have to go south but we can't have him going out to look for Birra-ga's cave. Greer follows our look.

I eyeball Greer. 'Isn't Jack coming with us?'

'He has his own affairs here.'

Beside me, Mularabone goes all loose, like he's getting ready to throw a punch, or take one.

'If Jack's not coming with us, we're not going.'

Greer stares at me. I stare him down. I can see my tracks leading forward, being obliterated as I step into them, and my track leads straight through him. There is a valley in his heart and I'm wandering along it with a grenade in each hand. Greer can see I've already pulled the pins. His eye is trained to notice such detail. He glances over to Mularabone who gives him the tiniest of nods: Jack should come. Greer turns to Jack and tries to keep his voice conciliatory.

'Get your shit, Jack. You're coming.'

'There's no way I'm –'

'You're coming with me, lackey boy!' I spit at him, pressing my advantage.

'Shut up!' Greer cracks at me, his voice hard and loud, and his stare crazy. He turns back to Jack, who looks even more pissed off. 'You've got thirty seconds,' he says and climbs into the vehicle.

Jack spins on his heel and goes over to where troopers are checking the weapons on this armoured fighting rig. Greer gives Mularabone and me a look: you're right. Jack grabs out a pack and comes over to us. Mularabone and I climb into the vehicle. Greer has his usual driver – so the only place for Jack is in the back, the open tray. Mularabone gives me a little slap on the shoulder. We hear Jack in the back on his comms. It is a short, terse conversation with his 2IC.

Over to the east the sun is just coming up. The compound lights go off. We drive out slowly.

Thirty-five: Brothers Going South

We drive out through the stunted gums and sandbags bristling with machineguns that surround the base. Our eyes go out to the remains of the dam structure. The water finished the job that we started, and there are concrete blocks as big as cars washed halfway down the valley. There are a couple of big earthmoving machines moving down to where the river is flowing through the gap. Above the wreckage we can see that the Country that has been freed from the weight of the water is beginning to dry out.

Behind the wire and other defences of the compound, there's not a single structure that isn't peppered with bullet holes, or even more substantial damage from exploded grenades. There are still wet marks on the ground from where men have lain and bled.

'He's a one-man wrecking ball, your mate,' says Mularabone.

'Not my fucken mate.'

'Report said they were attacked by a fire-team of thirty,' says Greer.

'We were well trained,' says Mularabone, and somehow makes other meanings of words not said about The Sarge reach out to me, and to Greer. This is something we have learned from Warroo-culla and Birra-ga. Greer and I both nod, instantly understanding that this reaching out, and these meanings, are not meant to unfold on a conscious level. But we know that we already feel like a team.

It takes about five minutes to get to the runway where a Water Board corporate jet is waiting for us. The red dust is still asleep and hardly stirs at our passing. In another hour this journey would create a mini dust storm. As the vehicle swings into the open and heads for the waiting plane, Mularabone and I notice the armed men in the tree line. It sure don't look like they are in total control of the countryside, or they don't expect to be. The vehicle pulls up next to the jet. Jack jumps out of the back tray.

We climb onto the plane. The chairs are big and leather and set out in an open plan. We've only just sat down when the cabin door is shut behind us and the jet engines start to rev. A young Djenga appears in the cockpit doorway in the uniform of a Water Board officer. He is very clean. He crosses to the cabin door and twists the internal lock into position.

'Good morning, gentlemen. I would ask you to strap yourselves in for take off. Please place all baggage and weapons in the overhead lockers. I'll serve breakfast as soon as we are in the air.'

Mularabone and I look at each other. We have no bags, packs or weapons. Jack stashes his assault rifle and pack above his seat.

The jet goes to the top of its taxi and turns and the throttle goes down. I swivel and look out of the window, and look at the Country flashing past.

I get this pang deep in my heart, like I'm never gonna see this Country again. My Country. It cuts me. I can hardly breathe; the more I try to force air into my lungs by bellowing out my ribcage like a didj player, the more faint I become, until eventually I start to feel like I am leaving my body.

There I am, down there, sitting in my leather armchair, seatbelt buckled low over my hips, a lump in my throat, tears in my eyes, and a vice gripping the organs at the base of my stomach until the pain is white hot. There I am, staring through the window, leaning into the little porthole, looking down at that beautiful red dust Country as the jet plane lifts up and away. The river shines silver in the morning sun, snaking its way below the smashed dam and filling up the valley.

There I am staring down to see a lone figure standing right out in the open, past the end of the runway. I flick my eyes back to Greer and Jack. They aren't looking. I look back at the lone figure getting smaller and smaller. I stare at the person on the ground until I am back in my body and looking down, and feeling the connection, and knowing it is Nayia.

She is dancing in the morning sun. I drink her in and hold her in the hollow cheeks of my mouth. I swirl her around, tasting her, feeling out her contours with my tongue and lips. Then the jet banks, turning away south, and she is gone. I spit her gently into my spirit hand, and press her in against my chest, pushing her through the warm curtains of my flesh until she is hard up against my beating heart. She curls up against the heat and the motion of that never-ending organ, and, like a child in a womb, is lulled easily off to sleep.

The front door opens and out comes the Water Board officer with four self-contained meals in silver trays stacked on top of each other. He hands one to each of us, starting with Greer. He doesn't look directly at Mularabone. He puts a big pot of coffee on a shelf next to the door.

'Flying time will be two hours.'

Greer gives him a nod and he disappears back into the front section of the plane. Mularabone and I give each other a little look. We help ourselves to more coffee. We eat our pre-packed Water Board breakfast in silence. It's like being back in the cadres for a moment, it all tastes like shit: warm and moist – and therefore food.

Finally we are full. We sit back. We wait. We watch Greer.

He takes out a briefcase and fills in a few papers. We watch his hand move his pen across the paper. He puts the papers away and inputs a few things into his handheld computer. He drinks coffee.

'I have been taken off all other missions, to give this one the highest priority,' Greer says.

'What other missions?' asks Mularabone.

For a moment, a hardness flashes through Greer's eyes, and then is gone, replaced by his soft, diplomatic smile.

'We asked our computers to come up with names,' says Greer.

'And they came up with ours,' I say.

'Complete with vision of you confessing,' he adds.

'To what?' I ask, looking directly at Jack.

'Confessing to whatever I asked you to,' Jack replies with a smile.

'I've been trying to meet you for a long time,' says Greer.

Jack looks away, out the small window. Greer isn't telling us anything. We know the drill; this conversation is for Jack's benefit, to mask our true purpose. This is just protocol. I look out the small window of the plane. Beneath us the red country is laid out like a massive sand painting. My eyes follow the contours of the land carved out by primordial water flows.

'You were with my brother when he died?' asks Greer.

I look up to meet his direct gaze. I nod.

'Friendly fire?'

I nod.

'He loved you lads like sons,' says Greer.

I nod. My tongue seems to have turned to mud. I glance over at Jack. He looks lost. The figure inside his eyeball is slumped at the base of the dead tree. The figure's head is down. He might be weeping. I look down at my hands. I remember my father washing his hands in grog, wringing them over and over in the bowl of clear liquid until the grime was gone. Jack is looking at his hands too. For a moment the cabin is full of the stench of grog and blood – and then it is gone.

'Are you two really brothers?' Greer asks.

Jack snorts.

'No,' I say. 'My entire family were killed in a frozen urine accident. No survivors ... A Water Board jet was flying over, maybe even this one, and they jettisoned some urine into the stratosphere, which froze, and plummeted out of the sky and ...'

'There is a story about two brothers ...' says Greer.

We wait for him to say more. The jet starts to level out. Greer is saying nothing more for now. We listen to the jet engines whine.

Mularabone finds a little compartment under the armrest of his chair. He flicks it open to find a pair of black silk eyeshades. With a huge smile, he digs them out and slips them on. I follow suit and slip behind the veil of personal dark.

'It's like having your own camp,' he says to me in Language.

I laugh, one, because I understood him, and two, because he's right. Under my dark shades I feel safe. I'm like a child covering my eyes to make the Hairy Man go away. And like the child, when I can't see the horror, I can easily believe that it is gone.

I put my hand over my chest, and I can feel both our hearts beating, Nayia's and mine.

Ghost of History: Me and Wobbegong Down by the Darbal Yaragan

Bright Eyes and I jump down from the cutter. We're on the south side of the Darbal Yaragan just below Manjaree. The marines follow us.

Fremantle is there with the Birdiya of Beeliar, and a large group of warriors. He has two cannon set up on the beach.

'Ah, Conway. Just in time.'

'The last of the 63rd are secure out on Wadjemup, sir.'

'I do wish you'd finish with the "sir".'

'Not easy to shed a skin, sir.'

Beeliar goes down the beach and places his wooden shield against a log. His shield, and that of Bright Eyes, is much smaller than the other warriors'. He comes back and speaks to his son in Language. Bright Eyes fits his spear into his throwing stick. The shield is about sixty yards to our front. Bright Eyes takes a few paces' run-up and throws his spear. The shaft flies from the woomera, curls, and then uncurls in midair, and then slams into the shield. A collective 'Oooh' rises up from the watching marines. Fremantle applauds like he is at the opera.

'Bravo! Bravo!'

The Birdiya picks up his nulla-nulla and shakes it with a 'Yaaaaah!'

Fremantle looks at Bright Eyes' shield, and points with his lips down the beach. Bright Eyes trots down the beach and sets his own shield next to his father's.

'Would you care to do the honours, Mister Conway?'

'If you would leave off with the "mister", it would assist the process, sir.'

'Touché, Mister Conway.'

One of my marines hands me his Brown Bess musket. I pour in some powder, bite open a cartridge, keeping the ball in my mouth, pour the remainder of the powder into the barrel, spit the ball in, push in the paper wad, and ram the load home. I take aim and fire. There is a resounding report and Bright Eyes' shield is flung backwards several feet. All the warriors run down the beach to inspect the damage. The round has blown a big hole in the shield, almost cutting the shield in half. The Birdiya shoves his fist into the hole, and nods grimly back to us.

'All shields,' calls Fremantle. 'All woornta!'

The Birdiya nods and all the warriors prop up their shields on the logs. They all come back to where we are at the cannon.

'Gunner! In your own time!'

The gunner pours in the powder, loads the canvas bag full of grapeshot, and rams it home.

'Prepare to fire! Fire!'

This time the report is so loud that many of the warriors fall to the sand, covering their heads. The Birdiya and Bright Eyes run forward to inspect the damage. Each warrior picks up his own shield. There is not a single shield not penetrated by at least one of the three and three-quarter inch lead balls. The Birdiya looks back to us. He shakes his nulla-nulla at us, 'Yaaaaah!'

Bright Eyes strides back to us and glares at me. I glance at Fremantle; the shields as targets were his idea. Fremantle gives me a nod. He's made his point. Bright Eyes throws his shot-up shield at my feet, his eyes still blazing. I can see a large chunk of the woornta blown away. The remaining surface is covered in intricate designs. Bright Eyes yanks the Brown Bess musket from my grasp. He steps over to the marine who handed me the weapon and divests him of his pouch. He turns back to me, and with an open palm shoves me backwards onto the sand. He turns and heads towards his camp, motioning for us to follow. The Birdiya and all the other warriors are already heading back.

'Still dreaming of beer, roast beef, and dancing girls, Mister Conway?'

I pick myself up.

'I don't care if they don't dance so well, sir.'

I look down to see the tiny jumping spider from the leaf in the river. The spider is clinging to the sleeve of my Royal Marines jacket. As I step off, the spider jumps off to land on my upper boot.

Overhead, Wardung sings out: 'Arrc! Aarrrc! Aaarrc!'

I catch up to Fremantle as he strides into the main camp. The Beeliar Birdiya is laughing by a big fire with his wives. Bright Eyes sits close by holding the Brown Bess, and joins in the mirth. We approach him and he motions us to sit. We're offered damper and chunks of cooked, still-warm meat. I'm reminded of going to my aunty's place in Plymouth as a child: she was always trying to fatten me up, and didn't seem happy unless I was eating. Her butter cake really was something special. This is a memory of the child Royal Marine. I'm going deeper. This is what Birra-ga was talking about.

We sit and eat with Beeliar watching over us with an expression just like my aunty's. I'm still eating when he leans in to speak to me. He is close enough to touch me on the upper arm as he speaks. He speaks slowly and evenly, and then his eyes start to lose focus. Then his voice is inside my head. Inside my head I understand his Language completely. It's like I'm falling into a mirror: everything on the other side is a reflection but has its own life and way of being. Everything is exactly the same but somehow very different.

The Birdiya gets his focus back in his eyes and I am released from his discourse. It's like he was holding me firm by the shoulders and suddenly lets me go. I sink back. I still haven't mastered the art of sitting on the ground without my spine collapsing, like the Countrymen do.

'Did you tell the Duke of Beeliar about my dreams?' Fremantle says.

'No, sir.'

Beeliar looks at Fremantle; his head goes back, his mouth opens, and out comes a pealing whine/call/yelp that reaches out and curls a circle of unease around all of us. It is so frightening, that dingo call, curling, snarling, and breaking, then rushing into the shore, all foamy and bloody. Fremantle is fixed by Beeliar who drops his head and smiles at him. Now Fremantle is in a whole other world. Everything he thought he knew now means nothing.

'Wobbegong!' says Beeliar.

'What's he saying?'

'Wobbegong,' repeats Beeliar. This time he jumps up and his feet do a slow stamp and his shoulders move like the carpet shark on patrol over the seaweed. Beeliar transforms into the shark for the tiniest of moments, just enough to give us belief, then he's there laughing at Fremantle. Wobbegong.

'Wobbegong!' says the Birdiya and points at Fremantle with the knuckle of his right forefinger, his finger curled back towards himself.

'You're saying I'm like that shark, the brown, speckled one?'

'Wobbegong.'

'He's saying you are that shark, sir.'

Fremantle turns to the Beeliar Birdiya. 'Boom!' he says.

Beeliar nods. 'Wobbegong: you, me – fishing in the river!' he says.

We are trying to free our Empire minds so we can understand.

He turns to me. 'Conway: you go,' he gestures to Bright Eyes with his lips, 'listen to water!'

He nods again. The Duke of Beeliar has spoken. This is the end of it for him.

Bright Eyes hands the Brown Bess to his father. Beeliar examines the firing pin. He reverses the musket and looks down the barrel.

'What is happening, Captain Fremantle?'

'Pilgrimages. You and I have different paths now. I am going to learn about fishing in the river, the Darbal Yaragan. You are going to learn to listen to water.'

Already I'm standing. Bright Eyes is gathering up his spears and thrower. Everyone's flesh has the texture of water. The Birdiya sees me looking and breaks into fresh laughter.

'By the time you get back, "Captain Fremantle" will be gone. And all that will remain will be Wobbegong. Mister Conway, you will be gone too. Then you will be Holy Water. Did you know that's what your name means?'

'Yes, sir.'

I drop my eyes before Captain Fremantle, respecting him as my birdiya. We have come on a long journey since I pointed with my lips, that first day on the beach at the river mouth. Now I am the novice, and Fremantle is the master. Now Charles Wobbegong Fremantle has the steerage of this unfolding mystery, partners with the Birdiya of Beeliar. Fremantle claps his hand on my shoulder. I look up, and he signals with his lips that Bright Eyes and I should leave on our water listening-odyssey. We turn, and go.

Thirty-six: Landing Down South

The angle of the aircraft alters in the air and there's a change in the note of the jets. We must be coming down for our landing approach. I take off my eyeshades. Mularabone is still asleep. I always admired his ability to sleep wherever and whenever he can. If he has ten minutes before 'GO' – he'll sleep for nine minutes and fifty seconds and then be wide awake. Jack also has his eyes shut. Him – I don't know if he's ever really slept. The rings under his eyes are dark and permanent. The Nyoongars in the tank called him Coomal – the possum, because of this feature. Like possums, Jack is a nocturnal animal. I think of him more as a bat; a vampire bat – like those angry little pale fullas from Larrakia Country. Greer is leaning over his personal computer. He has that stiffness in the chest and lower back that gives him away as Water Board Special Forces. Men who have worn a uniform for a long time retain a memory of it in their bodies. He looks up at me and holds my gaze.

When he tries to go deeper, he appears surprised to be confronted by the impenetrable soldier's look. I learned this look in the Royal Marines.

'I knew your father,' he says quietly.

I hold his gaze but don't react.

'We weren't friends,' he adds.

'Not brothers,' I say in a faraway voice.

'Why do you say that?'

'You're the second person to say that to me about my father.'

The door to the cockpit opens and the clean young Water Board officer steps out. He looks at us and then hesitates.

'Excuse me, sir ...'

'It's all right,' says Greer.

I glance at Jack. Everything looks a hell of a long way from all right with him. That fidgety little bastard is pacing back and forth in Jack's eye, flicking some metal thing in his hand out and then in again.

'We'll be on the ground in ten minutes, if you would care to strap yourselves in. Thank you.'

He turns and scurries back into the cockpit. Greer busies himself with putting away his stuff. Jack sits forward. He pulls a pistol from his belt and checks its readiness. Satisfied, he puts on his seatbelt, still holding the pistol in his right hand, pointing it at Mularabone and I. Mularabone stretches, and takes off his eye shades.

'I was close with your father. We were like brothers. That was before the grog.'

'He always had grog,' I say.

'Not always,' says Greer.

'Is there grog here?' asks Jack.

The jet touches down.

'If I catch you drinking, I will kill you myself,' says Greer quietly.

I look out the window to see the Country racing past us as the plane begins to brake. I can feel the Darbal Yaragan calling to me like I am a tidal flat, and that river is the moon. If I don't bend and go with the attraction, my whole heart will be sucked from my body – and stick to that river like a nail to a magnet. That's what I feel like – a nail ready to be hammered in. Like my whole purpose will be realised if a cosmic hammer smashes me on the head half a dozen times to push me into this earth, this wood, to make a join.

Thirty-seven: Trick of History

The clean Water Board officer comes out of the cockpit and releases the outside door. The bright morning sun floods the cabin and we stand to exit.

We go out in front of Jack as he gathers up his weapons and his pack. Outside there are armed Water Board troopers everywhere.

Two troopers come over and fall in with us. I look past them to the nose of the Water Board jet. There is a fulla standing there. He looks completely out of place in his traditional dress with full paint-up. The only part of his body not covered with white clay is his eyes. He looks at me steadily.

Mularabone follows my eye line.

'Who's that?' I whisper.

'Spirit fulla. Look again, coorda.'

I look again. I see the spirit fulla with his beard and prominent forehead bump: the old Birdiya of Beeliar. My hand asks the question of Mularabone.

'He's waiting for us, coorda.'

Over near the airport buildings we see a high wire fence, topped with razor wire, stretching in every direction to surround the airstrip. Behind the wire, just beyond the buildings, there are hundreds of Countrymen standing silently, watching us.

Jack turns to one of our assigned guards. 'What's going on here?'

'Dunno, sir. They all turned up this morning.'

Mularabone and I feel the scrutiny of that mass of dark brown eyes. They all look like strong men. Their bare chests are firm, scarred up, and well muscled. They all have nose-bones.

I glance back to the front of the jet and the spirit Birdiya is gone.

All around us there are other Countrymen doing the work of the airport, carefully watched by the Water Board troopers. They unload our plane and others, and carry out refuelling. This place is nothing like a civil facility. I'm reminded of the ancient Romans and their slaves. Sooner or later history will spew up a Spartacus.

Jack is eyeing the silent mass of Countrymen beyond the wire. He draws his pistol and aims it at the wall of dark brown flesh. There is no reaction from the Countrymen at all.

'How many bullets you got, Jack?' asks Mularabone.

Jack's head and eyes snap around to regard Mularabone. The pistol points at Mularabone's head. Mularabone holds his gaze, smiling his cheeky smile.

What now? he seems to ask with that smile.

The mass of Countrymen watch this action without blinking.

But Jack has nothing to say. He puts the pistol away.

'Go with Jack and recce from the air,' says Greer. 'We'll have a full briefing when you return.'

There is something in Greer's tone that immediately gives Mularabone and I the renewed understanding. This is the tone Fremantle used when he directed me to go on my water-learning odyssey with Bright Eyes. Mularabone knows this tone well from Birra-ga and Warroo-culla leading him and others into ceremony. Boys often have little or no warning before being taken to the men's camp in the middle of the night to begin the arduous journey to manhood. Now we all know that Jack is part of this, part of the layering of the dreaming of the two brothers; the grog dreaming. We jump into Greer's distraction.

'Why with Jack?'

'Jack's been here before. Haven't you, Jack?' Greer turns and walks off.

'Get these two into the chopper. I'll be there in a sec,' says Jack to the troopers, and follows his boss to the airport buildings.

I get that certain feeling and glance over to the waiting helicopter. Sitting in the front seat is the spirit Birdiya. Even from this distance he seems to be wearing a wry smile.

The troopers prod us with their weapons. We amble off towards the chopper. It is a small but heavily armed jet-copter, an eight-seater. By the time we get over to the machine, the spirit Birdiya is nowhere to be seen. We are strapped in and waiting. The large group of Countrymen turn and disappear into the scrub behind them, and in moments it's like they were never there.

A minute later Jack strolls over with the pilot. They climb in and the pilot fires up the rotors. We take off and head for the coast.

Below us we see hundreds of small settlements, with their individual huts clustered around a central, larger building. Each grouping has a responsibility over a certain water source, and a certain industry, and all of those are linked to the main port near the mouth of the Darbal Yaragan. The main roads are the Nyoongar highways that have been expanded. There are no square grids of streets and roads on Nyoongar Boodjar.

'Jack. Take us down the river.'

'We can't go down the river. It's dangerous.'

'That old fulla Rainbow Serpent can spit fire, coorda,' Mularabone warns.

'I know, bruz. Jack is too scared to fly over it.'

Mularabone and I are laughing.

Jack switches off our headphones. There is a heated exchange between him and the pilot. Mularabone flicks his hand open with one extended finger: Why? I touch my heart with three fingers: Feeling; I got a feeling.

The flying machine crosses the coast. Out to sea we can see the Koort Boodjar, Wadjemup. That's where Fremantle and the mob set up the station to 'process' all the Europeans who arrived, readying them to take their place in the new and evolving society. Assessing who was going to be able to make the leap of faith and who was not. Despite the opposition on both sides, they made it work. Jack switches our comms back on. I glance at Mularabone. He makes a sign with his hand in his lap: Child! I almost get the giggles. We'll be flying down that river all right. Jack has completely fallen for Greer's distraction. Now that I've got him to give ground, I wade on in with my navy cutlass.

'Seems to me, Jack, any success you mob have had is all on the backs of the Countrymen; their structure, their industry, their society ...'

'But without our technology ...'

'It was already working, Jack. How's the water supply here?'

There is no reply from Jack, just the wound-up whine of the engine, and the thudding of the rotors. The chopper is approaching the river mouth. I look down, half expecting to see Fremantle and me on the cutter, racing for the opening, not seeing the reef there. But there are only the foamy swells marching onto the sand.

'How are the water supplies in your cities, Jack?' I press my advantage. 'That's why Greer got us here. Your mob have fucked everything up.'

The chopper wheels down low and turns eastward above the river. The troopers on the automatic guns both cock their weapons.

'It was other countries that warmed the globe, not us. And besides,' says Jack, 'it was only a trick of history that allowed that first settlement to survive. The English sent two man-o'-wars to deal with the rebels. If they hadn't been lost at sea, this whole story would be different.'

The chopper belts along, low over the Darbal Yaragan. On our southern side is Dwerdaweelardinup. The Dogs. We take the left-hander past Garungup and keep going.

'Lost at sea, Jack?'

The whole problem of writing history down is exactly this. Who writes it down? Many current events fly so in the face of contemporary beliefs that they must be filtered to be written down in an acceptable form. In many instances this filtration process turns the actual events into fairytales, or worse, completely subverts the original events. Djenga seem to be good at this nursery version of history.

We take the right-hander and then the left.

'Put the radar into the water,' I tell Jack.

'What?' he says, not sure if he's heard right.

'Put your imaging radar into the water, and I'll give you an education.'

Jack nods tersely to the pilot. I've got his curiosity up now. He won't be able to resist proving me wrong. We cut down, below the huge cliffs to our right. The troopers with us are gripping their machineguns tightly. Below us, the deep water is about to open up. I lean forward, straining against the seatbelts so I can see the radar screen between Jack and the pilot, and ... bang! There they are. Flashing on the screen in sharp green outline are the foreign objects in the water. Their shape is almost too perfect. The two warships sent by the British government to deal with the Swan River Rebels, side by side on the bottom of the river.

Jack switches off our comms. He and the pilot are talking. The chopper wheels around for another pass. Maybe they don't believe their own equipment. We come in real low and slow down right over the spot below the cliffs. It is deep. The deepest spot in the river. But there they are, sitting on the bottom as if sunk only yesterday, masts still on the ships and all.

Jack and the pilot are still talking when the rocket is fired at us. Everything goes into slow motion. From up the cliff comes the fiery projectile and hits us right in the tail. We get a glance at the two Countrymen there, as there is an explosion and a big shudder behind us, and the chopper goes into a spin, sideways and down. The two troopers on the guns open up and the rounds spray the cliff and water in a crazy arc around the downward spiralling helicopter. The back end drops and smashes into the deep green, flipping us over and in we go, upside down. The guns fall silent as the water gets hold of us and sucks us down. The water is cool and clear. The temperature drops sharply as we descend and the pressure on our flesh increases. We're still strapped in.

Finally we are down in the dark green cold and the machine around us comes to a rest. Mularabone and I hit our release buttons. We push ourselves out and away from the chopper and start to swim. Above us, there is nothing but the serene green of the Darbal Yaragan. Below us, the shape of the helicopter is shrouded by swirling mud and silt. I get the feeling about a direction and, instead of kicking directly for the surface, I go in toward the submerged cliff face. Mularabone is right with me like my wingman, like he was waiting for me to do something like this. I hold onto the rockface, and start to inch upwards, and then ahead of us is the hole I knew I'd find. I kick into it, with Mularabone right behind me.

It is a tunnel into the cliff that heads away, upwards at a slight angle. As we go upwards, we see the light at the top of the tunnel. We kick out for it, feeling the pressure subsiding in our ears, and in moments we break the surface.

We're in a grotto. There is a sandy beach, and a light-filled tunnel snaking away above us. We drag ourselves up onto the underground beach, heaving and wheezing.

Down the tunnel come two Countrymen. They're both carrying automatic weapons. They greet us like long lost relatives.

'Eh! Eh! Welcome to Country, yutupella!'

And all four of us are laughing. Mularabone and I pull ourselves up and look back into the water.

'Ya reckon they got out, coorda?'

I shrug. Jack and the pilot are both trained.

Back in there, in the depths, there is a helicopter sitting upside down on the deck of those 1830s British warships. There is a certain poetry in that. Military history is the same as family history: if you don't learn from your mistakes, you are destined to repeat them.

Above us, we can hear the sound of other choppers, and heavy weapons firing.

'Your mob gonna be all right?' I ask.

'It's just us two, cuz. There's no one else here. They're firin at nuthin.'

This is a big joke to the two local lads.

'We're just teasin em, anyway. We won't start up big til yutupella are ready.'

'When your slate is clean,' adds the other lad, and looks right at me.

It's not surprising that these men know everything about

us. This is what Uncle meant: the Country speaking up. We are all little lumps of clay moving around. We are the Country. What the earth our Mother knows – we all know.

Dreaming 44: Value of Concrete

I'm standing on bare concrete. It's a ramp. Everywhere is concrete. Concrete ramp, concrete walls, and a big, thick concrete parapet shielding the emergency drop-off point from the busy road I can hear beyond. A car horn beeps, one of those loud and sudden air-horns, and I jump, that old flinch from my childhood creeping back in. When he would sneak up behind me and shout suddenly was curiously more terrifying than when I got hit. Getting hit is easy. You don't have to think about getting hit. You don't have to react, to feel the fear.

I move to the side of the concrete ramp, where there is a narrow pavement barely wide enough to accommodate my body, so that I have to lean into the wall, press myself against it, to avoid being run down by the oncoming ambulance. As it slides past me I see that it isn't an ambulance but a big black limousine. It screeches to a halt. The back door opens and a short stocky man in a dark suit gets out. He looks straight back at me, his dark eyes ablaze with some dark emotion. I steady myself with my chunky concrete hands against the concrete wall and return his gaze.

The big black car roars off, disappearing down the ramp on the other side, and into the traffic. The concrete beneath my feet is humming with the vibrations from the unseen vehicular traffic. The man starts to walk towards me. It's like someone took 44, and put him into a wool press, compressing his bulk down into this stocky, suited version of his old self, shorter but three times as wide: 44's little brother. I glance back down the ramp. There is nowhere to run.

'You lookin for something?' he asks, as he gets closer, his hand straightening his double-breasted jacket.

'Nuh,' I offer, my voice barely a croak.

'Where's the child?' he demands as he stops, six feet in front of me.

'Where's your brother?' I shoot back.

'My brother?'

'44.'

'He couldn't make it. Where's the child?'

'What child?'

In my eye he sees the ute driving on the road on the edge of the cliff.

'Where's the fucken kid?' he asks again, and to emphasise his redneck accent, his hand dives inside his pure wool jacket and withdraws a .44 magnum gas auto desert eagle.

'I'm not gonna arks ya again,' he says, flicking off the safety catch.

'The child is not for you,' I say evenly.

He fires the weapon and the big slugs slam into my chest. It's like being cracked with a baseball bat.

Once! Twice!

I use the momentum to turn and run down the ramp. Two more bullets slam into my body as I run, propelling me faster down the concrete ramp. At the bottom of the ramp there is a small wooden door set into the concrete wall. I hit the door running, slamming into it, leaving a huge blood-and-gore smear, as I push down on the door handle and fall inside. I spring to my feet and snip the lock on the door behind me. Outside, I hear him trying to work the door handle, and swearing through his failure. I get up and start to walk.

'Canapé, sir?'

I look up to see a waiter in black tie and jacket offering me devils on horseback on a silver tray.

'Give me ya jacket!' I say, and rush him, divesting him of the garment before he can protest. I slip it on and it covers my sucking chest wounds nicely.

I move into the crowd of people in dinner suits, drinking and eating. I've gotta find another exit. The canapés look pretty good. Through the crowd, on the other side of the reception room, I think I see Mularabone, standing by another door. I make my way over, with only a few big red drips on the carpet to betray my pathway. I get to the door. I think I hear women's voices. On the door is the number 44. None of the Djenga who are drinking notice me at all.

But at the door, there is no one. As my blood drains away, my senses are playing tricks on me. I open the door and go through. I find myself in a car park, dark and quiet. About twenty feet away there is a man standing, leaning against a car, and smoking. I go straight up to him.

'Eh, bro, got a smoke?'

I hear a noise and look back to see Stunted 44 coming through the door.

'Grab him!' yells Stunted 44. 'Grab the fucker!'

He runs up to me and punches me in the heart.

Agony shoots through my body. His fists are as hard as jarrah. I sink to my knees. I open my hands, and as he goes for the last big punch, I catch his fist in my hand. He tries to wrench his fist from my grasp but I easily hold him. He is a sad, strange, funny little man, just pretending to be a gangster. The smoking man who has remained nonchalant during the attack on me, reaches out and ashes his cigarette on Stunted 44's head. I jerk him in close to me. I can smell the grog on his breath. It goes up my nose like a tiny willy-willy. That grog willy-willy is in my brain, and I clench my fists to hold firm against the chaotic grog wind.

'You better watch your back, little brother,' I say.

'He'd never hurt me,' his voice says, but his eyes are looking around for a place to hide.

'I am the child,' I say.

I let him go. He slides down my body to the cement floor.

'This is the last time,' I tell him.

'We'll see,' he says.

A car in the car park switches on its headlights, blinding us.

Thirty-eight: Just in Time

Light streams into the tunnel from above Mularabone and me. We pick our way upwards towards this light. As we get to the entrance of the cave, the two Nyoongar lads ahead of us step into that light, and effectively disappear. My head throbs as though those rotor blades are still thumping away, only now deep inside my skull, holding up my body against the inevitable pull of gravity. My mind is wandering to those other times when I have wanted to wish away this inevitability. It's like trying to wish away the desire to breathe. When I was a child, I thought that if I said it backwards, then I could defeat the force. From my knowledge programs, I already knew that gravity was made up of two forces, one going away from the centre of the largest mass, and one going towards the centre: so all I had to do was negate the force pulling us into the earth, which I easily did by saying gravity backwards to myself over and over –

'Ytivarg! Ytivarg! Ytivarg!'

And then I could float around inside the van for hours, or even days, until Mum came back.

I notice that Mularabone is shivering so violently his teeth are clattering like a mob of old blokes tapping boomerangs together in a chaotic storm pattern. I look down to my own body, shaky and unsteady with each faltering step. The shock must be grabbing at us. Below our feet, the ground changes from hard limestone to soft sand, and the effect on both of us is immediate. The process of our bodies going into shock always intrigues me. This process is part of the survival mechanism of the organism that harbours our spirit. This shock mechanism can also kill the organism. To come out of this shock we need the support of others around us. At the level of the animal organism that we call human, we fundamentally need a community of other souls to facilitate our survival. Some believe that it shows our propensity to destroy ourselves – like the way that the iron molecules in our blood, given a choice, would choose to attach themselves to a carbon monoxide molecule, and not oxygen, therefore killing us. But I reckon that it just shows that we need each other at the most basic of levels.

We start to sink. Sink down like we are going underwater again, or into some unknown quicksand, soft and dry and deep as deep. We are still making for the entrance with its waterfall of light cascading in, but with only a few steps to go, we know we can't make it. My head begins to arc forward and down, as though it is simply far too heavy for my spindly body to hold it up. As my eyes come down, I see there is one very old man sitting just inside the entrance. He has a white paint-up, except around his eyes, almost like the spirit birdiya we saw at the airstrip. From his eyes, I see he is a dreamer. He has a pile of blankets next to him, and he is smoking a clay pipe.

There is a soft 'thunk' beside me as Mularabone hits the sand. I am still watching my brother as the white sand claims me.

We lie there like felled trees, and I hear Mularabone start to giggle. I catch it almost instantly, this hysterical mirth.

'What are you laughing at?' I finally get out, as I heave for breath in between my debilitating giggles.

'I just ... didn't ... know ...'

And the laugh claims him until it giggles him down to silence.

I lie there too, until the laugh in me is all spent.

The Dreamer is leaning over us, covering our bodies with blankets, smiling all the while. For the briefest of moments, our eyes touch each other. The warmth radiating from the Dreamer is palpable. It is like the love a parent has for their child: love that can only be realised in the moment of letting go.

'Just in time,' he says into my ear, in English.

The two young fullas reappear with respirator gear in their hands. The Dreamer waves them off with a tiny shake of his head. They place the respirator gear next to us, and leave again through the curtain of light.

I close my eyes.

The Dreamer lies down so that his head is right in between Mularabone and me. I can hear him whispering an incantation.

Dreaming 44: Finish Up

44 is still half in the dark of the tunnel below me when he stops. He props on one foot and sits the Winchester .44-.40 into the crook of his hip. He almost looks comical, like he is playing at being himself and doing it in an unconvincing fashion.

'Howdy, boy!' he booms.

I half expect him to start twirling his moustache; his playing of himself is so over-the-top.

'44,' I acknowledge with a nod and a smile.

There is a silence. A silence filled by years of silences, as we take each other in. 44's face is grim. He shifts on his feet. 44 looks like an old man in pain. Like there is no way that he can hold himself to get comfortable.

'You wanna do it here, in front of your little friends?' he asks and takes a few steps forward. He seems genuinely curious. I look down at the three sleeping bodies.

'What? No fancy backgrounds?' I shoot back.

44 looks stunned.

'No utes, no sand dunes, no cornfields ...'

44 looks at his feet.

I make a study of the black baseball cap on his head. I always wondered what it says on the front. Just can't make it out. It's black embossing on black.

'That concrete really took it out of you,' I offer as some kind of conciliatory gesture.

'I don't really mind where we do it,' he says.

I turn and step into the waterfall of light. I close my eyes from the blinding whiteness, and stand stock-still. I feel 44 moving up the cave, across the sand, and step into the light.

I open my eyes. I can see fine now. My eyes have adjusted. 44 is two metres in front of me, the lenses of his black-rimmed glasses glowing like headlights, as though the terrific light around us is also coming from his eyeballs.

'I can't see,' he growls.

There is no subterfuge. Just a sick old man complaining to his nurse.

I make a hand signal, and the tremendous light is gone like smoke blown away. It is the half-dark of sunrise when it is getting light, but the sun hasn't come up yet.

'How's that?' I ask.

'Better.'

'We can't have you not being able to see, can we?'

He wants to play parent-abandoned-in-his-hour-of-need, but lacks the acting skills. The weapon comes off his hip and he cocks it in one easy motion, and brings it to his shoulder.

I throw my hands up.

'Oh, no! Not the face! Not the face!'

I look over my hands and 44 lowers his aim from my forehead to my heart.

I smile.

He fires.

The click of the hammer hitting the empty chamber is as loud as a howitzer.

44 looks down. He works the lever action to reload.

Aims. Fires. Nothing.

He throws the weapon down and his eyes meet mine.

'Unloaded it while you slept,' I offer, not wanting to kick the man while he's down, but just trying to give him something that his heart can accept.

44 reaches behind himself, and pulls out Stunted 44's .44 magnum gas auto desert eagle. He fires the weapon, and it clicks empty. He tries to reload. Empty. He tosses the weapon. He looks up, as if seeing me for the first time.

44 dives for his right-hand boot. Looking for the knife that isn't there. His hand feels around, as though the knife might still be there.

44 looks at me. I can see he is not beaten. He looks around wildly, and some unknown wind blows across us, standing on the sand outside the entrance to the cave.

There is a pump-action shotgun leaning against the cave entrance.

44 crosses to it and snatches the weapon up. He checks the chamber, and, satisfied, brings it immediately to his shoulder.

I dig my toes into the sand and brace.

Blam!

The charge hits me in the centre of the chest and the momentum nearly knocks me off my feet. The ball-bearings spin me as they hit me, back to the left, and I glimpse the spray pattern explode out of my back. I look to the ground to see that my blood has fallen to highlight the sand painting that is there.

44 is looking over the shotgun. I get the giggles. It builds quickly until that laugh has me, shaking me like a rag doll.

'You always ... were ... a ... good ... shot ...' I get out, and laugh and laugh.

44 throws the weapon to his shoulder and the charge smashes into my head, tearing half my face away. As I laugh, my laughing makes a gurgle as it comes out of the place where my nose and mouth used to be.

44 pumps another round into the chamber.

'You wanna try for one of my backgrounds?' I ask in a clear voice.

The light comes right up to reveal that we are standing on a vast sand painting. We are now both naked. I am standing in the centre of a group of concentric blue circles. 44 is standing on yellow ochre circles.

I walk straight up to him, following a line of white dots. Without clothes, 44 has spindly legs, and a big soft gut that hangs off the front of his body like a giant white kangaroo tick that has sucked all the goodness out of him.

44 reaches out with both hands to get me by the throat. The look on his face reminds me of Molloy in the river of blood, who wanted to kill someone before he died. Anyone.

I look into his eyes. I search for something. Anything.

I find nothing.

His fingers clamp onto my throat. I look down to see that my face and chest have healed, and the shotgun wounds are gone.

I reach into 44. I shove my hand straight through his breastbone, push aside his heart, or whatever that slime-covered thing is taking up that space, and grab him firmly by the backbone. His eyes go wide, and his fingers increase their grip.

I start to shake his spine. Once I start to shake I can't stop. The shaking gets hold of me like the rhythm of a dance that I knew once, and now have to remember. I stamp out a few steps. I shake.

The pressure from my throat melts away. I look 44 deep in the eye, and I shake him until his arms fall off, and then his legs, and then the flesh and bones from his torso, until finally, it is just him looking at me longingly for one last time out of those dead eyes.

I shake. I shake. Until I am just holding onto a spinal cord.

I keep shaking, and the spine comes apart, and the bones pile up at my feet. I look down and they are already dry and white. I open my hand to let the last two vertebrae fall. Then I stamp on the bones with my dance, and crush them into dust.

Thirty-nine: The Waterboys

Water pushes against my eyeballs. Way up on the surface I can see my body floating languidly, surrounded by a phosphorous glow at my extremities. My body: broken, but still good. I notice my fingers play with the water, the way a lover might lazily allow his fingers to play over his partner's sex, in the bliss of a post-coital cloud. I lazily kick my fins, and propel myself unhurriedly upwards towards the light, and that relaxed, floating body of mine.

I feel the soft sand at my back, and the weight of the blanket on me. Mularabone stirs beside me. The Dreamer sits up. I haul myself up to sitting, and look to the Dreamer. He has that same look in his eye that Aunty Ouraka had when she awoke to see Nayia-Nayia and I looking deep into each other, across the fire. His eyes seem to say: Well, now that we got *that* out of the way ...

He gives me a tiny nod, and gets up and leaves the cave. The two fullas who dropped the chopper step in and sit. They both have pannikins of steaming soup, which get handed to us.

We drink our soup and look out of the cave. There's a pile of sand just outside. Obviously someone had to put out a fire by piling sand on top of it. Probly to hide the heat signature from the Water Board troopers looking for us. I look to the two Nyoongar warriors. They are watching us. Mularabone applies himself to the soup. The soup is full of vegetables and local herbs. As we sup, we can feel it going into our bodies.

I can discern each vein and capillary in my body, and feel the warmth of the soup as it travels down to nourish my extremities. I always feel the cold in my fingers and toes, and now it's the opposite feeling, with those outer edges of myself warming first, and spreading back inwards to my core. I feel so light that I could float away, and so heavy that I could melt down into the sand.

I look out. In my dream, the sun was just coming up over the pile of sand that once was 44. Here, the sun is setting. We have slept through the bright sunlight with the Dreamer right here between us.

We get to the bottom of our pannikins. I have barely swallowed the last mouthful when the pannikin is whisked away by the young warriors. They stand over us with an air of expectation. Mularabone and I exchange a look.

'They'll be waiting,' says one of the young fullas, and they both step out of the cave. I notice that they are not carrying their automatic weapons.

'We better not keep them waiting,' says Mularabone with a grin.

We get to our feet like old men who have been sitting for days. But once we are up, we feel good. We feel really good. The young fullas start to move off, and we follow.

'Who will be waiting?' I ask out aloud to no one in particular, and no one in our little group feels the need to answer.

We pick our way along the path threading the rocky, lightly treed ridge. Thirty metres below us on the left, is the dark water of the Darbal Yaragan. In those depths rests the pride of the Royal Navy from three hundred years ago, and one attack helicopter upside down on the poop deck of the larger of the two man-o'-wars. A bit further along, we follow our guides as they turn to the right, and go into the trees. As the ground slopes away to the low flat area down near the water, we start to hear the singing.

There are a lot of voices singing over clapsticks in low, subdued tones. In only a few metres of travel, the trees begin to open out. Below us, on the open ground, there are maybe ten thousand people, maybe double that number. There are a few grass trees on fire, sending thick, sweet smoke skyward, and lighting the whole scene with flickering oranges and yellows.

Everywhere there are men and women wearing different paint-ups. Down near the water, there are a group of men adorned with pelican feathers, stamping out a dance right on the beach. They flow this way and that; the distinctive pelican head movements of the men shine through, as they hunt in the dance, and ride the wind currents expertly to survey their world of air and water.

As we start to move through the press of humanity, following our young guides, everyone begins to fall silent. They stop what they are doing, and watch Mularabone and me as we go down to where the main fires are. One of the young warriors gives us a hand signal as we walk. Mularabone and I take off our shirts and drop them casually, without interrupting our walk. The big mob parts ahead of us, and then closes around us as we move through. Finally we come to a rest near where the elders are sitting in proximity to two large fires. We see the Dreamer from the cave, sitting in a group of senior men. The Dreamer gives us a big smile. We stop. The silence of tens of thousands of people who have been given no cue beats down on us even louder than the silence of empty bush, or the silence of a clean river. This silence is a stillness that suddenly comes over all of us at once. I allow myself to sink to my knees, and Mularabone follows suit. I drop my eyes to the earth in front of me so that the senior men know that I submit to them. Submit to the Country.

Another old man stands by the fire. He has a distinctive storm-like paint-up over the shining ridges of scar that wind around his abdomen in a tight spiral. When he speaks, he effortlessly lifts his voice so that he touches the ear of all present without shouting or straining. His voice gives him away as the direct descendent of the old Birdiya of Beeliar.

'The Waterboys have come!'

The cheering and thunderous applause breaks over us. It is a great joy – but a heavy joy that beats down on us like the weight of a child too heavy to be carried, and there is a long way to go.

I have to work hard to get air into my lungs. I glance over at Mularabone. Like me, he has tears streaming from his eyes. They run down our cheeks and into the river sand. They plant themselves deep. That heaviness goes, and we start to laugh. The laugh comes easy. The Birdiya, grabs our laugh, and runs with it. It flows outward like a wave in this vast river of people. We are still on our knees, and laughing for pure joy. Around us, the bush and the river shakes with the laughter of ten or twenty thousand people. The bush is laughing with us, the river is laughing with us, and the earth laughs with our joy. The Birdiya comes over to us and, with a hand on our shoulders, motions for us to stand. We come to our feet and the crowd roars, and then falls silent.

The Birdiya smiles, almost as if he is embarrassed. His palms open out.

'As you can see, we have been waiting for you.'

The Birdiya pulls us each into an embrace where he rubs his chest on ours, so that our spirits can touch. This Birdiya can trace his ancestry all the way back to the river. His spirit is like the river itself, part of something much bigger.

The Birdiya turns very slowly and looks back to the main

fire, where he came from. A man slowly stands. Like all the men at that fire, he is covered from head to toe in red ochre, and is wearing only a naga.

The Birdiya looks back to me, and smiles – as if he is daring me to look with my heart, and not just my eyes. My eyes go back to the standing man. His paint-up leaves no flesh uncovered. Painted up with red ochre, a white man is barely discernable from a black man. It is the way he holds himself. Reminds me of someone. Then I get it. The man is Greer.

I look back to the Old Man, and his eyes, and his smile, say – 'Yeees.'

'We brought you here for the dance,' the Old Man says to me.

I look to my brother.

'I can't dance.'

'You're a man.'

There is no time for me to protest. We are surrounded by young fullas who start applying ochre to our torsos. As they rub on the ochre, and make certain designs, they start to sing. This song is picked up by the senior men, and then the entire gathering, thousands upon thousands of voices, join in, and sing the ochre on to us. The song laps at us like a great ocean. We feel the sand of our beaches start to get moved around. We know we are part of this endless exchange between the land and the sea.

I look to the Birdiya.

What dance? I implore with my eyes.

The Birdiya is faraway in the song.

The painters step back, and their song dies away. Mularabone and I look down to see the designs painted on my body. There are marks on the red ochre that I have only seen before in dreams within dreams. I am excited now, but frightened too. With great privilege comes responsibility.

The Birdiya raises his hands, and a hush comes down on the huge gathering. The Birdiya speaks in Language. The words are living things that he does not create, but harnesses them from the night around us; he makes meaning with them, and then sets them free to roam out over the heads of the multitude. Looking into the mob around me, I notice that there are Djenga all through the crowd, painted up, and indistinguishable from our Countryman brothers. There are murmurs in the crowd like sporadic bushfires starting up, and then the Old Man turns his countenance on us.

He looks deep into me, and pronounces: 'Fremantle – Wobbegong!'

There is a noise from the huge mob, somewhere between a cheer and a growl.

He looks into Mularabone, and pronounces: 'Conway – Holy Water!'

The Birdiya then begins to dance out a step.

Clapsticks and kylis quickly join in, and all around us we can feel the stamping dance take hold of the people. We can feel it because it is taking hold of us. For a moment there is a rush of confusion in my mind. Then I just accept where I am. I was born to be here.

A song is begun by the senior men at the main fire, and in moments, thousands upon thousands of throats join in. The whole place rings with this song.

'Remember!' the Birdiya calls out to us. His joy is like a living thing, shining out through his eyes and swirling all around him.

'Remember! Remember, Fremantle! Remember, Conway!'

And then the song starts to come at us – up through our feet, as they stamp out this pattern on the river sand. I get the flush of water-heat crawling up my spine, and crackling around behind my ears. I feel sure my head must explode into flames at any moment. My feet stamp out the rhythm. My shoulders start to sway in a specific pattern. The remembering that the Birdiya is talking about does not need any thought processes. It's not a memory that lives in the mind, but in the muscle memory, in the flesh, the water itself. And in the spirit.

I reach out to my brother Mularabone, and touch him on the shoulder. I invoke our connection forged in shared dream memories. I feel the heat travel down my arm. I give this heat to him, this power, this child. His body drinks the heat in like a hunger that he always knew would be satiated. We stamp down to the water. A huge handful of grass tree sap goes into the fire and a roar of sparks lights us up, before the thick, sweet smoke engulfs us. With our extremities we are feeling for the presence of our great benefactor whose river home sustains us all. It is the Waakul who gave this dance to Fremantle and the old Beeliar Birdiya for them to celebrate.

We dance it out. I play Fremantle with his mad Wobbegong shoulders, and Mularabone plays me, with my light step and faraway eyes.

The dance holds us in a pattern, and then we whirl back upon ourselves, and break the pattern with another stamping set. The thousands of dancers all cry out as one, and my own throat open at precisely the right moment with precisely the right sound. The smoke flows through our bodies as we dance, and remember. Dance and remember. The earth beneath me vibrates and hums like the living instrument that it is. The smoke has me. The song has me. The dance. The clapsticks. The people. The Country.

My feet sink into the sand up to my knees with each stamp, and the thick smoke swirls around me closely like a blanket – and everyone around me starts to lose their shape – as I am thrust through the walls to another place.

It feels like a victory, this jumping – I am that little jumping spider, and after I step off, and before I land, there is this triumphant life in between.

Ghost of History: Smoke and Water Dreams

I move again. My feet and shoulders still have the memory of that dance by the river flowing through me like a torrent. Now my movement is just a shuffle. It's only a small fire but that old smoke is following me. Maybe the smoke also has the memory of that dance by the river. There is no wind to speak of. It's my third move, and still that smoke homes in on my face and eyes, remorseless and relentless as that rocket that shot down the chopper into the deep water where the warships lie quietly on the bottom.

I look through the smoke to Bright Eyes. He's quiet now. But my head and heart are full of his words and songs. We followed the water under the ground all day, and he taught me how to read the signs in my blood as surely as he showed me those emu tracks in the sand. As if he's heard my thoughts, Bright Eyes looks up and straight back at me with the smoke still swirling around my face. His face softens a little. Maybe this smoke that won't leave me alone is amusing to him.

The stars above me sing of endless possibilities. They tell me that I can shine. They tell me that light can be seen aeons after the processes that made the light have faded from existence. They are a reflection of the water story I've been immersed in all day. This story is fundamental to our existence. Accepting this is what others might call faith – but it is a simple act of recognition. It is something Fremantle said to me on that first day that we set foot on this Country.

'Maybe these people know something.'

I decide to embrace the smoke. Maybe the story in the smoke will speak to me. It has before. I open my eyes and they stream salty tears as the smoke bites. I open my mouth and let the smoke all the way in through my nose and throat. It sets me off in a coughing fit. I cough and cough, until the cough itself becomes like another kind of smoke, and the cough that this smoke sets off is a laugh. I laugh with my burning throat and weeping eyes – until I start coughing again, and then finally fall silent.

I sit. With my silence, the smoke leaves me, and trickles away gently, straight up into the night sky. I look up, following the smoke stream, and watch it lazily dissipate into the stars.

At my back is a huge blue-grey rock set into the side of the hill where we are camped. That rock makes me feel secure, too.

Bright Eyes throws some more wood onto the flames, and lies down. I rock back into the little nest I have made for myself.

I go straight to this dream. I am sucked down into it like it is a powerful undertow in huge surf. I am standing on top of the big rock behind my sleeping body. The world does not seem very different. I am painted up like I'm still back at the big Wobbegong corroboree at the Darbal Yaragan. I can see right across the Country that Bright Eyes and I have traversed. I can see across the red-dirt Country, with the string of rock holes we've been following, brimming with life-giving water that hums through my secret veins, over the hills, down past the wetlands, and swamps, right down the river to the very opening to the sea where Fremantle and I first arrived, and went sprawling into the drink.

All along the river, I can hear the children playing. I can hear them laughing and calling out to each other in their games. The sound of these children is the pure sound of joy. Our joys. Our treasures. It is a hot day along the river, and the adults relax in the shade, groom each other, or sleep.

It is to the river mouth that my third eye is drawn. There are two tall ships retracing our earlier pathway. With the wind blowing in from the west, they are belting in towards the river mouth at full sail. Man-o'-wars. They're big. Colossal warships that speak of the wealth and the terrible power of the Empire. The lead ship looks about seventeen hundred and fifty tonnes, with eighty-four guns, and at least eighty-four Royal Marines on board. To the rear of that is a two and a half thousand tonne monster, with one hundred guns, and one hundred Royal Marines on deck. They plough on towards the river mouth, and are increasing in speed. I get a feeling of grim satisfaction as I see that their course must run them onto the reef guarding the entrance to the river. At this speed the first ship will go onto the reef, and the second will smash into the wreck.

I'm bracing for the crunch of the hit, for the limestone reef to tear into the hull of the first warship, putting a little bend into my knees, as if I was on board myself. But nothing happens. The great warships bear into the mighty Darbal Yaragan as if the reef was not there. They are taking in sail, but still moving very briskly as they fly up the river like great birds of prey.

The firing starts. Some kids are playing. Kids are yelling back to their parents when both man-o'-wars open up with everything they've got. I see the grape and cannon shot tearing into the flesh of the mob by the river. The marines line the deck, and pour musket fire into the camps. The family groups try to gather up their kids and run, but the cannons are reloading and firing, and there is no chance, no hope. Further up the river, as far as the springs at Goonininup, people are hearing the firing, and trying to flee. But these ships are too fast, too big, too deadly. Some people are mesmerised by the vision of the warships, and are standing staring when they are cut down by withering fire. I see the depth sounders at the front of the first ship, taking soundings, and calling them back at a speed I have never seen before. The marines fire and reload, fire and reload. They point out targets to each other. They laugh at the antics of the wounded Countrymen crawling in blood across the sacred earth.

Then I see the Birdiya of Beeliar. He is running. Not away from the massive warships, but down the beach, straight at them.

I hear him shouting from here: 'Warra! Warra!'

He is knee-deep when he fits his spear onto his throwing stick, and his body coils for the throw. The Royal Marine commander sees him, and at a shouted order, a hundred musket balls find his body and fling him backwards into the water of the Darbal Yaragan.

I take off at a run. I fall off the big rock – down, down, down, and smack into my body by the fire.

I sit up. The fire has died down. Bright Eyes is sitting up.

'Brother,' I say quietly.

He doesn't hear me. He is faraway. He has his own dream smeared across his eyelids.

'Brother.'

I take a dry branch, and chuck it on the fire. In a few moments the leaves smoke, and then take, the flames roaring up to expose us to the night.

I make no attempt to meet his eye. We gather our stuff, and run away into the night.

Ghost of History: State of Grace

We've been running for days. For weeks. I don't know. That old sun rises and falls. That moon waxes and wanes. This earth spins. This running is something deep inside of us, down low in the guts. This running is like being pulled along by some whisper-thin cord extending out from our lower bellies, and stretching away before us – pulling us towards our destination as surely as a river is drawn to the sea, linking our feet perfectly to our own spoor that dissolves behind us.

We're coming down the hill towards Beeliar's beach camp when we see a big mob of young people all heading the other way, up the hill, away from the water. Everyone is carrying all his or her gear.

I can see Fremantle down there at the beach, wading out to the cutter, which is just out in the deeper water of the river. We go straight down the hill, threading our way through the big mob heading up to the higher ground. My hand traces an arc up through the air and I call out:

'Wobbegong!'

Wobbegong turns to look at me. 'Holy Water!'

But I have come to the end of the cord pulling me from deep in my belly, and now my feet are battered and tired, my boots having long since fallen apart, and I go sprawling in the dust, rolling over myself, and finally slapping into the water of the Darbal Yaragan. I am lying there spluttering, and Wobbegong is above me, grabbing me, and hauling me up.

'Ha! Ha! What took you so long?'

He laughs a full-throated laugh, and pulls me into an embrace. Wobbegong grabs Bright Eyes' hand and shakes it, and they both start laughing afresh.

'Come on, we've gotta go with the tide,' Wobbegong says.

With that, Fremantle grabs me and drags me through the water to the cutter. We are pulled up the side by strong hands, and then the sailors quickly apply themselves to the sail, anchor, and wheel. I collapse on the deck. Fremantle sits opposite me, and offers me some damper. I accept it and bite and chew. To me, it is ambrosia. Bright Eyes takes a chunk and hoes into it.

I can't take my eyes off Wobbegong. His beard is long, his hair is long and tinged with grey, and his bare chest and arms are firm and filled out with muscle. I glance at Bright Eyes, just to check. He seems the same. Some of the other men on the boat I vaguely recognise from the marines – but everyone looks so different. Everyone looks older. Everyone looks stronger, healthier, and happier. Wobbegong catches the little puzzle in my eye and laughs again. No wonder he hit it off so well with the Birdiya, they're both as mad as cut snakes.

'Have you learnt the Law for water?'

'I have begun to walk the path,' I say. 'Have you learnt the art of fishing?'

'Before the sun sets today, we will know,' he says.

How long have we been gone? Wobbegong shrugs as though he has read my thought, and decided that it has no relevance.

'They are coming for us,' he says with a smile. But his eyes are as hard as stone.

'I know. I had this dream.'

Wobbegong pounces on this like an excited puppy.

'Did you see who?'

'No.'

'Which ship?'

'No.'

He waits. But I am chewing now. Already I can feel the strength flowing back into my body.

'You want water?'

I nod, and he pushes a wooden bucket across the deck towards me. Perched right on the lip of the bucket is a bright green praying mantis. The mantis has a little swaying motion, like some little dance, completely independent of the movement of the boat beneath us. As I reach for the bucket, she takes off and flies up to the yardarm. I look to Wobbegong.

'They eat their husbands,' he comments.

'Give me a Parisian dancing girl, any time.'

There is a metal ladle in the bucket, so I grab it and spoon some water into my mouth, then offer it to Bright Eyes. The water is cool and clear.

'From the holy spring,' I say. 'The springs where the spirit dogs drink.'

'The guardians of the river. Fitting, don't you think?' fires back Wobbegong, pleased with himself. 'They called out to me.'

I have another drink, and roll the water around in my mouth, allowing the fresh texture of the living water to caress me.

'Well, what did you see?' Wobbegong says.

'I saw two ships.'

'Two?'

'Yes.'

'Damn.'

'Indeed.'

'What rating?'

'Two thousand five hundred tonnes, one hundred guns ...'

'A first-rater ...'

'And one thousand seven hundred and fifty tonnes, maybe eighty guns ...'

'Oh, Lordy ...'

'You must have really upset someone at the Admiralty.'

'It's my brother. Cottesloe doesn't want me to shame the family name again.'

I see a shadow cross his eye. Something dark and dangerous. He looks away up the river. I'd heard the rumours about Fremantle, how he got his commission – why his family wanted him as faraway from England as possible. But I decided to take him on his merits as a commander. Not my place to judge him.

Now it makes sense. Only Lord Cottesloe could arrange for such overwhelming force to be sent to deal with our treason. If I had command of those two potent man-o'-wars, I could take this whole Country. But this is a thought from the ever-shrinking Royal Marine part of my mind.

We are moving pretty fast now. We have the tide and the wind with us.

'Where is the Birdiya?'

Wobbegong gestures back up the river with his lips. 'He has been off with the Holy Men for days. They are singing and dancing. Something really big, you know. Proper. All the mob has been told to move to higher ground.'

'That's what I saw in my dream. The water was so high that even the first-rater sailed straight in, over the reef.'

'Ah-ha!' Wobbegong jumps up and dances a jig on the deck. His enthusiasm is crazy. 'You will be getting everyone off Wadjemup,' he tells me. 'While you have been away walking the water song, we've been running the Birdiya's healing program out there. So there are only the healers, and the new arrivals there. Since you have been gone, some eighteen ships have arrived. Fifteen hundred souls. Some have joined us, but many have gone the way of Irwin, Roe, Dance and Wittenoom – put back in their ships and sent on their way ... And some went the way of Stirling ...'

I look out at the shoreline slipping past. A pair of pelicans soars overhead, up high and travelling fast, tracing the river path in the sky with barely a movement of wing.

'What will you be doing?' I say.

'I will take to the *Challenger*. I used to be in the Royal Navy, you know?'

'When will the man-o'-wars get here?'

'Today. The Dreamers have seen it ... And you have arrived.'

'Is it just you and I?'

Wobbegong looks right through me. I remember that he is from the ruling class of the greatest empire the world has ever known. Even if Lord Cottesloe arranged for his commission, Wobbegong has always been an exemplary officer. Right up until the very instant that he fell into the water at the river mouth of the Darbal Yaragan in Nyoongar Boodjar.

'Holy Water.'

'Wobbegong.'

Wobbegong laughs again.

'You seem so happy. Radiant,' I say.

'Do you believe that Jesus was morose in Gethsemane? I believe he was ecstatic.'

'A state of grace,' I agree.

'You never judged me, Holy Water. Even before.'

'Not my place.'

'I shamed my family.'

'Then you don't need shame from me.'

'I will have to pay for what I have done. I don't mean

Stirling. There is no hiding from who you are.'

I look away, to the shoreline going past, and to the mass of waterbirds feeding in the shallows.

'This is right, Holy Water.'

'I'll not kiss you in the garden.'

'You will if I ask you to.'

I look over to Bright Eyes watching us.

'I saw one, you know,' Wobbegong says.

'What?'

'A wobbegong.'

I look to him. For a moment, his skin is rough like leather, and blotched with brown, and gill slits flair open on his neck. I see this through my many spider eyes.

Then we are just two whitefullas who have stepped off the edge, turned our backs on everything that was so painstakingly taught to us by the Empire, riding down a big river in a little boat, on the underside of the world.

'Wake me up when we get to Wadjemup.'

'Sleep, my brother, sleep.'

And with the run across the Country seeping out of my body like the tide going out, and the water humming beneath the hull, I close my eyes and drop off. This time there is no dream to be had. No dream to strive for, or be sucked into. History is a dream. It is crackling all around me like a wild bushfire. It is bubbling through me like an underground brook first breaking through to the surface.

Ghost of History: Wobbegong and Holy Water

It feels like seconds later when Wobbegong is shaking me gently by the shoulder.

'Brother,' he says, in the exact tone of voice I used to Bright Eyes beneath the mammoth blue-grey seeing-rock of the interior.

'Coorda,' he repeats.

I open my eyes, and the cutter runs straight up onto the white sandy beach, and comes to an abrupt halt. The sailors are already taking in the sail, and readying the boat to be turned around, as I get up, and go over the side. In another time, a lot of orders would have had to be shouted for such a process to occur. Now, no instructions have to be given in clipped accents and then relayed down the line in rougher cadence; everyone simply knows what needs to be done, and is getting on with it. Fremantle doesn't even look back at the crew, as if he knows that they are onto it. Fremantle is already up the beach, and in conference with a Nyoongar fulla there. The entire beach has an air of quiet resignation about it, and resembles an orderly evacuation prior to the arrival of hostile forces, that we have both seen many times in Europe and South America. That the whole operation is orderly, and being enacted with military precision, is the surprise. Offshore there are several ships riding at anchor, with two longboats rowing in to where the cutter is already beached, and everywhere, people are quietly going about the business of preparing to depart.

As I approach Wobbegong, I realise that he and Bright Eyes are conversing in Language. Already the new society has become bilingual.

'Holy water – you need to get everyone off the island. You have the *Calista*, and the *Sulphur*,' Wobbegong says, indicating two ships riding at anchor out in the little bay, in closer than the *Challenger*.

'The ships will transport them down the coast to a camp we have set up south of Manjaree. Then you follow them in the cutter. I will draw the man-o'-wars up the river in the *Challenger*, where we will destroy them in the deep water below the cliffs past Niergardup.'

I remember well the pelican dancers at the pelican place, Niergardup.

'I am coming up the river, as well,' I say.

'We have trained for this, Holy Water. All hands know what they have to do.'

'And I know what I have to do.'

Wobbegong gives me a look. For a moment we are back around that fire at the camp near Manjaree, trying desperately to explain to the Birdiya, his brothers, sons, and nephews, that white people will turn up and destroy everything good about their world.

'You're right, Holy Water. We're only up against two of the most powerful warships ever commissioned. There can't be much risk.'

'We do have the twenty-six guns of the *Challenger*.'

'Twenty-eight.'

'I stand corrected.'

We stand grinning on the beach, while somewhere out to sea those terrible warships are bearing down on us. Wobbegong grabs me firmly by the shoulders. He looks into my eyes, like he is trying to find something that he lost a long time ago. Something small and vital. Trying to find out who I really am. Maybe he's always known.

'Thank you for coming back,' he says. 'I'll see you on the other side.'

I'm looking into his eyes, trying to find him. He's spent his life running away from something, and now he's running towards something. Wobbegong turns, and strides back down the beach to a waiting rowboat. We are two men who are all alone, but together in this thing forever. He is almost at the boat when he turns around.

'Holy Water!' he sings out. 'Holy Water! The Birdiya is teaching me to dance. Look! Carpet Shark Dance!' he yells, and breaks into the step the Birdiya has taught him – throwing his shoulders into the swaying, patrolling movement. Bright Eyes yells out with joy, and starts to clap out a rhythm. I join in. We are shedding our Empire skins. Even the two Djenga sailors waiting by the rowboat are clapping and stamping along with the great man's exuberance.

'Wobbegong!' Bright Eyes calls out. 'Wobbegong!'

Wobbegong beams up at me. He is not running towards something – he is swimming towards his fate. Swimming through the holy water. He finishes with a flourish, and then waves the dance off, turns, and jumps into the rowboat without a backward glance.

The two Djenga sailors in the wooden boat apply themselves to their oars, and the little rowboat pulls away towards the *Challenger*. Wobbegong sits upright in the little rowboat. That Royal Navy is still stamped all over his posture – I doubt he could slump, even if he tried. He is still shirtless, but he has donned his Royal Navy captain's hat. He stands up to buckle on his cutlass.

On his ship, I can see that Wobbegong has had the *HMS* scratched off, and now there are three large concentric circles painted in red before the name *Challenger*.

Ghost of History: Mutiny

I turn, and walk with Bright Eyes back up the beach. There is a cluster of limestone buildings, and people moving everywhere. There is a big mob of Djenga, maybe three hundred souls, sitting in the shade just above the beach. They are just sitting, not really talking, or doing anything in particular – but just sitting. There are a lot of men, with some family groups scattered throughout. This is nothing like the confused scenes on the docks of London, Liverpool, Portsmouth or Plymouth, when these people left England.

There are also many armed Countrymen moving around, some with spears, some with muskets. There is no mistaking we are on a war footing. The armed warriors go about their business with quiet dignity and discipline. If I were still a junior officer in the Royal Marines and these were my men, I would be proud of their conduct. Standing here on this beach at this time, I cannot say for sure whether or not I was ever an officer in the Royal Marines. Those memories seem faded now. The sense of calm is all-pervading. I have faced the prospect of battle many times, and I know that it is not always like this.

'Let's get them into the longboats – thirty to a boat,' I say, 'and start to ferry them out to the ships. Fill the *Sulphur* first; then she can get underway as we load the *Calista*.'

Bright Eyes gives me a funny look. Maybe my voice went all 'Royal Marine' on him. I half expect him to reply, 'Aye-aye, sir' – but he just grins and turns away. He speaks rapidly to a group of warriors sitting on the beach. They respond by jumping up and moving to the mass of Djenga in the shade, and start getting up two lots of thirty. Down on the beach, the sailors ready the two longboats. I catch Bright Eyes' bright eye, and indicate with my lips the two longboats on the beach, then do the question sign with the fingers of my right hand. He nods and grins back: yep – only two longboats. That is a bit of a setback; Wobbegong must be using the other longboats somewhere in his crazy plan. That's if there really is a plan to anything.

I go up past the waiting Djenga in the shade. There are four massive mia-mias made from bent-over trees, and filled out with interlaced branches for the walls. They have openings in the front, and fires going in front of these openings. There is a group of Nyoongar women wearing skins sitting around one fire, cooking some fish. It smells good. I go over to the other group, which is all men. I am quickly waved down to sit by the fire, and offered some fish by the men.

I could laugh. There are massive war machines bearing down on this tiny island in the Indian Ocean, and these fullas would like to sit and eat and share a joke. I sit. The fish is sweet and good. Bright Eyes comes over.

'Brother, I need these men to travel on the next longboat, and the women, too.'

'We will need different boats,' he comments.

I nod my agreement. Acceptance is better than under-standing. If they need to travel separately – then they need to travel separately. I'm wishing that I had gone through the healing and orientation ceremonies that the mob has been running out here. I can see from three hundred Djenga sitting silently in the shade that something extraordinary is going on. They aren't beaten-down quiet. They aren't quiet through fear. They are just quiet. All there is to do is wait. So they are waiting.

After today it will all be different. Either we will be crushed, or no more boats will arrive from England, from the Empire. Not sent by the government, anyway. There is no middle ground. We have stepped off the edge.

We mosey on up past the limestone buildings. They have the appearance of being giant soft-stone igloos, squatting on the island like nesting seabirds. These buildings speak to me of how long I was gone with Bright Eyes, learning his secret water songs.

'Djenga camp in there. Bring them out for ceremony, and training,' says Bright Eyes.

We come to the edge of a big clearing. It is obviously a dance ground, with fires off to the side. There are large mounds of earth placed in a symmetrical pattern, and some of the mounds have wooden sculptures or painted sticks set into them. On the far side there is a beaten pathway to a large enclosure. I indicate the buildings and fences to Bright Eyes. He holds two hands together in front of him like they are manacled, and drops his head in the manner of a prisoner. I nod. As we approach, several Countrymen rise from the shade at the side of the path. They are painted up, and all carrying four or five spears, with nulla-nullas thrust into their hair belts. They look serious.

'Some Djenga cannot change their hearts,' comments Bright Eyes matter-of-factly, indicating the buildings beyond the fence with his lips.

These square-looking buildings are much more like what I would expect to find in a fledgling British colony. The Empire always has a need for courthouses, jails, barracks, and hospitals. Whereas in England, they need their factories, big and bleak and square. And where you have factories, you have tiny workers' cottages, and somewhere, not far-away, probably on the tip of a hill surrounded by perfectly manicured gardens – a large country house. Here we just have the Country. Boodjar.

'How many?' I ask, my mind trying to compute numbers on board ships and longboats.

'Maybe hundred, maybe two,' my new brother guesses.

I march up to the wooden gates fastened with a huge lock. I want to look into Molloy's eyes. I need to see what is there. I indicate with my head movement that I want to look inside. I want to know what I'm dealing with here. A Countryman comes over, takes the large key from a rope around his neck, and undoes the lock for me. He pulls a nulla-nulla from his belt and offers it to me. I shake my head, but he insists, and presses the heavy club into my fist. I step inside the gates with Bright Eyes. Behind us, we hear the unmistakeable wooden clicks of gidjas being fitted into woomeras, ready for action.

Inside, there are four low, square buildings set back from the gate, and between them and us is a wide, shadeless parade ground. There are a lot of wretched looking men sitting to the side of the buildings in the small amount of shade offered. We don't go any further. Three men get up and break away from the group and stride towards us. That stride says it all. That stride speaks of uniforms worn, of campaigns fought, of fortunes made, of power, and the arrogance of the Empire. Bright Eyes shakes out to my side and loosens his arm muscles a little, as if preparing to club these gentlemen with their raised chins right into the ground.

I'm thinking of the Tank, Mitch the Blood Nut, and all those other rednecks.

'Who are you? Have you come to free us?'

The voice startles me. It is Bunbury. Bunbury, Bussell, and Molloy. Voices from the river of blood.

They stop just in front of us and stand formally, as though

we have come to fight a duel. As though I have besmirched their honour by describing them as rapists and murderers on a mass scale, in mixed company at a regimental dance. History is choosing different ghosts to remember, to be haunted by. Different heroes.

'You will be moved off the island later today,' I say. 'You will be given a ship, as well as food and water, to make Van Diemen's Land. Like all the others.'

'What others?' barks Molloy.

Him I know. Him I will give to the weight of the nulla-nulla without another thought. I look him directly in the eye. There is nothing. No story for me to read.

'The others with hearts of stone,' I say flatly, already disappointed with myself. Why are we so conditioned to hate? Hating makes us just like them.

'This is mutiny,' says Bussell. 'You will all hang.'

'This is revolution. The Country is speaking up.'

'Stirling claimed this land for the Crown.'

'No authority,' says Bright Eyes.

Bunbury ignores him and continues on.

'Where is Stirling?'

'Finish up. Dead,' Bright Eyes says.

'I want to see Fremantle.'

'Captain Fremantle no longer exists.'

For a moment I think the three of them will burst into tears and throw themselves on the ground like spoilt children. But they don't, of course. These men are so certain. So firm in the belief of their own righteousness. Which is why this Country doesn't want them.

'I know you,' Bunbury says.

'I think not.'

'I know you. You are a Royal Marine.'

'Holy Water,' says Bright Eyes.

'You will hang. And I will live to see it,' spits Bunbury, but he doesn't sound as sure as he wants to.

We turn and go, with Bright Eyes hoping that the Englishmen might set upon us as we leave. I can feel his loose readiness by my side without looking at his body language. Unlike Wobbegong, he never wanted to show them this mercy.

Ghost of History: Running on the Wind

As we get back down to the mia-mias, I see that Wobbegong is getting underway in the *Challenger*. The sails begin to fill with wind, and the ship starts to move in a northerly direction. He is taking a punt on where the man-o'-wars will come from. Not many military commanders in the history of the British Empire have taken their main intelligence from their 2IC's dreams. While I'm thinking this, the longboats are returning to the beach empty, and the Nyoongar mob are getting ready on the shoreline. The sun is high now, and I am feeling tired again. In my head I am hearing Mularabone's voice from our time in the cadres – 'When there is nothing to be done – do it.' I also hear a voice in my heart. It is muffled and faraway. But I need to keep my spirit here – so I banish these thoughts. Soon I will be seeing her again. It is the way of things. It must be. I sink down into the soft sand and the cool shade. Bright Eyes lies down in the shade near me. I hear constant singing, and sense the dancing onshore as if I were able to feel the vibrations coming to me down a thread of web, forever long and invisible. It is constant and insistent, if anything, it is building in intensity. There is smoke everywhere on the mainland – it is like the mob have fired everything. The Country is speaking up.

I sit up. As if Mularabone is reaching out across the space between us, I suddenly have the power to be completely refreshed, and wide awake. I'm so awake that everything around me seems new and vibrant, and shimmering with hidden power. There is a great and secret power permeating everything today. Before today. It began with that dream, and that run back from the water pilgrimage with Bright Eyes. And ended with this day, where there is something in the air, and the water. We can all feel it.

All the Djenga are gone. I can see the last of the two longboats unloading at the second ship. The first has already sailed, running southward down the coast.

Bright Eyes is still asleep. I reach out to gently touch him on the ankle, but before my hand reaches his flesh, he sits straight up, grabbing for his weapons. He looks me straight in the eye. It is like that moment, watching the footy with my mates, when I looked into the mouth of the beer bottle and saw Mularabone's eye, saw him wink at me.

'We go! Now!' he says.

'How many still here?' I ask.

He indicates the fullas by the cutter on the beach. They are the guards from the compound. Everyone is getting the cutter ready to make way.

'Djenga warra?' I ask.

We look back up the beach towards the compound. I stand.

'We go! Now!'

As if on cue, there is a huge roar from the direction of the compound.

'Go!' Bright Eyes shouts.

We all take off down the beach. The fullas are pushing the cutter out. Some sailors are trying to get some sail out. We hit the water at full run. The warriors get on, and the cutter has enough water. Behind us, the whitefullas who all failed the induction course come running and yelling down the beach. We are chest deep, and grabbing at the moving boat when the angry mob hits the beach. A volley of shots is fired from up on deck by Countrymen and Djenga alike. I look back to see eight blokes get flung onto the sand. I grab at the wood of the cutter. There is no hold. The boat is slipping away from me, I can feel it going, when Bright Eyes reaches back and grabs me. With his other hand he is holding onto the rope ladder. He drags me through the water towards him, and I get close enough to grab the rope. One whitefulla keeps coming. He is yelling and almost on me. I am the last one to get to the boat. I am hauling myself up the rope ladder when his hand gets hold of my ankle. Bright Eyes is half out of the water. He pulls his nulla-nulla from his belt, and smashes it onto the top of the whitefulla's head. He lets go, and sinks away into the water. We are away. The Djenga are waist-deep behind us, and still looking like they want to have a go. One of the painted-up fullas from the compound guard fits a spear to his woomera and steps up to the rail. He gestures at the fullas in the water like he is about to throw, and bears his teeth. They stop running. They stand in the water, watch us sail away.

Then we hear cannon fire from the north. The Countryman at the helm looks at me. I remember him from that very first day when we hit the reef. He was the first Nyoongar to get to Wobbegong.

'Head straight for the reef,' I say.

'Aye-aye, Boss.'

I turn to Bright Eyes. 'Do we have a glass?' I mime putting a looking glass to my eye.

He smiles, and looks sheepish.

'Where is it?'

He smiles, and looks at the deck. 'I gave it to my new wife. Young wife,' he says, and smiles again at the memory of the moment.

I don't know what to say. Bright Eyes laughs. I try not to laugh. I am feeling the gravity of the situation. At least, I am trying to. We could all be dead very soon. These fullas are acting like we are going behind the sports shed to see the new kid make the school bully piss. There is more cannon fire. Then I make out Wobbegong. He is in close to the mainland, and has just come around, to tack back into the wind. He's trying to buy us time. He wants to take the killers back to the north side of Wadjemup. I can see the man-o'-wars now, too. In full sail, as they join the pursuit, they are like two magnificent ladies at the races. They are gaining on the *Challenger*. He'll never make it. Maybe he hasn't got a glass either, and can't see us.

'Make a fire!' I shout.

Bright Eyes comes in close, the question in his eyes.

'Make a fire! Up the front! Use anything! Make smoke!'

He runs down to where I'm pointing. There is a warped piece of timber slightly protruding from the bulkhead. He grabs at it, and in few moments works the plank free. Once the wood is exposed, he smashes into it with a small axe. A Djenga still wearing a Royal Marine tunic throws Bright Eyes a flint. In seconds there are sparks, and a flame flicking into the splintered wood. These mob know about fire. The other Djenga are looking at me like I'm mad. These two other Countrymen tear into the bulkhead, and the flames and smoke grow quickly.

My eyes go back to the *Challenger*. She is ploughing into the wind like a pelican. I look back to the fire. The whole boat looks like it is on fire.

The side of the first magnificent lady spouts smoke, and a few seconds later the report of the cannons reaches us. I think I see water spouts. This wind is picking up out of nowhere. They're still out of range.

Then the *Challenger* turns again. Wobbegong has seen our smoke. He's going to drag them across in front of the island, and then make a straight run for home.

'Can we put the fire out?' I yell to Bright Eyes.

He looks at me, and then at the raging fire. Now everyone is standing back from the flames. The strong off-shore winds are keeping the flames off the main part of the cutter.

I look back to the warships. The first-rater is following Wobbegong, whilst the other is heading straight for Wadjemup. Then I look to the looming shoreline. The fire on our boat has been taken as a trigger. From here, as we race in, it looks like the entire Country is on fire. Smoke pours into the vast blue sky as far as the eye can see.

The *Challenger* must adjust again. Wobbegong is right on the line. He turns, and runs for home several leagues behind us.

The smaller of the two massive man-o'-wars powers past the island. We can just make out the mass of whitefullas shouting on the beach. Then the warship sails into view, and again we see the puffs of smoke as the ship opens up before we hear the cannon fire. Thirty or so cannon pound the beach and every visible structure on the island into rubble in a matter of minutes, the barrage is so intense. There is no more movement on the beach.

I look back to the fire on our own boat. We are never going to make it. We will have to go into the water and get picked up by the *Challenger*. But if he stops for us, he'll be caught by the warships.

Ghost of History: Wobbegong Hunting

The sun sinks low in the sky. All the Countrymen on board suddenly start slowly stamping. Everyone can feel something coming. Something beyond us all. Bright Eyes turns back to me.

'All you Djenga! Get down! Eyes closed!'

And he demonstrates with his hands over his eyes, and holding on tight, in case any of us doesn't get the picture. We do. By now, we are not who we once were. All us Djenga drop to the deck, and cover our eyes with our hands. Through our hands, we feel the intense light that flashes. Not all white light, but flecked throughout with brilliant and deep colours like pinks, greens, and all manner of purples. Behind my ears, and all down my spine begins to heat up. Fast. It is like I have some internal fuse, and someone has lit it. In moments, the feeling is at white-hot intensity.

Then the whole boat shudders. We feel the passage of something huge beneath our little flaming boat.

'Holy Water,' I hear a voice say.

I am screaming. It is the heat down my back, and behind my ears. The pain is intense, and the smell of my scorched flesh fills the air. I feel the back of my head where all my hair is singed off.

'Holy Water,' Bright Eyes says again.

I open my eyes, and the cutter is really flying. We are being lifted on this kind of king tide that fills the horizon.

'Steer the boat,' he says matter-of-factly.

I look up, and there is a huge body of water bearing down on us, a wave with no peak, and extra back.

We are almost at the river mouth. The water is rising as we approach, riding on this even bigger wave. We go over the reef, with plenty of water between the limestone and us. Once we get into the river, the smoke begins to close in around us. Visibility drops. I am steering by instinct. I've never been in a boat travelling this fast before. We are flying. Everywhere on the deck of the cutter fullas are hanging on to whatever they can. And all the while, the fire rages at the front. The cavity from the fire is looking deeper now. Travelling at this speed, we could have all sorts of other pressures on the hull. With that fire still burning, we can't last long. I look back to see the *Challenger* similarly driven along on this massive wave.

'Brother, how is the fire?' I call to Bright Eyes.

'We have to go onto ground ... Soon.'

'Everyone get back! And hold on!'

Even if Wobbegong knew about this, he could never have told me. It does sound a little far-fetched.

The reverse-flash-flood-massive-tide carrying us upriver tugs at the cutter, and I have to fight the wheel to stop the huge current from dragging us sideways.

Behind us, in the smoke, there is cannon fire. An exchange.

Dead ahead, there is a break in the smoke. I see there is a place where the bank doesn't look too steep, and the current looks a little less manic.

'Here we go!' I call, and steer the fire straight at the bank. The cutter turns to go in, and we are almost there, when the current grabs the rudder, and flips us, smashing us backwards onto the shoreline. The boat hits with a crunch, and we are all thrown clear to a man, the speed we're travelling at is so great. I land on top of the Nyoongar helmsman. He smiles up at me.

Just like old times.

'Get up the bank, and get down!'

We scramble up the last bit of the lip of the river bank, and hurl ourselves down behind it. I throw my head up for a quick look – just in time to see Wobbegong, standing on the deck of the *Challenger* as she sweeps past us, and into the smoke. He doesn't see me. And in that moment I know that I am in the presence of a great spirit. In that picture – he is Charles Wobbegong Fremantle. He is standing, shirtless, on the deck. His torso is painted with the brown circle designs. He stands erect, and calm. Set into his features is the firm knowledge that he is exactly on his dreaming path. Exactly where he is meant to be. And then, the wild torrent of water carries him away into the smoke before the next bend in the river.

'We've got to get to the place.'

It is Bright Eyes in my ear. We take off at a trot along the river – but further up the bank from the rampaging water. The smoke closes in around us. Twice, we hear the sounds of English voices calling out from the river. The smoke blurs direction. But our running direction is sure. We break into single file behind Bright Eyes. This is his Country. He stretches us out, and I lean into my run. I was born for this run. The burns all down my back and behind my ears ache with each step I take.

Ahead of us, there is cannon fire, and the pops of small arms. It starts sporadically, and then it sounds as if every weapon is being fired at once, as the cacophony builds, and then drops away to nothing. There is one lone cannon shot. Wobbegong is dancing.

No one speaks. We just run. Behind us, out past the smoking carnage and the stillness of Wadjemup, the sun is dropping below the horizon. My breathing feels good. The smoke begins to thin. We run. There is another massive exchange of fire from up ahead, and then quiet.

When we eventually burst through the smoke, we are just before the place. The smoke clears quickly because the wind has suddenly swung around, and is blowing back out to sea. I draw level with Bright Eyes.

'Gonna spit em out now,' he says.

I look to the river. The terrific flow has stopped completely. Whatever it was that travelled up the river so fast, pulling the massive amount of high water with it, must be way up the river by now. I know what went under the boat. We all do. I look ahead. Around the corner, where the spit would be when the water level is normal, I can see the *Challenger*. She is run aground, and completely on fire. The two massive English warships are out in the swollen body of the river. Two boatloads of marines are rowing steadily towards the burning *Challenger*. The *Challenger* appears empty. And the fire is very uniform.

But now the river water is really changing. All around us, the setting sun blasts the smoke with bright pink, and then I see Wobbegong. He is in a little rowboat with two Countrymen, and is rowing across the river, from the other side – towards us. He is using the changing current, and has started a long way upriver. Behind the rowboat, there is a mess of rope in the water. I can see other ropes tied to the shore further along. He's putting the finishing touches onto some improvised net barrier system. Wobbegong feeds the rope out the back of the rowboat as the Countrymen struggle to keep the craft on course in the changing current of the swollen river.

We pick up our pace. He might need us. And suddenly the river is really roaring back out to sea. Looking down river is like looking down a hill. This water is going out faster than it came in. The marines in the longboats have no chance against it. They struggle with their oars. I can hear the coxswain shouting at them.

Wobbegong looks like he is going to make it. He has judged the flow right. He is setting a massive net across the river. Big net for big fish. Big lure for big fish. The two fullas rowing are going like mad.

We take off for the place where he must land. The huge warships are now caught in the current. But they've seen Wobbegong. Two shots go off. Range-finding rounds. One smashes into the bank, and the other cracks a massive jarrah tree on the shore. They fire two more. They have the range, but the current is grabbing at those man-o'-wars like they are toys. The splashes are forty feet upstream from Wobbegong. We run until we get to the spot. The whole ship opens up, and we throw ourselves into the mud. There are spouts everywhere, and Wobbegong is thrown into the water. Now the warships are close enough for us to see the marines taking aim with their muskets. Wobbegong is swimming. He is swimming with the rope. The Englishmen are firing at both of us. I am running into the swirling river water. Wobbegong reaches the edge, and passes the rope to me. I hand it to Bright Eyes, and instantly the whole team pulls on it, to get it as tight as possible, and then he secures it to the broken jarrah stump as if he's been a lumper all his life. Wobbegong is lifting himself from the water when two rifle balls smash into him. He lurches forward, into my arms, and we fall in a heap. We slop around in the mud and the blood. I look down to brother Wobbegong. Two big chunky red holes punctuate his carpet shark paint-up. I hold him, propped up in my lap. The water plays all around us.

Out in the dropping river, the massive warships hit the ropes.

'It'll never hold,' I mutter, overwhelmed by the sheer size

of the man-o'-wars.

'Doesn't need long,' Wobbegong says, and points upriver with his lips.

In the river there are two longboats. In the fading light we can see the boats piled high with powder kegs. A big nulla-nulla to stun big fish. The rope out in front of us starts to go taut, as the colossal warships get caught in the massive rope barrier, and the river roars back out to sea. The rope stretches. The drifting longboats look like they will hit the warships dead-centre. We hold our breath.

Then the longboats bump into the warships. The fuses burn down. It is a dance. The explosions rip the night apart. We are all flung back. I land hard on my burns, and yelp with pain, still cradling Wobbegong. The rope is gone. The warships are dragged under the water as if sucked down, their guts torn out by the blasts. There are no screams or shouts. One moment the boats are on the river. Then sinking. Then gone. Finish.

The water drops at breakneck speed. The night comes down.

Wobbegong feels cold in my arms.

'Let me go into the water.'

'I can't.'

'Let me go out to sea, Holy Water. That's where I belong.'

I lean down and kiss Wobbegong on the forehead. His skin is leathery.

I open my arms, and push Wobbegong out into the current. My beautiful brothers just behind me see his carpet shark tail flip, as he turns and goes back to the deep.

Wobbegong has gone back out to sea to hunt.

Forty: Two Brothers

I squeeze my eyes tightly against the invasion of smoke. My feet stamp out the last of the dance, and there is a big cry from the other dancers all around me. The music and singing stops, and people drift away to more peripheral fires, and smaller family groups down by the edge of the bilya.

I feel spent from the stamping dance, and from the constant jumping and landing, and the dream country in between.

Mularabone is right beside me. We go up to where the main fire is, and sit in the soft, cool river sand to feel the flames heat our faces. Greer comes over and sits behind me.

All the hair is singed off the back of my head in a half-circle pattern, and there are straight-line burns running down either side of my spinal column, with another half-circle down below the small of my back. Greer has some herbs, which he has ground up in a piti. He takes the pungent concoction and applies it to my burns. The sting goes away almost instantly, as I feel the open wounds sucking at the offered healing. I notice that there is another old fulla sitting behind Mularabone, and rubbing the salve into his burns. Mularabone gives me a lopsided grin. I reach out, and we hold hands like schoolboy friends from another time.

'I can feel that old water now, my brother,' he whispers.

I nod. I remember that heat transfer in that sacred dance. Them old men never stop thinking. As if he hears my thought, the Birdiya moves over and sits very close to us. He touches us both on the upper arm and beams at us.

'You wanna see the Eastern States?'

My eyes tell him that I do.

'You come!'

We all get up and follow him. He picks his way through the mob, who are now all starting to cook fish. The aroma of fish being cooked floats around us. The Birdiya walks straight at the rocky cliffs at the edge of the bush, near where we slept, and where 44 and I met on the sand painting. As we get close to the rock face, I notice a small opening, only half our height, and into this hidey-hole we go, one at a time. As soon as we get inside, there is room to stand upright again. My eyes don't get a chance to adjust to the dimness before the Birdiya hits a switch, and a line of green tactical lights marks out a pathway on the floor, like in the corporate jets of the Water Board.

Only a short way into the tunnel, the Birdiya makes a sharp left turn. I follow him, and quickly find myself in a large chamber. Mularabone and Greer are close behind me.

The Birdiya hits a button and a huge control panel flips out of the wall.

This reminds me of the first time that I met Uncle Birraga.

'You wanna see Melbourne?' the Birdiya asks with a mischievous grin.

I find myself shrugging: 'How?'

His fingers fly across the keyboard, and a large screen drops down.

'Satellite!' he announces with a flourish. 'We got satellite!'

And he laughs as if he has told the funniest joke of all time. The screen drops down, and is barely in place before the snow-dust crystallises into an image. We're looking at a satellite image of a streetscape. It's as clear as if we were flying over in a Water Board attack helicopter. It's daytime there.

'When was this taken?'

'Earlier today.'

'What am I looking at?'

'Fitzroy Street, St Kilda.'

The streets are deserted. No people. No vehicles. Grey dust coats everything. The edge of the bay that we can see has an oily, sickly-looking surface.

Greer steps up to me, and puts an arm around my shoulders, like I am his son.

'The Old Man likes to look at this place. It is the beginning of a big Dreaming for us.'

'Us?' I hear myself ask with a faraway voice.

Greer's proximity to me is having an effect. I don't feel strange, though. His spirit is familiar to me, because of The Sarge. He wants me to think about the nature of brothers and brotherhood.

'Conway, you must not think about what separates people – Countrymen and Djenga, white spirits – but what unites us, what is our common ground. We need this "Us" thinking now, more than ever.'

'What Dreaming?'

'Grog.'

The word goes into me like a barbed spear. I remember that night after The Sarge ... And watching the footy with me mates.

'The Water Board troopers made me drink,' I stammer out, and my voice does not seem to be joined to my throat at all.

'It's all right, my nephew.'

The memory of that grog sends a shiver through my body.

'That grog ended up making us stronger,' Greer says. 'Uniting us. When it first came across, it began to destroy us. Us; the Djenga. We had no Law base to fight it from. The Mob didn't suffer. They didn't need it. Then we realised how it worked. There are malevolent spirits in this Country, too. This balance is the way of things. The spirit in the grog releases them, and unites them into one destructive force. So the old people decided to start putting Djenga through certain Law – to give us the strength base to fight them spirits from. Old Fremantle saw this coming.'

'Some of my old people used to drink there,' chimes in the Birdiya, and indicates the place on the screen with a nod of his head.

'Then the Djenga brought it back here. Once you have that first sip – grog's got you. Grog will destroy you. Grog will destroy your children and their children – forever! So we fight. Kill them grog runners. Burn em. Smash em. Nyoongar Law now. Nyoongar Boodjar. We can't have that grog release evil into the Boodjar. We are the Boodjar. Strong Country now.'

'Can I see more?' I say.

The Birdiya hits the controls and the image pulls back so that we are looking from a greater height at the vast waterless wasteland. But even in that dried-out Country there are two small green dots where the Country looks healthy.

'What's that?'

'Boonwurrung,' says the Old Man with a grin.

'And that other one?'

'Wurundjeri.'

I'm starting to get it.

'People always bin livin here,' the Old Man says.

I feel tired. All in. Bone tired. Mularabone likes to say that beauty is only skin deep – but ugly goes right to the bone. This is tired that goes right to the bone.

Without a word, Greer turns and walks deeper into the cave.

Mularabone follows. He takes a few steps, then turns back to me. 'Whatchawaitin for, bruz? A royal invitation?'

I follow, and can only manage a weak smile. We turn down

into a small tunnel, where we have to duck our heads. I brush the wall with my shoulder, and the limestone is cool and dry. A little way in we come to another cavern. There are camp beds set up everywhere. I go to the nearest cot and sit down. The beds are low to the sandy floor, and with my knees high, and the tiredness all over me like a rash, my head hangs between my knees. Greer sits next to me. Mularabone sits on the cot closest.

'Big day tomorrow,' comments Greer.

'What big day?' asks Mularabone.

'Jack.'

A silence comes upon us three, sitting in that cave on those low beds. I look at the sandy floor of the cavern. The green light overhead flickers for a moment.

'It's not over,' I say.

I look to the others. They are all resigned to this fact.

'Greer, you know, there are a lot people who haven't told me their names. Titles, or whatever, but ...'

'For your protection.'

'Thanks, Uncle,' I say, and his strong hand squeezes my thigh.

'You are coming at the history from our side.'

'When you first came north for us, you didn't take us,' says Mularabone.

'Jack had us,' I say.

'You weren't ready,' says Greer.

We sit there lost in our thoughts. I am standing on the shore looking out, watching the water being sucked out to fill out a big swell coming. I wait. Greer breaks the silence.

'In the grog dreaming ... there are two brothers ...'

Flying Dream: Spirit Dreams of Love

I feel light. I have no weight. There is a tiny but familiar voice calling to me from far away. The voice calls on me to fly, fly, fly. I lift myself up and out of my body – but despite my lightness, my feet are still anchored to the river sand.

I glance down at Mularabone. His body is there – but he is gone somewhere else. His empty body glows from within, and blue circles radiate on his brown flesh like a blue-ringed octopus that feels threatened.

I half expect to see the spirit of The Sarge bearing down on me with his gleaming blade. But there is nothing. No one. Just me standing above Mularabone's body with its glowing blue rings.

The faraway voice is gentle but insistent – and calls to me over and over. I step up onto my camp bed and spread my arms like an eagle. I allow myself to fall into the spirit-air so that I can find an air current, and ride it. But nothing happens. I fall straight to the sand, and my body and face hit the earth, forcing a grunt from my near-see-through body. I've gotta get outside.

I follow the low-roofed tunnel back to the control room with the satellite screens. Two warriors are slouched in the corner with automatic weapons in their laps. They sleep peacefully, their breathing slow, deep, and measured. I continue until I get to the small opening, and step out into the eerie light.

Out to my left, there are three figures standing in a thicket of bush. They watch me but I can't make out who they are. The sky has a bluish tinge to it, the same blue as the glowing rings on Mularabone's sleeping body. The sand is light brown, and has designs marked out on it in reds and greens. I walk down towards the Darbal Yaragan. The low glow of quietened-down fires is all around. I see a boulder that I never noticed before, and climb up onto it. It was putting my arms out, I decide, that was wrong. I'm not a bird. I focus myself and drop forward off the boulder. I have no relationship with gravity – and yet still I fall straight down. This time, I don't hit the sand, but hover just millimetres above it.

I think I hear giggling from the bushes but I don't look up. I've gotta get up into the air. I arch my neck and head back and take off, and this time I start to gain altitude. But my arch is too tight, and I go right over in a loop-the-loop, and this time smack into the sand! Now the laughing from the bushes is definitely not imagined. It tickles at my extremities like hairy little spiders running across my spirit-flesh – and I laugh, too, in spite of myself. There's nothing funnier than someone trying too hard, especially if they cause themselves a little bit of pain as they do it.

Then I hear the tiny voice again. It is Nayia-Nayia calling from across the other side, a distance vast and unmeasurable. My face has a secret smile that shines out of my multiple eyes so that my head has a glowing halo of joy. I gather my eight legs beneath me – and launch myself straight up into the bluish night.

Up here it's cool and sweet. The stars gather around me and I allow my hands to drift out and lightly brush them as I fly past. The burns on my back and skull glow like the stars themselves, and those playful stars recognise me as their brother, and call out their good wishes as I rush past. Down below, the Darbal Yaragan is a child's painting, plastered across the fresh canvas of the Boodjar.

She calls again. Out of my throat comes a long-forgotten song, a gift given to me long ago, in another time, and another tongue.

And there, way out past the horizon I can make out a tiny glowing speck that must be Nayia-Nayia – hurtling towards me. As the song dribbles from my heart, I speed up, and we lock onto each other like missiles. My hair flows out behind me like a single thread of web, and the spirit atmosphere buffets my naked soul, as we hurtle towards each other on our unstoppable trajectories.

Our eyes lock onto each other, into each other, drinking in each other's spirit-flesh as the distance between us closes at an incredible rate. Then there is that moment, and I know we both feel it – a tiny moment of hesitation before the impact. What flashes through our hearts is unknowable. Is there trepidation of the impact, or just the age-old desire to draw the moment of love contact out – to draw it out ... forever?

Our spirits melt into each other and we tumble across the limitless sky. We tumble over and over, drinking in the bliss, drowning in the love-water, dying in it, being reborn from it like iridescent dragonflies, and pouring ourselves in again and again, until this love is all there is.

Forty-one: Make More Spear

I rub my face. I feel light. I look at the cot next to me. Empty. Mularabone is already up. I've still got the remnants of last night's big dance paint-up on my flesh. It's all flaky. My skin itches.

I haul myself to my feet and retrace my steps out of the sleeping cavern. I come into the control room, and there are those two fullas working on the satellite system. The screen is down and there is an image of the fortified airfield on it. Everything looks still. The two lads don't look up as I go past them, down the passage, and out into the pre-dawn light.

I keep walking as though I am on a track. I go down to the water, walk out until I am waist-deep, and then fall forward, straight into the water. The burns on the back of my skull and down my back start to tingle and then sting. Out in the river, a big pod of dolphins is cruising past. They are unhurried and peaceful, and I hear the sharp little hisses as they breathe out and in before diving again. I take a deep breath, and turn back to the bank. As I walk, I rub my skin, and the paint comes off me and clouds the water.

I just get back to the shore when the little boat rounds the bend, and heads for where I am. For a moment, I expect to see Fremantle at the helm, but then Mularabone waves to me from the stern. Mularabone's wave is like a smile.

I stand ankle deep, and Mularabone aims the boat for the beach. I step out of the water, sit on the beach, and wait. Uncle Greer walks down the beach and hands me a big chunk of still-

353

warm damper. Uncle Greer is giving me that smile that Aunty Ouraka gave me when she awoke to find Nayia-Nayia and I staring into each other, falling into each other, over that fire.

Mularabone takes in the sail, and the little wooden boat beaches itself right next to us.

'Jeez, you Djenga like the cot,' he sings out, beaming at me.

'Who you calling Djenga?' Greer sings back.

'The day's half gone!'

I shake my head in mock indignation. Mularabone is relentless. He grabs the damper from my hands, bites off a chunk, and throws the seed cake back to me as he heads off up the beach.

'You hungry, brother?' I say. 'Help yourself.'

'I'm right now,' he says working the dense bread around in his mouth.

'You're in a mood, bruz,' I call after him up the beach.

'Going home, bruz. I gotta go pack!'

I watch him as he goes up to the Birdiya, who sits by his big morning fire. The Birdiya gives him two kylis with two distinctive white stripes near each end. Mularabone hugs him, and then dances down to us.

'Right! I'm ready!'

We quickly turn the boat around; push it out, and we three jump on, with Mularabone immediately letting out the sail. Mularabone aims the boat upriver, and the sail quickly fills.

I look back to the Birdiya on the beach. He sees me looking, jumps up, and parodies my Wobbegong dance from last night, before dissolving into the sand in a fit of mirth. Lying there, he gives me the goodbye wave. I give it back to him. He twirls his enormous nose-bone, and smooths his beard, before one of his sons comes across and hauls him to his feet. I turn back to the boat.

'Are you coming north?' I ask Greer.

'I'm flying the jet,' he says with a smile. 'It has begun, Conway. They can't remake the dam.'

'Why not?' I ask.

'Things have changed.'

I look to Greer, but he is not saying anything else. I'm wondering what was happening at the big Law meeting where Old James did the healing on me.

'What about Jack?' I say.

Greer and Mularabone both look away, up the river where we are heading.

'Here, take the wheel,' calls Mularabone.

I move down to the back of the boat and take the wheel. Mularabone moves up to the front. He sits on the prow and lets his feet dangle in the water. He starts to tap his new kylis, and busts out with a song that I've never heard before. I steer the boat up the river, and enjoy the sunrise that we are sailing towards.

Each freshwater spring that we sail past heats the burn designs on my back, and pulls my eyes like a magnet – and I see Mularabone's head swivel too. He really can feel that water now.

The sun is only a little way up as we beach the boat near the Water Board fortified airfield. The three of us jump off the boat, and go up the well-worn track with me leading. Without warning there are warriors everywhere – painted up, nose-bones in, all carrying kylis, or clapsticks in the place of weapons. No one speaks. The men watch us pass in silence, and then fall in behind.

When we reach the airfield, it looks like a cyclone has torn through it in the middle of the night. The razor wire is gone, and the fences are lying down. The buildings look ripped apart, gutted by some invisible, heatless fire, and the whole place is deserted. There is no sign of all the Water Board troopers of a few days before. The Water Board jet stands alone on the runway.

'Is there enough fuel?' I ask Greer.

'Enough to get home,' he says.

Then I see him.

Jack is standing shirtless and alone in the middle of the runway between the jet and us. We stop. I can see the weapon in his hand. I look back to Greer. He gives me nothing.

Mularabone, my spirit-brother, steps up close to me. 'Brother, make more spear. I am your spear.'

I don't look back. If I do I might see Mularabone standing straight and true, the wooden shaft of him tapering to a stone tip, welded on with the age-old gum technology. He starts to lightly tap his kylis, the gifts from the Birdiya. Behind us, another four hundred sets join in Mularabone's rhythm, measuring out our heartbeats.

Clack-clack! Clack-clack! Clack-clack!

The sound rings across the tarmac, reaching out for Jack's heart – daring him to share our rhythm.

I stride out for my brother. I step out, and behind me the men break into a song. I don't look back, but I feel Mularabone a few paces behind me, as surely as my shadow. I hear his voice singing down low, almost a whisper. I stride across the runway, with Mularabone as my shadow, and the other singers waiting where the fence used to stand.

When I am three metres from Jack, I stop. It is his twitching hand on the weapon that stops me short. My eyes go to the scars on Jack's shoulders and upper arms. I have the same marks, made by the same blade. Jack will follow his path to the end, I see that now. I saw the fidgety little bastard in his eye weeping on the plane. Our path is changing. We are brothers. There is a power between us. I will walk my dreaming path right to the end. Where we began.

'I see you've brought your pet,' Jack says, and indicates Mularabone with his lips. To see that Countryman gesture on Jack's flesh is somehow sweet, even in this moment – especially in this moment.

'I see you've brought yours,' I reply, and indicate his weapon with my lips.

In Jack's eye, that fidgety little bastard is getting restless. He plays with his yo-yo, and chews gum. Jack's fingers flick the safety catch of his weapon off. Then on. Then off.

He brings his weapon up and aims it at my heart.

Clack-clack. Clack-clack. Clack-clack.

The fidgety little bastard in Jack's eye is beside himself with anxiety. He throws down the yo-yo. He spits out the gum. He is speaking, but I can't hear what he is saying.

'You didn't bring a gun,' says Jack.

'I brought my spear.'

'Who brings a spear to a gunfight?'

But Jack isn't sounding as steady as he wants to. The little bastard in his eyeball is abusing him, screaming at him to fire, to shoot me down.

The song from the men is putting a strange shimmer across the runway. I slowly reach back with my right hand. My hand touches Mularabone, and he dissolves into my fist, like me turning to balga sap in that Old Man's hand on that dance ground in Walyalup, all those dreams ago. I arch my body, my hand back and low, my front foot planted – and I fling him, Mularabone my spear, fling him right into Jack's eye. He goes in straight and true, diving into the black pool with only the tiniest splash to mark his entry point.

Jack is paralysed with fear. His weapon still points at me, but it shakes, drawing a little figure eight in the air. His other eye flickers madly, trying to turn back upon itself so that he can see what is happening – and then back to me with some insane appeal when he can't.

Inside Jack's eye, the fidgety little bastard is trying to get away from Mularabone. He wasn't expecting this. He scrambles backwards across the black sand to the dead tree. He tries to go up it, but the brittle branch breaks off this time, unable to take his weight. He scrambles across the sand, pulling a knife from his boot, and slashes madly back at the pursuing Mularabone. Mularabone is relentless and methodical. He doesn't hurry – just presses forward. The fidgety little bastard gets to his feet, but his boots are stuck now in the spat-out chewing gum, as surely as he was caught in one of my massive webs. The fidgety little bastard slashes again with his blade, and Mularabone easily slips under it, and hits him with both heavy kylis simultaneously. One blow knocks the knife free, and the other delivers him a terrific blow to the abdomen. The fidgety little bastard is scared now. Bullies always are. Mularabone hits him on the back of the neck, and down he goes.

Jack writhes in agony but somehow keeps his feet, and somehow keeps the weapon pointed at me. I can see his finger tightening on the trigger.

In the left eye, Mularabone is still calm. He is not in a blood rage. He is just doing what has to be done. He stands over the fidgety little bastard and smashes him with the jarrah kylis over and over. He stands over the body of the fidgety little bastard. He bends and presses the curved end right into his eye so that it goes deep into the skull of the fidgety little bastard. The blood that flows is dark and chunky, and the bits of bone that fly up are thick and messy like rotted algae. Mularabone smashes the body until the fidgety little bastard is no more. Mularabone slips his kylis into his hair belt, picks up the mashed-in remains of the fidgety little bastard by the feet, and swings it round like he is casting out a fishing line – once, twice, and out.

Jack drops his weapon, and it clatters on the tarmac. The dark stuff explodes out of his left eye, as though the eye has been shot out from inside. He sinks to his knees; his deep sobs shake the airfield, and Mularabone is standing back beside me. Jack's hands go up to his eye, as the dark grease oozes out. He sobs and sobs, the tremors shaking his body to the core.

I go to my younger brother, kneel with him, and take him in my arms.

The song dies away. The ceremony is done.

The jet starts up for the last time.

Nyoongar Boodjar Regional Map

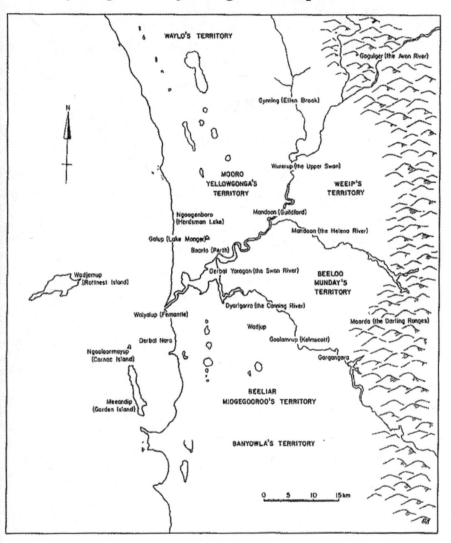

Map generated by R.M. Lyon in 1832 showing tribal boundaries and place names of the Swan River area by information provided by the prisoner of war, Yagan, whilst kept on Carnac (Ngooloormayup) Island.

Aboriginal Words and Their Meaning

The words listed below originate from languages spoken in Nyoongar Boodjar, unless otherwise stated. There are variations in spelling of many Aboriginal words, perhaps reflecting regional differences in pronunciation, though more likely reflecting the inability to capture the pronunciation of the language correctly with an English spelling system.

birdiya – *Law boss, boss man*

boodjar – *country*

bungarra – *racehorse goanna*

coomal – *the possum*

coorda – *brother*

corroboree – *an assembly of sacred, war-like or festival character*

Darbal Yaragan – *darbal – estuary; yaragan –river; now also Swan River (alt. spelling: Derbarl Yerrigan, Derbol Yaragan)*

didj – *didgeridoo; wind instrument, long wooden pipe*

djenga – *whitefullas; white people; literally: white spirits. It is thought that some Nyoongar believed that the Europeans were returned spirits from the dead, because of their paleness, dress, and powerful weapons. This is a term for whitefullas that historically was only in use for a short time after the arrival of the settler/invaders, to be replaced by the Aboriginal English word wadbulla (whitefulla).*

Garungup – *place of anger. Place name for the western bank of the river at North Fremantle, where the river is wide, not far from the Waakyl cave.*

gidja – *fishing spear*

gudia – *white person (origin: Aboriginal English, Kimberley region)* inkata – *clever man, important man (origin: Arrernte)*

jilba – *warming season on the Darbal Yaragan (August–September); one of the six seasons of the Nyoongar calendar*

kartwarra – *crazy*

kodja – *stone axe*

kyli – *boomerang*

maban – *clever man, holy man, man of high degree*

mokur – *the cold, wet season with westerly gales on the Darbal Yaragan (June–July); one of the six seasons of the Nyoongar calendar (alt. spelling: makuru)*

naga – *ceremonial loin cloth (origin: Yolngu)*

ngumari – *tobacco*

nulla-nulla – *club or heavy weapon*

piti – *carved wooden bowl*

redneck – *a hater (white man) (origin: American English)*

Waakul – *Rainbow Serpent who gave Nyoongar their law and culture and lands; lives in the Darbal Yaragan*

wardan – *waters (the ocean)*

wardung – *crow*

warra – *bad, wrong*

waru – *fire*

woomera – *throwing stick with a notch at one end for holding a dart or spear*

woornta – *shield made from wood, usually marked with designs pertaining to men's business (the smaller the shield, the cleverer the man)*

yandi – *oblong carrying dish/tool*

yutupella – *you two fellows (origin: Aboriginal English)*

yuwai – *yes (origin: desert languages)*

Fictional Characters' Names and Their Meaning

Birra-ga – *man-killing stick (origin: Wiradjuri)*

Conway – *holy water (origin: Welsh)*

Greer – *the guardian (origin: Scottish)*

Mortimer – *still water (origin: Old French)*

Mularabone – *muddy water (origin: Wiradjuri)*

Nayia-Nayia – *angel from above; the chosen one (origin: Gooniyandi)*

Ouraka – *wait awhile (origin: Arrentrnte)*

Thanpathanpa - *snipe (origin Wiradjuri)*

Warroo-culla – *moth (origin: Luritja)*

Acknowledgements

Thanks to Jane Cunningham, my first reader & sounding board who always believed in this story and me.

Thanks to Richard Frankland (Djaambi) for his encouragement and the many late night discussions of warriors, spirit, and dreams.

Thanks to Tom E. Lewis for his discussions of the Milky Way, revenge, and how the Country will affect us all.

Thanks to Kelton Pell & Geoff Kelso for stories & feedback.

Thanks to David Ngoombujarra for his talk of dog & whale spirits.

Thanks to Tall Fulla of the Gooniyandi for his talk of totems & his naming.

Thanks to Tara Wynne & Victoria Gutierrez for their notes.

Thanks to Georgia Richter who can uplift me, crack me up, or slay me with her timely 'hmmm'.

Nyoongar Boodjar regional map reproduced with permission of Dr Neville Green, author of *Broken Spears: Aborigines and Europeans in the Southwest of Australia* (Focus Education Services, 1994).

The Aboriginal words used in this novel are part of oral knowledge acquired by the author through a lifetime of listening. They are cross-referenced to the Map of Rottenest Island & Swan River (Wadjemup & Darbal Yaragan) published by Western Australian Local Government Authorities and the Swan River Trust, with research by Len Collard, Lisa Collard and Ian Henderson. Other useful sources have been A.W. Reed, *Aboriginal Words of Australia* (Reed Publishing, 1965) and Philip Clarke, *Where the Ancestors Walked* (Allen & Unwin, 2003).

A very special thanks to Kylie Farmer (Kaarljilba Kaardn) and Kathleen Yarran for the Nyoongar Welcome and translation (taken from the Nyoongar Welcome extended for the Perth International Arts Festival 2006):

I wanted to show the beauty of a 'welcome' – how open one's eyes should be to the beauty of our boodjar – it's more than a resource point, it's our home, our feeding ground, our shelter, our special places, our warmth ... our life! And 'our' is ngalla ... all of us, black, white, blue or brindle. We only have one boodjar. We share one boodjar.
 – Kylie Farmer (Kaarljilba Kaardn)

Also available from Fremantle Press

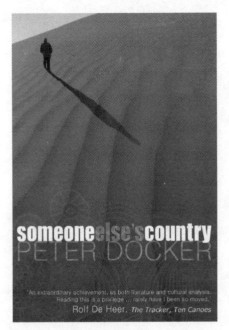

someone else's country

PETER DOCKER

'An extraordinary achievement, as both literature and cultural analysis.
Reading this is a privilege ... rarely have I been so moved.'
Rolf De Heer, *The Tracker, Ten Canoes*

On a remote cattle station a small boy begins a profound journey into an Australia few whitefullas know ... This is a journey into another place—a genuine meeting ground for Black and White Australia, a place built on deep personal engagement and understanding. A fearless, funny and profoundly moving Australian story.

'Written in hotel rooms while working as a professional actor in various indigenous film, television and theatre productions, Peter Docker's Someone Else's Country *is a deeply sensitive and at times intensely visceral engagement with contemporary indigenous culture ... it is also a powerful historical document, which has at its heart the struggle of a non-indigenous author trying to find an authentic position from which to discuss the indigenous culture ...'* — Australian Book Review

This book is written from the inside out. And that's what it did to me — turned me inside out.' — Pete Postlethwaite OBE, Usual Suspects, In The Name Of The Father, Liyarn Nyarn

First published 2011 by
FREMANTLE PRESS
25 Quarry Street, Fremantle 6160
(PO Box 158, North Fremantle 6159)
Western Australia
www.fremantlepress.com.au

Consultant editor Georgia Richter
Cover design Allyson Crimp
Cover photograph Duncan Walker / Getty Images
Printed by Everbest Printing Company, China

National Library of Australia
Cataloguing-in-Publication entry

Docker, Peter, 1964–
The waterboys / Peter Docker.
1st ed.
9781921696947 (pbk)
9781921696954 (ebook)
A823.4

Publication of this title was assisted by the Commonwealth Government through the Australia Council, its arts funding and advisory body.